Praise for award-winning author Hope Clark

"Author C. Hope Clark brings to life . . . endearing and strong-minded characters that linger in your mind long after the last page is turned"
—*New York Times* bestselling author Karen White

"Edisto Jinx has all the elements current mystery/thriller readers love"
—*Killer Nashville Magazine*

"Award winning writer C. Hope Clark delivers another one-two punch of intrigue with *Edisto Stranger*, the fourth book in her popular Edisto Island Mystery series . . . Clark really knows how to hook her readers with a fantastic story and characters that jump off the page with abandon. Un-put-downable from the get-go, this is a mystery that will certainly not disappoint those who are already fans of the author as well as those that are reading her for the very first time. Once again, I overshot my bedtime by a mile several nights running but, as always, reading Clark's latest was worth every missed wink of sleep."
—*All Booked Up Reviews*

The Novels of
C. Hope Clark

The Carolina Slade Mysteries

Lowcountry Bribe

Tidewater Murder

Palmetto Poison

Newberry Sin

The Edisto Island Mysteries

Murder on Edisto

Edisto Jinx

Echoes of Edisto

Edisto Stranger

Newberry Sin

Book 4
The Carolina Slade Mysteries

by

C. Hope Clark

Bell Bridge Books

Bell Bridge Books
PO BOX 300921
Memphis, TN 38130
Print ISBN: 978-1-61194-877-6

Bell Bridge Books is an Imprint of BelleBooks, Inc.

We at BelleBooks enjoy hearing from readers.
Visit our websites
BelleBooks.com
BellBridgeBooks.com
ImaJinnBooks.com

10 9 8 7 6 5 4 3 2 1

Cover design: Debra Dixon
Interior design: Hank Smith
Photo/Art credits:
House (manipulated) © C. Hope Clark
Sky (manipulated) © Dary423 | Dreamstime.com

:Lsnh:01:

Dedication

This book is dedicated to the Newberry Friends of the Library who have mothered, endorsed, and befriended me since my first novel. They are jewels and sweethearts, and I cannot thank them enough for being such lovely people. And specifically, to Sue Summer, the epitome of Newberry history, stories, and tales, whose knowledge actually enticed me to place this book in such a quaint, small, Southern town.

Chapter 1

HARDEN HARRIS pointed to a wooden chair in the tiny, dark paneled lobby of WKDK radio. "Park it right there, Ms. Slade."

The two ladies with him paused at the delivery, as did I, their gazes uncertain. Mine, however, wanted to laser Harden into micro-flecks of ash. Red-faced, I couldn't let the remark slide, even if he was my boss. "Pardon me?"

Harden had disrespected me for close to six months now, and something had to change. I wasn't his clerk. I was a special projects representative, a unique title delegated to troubleshooting . . . a job I did pretty damn well when allowed off my leash.

Harden and I were supposed to represent USDA on the morning radio show in a goodwill appearance of the state director, and me—his supposed right-hand lieutenant. We were to be a united front of federal assistance and gratitude to the taxpayer and the agrarian community.

"Don't need you in this interview," he said, then smiling, he preceded the guest-of-honor, who happened to be one of our own, and the DJ host into the next room. Etiquette dictated he should let them walk through first, but etiquette never stopped the man before. *Idiot.*

The women's over-the-shoulder looks pitied me.

I assumed my seat, which at least gave me the best view of the three and their show via a window in the wall.

A ditty played with a group singing WKDK 1240-AM, then the raucous yet radio-perfect voice of the older woman took over. "Lottie Bledsoe here with two quick public service announcements, y'all. A set of keys with a Disney keychain was found in the Walmart parking lot. Go to customer service to identify them. And the Baldwin farm in Silverstreet reports two of their llamas escaped the pen, so watch your driving in that area." Then another version of the station jingle introduced *The Coffee Hour by Lottie.*

Introductions were made. The middle-aged lady DJ threw out a one-liner, and Harden leaned into the microphone and laughed like the son-of-a-bitch was on a late-night talk show. Then he grinned all saccharin at the guest of honor. I almost threw up a little in my mouth.

The three gathered around the radio station's table of mics. Harden had given the younger woman's tightly covered ass a thorough once-over, however, before she slid into her chair. No matter what he thought, no way in hell that sweet little thing should give Harden a second glance. The toned, tanned thirty-two-year-old guest sat across from him, feigning interest, her 34D cleavage riveting his attention on what looked like a man's class ring on a chain dangling between her breasts. She didn't dress much differently than I did in my mix and match separates, but her shape would flatter overalls.

Still angry at Harden, my stomach flipped and wouldn't settle, rocking with a queasiness I didn't need. Damn that man. He'd worn my patience thin long ago. *Deep breaths, Slade. Deep breaths.*

Ugh, not working. The burning built in my gut. I quickly scanned the room for barf options, chagrinned, mystified, and insulted that I'd let this man irritate me so. A trash can in the corner, and hopefully a restroom down the tiny hall to my left. But after a down-to-my-navel inhale, the problem seemed to ease.

To get to Newberry, South Carolina, I had ridden the thirty miles up back roads in my own truck so as not to be confined with Harden's body odor and cigar stench. Even so, those smells were having an effect. Another breath . . . whew . . . better.

Cigar scent always stank when I was pregnant with my son— Oh dear sweet, sweet Jesus. The WKDK advertising calendar on the wall to the right of the window grabbed my attention. I ticked off days, calculating, my heart slipping with each overdue number. *No damn way.*

Please let it be stress. Please, please, please . . . think of something else. Harden . . . dwell on him. Envision him being all kinds of stupid on the air.

Harden had yanked me out of investigations and assigned me picayune tasks out of spite. Spite and the fact that a couple of his old friends still occupied jail cells from a real estate scam I'd unearthed almost three years ago. Their transgressions were the most egregious of the old scam, but the friends would be out soon. Too soon. Since that case, and since rising to state director, Harden had riddled my days with minutiae or assigned me one duty then reassigned me to three more. Sometimes without even telling me, which led to continual chastisement for jobs I didn't even realize I was supposed to do.

I slid the chair a couple inches left for a better view of the show. A graying radio guy I hadn't met yet sat behind the big picture window of the interview studio. I stiffened when Harden caught my movement, as if I were a child waiting outside the principal's office and needed to be monitored.

Surely my stomach issues were boss-driven.

In my work, or rather the work I did before Harden's leash, I walked a fine line between examining issues for my politically-appointed boss and calling in the real badges when things got too dicey for a non-LEO like myself. I usually erred on the right side of that fine line. When I ultimately needed that badge, I called Senior Special Agent Wayne Largo. That hadn't been for some time now . . . not that we didn't see each other otherwise. As in a lot of seeing each other.

A baby would thrill that cowboy down to his boots . . . .

Stop. Think of Harden.

When my previous boss died, they put this twit in her place, showing me how little gray matter it took to work in federal wonderland in Washington D.C. The Beltway feds weren't famous for their genius.

"Now, Mr. Harris," Lottie continued. "Talk to me. What made you travel all the way to WKDK and speak to our audience about Cricket Carson?" Miss Lottie dropped Harden a wink. "Other than she's one of Agriculture's prettiest employees?" Radio guy laughed to himself from his sound-proof room.

Bless her heart, the woman was rocking this show. I liked her. Her gray-blonde shoulder-length hair curled under in a style that said she slept on those pink foam rollers. Fluffier than the average person, about sixty in age, with a pre-Civil War lineage per her bio on the radio's website, Lottie Bledsoe had sense enough to sit between the two people and pretend one wasn't an ogre and the other a siren. All of them seated in a room made cozy like someone's half century-old living room, except for the wires and mics.

"Miss Carson's remarkably effective in her job," Harden replied. "While Newberry isn't the largest county, it's agriculturally critical. She keeps farmers thriving." The imbecile grinned big again, like facial expressions mattered on radio. "We are thrilled she works for us."

If he were so thrilled, how come I'd never heard much about her before? There were only a couple hundred USDA types in the state, and if she were half as good as she looked, I couldn't see this one being all that Jane Doe common. I'd have to ask Monroe about her.

"And Cricket," Lottie said, turning to her other guest. "Most of us saw you grow up here, are familiar with your momma, and remember your daddy Grady and his dairy. Is he the reason you do what you do?

You're a pretty little thing and not exactly who city folk would expect to see getting her boots dirty in the fields."

The young woman straightened, shoulders back in beauty-pageant fashion. I wanted to sneer but couldn't help but find her cute. Then I felt catty. Who said a county manager for the U.S. Department of Agriculture couldn't pull off adorable? Good for her, frankly. Harden wouldn't even be here if she'd been a forty-year-old beanpole of a man in wrinkled khakis.

"I love my county, Ms. Bledsoe," Cricket said in a charming drawl that made you want to eat her up. She lifted the ring from around her neck. "I still wear Daddy's 4-H ring to ground me with purpose. Daddy farmed here his whole life and his daddy before him, and the Newberry community embraced Momma and her business endeavors. How could I not come back here after school and help make us stronger?" She dropped the ring, laying her fingers on her chest. Harden's brows raised. "These people need a voice," she continued. "And if I can be that voice, I'm happy to oblige."

Harden's tone dropped in an attempt at masculinity. "And USDA appreciates you. Farming is a tough job, but at the heart of it all, you'll see a vibrant community contributing to the future of our nation's health and food security . . . and Cricket Carson is symbolic of that contribution and renewal of our rural community."

Verbatim straight off our website. Clumsily, Harden reached into a bag he'd set on the floor. "And in honor of that appreciation, and the remarkable job you've done for Newberry, we'd like to present to you this plaque from the agency."

"Oh my, oh my," Cricket said, all breathy and appropriately stunned.

"Fantastic," Lottie said, staring up at the big plate glass window between her and the radio guy enthroned amongst wires, buttons, and technology. "Now let's take a caller." Hesitating a moment, radio guy then pointed at Lottie.

"Listener, you're on *The Coffee Hour*," she said. "What comment do you have for our USDA guests this morning?"

A female voice blasted back in response. "I want to ask how you think you can possibly throw accolades at that bitch when we all know—"

My mouth fell open. Radio guy cut her off, mouthed *sorry*, and fingered an okay signal through the glass.

Wonder what that was about?

"Oh, not sure what happened there, but we seem to have lost our caller," Lottie said, so slick. "While we try to get her back, let's take the next phone call."

Yeah, I bet radio guy would screen his calls harder now.

A woman spoke of her family's experiences with agriculture. A man asked about an upcoming financial program to see if he qualified. Routine stuff.

Suddenly, radio guy sat frozen, listening to something over his headset. A bit of color left his cheeks. After a few words, he looked back up, pointed to the clock, and made a wrap up movement to Lottie through the window.

Lottie smiled. "Well, we're grateful you chose WKDK to present this recognition to Cricket Carson. What a wonderful honor for one of our own." She launched into a rote announcement about the station, its sponsors, and the next guest for the show. The engineer then segued into "Brandy," an '80s song I only knew from my mother's first-generation iPod, rarely dusted and propped on a Bose speaker back home in Ridgeville.

Interview over, they all stood, but Lottie exited quickly, rounded the corner to the control room, and opened the door. "What's up, Jimmie?"

Harden had Miss Cricket cornered at the moment, so I sidled closer to Lottie.

"Hoyt Abrams was found dead at Tarleton's Tea Table," Jimmie said.

Lottie recoiled a step. "Hoyt? What the heck was he doing out there? How did he die?"

I eased even closer as Jimmie said, "They think heart attack, but that's pretty unofficial."

Oh yeah, so much more interesting than Harden and Cricket.

"But . . ." and Lottie paused, stymied.

Jimmie shrugged. "Found him lying there all dressed up like he was headed to a meeting."

"On a weekday when he ought to be in the fields?" She was right. It was planting season. Lottie's mind seemed to be working through something.

She must've been familiar with the guy, poor thing. While I found it odd a farmer dying in a tea house, maybe he was meeting his wife for a date. Actually, kind of sweet.

Jimmie attempted discreet. "Are you—"

"Damn straight I am," Lottie replied.

I had an idea about her plans. And was Hoyt one of *ours?* While Agriculture touched most farmers, not all participated in our programs. However, if one owed us money and he kicked the bucket, we needed to know. Harden would never let me check. He'd revel in blocking me from the first halfway interesting opportunity that had come along in a while.

Not that he had to find out.

"Time to go, Slade."

I jumped at his order, growling under my breath at the devil catching me by surprise. "We came in two cars, so don't let me hold you up," I said, itching to hang around and talk to the lady DJ. This was the closest semblance to an investigation I'd had in ages.

"Follow me back to the office," Harden said. He hitched up his pants over a middle that taxed the belt, wedging into his crotch. "I have some tasks for you."

I watched Lottie still talking to Jimmie. "I'm taking an early lunch and going by my house on the way. Family stuff," I said.

Cricket slid into the conversation. "It's past eleven, Mr. Harris. Why don't you take your award-winning county manager out to lunch? Give Ms. Slade a break. I want to ask you about the new farm bill and how it'll affect my farmers. Where would you like to eat?"

Good heavens and bless her heart. What didn't this girl do well?

I turned to Lottie. "What's that upscale place near the square?"

"Figaro's," she said.

"Yea, Figaro's." I smiled at Cricket. "I think the state director ought to spring for something decent."

Cricket winked at me.

Owe you one, honey. Take him all afternoon, if you like. Just take him away from me.

The girl took Harden's arm. "Ever had crème brûlée? To die for there!"

From his blank look, I was pretty certain he didn't have a clue what crème brûlée was. Everyone shared thanks and nice-to-meet-yous then the pair exited, her chatting up a storm, him awkward at such a fine young thing on his arm. I held back until the door closed, then exhaled the nervous breath I'd stifled too long.

The radio guy released one of his own and returned to his chamber with the oldie's ballad about to run its course, the public in need of his satin-coated announcements. Lottie, however, cocked a look at me. "Bet

I could dig up a story about you two," she said.

"Bad plot, trust me," I said. "Who's the dead farmer? My condolences if you knew him."

Lottie crossed pudgy arms and stared down her nose comically. "You're Carolina Slade, right?"

"Right."

"You were supposed to be the Magnum PI of farm business in this state. So what put you in the doghouse? Whose dick did you step on?" Then she nodded to the door. "His? Not seeing much of a challenge there."

God, I loved this woman. Favorite aunt kind of material . . . that you could drink moonshine with in china cups while laughing about the rest of the family.

I scurried over to glance out the skinny window next to the front door. There was no parking lot because WKDK sat beside a tiny, rarely traveled hardscrabble road. Everyone just parked along the edge, mashing the weeds. "They're gone." I spun around. "Where's the murder?"

Her eyes widened then so did her grin. "You wanna come with me to Tarleton's Tea Table?"

"How far is it?" I asked. And how distant was it from Figaro's? The town of Newberry counted ten thousand people tops, and if the tea house was near the restaurant, I didn't want to risk being seen by Harden who'd expect to find me back at the office by the time he got there. I'd come a pig whisker's width of being shipped out to the McCormick County office not that long ago, but the governor had dropped enough hints to quash the order. My kids didn't need me driving ninety minutes each way to work.

Lottie darted into the interview room and returned with her purse, her speed belying her built-for-comfort size. "I'll drive. Come on."

She shifted the stick transmission into gear almost before my passenger door of her tiny Prius closed. Gravel skittered under her tires, our elbows knocking when the car headed north off Smith and onto College Street, now lined with rose buds ready to pop in another couple weeks.

April brought sun intense enough for sunglasses but not the heat. Azaleas still retained their pinks and purples around the outskirts of the cemetery across the street, and dogwoods exploded in white.

Figaro's was south, toward the center of town and in the opposite direction from where we headed. I relaxed with relief.

"Good interview," I said, making nice . . . and wishing she'd been more of the late model caddy gal I'd envisioned. Wishing for almost any make of car bigger than this.

She cut loose an explosive guffaw, deafening as the sound reverberated off the low ceiling. I held back the urge to cover my ears. "Air time, honey," she said, her laughter continuing to peal like thunder. "Cricket appreciates its value. And Cricket's a drawing card. I'm not sure whatever it is she did to merit that award, but put pants on anything and it's hers."

She slowed to catch the change of red light to green without stopping, then the car picked up speed as buildings and homes of the small town thinned the farther we went. I'd ridden on tractors with more horsepower than this. But despite the vehicular challenges, I wasn't letting go of her comment. "So, what's Cricket about? That caller wasn't too fond of her."

"Hah, there's the investigator I've heard of. Half the women in this town have been wanting to talk to somebody like you."

Gossip. I loved it. Beat the hell out of whatever Harden had planned for me this afternoon. "So why didn't any of you Newberry talkative types just pick up the phone?"

I'd been to the town before . . . twice. Once to see a Christmas play with the kids at the Opera House, and another time to eat at Figaro's with Wayne, since we sort of, kinda hid our relationship from the average person around Columbia proper. We worked together often enough for someone with a bone to pick to fuss about conflict of interest, and with Harden Harris in charge, we tiptoed more cautiously than ever to avoid creating our own USDA gossip. The USDA Inspector General's office could transfer him just as easily as Harden could ship me.

Then I remembered my manners. "Are you related to the dead man?" I doubted it, because she seemed too full of excitement. "And why are we breaking all the speed laws to get there if he's dead?"

She wheeled around a slow late-model truck, shifting gears. "I'm the newsmaker in this county, honey, and definitely not as well-loved as Miss Priss we interviewed this morning." The rural population thinned as we traveled, with a house every quarter mile now, most with American flags unfurled on porch or post. More azaleas dotted front yards, shouting with the color they'd put on for nature's recent and perennial celebration of Easter.

Who put a tea house all the way out here? Maybe we were headed to a neighboring town.

Lottie went faster as if to make her point. "Speed to the news is everything. Radio, magazine, newspaper, and every meeting and club in the area rely on me for the news," Lottie said. "When I show up, people snap to attention. They can tell me the truth and spill the facts, or I'll find another means and tell it my way. They understand that." She pointed at me and swerved a little. "Oh, sorry. For example, I'm still working on an expose on the singer James Brown's estate. I'm telling the story nobody wants to hear on that one. But, my husband's family owns three stores around here, and his legal practice dabbles in most everything. Of course Cricket's mother runs a good deal of this town with all she owns. Don't believe that poor-pitiful-me story about Momma Carson, either. That woman blossomed after her husband died."

My smile broke out. "I want to be you when I grow up."

She tapped her stubby fingers on the steering wheel. "You are who you want to be."

"So, the farmer?"

"I have my suspicions."

"Which are?"

"Let's get there and see. Only one more mile."

Her hybrid, economy, energy-saving bug of a car hit eighty.

"Eager, huh?" I asked, clandestinely slipping a hand over the door handle since this car would crush like a cardboard box if it slid off the road and rolled into any of the ditches. She had a death grip on the steering wheel. I was glad. "This *is* my speed," she said. "Life is terribly short to take it too seriously or live it too conservatively."

"We talking politics?" I asked.

Her scowl glared almost cartoonish. "I vote the person, honey. Nobody labels me without permission. I just squeeze all I can out of the minutes the good Lord gave me and call it efficient."

She bore left then found a dirt road that appeared little more than a fat path, already blocked with emergency vehicles . . . an ambulance and three county patrol cars. No blue lights.

After sliding the vehicle behind a cruiser, she jumped out, her breaths heaving an ample bosom. "We gotta walk a little ways."

The trees weren't dense and brush wasn't high. The major portion of the forest floor lay packed from enough traffic to keep it clear. No buildings, except for some small houses several football fields away.

Marching, she waved her arm and hollered, "Royce? I see your car back here. Where the heck are you?"

"Damn it, Lottie, do you have a scanner or what?" boomed a voice a few dozen yards in.

We trotted under a handmade wooden sign that read Tarleton's Tea Table. This was the tea house? Where the heck was the house?

"I already heard it's Hoyt," she hollered. "Heart attack? He had his sixty-fifth birthday not two weeks ago. Thought he had more substance than that."

Dang this woman could walk fast.

A fiftyish gent in a black, short-sleeved uniform appeared from behind some trees and held his arms wide. "Can't come in here, Lottie, and you know it." Another deputy strung yellow crime-scene tape. Judging by the plain clothes and case in his hand, the coroner walked up.

Which meant the body hadn't been moved yet. Which meant Lottie was quite connected for someone to locate her at the radio station quickly enough that she got here before the coroner. Wish I had connections like that.

"Heart attack or not?" Lottie asked Deputy Royce.

"Can't say."

"Maybe not?"

"Lottie, please. Show some decency. He's still warm, and his wife hasn't been informed, so we don't need your interference."

She rocked her head. "My concern *is* for his wife, Royce, and you understand why."

Royce slowly shook his head. "Hoyt wasn't a bad fella."

"No, but he wasn't too solid a husband, was he?"

While my new friend, the unofficial town crier, peppered Deputy Royce with questions, I studied the site. Why would anyone come back here?

Amidst the pines, an outcropping of three large rocks rose eye level and higher, smooth from years of touch. One stood particularly flat on top as though designed to sit on.

I strode up to the deputy, attempting to get a word in edgewise between the two. When Lottie took a breath, I slipped in my question. "Where's the farmer's vehicle?"

They both hushed. He wasn't surprised. She suddenly realized my point. Without a vehicle, he'd likely met someone elsewhere then come out here . . . the other person had probably taken off, most likely when Hoyt decided to meet his Maker instead of doing whatever it was they'd planned to do.

"Was he all gussied up?" she asked. At the station, Jimmie'd talked about the body found as if dressed for an occasion. "Or was he maybe missing some of his clothes?"

My, what led her to say that? Apparently, Lottie was already latched ahold of something I wanted to learn more about.

"You know I can't give you details about the body," he replied.

Either meant he was out of place. I took note.

Lottie clicked her tongue. "It was a matter of time," she said. "Just a matter of time." She tugged my sleeve. "Glad you were here today, Miss Investigator. I've been meaning to call you about this."

About what? I wasn't sure this was Agriculture's jurisdiction, but with Hoyt being a farmer, I'd go with it as long as I could. Or at least until Harden heard about it.

"Trust me," she said. "Hoyt wouldn't have died except for you federal agriculture people. It's your problem through and through." She smacked my shoulder. "Welcome to Newberry, child."

Chapter 2

IT WAS BARELY noon, but under the pine and oak canopy, the April air contained a coolness still requiring long sleeves. Lottie, however, churned up on a mission, shed her sweater and laid it on a gum tree stump. She returned to craning long and hard to see over the police tape and into the woods, pacing one way, staring, then pacing back the other. "Damn, they covered up Hoyt. Can't see squat."

This woman had to be kin to somebody on the police force to catch a tip on a body so quickly. And she hadn't lost too close a friend in Hoyt from the way she carried herself.

Like a shadow, I trailed my newfound mentor, turning when she did, grateful for my flats. Wondering why Lottie seemed way more than a little nosy. Finally, I punched in a number to my State Office in Columbia.

"Monroe?" I asked when my party picked up. "Need your help."

"You haven't killed Harden, have you?" he said, with no attempt to hide the humor. "In that case you need your badge guy."

"Huh." I almost stepped in poison ivy and sidestepped. "If I could make Harden disappear, I would. I'm in Newberry."

He snorted. "Harden already told us. We're taking bets on which of you comes back in one piece."

"He's dining with *Cricket* at the moment."

"Ahh, so you met our wonder girl. What'd you think? Be nice."

"What, because she's younger, prettier, fit, charming, and too good to be true, you think I can't like her?"

Monroe Prevatte was a coastal Carolina man from Aynor, an agrarian bump in the road in a county more recognized for Myrtle Beach. A friend for most my career. With a striking, prematurely white head of thick hair, he hated wearing socks with his docksiders, but he did at the office. Most Lowcountry men felt that way. Tanned, with a preference for tightly creased khakis and pastel shirts, polo or buttoned with sleeves rolled three-quarter, he had the looks. Most women in our Strom Thurmond Federal Building headquarters gave him second glances, but he returned them only to one woman. Me.

Not that I encouraged him. His competition was the federal agent he mentioned, whom I'd grown intensely fond of through our crime-solving escapades. Monroe didn't have the itch that Wayne and I did for cases . . . an itch that not only fueled and antagonized my relationship with Wayne, but also spurred our diverse ways of analyzing crime. Monroe just preferred there wasn't any tension, competition, or drama. He was Lowcountry laid-back to the bone.

"You at your computer?" I heard scratchings and looked up, catching a pair of squirrels chase each other about twenty feet up a pine. "Look up Hoyt Abrams in Newberry County. Is he one of our farmers?"

"Give me a sec." Tap tapping in the background. "Here you go. Yep. For his size he's not too heavily mortgaged, but there's a small six-figure balance." He hesitated. "Dare I ask why?"

"He's dead."

"Oh wow, but . . . okay."

"As in mysteriously."

"Um, Slade," he warned.

Lottie ducked under the tape thinking Royce wasn't watching, but he spun and motioned her back.

"You can't tell what I'm thinking, Monroe," I said with a hint of annoyance.

"The heck I don't. Don't go behind Harden. Your career slides on some mighty thin ice these days."

Yeah, it did, and I'd go bat-shit crazy if this was the speed I had to endure into retirement. "They think he just had a heart attack. Monroe."

"So why does that need your attention or seem mysterious?"

Lottie threw another glance my way, too impatient not to express her need to talk to me. Uh oh, hand on her hip. Like right now talk to me.

I headed her way. "Got to go, Monroe. Don't tell Harden. Okay?"

"Slade, think carefully about this. I sorta like having you around."

With a smile I motioned one more minute to Lottie. "Aww, thanks, Monroe. But it's not my fault. Some locals caught me while I was over here, and they're bending my ear. I just feel obligated, you know?"

"Slade—"

"Bye, Monroe."

Pocketing the phone, I turned to my new friend. "Haven't known you three hours, Lottie, and I can already tell your brain's trying to digest something it can't swallow. But answer me this first. How did you find out so fast?"

Her finger started wagging. "No, ma'am. A reporter doesn't reveal her sources."

As an umpteenth generation Newberrian, she was probably related to half the police department, sheriff's office, and coroner's office. I could see them around the holidays, swilling eggnog, tallying the favors they'd done for each other. "Is your husband on the force?"

"Nope, an attorney, remember, and that's all I'll say about who keeps me informed."

"Then I'll ask something you can answer," I said. With a shrug I pivoted around with an obvious scan of our surroundings. "What is Tarleton's Tea Table, and why does anyone come here? Much less die here."

"Exactly," she said, with a swish of a fisted hand.

"Exactly what?"

She shook her head as if erasing and starting over. "Okay, okay. Let me back up and educate you, honey."

I wondered if I needed to sit for this as Lottie didn't seem short of words when she took the floor. She stood firm on the crushed oak leaves, the scent of pine and spring growth filling the air, and took a straight-backed stance, obviously having given the talk before. "Right here on this very place, British Lieutenant Colonel Banastre Tarleton camped in January 1781, preparing to attack American General Daniel Morgan."

Wonderful. A friggin' history lesson. I hunted for a seat.

She shook her head. "The short version, I promise. Anyway, Tarleton was a bastard. Think of that horrible redcoat British soldier in *The Patriot*. The one chasing Mel Gibson."

The cutthroat colonel with the plumed hat. "Got it," I said.

"Only Tarleton wore green. Really arrogant. Anyway, he was headed to Cowpens to nail Morgan, right? Well, one or two lovely American wives, one a widow, delayed the son-of-a-bitch. Didn't want him in their homes, so they served him tea out here on the flattest rock. At least most think it was just tea. Some of us wonder since they weren't exactly held up for an hour." She waggled an eyebrow. "They waylaid him long enough for Morgan to beef up his forces and win the Battle of Cowpens when Tarleton finally arrived." She inhaled and spread her arms wide. "Big turning point in the Revolutionary War. General Cornwallis never forgave him."

"You learn something new every day," I said, fighting to keep from sounding impatient. "Now, what does that have to do with our deceased Mr. Abrams?"

She scurried a few yards around the tape, her cotton shift again snagging only this time on pine bark as she peered toward the rocks. Made me grateful for my slacks.

"He doesn't have his shoes on, and his hair's all disheveled," she said, then motioned toward who appeared to be the junior deputy guarding the body now. "My nephew lifted the tarp a second for me."

I understood her source now, but what did it matter about his shoes and hair?

She cocked a hand on her hip. "You telling me *y'all* don't have an inkling of what's going on out here?"

"Y'all who?" My shrug was apologetic. "If you're talking Agriculture, I guess not. Personally, I thought Tarleton's Tea Table was a tea and coffee house."

A dramatic sigh. "And we pay so many taxes to you people."

"Hey, I'm trying to follow," I offered, no longer feeling the love and regretting staying for as long as I had.

She narrowed one eye, in a Popeye sort of way. "Keep up with me, honey. Guys are ga-ga over Cricket. It seems that the guys closest to her get perks, or so say people around here. All these farmers hear who gets what from Uncle Sam, and who probably shouldn't be getting checks they aren't qualified to receive. Rumor has it your county manager seems overly affectionate to particular clients, especially the successful operators." With a nod toward Hoyt, she added, "Like him."

Which made me look at the tarp in a whole new light. "You're saying Cricket bangs farmers?" Eww. Not that some farmers weren't hunks, but I could count on one hand those I'd bat my eyes at, and I'd met hundreds.

But Miss Cricket had been at the radio station, unless she did her dirty right before, cleaned up, and kept her appointment with us. Wow, that would be cold indeed, and close to impossible.

I just wasn't buying her being the femme fatale. Too simple. Admittedly, farmers didn't always wear the white hats, but there were too many jealous wives with the potential to rain revenge down on Cricket's pretty head. Besides, Cricket had the package to snare someone way better than Hoyt, may he rest in peace.

Lottie raised those blonde brows again. "Like I said, lots of wives and ladies around here have been meaning to call y'all about all this."

"Yet they haven't. Any others die?"

She cackled. "No, or you'd have heard about it. Lucky you were here today."

Not what Hoyt would call it, but sure, why not.

Normally we wouldn't care who raised whose skirts or unzipped britches, but if any employee of ours exchanged favors with clients we darn sure did.

Agriculture was a world with ample room for misappropriation. Loans made, paid, or delinquent, subsidies granted, foreclosures sidelined—that's why the government pounded ethics into us. Violations led to either an administrative investigation via me, or an IG investigation, usually Wayne. My first case had been initiated by an attempted bribe to me.

I knew how easily someone's name could be smeared. While I liked my first impression of Lottie, her credibility hadn't been proven, and might be sliding into the level of gossip. I wasn't sure I was willing to make Cricket the culprit just yet.

"Cricket was with us all morning," I said.

Lottie scrunched her nose, which made her mouth lift up in a weird pucker. "We don't know time of death, now, do we? Cricket had time."

That was a leap. "Being rather heavy-handed with Cricket's motives, aren't you?"

"Cricket's family is a rather motivated lot," she said.

People didn't stand a chance at keeping secrets around this woman, which made me wonder why we hadn't heard about Cricket before. "So," I said, "you think she rose early, came out here to meet her farmer at sunrise, killed him, then moseyed over to the radio show?"

Lottie gave my shoulder a soft backhand. "Funny, but no. Too linear, and I can't really say, but . . . well . . . ain't my job to figure it out, is it?" Then she stared at me, like she'd lobbed the ball in my court.

I volleyed back. "Something tells me you don't hesitate to stick your nose into things even if it gets dirty. Maybe even screw with the facts a little bit to juice the urgency?"

Not that I hadn't been accused of the same.

"Don't mind me, then," Lottie said. "Call it the prattling of an old woman. But I've reported it to you now."

I gave her a small snort. "You're not that old. And why not tell State Director Harris instead of me, while you had him here for the show?"

"The moment I saw how he treated you back there at the station and how he fawned all over Cricket told me not to trust him."

Which sort of endeared her to me again.

Deputy Royce had been studying us hard for a while, but now stalked in our direction.

"Um, your deputy's not happy," I said under my breath.

"He gets why I'm out here," she said. "Scandals crawl up my leg and sit on my shoulder, and I deem it my calling to give them the light of day."

The visual gave me pause.

Royce kept coming. He'd want my name, which Lottie would happily give even if I didn't. Time to make myself scarce.

"The boss'll be wondering where I am," I said, hunting for an out. To my surprise, Lottie conceded and waved to Royce that she was going, then led us to her Prius.

Maybe this was a case of some sort. Not the murder, but the whole USDA red-light madam suggestion. Lottie had basically delivered a hotline complaint to my lap, which used to be the type of work I did before Harden. The type of work he doled out to whomever he wished these days. *Hey, random dude, make a loan and while you're there, check out that embezzlement problem.*

I was trained to probe, with continuing adult-education by Wayne on the side, and I'd been sidelined too long. Bigger cases had originated with less. Trouble was I couldn't open an investigation without the nod of my ass of a boss unless I went over his head, which could easily scorch the bridge of my career. Lottie had already established a reputation of her own, which included pontification about all and sundry. Nothing to lose on her side when she went after a scandal.

Me . . . total opposite issue.

We strode back toward the Prius with Lottie babbling about Newberry trivia, like my visitor status gave her license to orient me. Ghosts in the Opera House, an old resident who relocated to Australia and became a cannibal, stories confirming Newberry's founding "mothers" were comprised of whores and their convenience to the railroad.

But her words faded as I studied the ground passing under my feet and sorted what I'd learned. Hoyt came out here with someone else, someone who didn't want to be seen with him, and then he'd had the heart attack. A secret business meeting or something else? No shoes hinted at the something else.

In knee-high weeds to my right, the sun glinted off something. A coin, glasses maybe. Out of curiosity, I gravitated to it. Trained to look first and touch later, I stooped down. A broken piece of china. The handle part. No dust, mud, or wear whatsoever on it. Then other pieces off in the weeds.

Lottie rushed over and leaned down beside me. "Royal Doulton. British, of course. They put real bone ash into their pieces. Any decent mother teaches her daughter how to read china."

My mother never taught me how to read china. But that teeny fact, assuming Lottie was right, made the find even more odd. "Why do people come out here?" I asked. "I mean, other than for the obvious history?"

"Tea parties."

I felt my leg being pulled. "Which is code for what?"

She lowered her voice, though I wondered why she bothered after the noise she'd already made out here. "Sex."

"On a rock?"

"Probably more on the ground, on blankets, on Sunday tablecloths. Think sex in costume. They act all prim and proper then *get it on*." She growled the last three words.

"Wow," I uttered for lack of what else to say about some folks' dedication to historical reenactment.

"Crazy, right?"

"Better go get your buddy Royce to look at this," I said.

With an excited *ooh*, Lottie hustled over to the tape, giving one of her trademark hollers.

Royce soon arrived, with a newfound glance of appreciation for me once I pointed out the broken piece, but he made no conversation other than, "Did either of you touch anything?" I saw no point bringing up that his guys missed the clue.

Then I dragged Lottie to her car so they could have a re-do without judgment.

Inside the vehicle, she gushed what-ifs and theories, some far-fetched enough to question her mental faculties, but I let her run with her thoughts while I sank into mine. Someone held a tea party for a farmer, for reasons not hard to define. Secluded in the woods, early in the morning when they wouldn't be found. Hoyt might've simply met a hooker in a squirrelly sort of tryst.

I'd been starved from sleuthing so damn long that this one now had me drooling. Might be nothing more than sex, but he was our farmer, and I convinced myself I had an obligation to determine how this death would affect the agency. Lottie hinted at something more, and woe be it for me to ignore a taxpayer and her concerns, especially since she understood who I was . . . and what I did. Maybe I could learn enough about the case for Harden to leave me assigned to it. And I could get Lottie, maybe Royce too, to request me over someone foreign and green Harden might threaten to send in my place.

As Lottie pulled back on Old Whitmire Road, headed south toward town, a smile spread across my lips. Even the nausea eased. Oh, this was good. A case that could pull me out of the office and back into the field. And Lottie could ask for me by name.

Chapter 3

LOTTIE BOUGHT ME lunch at The Palms on the edge of town. A meal I wolfed down so I could skedaddle toward Columbia in hope I'd get back to the office before my boss wondered where I'd been. A difficult feat considering Lottie couldn't stop talking about her lady friends, and how Newberry was the center of the universe. And how, after looking side to side around the restaurant, she would love to find fault with the Carsons, a tinge of competition in her voice when she spoke of Cricket's mother and her ownership of a respectable chunk of town.

My newfound DJ friend vowed to keep me apprised as she continued her snooping about Hoyt's death, reiterating he wasn't exactly the perfect husband. Admittedly, I left later than planned, still experiencing the quickening exhilaration of a potential case.

In the truck, I shut off the radio, surprised at how excited I still was. The death could mean nothing financially, and socially amount to little more than spouses jealous because Agriculture's Newberry representative was female and hot. But I smelled enough smoke to want to pursue the facts. Over my short career as an investigator, I'd learned to pay attention to gossip and the little prickles under my skin when something felt amiss.

Lottie swore wives nagged her about exposing whatever they thought Cricket was doing. Had our pretty-as-a-picture county manager abused her position? This could simply be an administrative case if it involved Cricket sleeping with a client. A scene normally in my wheelhouse.

But worst-case scenario, the local Agriculture office could support a criminal enterprise where hundreds of thousands of dollars in federal funds were channeled to certain people for God-knows-what in exchange. A serious vulnerability for Agriculture.

Farmers versus Cricket? Or Cricket versus farmers?

Or pure, crap-coated rumor mill material?

Wayne would laugh his ass off listening to my cogitating, and I'd give him that. But between the radio caller and Lottie, I felt we needed to poke around the edges. A one-day trip to check Hoyt's history in Newberry, maybe a few others like him. Most certainly interview Cricket.

Ironic that an award for Cricket put her on my radar. And sad that a man died. Mrs. Hoyt Abrams would have to be interviewed. I made plans. This was my case, without Wayne, until I had no choice but to call it a crime. At which time Wayne would enter the picture.

He'd get bossy. I'd feel challenged. Then we'd get rocky for a week or two or three. This always seemed to be the routine between us.

A pickup passed me. I was barely doing forty in a fifty-five zone. Either I didn't want to get back to work, or my Wayne memories sucked my attention from the road. Most of the time Wayne felt as natural to me as my favorite tee shirt, but there were still those few uncomfortable times when that attraction scared me to tiny pieces.

His engagement ring still sat in its closed box on my dresser . . . unseen. Delivered with a proposal last August when he and I barely escaped a shootout in the tiny, peanut-worshipping town of Pelion. He'd told me to take my time deciding. I had. I still did. I doubt he thought I'd take this long.

Even I was surprised that temptation hadn't made me check how many carats or what color gold. Was it even sized right? But I was afraid to test-drive it in case it wouldn't come off once the band passed that final knuckle.

Wayne occasionally turned a bit testy about the matter, and I understood that, but I was frozen in this middle zone. To the point that with my two kids in the picture, our *dates* usually occurred at his place, with the perk of giving me distance from that maroon velvet box.

Was my hesitation self-preservation or silliness? Scared to change something that wasn't broke was more like it.

In the meantime, calm, Lowcountry Monroe waited. Not that I'd told him about the ring. Unusual for a girl who chatted up life to avoid facing it sometimes, but a lot of my sanity was due to Monroe letting me vent about work . . . about life. He was such a damn fine listener, and I selfishly wanted to preserve that.

I parked in the parking garage across the street and trotted through the federal building entrance with a brief pause at the metal detector. Nabbing a second elevator after a herd of people piled into the first, I closed the door quickly to avoid stopping on other floors.

Agriculture consumed the entire tenth story of this gray concrete box of a stark structure with minimal windows. A contrast to the sea of colorful oddities who worked within. We swore the germ-infested air dated back to the 1979 ribbon-cutting. Ancient carpets stretched flat as paper in the public areas. I counted my blessings each and every day that I wasn't deskbound by my duties, despite Harden's desire to keep my butt glued firmly to my chair. I had applied to Agriculture to be outside, at least part of the time.

Whitney, my admin technician, managed my calls and ran interference for me with the front office, using myriad excuses with a shrewd creative bent. Her late-twenties appearance allowed her to pull off innocence like nobody's business, and I sent her random goodies as thanks.

I hustled to her desk. "Is he in?" The thought of Harden sent a rolling uneasiness through my gut again. See? My stomach troubles were all about him.

"Not yet," she said. "You okay?"

Regardless the reason, I needed an antacid. "Spent the morning sharing opinions with the boss, so what do you think?"

"Gotcha," she said. "So, how'd it go at the radio?" Meaning, who won.

Reaching into a cabinet, I shook out three Tums, hoarded for times such as this. "He made me sit outside and watch."

"Aww."

Her feigned pout made me laugh.

"Love the dangles today," I said, complimenting her six-inch beaded earrings, her trademark jewelry swinging against her neck as she typed. "Anything urgent come up while I was out? Need to head down the hall to talk to Monroe."

She gave a wilted, are-you-kidding look. We hadn't done anything *urgent* since Harden shackled me six months ago.

"Good, then." I headed back out the door. "Buzz me if there's a nuclear holocaust."

"Will do."

I took the outside hallway, rather than parade through the rows of cubicle-chained employees who probably wondered, like Whitney, who'd escaped Newberry the victor. Two dozen employees huddled in the same space tended to discuss each other's business.

Monroe's department took up the east corner of the floor. His staff liked me because Monroe liked me, which made it easy for me to come here for help or talk. Reaching his open door, I stepped in. "Knock, knock."

Monroe stood like the gentleman he was. "Come on in. Sit. Spill it."

My expletives and Kodachrome adjectives of Harden consumed several minutes until, breathless, I reached the gist of my mission, took it down a notch, and replayed the morning's events.

"He'll not be the only one with a heart attack if you don't get a grip," Monroe said, after hearing how Hoyt Abrams probably died. "Does seem odd how they found the man, but libido is a powerful instinct."

"With men, their IQ falls into their crotch. Women, however, want an emotional link . . . or have a motive."

"Profound," he said, humor bright in his eyes.

I scoffed. "But you agree I need to check out the Newberry operation, right? Just to put it to rest if nothing else?"

Come on, be on my side, Monroe. Tell me I'm right. Please?

He shrugged, eyes compassionate. The whole damn tenth floor understood I'd been shackled by Harden. "Somebody should," he finally said.

"Somebody?"

"Yes, probably you, but—"

"Somebody else is what he's trying to say," said a boom of a voice behind me.

I leaped in my seat at Harden sneaking up.

Monroe's face didn't hide his irritation. "Nobody said you needed to see me," he said, attempting to diffuse the issue. Monroe and I were equals in this little fiefdom, so Harden ruled the roost over him too. My friend had no dog in this particular fight and waited, rather than contradict Harden's assessment just yet.

I, however, stood and made my case. "I took the complaint. After that caller on the radio today, and once you left for your luncheon date with Cri-cket," I said, rolling her name out in two long syllables, "Lottie Bledsoe asked me to accompany her to the scene of a farmer's death this morning. Our county manager has been accused of stepping across a few lines professionally, but somebody could be attempting to blackball her, too. Either way, we should head off the damaging innuendo."

Harden and I had been peers until his recent promotion, often at each other's jugular. Both of us struggled to shed our old ways with the change, but the struggle lay more on my shoulders than his. I still saw him as a crook or at least as crook-adjutant.

Harden's glare took a few seconds. "We just gave her an award."

My hands dipping and diving, I pleaded the case. "All the more reason to look. We can say that the radio show prompted the caller, but we didn't want to be accused of playing favorites with Miss Carson because of the award. However we spin it we don't need to sit on our asses if there might be a mess over there."

"I agree," he said.

My mouth hung open like a hooked bass, then closed. "Um, good. I'll call Cricket Carson, and—"

"No, you won't."

"But you—"

Harden pointed at Monroe. "He'll do it."

Monroe's mouth hung agape now. "Harden, I'm up to my neck in community facility funding. Five projects in five counties with the deadline next week."

Shifting his weight to lean on the door, Harden crossed his arms, exuding his authority as he looked at Monroe. "Didn't you uncover fraud in Beaufort County last year?"

My friend Savvy's case on the coast. During a routine audit, Monroe noted falsified signatures in files and called me. If not for my fast and loose interpretation of my job description with a heavy dose of unconventional sleuthing, Savvy would've gone to jail. Monroe just got caught in my wake, and for a while he endured a pretty rough ride.

"I noted signatures, that's all," Monroe said. "Slade broke the case."

Harden scratched his cheek. "She just came back from Newberry, so the element of surprise is gone."

I held out my hands, palms wide. "We don't need surprise. We need expediency. Stop and think, Harden. This woman needs to be cleared or caught."

"Did you not hear me, Ms. Slade?" His voice raised, the words echoing in the small office.

"Yes sir," I said low, my jaw tight, a train wreck of accusations and curses piling up.

"Good." Moving from the door, he nodded with exaggeration toward Monroe. "In the morning, Mr. Prevatte. Two days, max. Then report to me, not Ms. Slade. Do you understand?"

"Understood," my friend repeated.

Our boss left.

Anger festered in me as I reclaimed my seat. Monroe asked a technician to bring us two coffees, then sat across from me with empathy. "Tell me again what went down this morning. I need a crash course in what you do, if you don't mind."

"You were with me half the time in Beaufort, so don't act so coy." Kudos to him for trying to make me feel better.

"We stumbled around that one, and you know it. Aren't there some basics? At least orient me to the people."

"Gladly," I said. "And call Wayne if you get over there and it gets weird."

"No," he said, resting his hands on my knees. "I'll call you."

ROUNDING THE CURVE toward home, the early evening sun made the purple Formosa azaleas at the end of my house shine neon bright. I slowed the truck, glancing to see if I spotted anybody. Even as tucked back off the road as my house was, people had found me before. Wayne's ex, his sister, a couple of drug dealers in a black SUV . . . I learned nobody was secluded unless they lived north of the Arctic Circle. But still I received my mail at a UPS Store in nearby Chapin where two ladies dutifully protected my address.

Somebody worked the grill on my patio, but the distance only let me count the bodies, not ID them. The sun had warmed, pushing temperatures into the seventies, so my sister, who lived with me, must have craved burgers. Which meant Wayne had to be holding the long-handled spatula. Two years younger than me, Allegra Jo Slade couldn't turn on a gas grill to save her soul. She'd called him, which was fine.

My sister fed the courtship every chance she got. Divorced, broke, and sort of my mother's favorite, she came for a short stay and never left. She'd have been happy to have married off Wayne and me a long time ago.

I debated whether to talk about Newberry. If I opened that Pandora's box, Wayne would ask for details and determine if it was his or not. I hated he was the only one who could play a trump card.

The USDA Inspector General's Office in Atlanta gave its field agents a considerable amount of autonomy. Wayne manned a one-man resident office on the fourth floor in the same Strom Thurmond Building I worked in. Convenient lots of times. A nuisance for those times I didn't want him to be aware of my cases.

I enjoyed my work and ran with a case as long as I could keep it in my grip. This time, however, Monroe held the reins. By the time I parked in my drive, I'd conceded Wayne needn't be informed quite yet. Not until if or when Monroe needed him.

Not my case. A bitter reminder.

With a quick glance in the visor mirror, I touched up the lipstick to perk up my pale. I still wasn't feeling so great. That subject I would *not* bring up. I didn't need two nursemaids.

I entered through the garage. Upon opening the door to the kitchen, the scent of things hot and greasy slammed into me.

My sister hovered over the stove, two cast-iron skillets popping grease. One with potatoes, the other with battered dill pickles. The latter my favorite, usually.

"About time you got here," she said. "Wayne's out back."

"Yeah." I quick-stepped to the cabinet where I kept the Benadryl for wasp stings and aspirin for headaches and snared the antacid bottle. I shook four tablets into my hand, popped them in my mouth, and chewed hard, desperately willing them to dissolve fast.

"Hard day?" she asked, turning the pickles. They could burn fast.

"Maybe a bit more than usual," I replied.

Ally was wilder, more social, and my only sibling. Also, the most irresponsible; which explained why she'd been living with me for seven months. She read people though, and right now she pretended she wasn't studying me like a final exam.

Skirting the kitchen bar, I hustled into my bedroom and changed into jeans and my long-sleeved Clemson tee shirt. Orange, of course, and bearing our 2016 championship football title across the back. A third of my tee shirts were orange.

My daughter Ivy blocked my way when I opened my bedroom door again, and my guard went up.

"Hey, Momma."

"Hey yourself."

She still didn't move. I waited, letting whatever plagued her gnaw good and hard. At fourteen, she drove me insane. Ally understood her. I pretended to. We all knew better.

"We're having burgers," she finally said.

I feigned surprise. "Are you kidding me? Seriously, burgers?"

The eyes rolled with a puff from her Miss Kitty pink lips. I chuckled. "What is it, Ivy?" Lip gloss to dinner. With family? Well, Wayne was sort of family. Ivy would love for him to *be* family.

"I invited a friend to dinner," she said, suddenly fascinated with her sneakers. Where'd she get those? Floral, cute. Another mall trip with her aunt, no doubt.

I squeezed her arm. "Glad to hear it. I like that you feel comfortable bringing friends over. Who is it?" Were we at eye level to each other? No wonder she had to go shopping.

When she didn't answer, I just said, "Let's go meet them. Where's your brother?"

"Down at the water, practicing his casting," she said, then dashed ahead of me to the back porch. Five years younger than his sister, Zack served as pure nuisance to her these days.

The double doors were propped open, and I glanced over at Ally in the kitchen before going through. She waved me on, meaning she had dinner under control.

Wayne met me at the stairs off the porch, the grill smoking from the end of the uncovered patio. Spatula still in hand, he gave me a speedy bear hug with a peck on the forehead. "Ally called me."

Though not short, I still had to stretch to kiss him back on the mouth. "I figured. How long before . . ."

But he was nodding in a slow, quasi-covert kind of way toward the porch. I stopped, struggling to read the language. "What?" I whispered.

"The porch," he said low, and a brow raised.

There in the glider sat Ivy and some lanky boy with hair three months past a cut . . . on the top of his head. The sides were trimmed up tight, accenting a ring on one ear. Some semblance of whiskers had been shaved to cup his chin.

"Dear Jesus," slipped out before I could catch it.

Wayne pulled out his phone and pretended to show me something. He bumped me with it when I couldn't stop staring at the punk kid next to my daughter.

"Overreact and you'll blow it," he warned.

"Hey, Momma," Zack hollered, on his way across the yard toward us. "See Ivy's new boyfriend?"

How could I miss him? Zack's question raised everyone's attention, so I walked back to the porch with a molded smile and stretched out my hand. "Carolina Slade. I'm Ivy's mom."

"Yeah, I'm Buddy, but they call me Bug." But instead of shaking my hand, he moved his around my daughter's shoulder. She stiffened, my presence conflicting her reactions in front of the beau.

"Which am I supposed to use?" I asked. "Bug or Buddy?"

"Probably Buddy until you get to know me better." He patted Ivy's shoulder, owning his property, flaunting, he intended to know my daughter way better than I cared to imagine.

"Let's go with Bug," I said, trying not to grit my teeth. "Because I suspect we'll get to know you pretty darn quick."

Not what I'd envisioned for her first puppy love. This kid would break her heart. That's what all first loves did. I just pictured someone more . . . all-American.

Gazing over his ripped jeans that had never seen soap, taking in his smart-ass you're-not-boss-of-me smile, then settling on the stud in the side of his nose, I made an executive decision. It'd be a cold day in hell before I thought of this impudent doofus as anything other than shithead, because I was sure that's what filled the space between his ears. The only question now was whether I showed him out before or after he'd eaten any of my fried dill pickles.

I reached over and lifted his arm off my daughter. "Humor me for now. At least until you get to know *me*, but hands to yourself, Bug. And that doesn't mean just in front of me, either."

He scowled. Ivy glowered. Ally's look said *what the hell are you doing?*

Which made me worry if I'd just thrown them together in a pact against me.

Chapter 4

WEATHER PERMITTING, my family often dined outside facing Lake Murray, a luxury afforded us by the insurance of my dead husband. Alan died at the hand of the man he'd hired to kill me, so I enjoyed the hell out of the view every chance I got.

Burgers medium rare were piled high on a platter on the wrought iron table. With the platter so heavy, Wayne motioned for each person to hand him their plate so he could dole out the main course. Our guest Bug, however, sat and waited . . . while Ivy handled his plate for him.

But Wayne wouldn't oblige. "Son, is your wrist broken?"

Instead, Bug studied his girlfriend, acting all deaf and dumb as a fence post, oblivious he was the topic of discussion.

"Hey, Bug," I said, tucking aside *shithead* for a more private moment. And, oh yes, I sensed one in our future.

The boy lazily turned his head toward me. "Hmm?"

Zack's eyes widened. Good. My parenting had at least taken with him.

"First, you will address me and every other adult in this house as ma'am or sir," I said. "Or at least Ms. Slade or Mr. Largo."

Brows pinching, he waited for my second point, which in and of itself was the most mannerly thing he'd done since we met.

"Second, you serve her," and I pointed to Ivy, "not the other way around. And before you serve yourself."

A limp hand raised, drooping with a point toward Wayne. "Thought he was serving us."

"Don't act like you don't understand what I'm saying," I said.

Even before I glanced at her, I felt my daughter's exasperation and utter embarrassment. To be honest, I might've exuded attitude toward me too if in her shoes . . . and her age, but I never would've brought home such a date. If I had, my daddy would've escorted him back to the car by his collar. "Manners are important in this house," I said. "Grandpa would've strangled any of my dates if they hadn't treated me properly."

Ivy blushed deeper.

Bug seemed oblivious.

"And your grandmother," I added, "might've sent you from the table."

And it hit me I sounded like my mother. Ally noticed, too, from the smirk crawling across her face.

Wayne served Ivy first, then motioned for the boy to follow suit. "There you go. Now, everybody eat before it gets cold. Burgers don't stay hot for long."

Awkward didn't begin to describe the next twenty minutes. Ivy nibbled at her food. Zack shot smug grins at his sister. Ally fought desperately to open lines of communication, but apparently, I'd burned the small-talk bridge for everyone. Bug ate like he belonged there, holding out his plate for seconds. Wayne left him wanting until the kid ultimately had to ask. Wayne also let him wait longer until he added *please*.

Once Bug finished inhaling that burger, Ivy rose and excused herself. The kid stood as well, never once using his napkin. I started to make Ivy thank her aunt and Wayne for providing dinner but let it go. Of course, expressing gratitude didn't cross the boy's mind.

Brushing her hand over Bug's sleeve, Ivy moved toward the patio doors. "We're going for a walk."

I stiffened.

She huffed at the unspoken. "Is that too much to ask, please?"

We lived semi-rural in these parts. No sidewalk but enough traffic to make you hug the weeds along the sides. "Be careful," I said. "Take your phone and answer my texts. Home by dark."

When Ivy didn't respond, I added, "You heard me, right?"

"Yes, ma'am."

She turned with Bug in tow. All of us waited until we heard them walk through the house to the front door. Finally, the door shut.

I honed in like a missile on my sister, the daytime caregiver, the aunt Ivy adored beyond measure. "Where the hell did she find him? And if you give me some *let her experiment* rationale, I'll toss your butt off the dock."

Rearing back in her chair, Ally held hands up in surrender. "Met him a half hour before you did, oh sister dear."

Wayne read my mind when I shifted my stare to him. "I introduced myself and got nothing, then they moved to the glider," he said.

Then I turned to my nine-year-old son. "Little man? What do you think?"

"I think he's an idiot, Momma." His eyes rolled up in his head, he drooped his shoulders, and spoke with his tongue stuck out. "My name is Bug. I am a slug." He giggled. "And, Momma, I'll snoop and tell you whatever you want."

Wayne fist-bumped him.

Zack started to stand and halted. "Can I go practice my casting?"

"Go on," I said. The kid deserved it after all that. "Don't get wet down there. The water's still too cold."

He scurried off, the late sun bouncing off the water with a glare. After tucking my legs under me at a light breeze, I snatched up two of the pickles and crammed them in my mouth, but froze after two chews and mumbled, "Anyone get the kid's last name?"

"Stillwell," Wayne said.

Thank God for the agent in the room.

Zack's rhyme stuck in my head. I'd be making fun of Bug's name for a long time. Well, hopefully not too long. "I need a beer, um, a root beer," I corrected. "Y'all want one?"

"You sit. I'll get it," Wayne replied.

With a flop back in my seat, I motioned to the door as he exited. "Now that's the manners I'm talking about. And how old was our ol' Nutty Bug? Sixteen?"

My sister pulled her cotton sweater around her. "Why didn't you ask?"

"Did you?"

"Yeah, Carolina, I did. He turned sixteen two weeks ago when he got his license. No big deal."

Only she and my parents used my first name. I wagged a stiff finger at her. "Don't. A two-year age difference is huge. You do not let them out of your sight when they're in this house, you hear me?"

"You just let them out of *your* sight."

Smart aleck. My voice faded as I added, "I haven't even had *the talk* with her."

Ally threw her head back and laughed. "Trust me, Sis. Ivy's way past that conversation."

I froze. "How far?"

"Knowledge, not experience. Don't lose your mind. She and I have chatted."

And with that I stared at her, my sarcasm clear. Ally's scruples hung a little loose at times with her visits to the nudist resort a couple towns over and questionable clothing advice to my daughter. "I cringe to think how you handled it."

"Better than you, apparently."

"This is what happens with too much spandex and rayon, or not enough. You aren't letting her sunbathe nude again, are you?"

Ally's dark shag shook in the negative. "Nope. You made that clear last year." She winked. "Plus, it's not warm enough."

Proof right there Ally Jo Slade would educate my daughter more sensibly and colorfully than I would when it came to boys.

I jumped at the movement beside me. Wrapped in a Koozie, a bottled root beer appeared. "Just talk to her tonight," Wayne said, scooting his chair out to sit. "Can we change the subject, or will that piss you off?"

"Depends on the subject," I said, taking a swig. My moods didn't flip on and off like a switch. They simmered.

"There's an edge on you this evening. Is this just Ivy or did you have a bad day with Harden?"

"Is there a good day with Harden?"

"Just like I thought," he said, putting his own bottle to his lips.

Ally swatted at a fly. "Are y'all going to talk about work? If so, I'm doing dishes. Y'all always forget I'm here when you talk work."

"I won't talk work," I said.

"Yes, you will," Wayne replied. "You always have to vent, and Harden's pushed your buttons." He squinted at me. "Ally won't understand, and you obviously haven't been able to unload enough on Monroe. My guess . . ." He took another drag from his bottle, still eying me, "is that he's not letting you investigate something."

My cheeks warm, I studied the lake. Busted.

"Yeah, well, on that note I'm going inside," Ally said. After a few noisy moments of stacking plates five high, the clattering of utensils piled atop, she disappeared. Wayne leaned back and continued with his beer, a quick glance saying he waited for me to speak my mind. Like Monroe, he was a sounding board, only his opinions carried more . . . opinion.

His foot tapped mine. "I'm not competing with you, Butterbean. Just trying to help."

"We might have a case, and Harden won't let me near it," I blurted out.

Wayne leaned back further, boots on the table support beneath. "Is he hiding it from me?"

There . . . that assumption right there irritated me. The fact he would ask that question. Not that he flaunted the badge and its clear authority, but it went unspoken he could.

The reason I hadn't wanted to tell him in the first place. Apparently I had a number of authority issues. Bug and I had that in common . . . and that irritated me, too.

"It just happened today. Still gathering information." The words fell out staccato, clipped, and I stared out at Zack.

Wayne came forward in his chair. "So he's letting you back into investigations? That's good. If you need my feedback, just ask. I'm not trying to—"

"He sent Monroe instead of me," I blurted.

He set the beer bottle gently on the table. "Another jab at you for sure, but Monroe isn't stupid. Did you tell him to call me?"

Even further removing me from the equation. "Yeah, if he had to. But there's sort of a body involved."

His boots hit the floor. "What?"

"Cool your heels. Might be a heart attack, but the locale sure lent itself to question. This morning the farmer was found dressed up, minus his shoes, at some Revolutionary War landmark behind a rock. A local told me our county manager is cutting deals with farmers via sexual favors."

Wayne sat back silent, mulling, the creaking rock in his chair methodical.

"The manager was in our presence at the radio station when the body was found."

"Time of death isn't that exact, Slade."

Time. I glanced at my phone for how long Ivy'd been gone. Dusk was falling.

"All right," I said, "agreed, but they cut a caller off the air because she wasn't fond of our perky little manager Harden took out to lunch, and I bet my view of the water that he continued his radio station flirtations over dessert."

Half a grin crawled up Wayne's cheek. "Not that you wouldn't mind catching him involved in something."

"You would too if you were me." I peered out at new movement. Zack had tangled his line in a low limb and was yanking it this way and that, dangerously bending the rod with a vengeance. "Zack? You need help?"

"No," he yelled back.

I kept watching his jerks and yanks, which were much more violent than necessary. "What's his problem?"

"His sister never brought a guy home before," Wayne said. "He doesn't trust the boyfriend."

Zack expelled energy through anger or schemes . . . had since his father died. He concocted solutions, not letting anyone in on the secret, though we always sensed something amiss. Easing back from the front of my chair, I finished my root beer. "Well, he'll be acting out for a few days."

"Kind of takes after his momma."

My lips flatlined. "Yeah, well, boyfriends can do that to a person."

"Let's not get childish about this," Wayne said.

Oh, he didn't just say that.

A shiver rolled across my shoulders as the sun began to fade. "Any suggestions how to pursue this case? God knows you wouldn't be able to leave here without advising me."

He frowned. "What the heck is wrong with you tonight?"

Damned if I knew. I tried to curtail my breathing which seemed rather loud at the moment.

Wayne and I never failed to discuss work, whether the conversation turned fussy or ran smooth as we linked facts and made headway. I clearly recognized that the advantages of dating a real agent made me look remarkably smart at times.

Wayne didn't wait for me to answer his question, which was great since I had no answer. I grabbed my phone and texted Ivy to come home.

"As always, follow the money," Wayne continued, offering basic direction I already knew. "Is each farmer eligible for the funds he or she received?"

"Have no idea yet. I already said it was early. What about the purported sexual favors?"

"What kind of favors?" he asked. "All I'm hearing is jealousy and gossip."

"Something along the line of the farmer being seduced and his reputation held hostage."

"But for what?" He shook his head. "So she looks better to the community? Gets an award? Come on, Slade."

My fingernail scratched at the wrapper on the bottle. "Has to be about more than that. What about kickbacks?"

"Again, account for where the money went." He pointed toward me then withdrew the gesture as if self-correcting. "That's how you solve the grand majority of any of our cases . . . and you should already appreciate that."

He was right. He'd be asking me regularly about Newberry now. Dropping hints of how he'd do it, which didn't help because, how was I supposed to tell him squat or take his advice if I wasn't running this case?

This clash with Harden wasn't his fault, but I wanted it to be somebody's fault. Not like I could yell at my boss about it.

I shot a second text to Ivy to get home.

"Monroe's actually a good choice here," Wayne added. "He audited files before and found fraud. Who says he can't do the same here?"

Right again, but not what I exactly wanted to hear. A frog croaked from up the cove, a few ducks splashing before settling down on the dead fallen trees to sleep.

He stood. "I need to head on back, Slade. It's getting on toward eight. You need to get the kids to bed, and I have an interview in the field tomorrow. Fraud case."

I rose and collected the bottles. "Which county?"

He took the empties from me. "You know better than to ask."

"I hate it you can ask me details on my cases, but I can't ask details about yours."

His head tilted. If he had a cowboy hat, he'd be eying me from under the brim. "I handle more than just your agency. Their business isn't yours. It's not a slam against you in any way, but . . . what?"

I had paused at the back door. "I think I get what's eating at me. The word *but*. It's always there. *You're good, Slade, but I'm better. You investigate, Slade, but I'm a federal criminal investigator.* It's completely unfair that I can't get through the gatekeeper of the sacred badges."

He exhaled and shook his head. "Let's don't go there. It's black and white, Butterbean. Admittedly, you've used skills and solved cases, really impressing me, but I'm—"

"Law enforcement," I said. I wished so damn badly that I'd applied to the Inspector General for one of those real jobs a long time ago. The cutoff age was thirty-seven, a date behind me now. The equivalent of being a nurse when you really wanted to be the doctor. Instead, I'd forever be the junior to his senior.

Why was I being so nasty? He could've grabbed a burger in town and not come out.

We finished in the kitchen and walked through where Ally lay draped across the sofa watching some mind-numbing reality show. Wayne thumped her on the head on his way out.

"See ya', Cowboy," she said. "Thanks for doing the burgers."

"Heard from Ivy?" I asked, fully aware Ivy might call her aunt before her mother.

"Texted. Home in ten."

On foot they couldn't be far, but it was darker than I preferred, so I messaged my daughter to come home now. No doubt she'd try to avoid a conversation.

Note to self to find out Bug's address, phone number, email, Facebook . . . ask if Wayne would run a check on him.

"Don't corner her too much tonight," he said, getting into his Explorer in the drive. He shut the door and rolled down the window when he started the engine.

"And how many children have you raised?"

"Come here."

Leaning in, I met him for a stiff kiss.

He half-grinned and pulled me to him again. "We could do this all the time." He gave me another peck.

I stepped back to let him leave. Instead of immediately putting the car in drive, however, a cloud fell across his face. "You could tell me no just as easily as yes, and we could quit playing these games."

To that I had no reply. He cocked an eyebrow at me and left. I watched his taillights disappear over the hill of my drive, hating myself for something I didn't understand. His being here to "do this all the time" scared me just as much as the thought of his taillights disappearing over the hill for the last time.

I hated myself right now.

Tears threatened, and I rubbed my eyes with the heels of my hands. I blinked then saw Ivy come into view walking down the drive. I waited for her, but she marched past me into the house.

Damn this Bug kid.

And Harden.

The outside coach lamp came on, its automatic eye reading the night. Someone inside turned on the light at the door. Slowly, I turned to go inside.

I had a case to drill down on, even if Monroe was the boots on the ground. He'd call me each step of the way.

Chapter 5

I WOKE UP WONDERING what the hell got into me last night. Besides the Bug. Wayne didn't deserve what I doled out. But a hint of queasiness slammed me back to the present.

No, today I wanted a clean slate. I would attempt to be reasonable with Ivy, whatever that meant. Call Wayne and test the waters. Dare I say apologize? My day was filled. No room to think pregnancy. Not yet. No, no, no. I wasn't going to start counting days on the calendar again. Today I had a case on my hands whether Harden accepted that or not.

A knock sounded on my door. "Coffee's ready." Ally.

I loved my sister, most of the time. Since her divorce last year, when our mother *suggested* she come stay with me a week to regroup, Ally decided to become a professional aunt and take up residence in my guest room. So, as retribution, I designated her my familial au pair, thinking she wouldn't last long being maid and nanny. Wrong.

And Ivy loved her more than she loved me.

Ally swore not, avowing that an aunt held more advantages than mothers when it came to being a buddy, and that I ought to count my blessings I had such a resource at my disposal. Sort of the way Wayne thought.

Damn, maybe they were right.

After I arrived at the office, my mind still churned about Ivy. I so missed the sweet child who curled up in my lap before bed each night, asking me to read Dr. Seuss at least twice before crawling under lilac sheets with a Tinkerbell quilt. And before that, the smell of prescription baby shampoo because of her allergies. And before that . . . gracious, this sappy stuff was so not me.

Focus on the case. Where would I start, or rather, how will I guide Monroe?

I tried to take another sip of coffee, and . . . couldn't. Caffeine had dosed me awake since college, to include while pregnant with each kid, albeit at half strength, so what was this?

I laid my head on the desk and groaned at the returned queasiness.

Shit. I couldn't be pregnant. Not at forty years old. And with Wayne at forty-six. He had no kids, and we hadn't discussed whether he wanted any, because we were sort of at *that* age.

Straighten up. Forget pregnancy tests or the lack of them because I didn't have the courage to actually stop at the pharmacy this morning. Forget the fact somebody would have to give up their bedroom to share with someone else. Or the scary, fleeting, there's-always-abortion thought.

I ran to the canteen and returned with a Coke. Better.

A quick call later, I learned Monroe didn't even come in today, so that meant he drove straight to Newberry. Then my fingers dialed Lottie's number before I could stop myself. She picked right up.

"Hey, Lottie, it's Carolina Slade from USDA. Have they determined anything about Hoyt Abrams? Or the china piece?" When she hesitated, I stared at the old government clock on my office wall. Eight thirty. I normally didn't percolate this early and realized Lottie might not either. "I didn't wake you, did I?"

The DJ cleared her throat. "Not in the least. Had a swallow of coffee caught there. My third cup. I beat the sunrise today." The words ran into each other, telling me she was bright-eyed and on full-octane caffeine. I wondered if she ever wasn't.

"Heart attack is cause of death," she said. "But the codger brought it on himself."

"How?" Questions usually taught as journalism guidelines were also recommended to agents who sought answers—who, what, when, where, why, and how. Spinning my chair around, I put hands to keyboard and listened while I sought whatever I could access in our system on Hoyt Abrams.

"The almighty blue pill, honey. No tests back yet, but all other conditions point to it in his system. That and the little single serving paper in his pocket with Viagra written on it. Makes you not so sympathetic toward the good old American farmer, doesn't it?"

Crap. My online access was limited. Not being a loan specialist let me only see some basics. Less info than Monroe told me over the phone.

"I don't know," I said. "Maybe he got it on with his wife that morning." Only twenty-four hours since Hoyt died, and Newberry had answers? Did I dare send Lottie to Monroe with this new info? Or him to her? Technically I should do one or the other. I told him yesterday who she was.

"Now those results are still unofficial, mind you," she said.

But damn efficient.

"But, nope, not swallowing the wife story," Lottie added. "No one takes their wife to the tea party rock."

The woman had a network, I gave her that. "Even your feelers have feelers, don't they?" I pulled up Newberry's town page on my screen, to gain a better feel.

"For sure. My people know people," she said.

I dismissed her with a puff. "No, your people are related."

"It's not a crime to have relatives."

Even her seriousness held humor, and I was grateful for her lifting my depressed state. "Ever considered that it's a crime to release sensitive information in an open investigation?"

"We don't tattle."

She sorta just did.

"And the tea cup?" I asked, doodling a cup on my notepad, a habit I often forgot I had until I later read clues all over my desk.

"Well, I wouldn't want to commit a crime releasing information and such," she said.

Ooh, such a sly player. "We're both past that point, I'd say."

"Well," she said, and lowered her voice. "Hoyt's prints and one other they can't identify. Real tea was in the cup, by the way."

"Makes sense."

"Of course it does. He died in the a.m. Only an alcoholic would drink that time of day, and Hoyt wasn't that big a social drinker so tea makes sense for a guy like him."

Sure, he can cheat on his wife during a picnic on a rock, but God forbid anyone think he's drunk.

"Plus it fits the role-play," she added.

Whitney's voice sounded outside my closed door. Shoot, she'd buzz me any minute. Then Harden's voice sounded loud and clear. "Tell her I'm here."

I slid my doodled notes into my top drawer. One day that habit would get me into trouble. The bubble-drawn words *Viagra* and *Hoyt* spoke way too loud for prying eyes not to want to pry more.

"Lottie," I said, lowering my tone. "Can I call you back? Our friend from yesterday is at my door."

"No problem. You're not informing him, are you? Not that I'm telling you how to do your job, but that man doesn't seem to think before he engages."

My phone buzzer sounded from Whitney.

A knock sounded then the handle was tried. Harden had the patience of a full bladder.

And he made me love the lock on my door even more. Locks kept good people honest and made bad people frustrated enough to leave proof of entry.

The handle shook again. "Ms. Slade, I need to speak to you."

"I'll get back with you today, Lottie," I said, hung up, and buzzed Whitney back. "Thanks for trying, but don't go anywhere. Okay?"

"Yes, ma'am. Good luck."

My heart pounded, and I felt exposed, as if Harden timed coming to see me because of my phone call to Newberry. But I'd called Lottie on my personal phone, I reminded myself. After a big collective inhale, I opened the door.

Harden's aggravation seemed to precede him into my office, and the scent of cigar followed. He didn't sit, and instead stood all big and bad in front of my desk which I retreated behind. "A television reporter's coming within the hour," he said. "Update yourself on GMO stuff and handle it."

Genetically modified organisms. A topic as polarizing as blue and red politics. I was surprised he even trusted me with the reporter, but realized Harden probably understood less about GMO than, say, Ivy's genius of a boyfriend.

"Send them to Clemson," I said. "We don't do research."

"Don't we have farmers with GMO crops? I'm pretty sure that's the side we're on."

I choked on my laugh and sat. "Most farmers plant with GMO seed, but we don't take a side in that, Harden. We help them stay in business financially, but don't get involved with their agricultural genetics ethics." Not that I didn't have my take on the whole non-GMO subject. We just didn't need this fight on our turf. "The senator might not like seeing us on TV, either," I said, referencing the politician in charge of selecting the person in Harden's job. He didn't have the job permanently yet, either. "We're money, not science, and his side of the state's mighty heated about this subject."

Still standing, he stared out my picture window to the prominent state capitol dome a few blocks over. He growled low as though to himself, almost an unconscious reaction, the unfamiliar politics of his new position always challenging to his naïveté. He'd been out of the field too long, had never farmed himself, and was hired more for his engineering degree.

"You talked to Monroe today?" he asked.

My smugness disappeared. "No, why?"

"Wondering if you'd been insubordinate yet."

Ah, he was just righting himself and clawing back to more familiar territory—dogging me. "Did Monroe go to Newberry today?" I asked, giving him his moment. Giving him a question he could answer right.

"*Hunh*," he said with a grin. "My order to you is clear: stay out of Newberry."

"But why?" I asked, tired of assumptions. Maybe it was time I forced him to articulate why he continued to keep me from the field.

"What do you mean why? Just the fact I said so is why enough for you."

I raised my voice before I could catch myself. "I'm not a show dog following orders and would like to understand why you won't let me get involved." He leaned on my desk, and I craved to smack his hands off my territory. I also wanted to stand and shout, *You are a walking wet turd of a moron!*

Instead I said, "I believe there might be a misunderstanding here."

"What kind of misunderstanding?"

Gripping the arms of my chair, I started to rise, to meet him eye to eye, and changed my mind. "I mean that the quicker you open and shut this case the better. Monroe is sharp, but he's not a natural investigator. And you've banned him from talking to me about it which will have him second-guessing himself." Like either of us would pay attention to that order.

With a gut-full of sarcasm, Harden laughed. "And you're the natural investigator?"

"I put your buddies in jail."

Oh Jesus, did I just say that?

Silence. And his skin seemed to blister from within.

My phone dinged with a text. Monroe. Panicking.

Where to start. Do I look at all the farm accounts? The big ones? The most recent? What the heck? Then, *!!!!!!!!!!!!!!!!!!!*

I could show Harden the message, punctuating my point, but he'd go after Monroe. No, couldn't do that. I was the one who got poor Monroe into this mess to begin with.

"Look, I'm just offering my services," I finally told Harden. "Might get Monroe back to the office sooner to handle those projects up for funding. Any of those of particular interest to the senator?"

Of course they were. Four of the five, and Harden knew that. State directors lived to kiss congressional ass in hopes they'd one day step into higher roles, or be rewarded, or whatever it was that drove the power aspirations of people like them. The attitude wasn't in my wheelhouse of personality traits. Law enforcement I understood. Define the evil, track it down, and take it out. That's what drove me.

Damn. I should've been offered that bribe sooner, met Wayne sooner, learned more about the IG's tasks sooner. I'd be in Wayne's shoes, and not seated here watching Harden mull over how to get rid of me. He stood sort of stymied, like I'd thrown too many options at a computer and made it crash . . . only computers didn't turn red.

"So, about the reporter with the GMO deal?" I asked, hoping his attention turned halfway back to what a senator wanted.

"Drop it."

Amen! "And Newberry?"

His sour sneer reminded me of a maniacal W. C. Fields. "No."

"Harden, please." For Monroe. Sort of for me.

"I can't decide which is more fun . . . stopping you from investigating or giving you grunt work. But as long as I'm your superior, your job will be whatever I dump on you. My choice, not yours. Is that clear?"

Cheeks heated, I stared.

He raised his voice. "Is that clear?"

Every sinew in me drew taut. "Yes."

The second he left, I shut the door and gave the lock a solid twisted click. He had to have heard it.

I'd crossed a line, and I might not hear the other shoe fall until it snapped my neck. *In for a penny* . . . I dialed Monroe. He needed guidance, and I needed to hear his voice. "Hey," I said when he answered. "Can you talk?"

"I can in a second. Hold on."

Assuming he walked to distance himself from Cricket hearing, I pulled back out my notes from Lottie and flipped past the paper with the Viagra scribblings on it.

"Okay," he said, winded. "Do I ask Cricket if she's made any loans she doesn't feel comfortable with? Or is that too blunt? And if I just start looking at files, what's the red flag? Her staff loves her." He gulped a short breath. "Everyone else in the county building thinks she walks on water. She drives a Honda, so it's not like she flaunts money. And she won an award from the state director just yesterday. She's wondering what triggered me to show up, and I can't tell her. Slade, all we have is gossip to go on!"

Monroe was too good a soul to interrogate anybody. He hated stepping on toes as much or more than missing Easter service. This job would churn him into a froth, and it was part of why I sneaked down to Beaufort to help him before. Back then I'd decided to ask for forgiveness instead of permission, but this time Harden had beat me to the punch and handcuffed me.

"Slow down, Monroe. Ask her why that caller complained about her yesterday on the radio show. You were listening to it, right?"

"Yeah."

"From different angles, get her to talk about why anyone would have an ax to grind with her. Act like you are on her side and your visit is because of that radio caller plus another disgruntled someone like her made a hotline call after the show."

"Did they?" he asked.

"No, but that's not the point." *Come on, Monroe.*

I heard his frustration, but the truth was that this was not straight-forward with a specific detailed complaint. There really might not be anything after all.

But we had to pursue this before another hot-headed caller accused us of a cover up. "Take this down, Monroe."

"Ready."

"Research Hoyt Abrams' file thoroughly. Did he have any financial problems? Was he qualified for the assistance or loans he received? You're familiar with auditing a file. But pull several files, and don't let Cricket see which one you're studying."

I gave him a minute to finish writing.

"Then look at Cricket's calendar. Make a copy. Send one to me, if you don't mind. Was there an excess number of meetings with Hoyt or anyone else? What stands out. Hunt for patterns and anomalies."

He *um-hummed* he was with me.

"Use the phone call, Monroe. Say that Harden was concerned about the dissatisfied caller, especially on the heels of the award. He didn't want the agency embarrassed. Ask her if there is anything we need to get in front of. We'd rather shut it down sooner than later. Tell her Harden, or rather Mr. Harris, is a politician, and the worst thing in their life is bad press."

That ought to take him half the day, at least. I added, "Go to lunch with her, if she asks. Stay friendly. She'll be more likely to slip up that way."

I heard a pneumatic door creak open in the background. "Hey,"

Monroe said, then came back to me. "That was her. Think she's checking on me?"

"Who gives a rip if she is, Monroe? Focus."

God, I wish I were in his shoes.

Monroe blew hard, and I felt bad. This wasn't his fault.

"Listen," I said. "My source says it's the bigger farmers, so if you need more to do, call a few of them. Ask if they are happy with the office. You are an auditor from out of town. Give them the feeling this is all routine to put them at ease. Promise them confidentiality but don't specify what you're looking for."

"That's good," he said. "Because I have no idea what I'm looking for."

Poor Monroe. He was so much happier behind his desk. "You can do this."

Big sigh. "Okay. I can do this."

"You said Cricket asked why you're there, but how's she really handling it? Describe her behavior."

"Curious but other than that she's a sweet kid."

"No animosity?"

"Not at all. Like I said, sweet."

But that could be part of the con. "Call me if you need me," I said. "In the meantime, I'm chasing down employees who are late paying their government credit cards."

"Poor Slade," he said.

"Yeah, there's one nefarious guy who bought his wife flowers."

He hung up in a brighter mood, but my stomach roiled. I began to doubt my initial opinion of Cricket and chastised my all-too-quick decision to fall into step with Lottie's sinister musings. *Don't rule out plain and simple gossip*, Wayne had said.

I could call Monroe back and tell him how to wrap up easily and leave, but Harden would love that. A built-in I-told-you-so at me for the next five years.

Maybe I could handle breakfast now. Scribble pad in hand, I told Whitney I'd be in the canteen then took the stairs down three floors. The crowd ought to be thinned out, and I might find a place to tuck away and call Lottie back.

The residual bacon aroma did me no favors, so I grabbed a fresh Coke and a cinnamon bun with all its illustrious carbs. I disappeared into the west corner behind a decorative wall divider, one of several that had been installed to give ambience to the concrete block walls and metal chairs that scrubbed thin patches in the thread-bare carpet.

I dialed. "Lottie? Can you talk?"

"Yeah, honey."

"Let's go back where we left off," I said, trying not to be heard as I ripped off a piece of bun. "What did you mean when you said role-playing?"

"Um, not now."

"But you said you could talk. What's up?"

"Mrs. Hoyt Abrams is what's up. She's sitting across my kitchen table from me, and she wants to know when you're coming back to town."

"Um, my boss—"

She lowered her voice. "You're not hearing me, honey. She's not even talking to Deputy Royce about this."

And I wouldn't expect her to. Royce handled the farmer's death, and Hoyt died of natural causes . . . well, natural with a little blue-pill assistance. Neither the sheriff nor the town police cared about what happened in Agriculture's jurisdiction.

"We have a guy over there right now, Lottie. She can speak to him. His name is—"

"And a guy from USDA is the last person she'd want to talk to," Lottie replied. "She wants a woman, and not the one you've got running Newberry County."

Chapter 6

WAYNE WALKED INTO the federal building canteen, and I cowered in my corner booth, trying to shrink into the size eight I always wanted to be. Lottie had the dead farmer's wife at her house, for coffee, with me on her phone's speaker, and I sure as hell didn't want Wayne hearing the details.

It would look worse if Wayne saw me hiding, so I got up and hustled to the exit, phone to my ear. "Can y'all give me a quick sec, Lottie? Someone just walked in."

"Here we go again."

"No, I just need to get to a more secure location." I muted her, cursing my decision to have this conversation here of all places.

Wayne stepped in my path. "Hey, how's it going this morning with Harden?"

"One skirmish thus far," I said, rushing by, guilt pinging my chest at his attempt to make nice, and me brushing him off. "Jury's out on the winner. Listen, I gotta go." I held up my phone.

"Monroe?" he asked as I fast-walked down the hall.

Later, I mouthed, entering the stairwell. Despite everything, I couldn't straight-out lie to the man.

Three floors up and breathless, I checked for signs of Harden, then made a run for my office. Whitney had worked for me long enough to not ask questions and flashed a sly grin at my effort to be covert.

With one hand, I grabbed the recorder from a drawer, then with the other I stretched to shut the door. I made sure the lock clicked shut, not caring for another one of Harden's morning interruptions.

A scorned spouse could be an investigator's dream. In South Carolina, the law stated one person could record another without their permission, as long as one of the two or more parties was a participant.

A button here and there, and recorder on. I spoke the date, time, and persons present as an intro, to be able to utilize the interview as evidence later, then took my cell off mute. "Sorry, ladies. Sometimes walls have ears."

"I can't imagine," Lottie said. "Let's try again, shall we?"

"How are you, Mrs. Abrams?" I began. "Please let me express how sorry I am about the loss of your husband."

"Not a problem," the wife said, her voice more angered than forlorn. "What do you need me to say about Hoyt? He loved his pecker more than me and exercised it elsewhere, often."

Whoa, Nelly. With that I double-checked the recorder. "I see," I said, to clearly indicate I'd heard her for the record . . . and to be polite. "Can we assume you had no idea of your husband's whereabouts yesterday morning?"

"I did not," she replied.

"Were you aware of him meeting anyone?"

"I was not."

"Can you tell me anything about why he was there or," I paused, "whether it involved . . . the farm in any way." I didn't want to mention Cricket and start a rumor that might not be true.

"I don't."

Well, we were headed nowhere fast. I shifted in my desk chair and winced, forgetting it had a tendency to creak.

Lottie interceded. "Slade. I can call you just Slade, right?"

"Yes, ma'am."

"When I said she only wanted to speak to you, that meant *speak to you.*"

"But we are speaking." This was like digging a pond with a spoon.

Lottie smacked her lips. "That means face to face. You can't trust phones."

Point taken with the recorder on my end. My mind ran scenarios to justify my going there without Harden aware. The ladies would never invite Monroe. I had tried. They only wanted me. There. Justified.

"When can you get here?" she asked.

"Um . . ." I wasn't sure and glanced at my calendar as if it could tell me. If I arrived after work, Mrs. Abrams might lose her nerve. If I left now, Harden might get wise. There had to be a way.

The wife spoke up. "She's no better than the rest of them, Lottie. Forget it."

Crap, there it was . . . cold feet. I leaned earnestly toward my desk, elbows on the blotter, as though the farmer's wife were there. "Mrs. Abrams, please don't feel that way. I would love hearing what you have to say."

"Apparently not."

I glanced at my wall clock. "It takes an hour from downtown Columbia, ladies. Can you give me that?"

Lottie chuckled. "That's what we wanted. Just took a pound cake out of the oven, so I think we can manage that long. You recall where I live, right? On Main Street. White with columns?"

A lot of old Southern homes were white with columns, also with azaleas and dogwoods, flags flying in front of rockers on the porch. So common in towns like Newberry where modernization was accepted at their convenience, not the other way around. "Street number?" I asked.

"1550," she said. "Come to the side door so we can hear you since we'll be all the way back in the kitchen."

We hung up. After slipping the small tape in my pocket from the recorder, not that it was worth anything, I pulled out my purse and breezed by Whitney with a quick order to call if anything came up. I wouldn't make her lie for me, so I didn't tell her my plan for the afternoon.

Then inside the stairwell, I called my sister. "If anyone asks, I came home because of a sick kid. They don't need more information than that. Okay?" Pausing two floors down I listened for footfalls. Not many government employees bothered with the stairs unless there was a fire drill. Ten floors were a lot of steps, but one couldn't be too careful.

Ally gave a tiny squeak of a noise through the phone. "Ooh, fun. Sure. Why? You on a trail?"

I fast-tracked my way down. "Can't say right now."

"Does Wayne know?"

"Um, just tell him you aren't sure where I am. How's Ivy?"

"At school. Ol' Bug picked her up today."

My brain shifted from my shenanigans to my daughter's. "He just got his license, for God's sake. And since when does she ride in someone else's car to school?"

"Since you messed with her guy last night. But this only was the first time, and in my defense, he showed up and she ran out and got in before I could stop her."

"And you didn't call the school to make sure she arrived?" I reached the ground floor and trotted outside, past the federal building guards.

"Trust her a little bit, Slade."

I tripped over the curb. "Trust, hell. We don't have a clue what kind of idiot Bug Stillwell is. Call the school."

She exhaled into the phone for my benefit.

I didn't care. She hadn't had to save Ivy and Zack from a kidnapper.

She hadn't had to calm them down after a criminal killed their dog on my first case. "Call me a tight ass if you like, Ally, but we don't take chances with my kids. You should appreciate why, and if you can't accept that responsibility, then pack it up and go bunk with Mom."

I'd never outright used Mom as a threat before, not that we hadn't joked about it. She didn't respond, and in the silence my flats clacked hard against the pavement on the way to the parking garage. My purse strap slipped off my shoulder, and I caught it, yanking it up and back in place. "It's the middle of the day," I said, needing to make a hard point. "If she never came home, how would that make you feel?"

"Like hell."

"Enough said. So, do you even remember why I called?"

"To lie for you."

"Right," I panted, staring at more stairs up to the second level of the garage. I should start packing sneakers.

"Are you in a race or what?" she asked.

"Trying to make an . . . appointment." Finally, I reached my truck and clambered in. "Text me once you confirm she's in class."

"While I'm lying for you."

Maybe I'd been harsh. "Sorry. This is new territory for me."

Ally gave me a *humph*. "Good thing I'm your favorite sister. I'll handle Ivy."

"I owe you."

The familiar banter with my sister settled my nerves a smidge. Time to get my head on straight. With a quick reverse, I was on my way. The interstate was less than a mile from here, and once on it, I could make good time. But I still couldn't get home out of my head.

Some days I wondered if free child care and half-baked house cleaning were worth Ally Jo. On others, she was exactly what God ordered. I worried most days if the kids would adopt her carefree hippy ways, particularly now with Ivy caught up in pheromones and flexing her teenage muscle just to piss me off. I was never a bad teenager, only had brief flashes of insanity. Ally, however, had defined irresponsibility in the name of loving life.

Not far past the Peak exit at the 95-mile marker, a couple of texts came in. Damn, I wished texts came in across your windshield or something. I couldn't stand not glancing over. I mean, it could be Ally, about Ivy. The phone was right there, in my cup holder . . . .

A horn blew to my right. I snatched the wheel to the left. "Sorry," I said to the guy in a Nissan, barreling off showing me his finger.

The phone rang, an unfamiliar number, and it came across my truck's sound system. "Hello?" I answered.

"Ms. Slade?" asked a man, sounding much like my father.

My pulse still pitter-pattering from the near miss, I responded, "Yes, sir. Can I help you?"

"I heard you were checking into Cricket Carson."

How the hell did he know that? Especially considering I wasn't the one doing the checking.

"Um," I stuttered, "I'm with her employer, but I'm afraid I can't really say much more than that. May I ask to whom I'm speaking?"

"I'm a farmer."

"Yes, sir?"

"In Newberry County."

Holy crap. "I see."

He coughed. "If we meet, can I expect discretion?"

What examiner didn't court a snitch, or a victim, or anyone willing to come forward? "Be happy to meet you. And I'll keep you out of it as much as I can."

Silence.

"Sir? You there?"

Then, "I have to remain anonymous."

What was I supposed to say? If he was an honest-to-goodness farmer Cricket screwed, in one fashion or another, his name would come out. "How about we meet, you don't tell me who you are, and we take it in baby steps from there. You can leave whenever you like."

"Meet me in the Lowe's parking lot on Harbison Boulevard at six."

"In the morning?" I asked, hoping.

"This evening," he said. "What do you drive?"

"A green F-150. Clemson alumni stickers on the back. And you?"

But he hung up.

Wonderful. The opposite direction from where I was going. Actually, fifteen miles on the far side of my place, making it an hour's drive from Lottie's. With it almost two o'clock, that gave me until three to reach Newberry. One hour of chat, two hours tops, then an hour back to Columbia in the middle of rush hour. I hoped these women talked fast.

The phone rang again. The same number.

"Hello?"

Nothing.

"Hello?" I picked up my phone to check for a connection, when a horn blared. The car gunned it and passed.

Crap! I'd strayed into the fast lane, astraddle the line. My grip on the wheel tensed all the way into my shoulders as I tried to ease back until a semi trumpeted a bellow on my right. I jerked left, across the fast lane, onto the interstate's edge before I caught myself. Every muscle clenched, waiting for that bumper-scraping, metal-grinding sound from hitting yet another car I hadn't seen.

Then suddenly the road noise disappeared. Shit! I'd left the asphalt for soft grass in the median. The truck slid as I fought to put wheels back on the road.

Opening eyes I hadn't realized were closed, I squealed as the wire cable safety barrier came at me fast. With a snatch of the wheel, I turned my truck back up toward the road. Slipping, holding my breath . . . finally the tires caught purchase.

I evened out and eased to a stop. Cars eastbound and westbound gawked at me parked where nobody was supposed to be, and my heart pounded like bongos in my ears. My God, I'd almost become my insurance agent's next nightmare.

About fifty yards back, somebody slowed on the opposite shoulder of the eastbound side, assumedly with the intention of checking on me. A social meet-and-greet in which I didn't care to partake. Didn't need the highway patrol arriving, which meant Wayne might find out. He always bragged about never breaking the governor's speed laws. Easy for him to say. Badges didn't give other badges tickets.

Think, Slade.

I hadn't exceeded the speed limit. Hadn't even touched the cables. Grass would grow back into the ruts I made. Not a mark on my truck, either, so who would be the wiser? For a second I gave myself credit for not hitting some poor soul, then guilt slid in like a snake. No phone call had been that important.

Unless this farmer had spilled his guts and split this immature inquiry wide open. I might have made an exception for my lack of driving skills in that case.

I eased back into traffic, humming. Then I quit humming, feeling stupid attempting to act normal when there was nobody to act normal for.

Then five miles down the road, about the time I felt home free from the near-crisis, a blue light lit up my back window. Damn, damn, damn. Had he seen me? Then why wait so long to pull me? Aww crap, I bet that

Good Samaritan called it in. Having a personalized tag labeled SLADE didn't help.

Proceeding to the Chapin exit half a mile down, I prayed the officer wouldn't hold the distance against me as I parked to the side of the off-ramp. The state trooper mirrored my move, angled, tight on my bumper.

God, I really hoped he hadn't seen me back there. And I hoped Lottie could keep Mrs. Abrams occupied. I was doing my damnedest to get there, with a farmer willing to meet me back in Columbia afterwards. I really had no minutes to spare.

Spit polished, the young man donned his hat and strode to my door, the epitome of starched calm. Troopers always looked fine.

I rolled down the window. A zillion cliché comments entered my head, but of course I chose the most clichéd of them all. "Did I do something wrong, officer?"

"Ma'am, are you all right? Someone called in your truck's tag. Saw you go off the road back there."

Heart pounding, almost hurting behind my boobs. "I'm fine, officer. My phone went off, and it made me look down." True that.

"You are aware that texting while driving is against the law, right?"

"Yes, sir, and I didn't answer a text or read it, but in that distracted second I almost wrecked, but didn't." I brushed hair behind my ear, and damn if I didn't batt my eyes. His head tilted a little. "Have you been drinking, ma'am?"

Yeah, I would ask the same question after that stupid response. "No. I'm headed to an appointment in Newberry."

"License and registration, please."

I froze a second, then remembered I needed to look in the glove box. What did Wayne tell me I was supposed to say? Oh yeah. "There's a firearm in there. In with my registration."

He nodded. Then as I collected the papers, I saw Wayne's business cards with their embossed gold Office of Inspector General shield. Holding my breath, I debated, then included one in the stack of cards I handed over.

Most of the time, locals looked up to state, and state looked up to the feds. A natural order of things with everyone aspiring to be a federal agent. Wayne put those cards in the glove box against my wishes, warned me to leave them there just for a moment such as this. Using one made me feel like I'd cheated on my taxes.

The officer took the items, flipped through them, then gave me a second glance once he saw the gold. "Who is this?" he asked, holding the card up.

I inhaled, panicked he'd think it a bribe. God, let me escape this ordeal as quickly as possible. Wasn't sure how long Lottie could keep Mrs. Abrams. Did I use Wayne's name or not?

"He's my fiancé," sort of fell out of my mouth.

"I'll be right back," he said, and returned to his cruiser.

I picked up the phone to see who and what had thrown me into this pandemonium. The two calls from the unknown farmer, assuming he was who he said he was. Maybe a mistaken butt-dial the second time. Then I scanned the texts.

Ally was first, saying Ivy was at school in one piece. Monroe was second, saying he still wasn't sure he was doing things in the right order, but would check in later.

Nothing that mattered. Except what I'd said to the officer. I lowered my head onto the steering wheel. I'd take a ticket all day long to avoid the lecture I'd receive from Wayne once that officer called him, but worse would be the reference to Wayne's *fiancée*. Not the best way for the guy to hear he was engaged. Especially if I wasn't sure I meant it.

Chapter 7

I ARRIVED AT Lottie Bledsoe's white Southern mini-mansion ten minutes late, going on three thirty. However, if not for sliding Wayne's business card behind my license, I would've missed the appointment altogether. Seemed a fair trade, I guess. I got on my way, and the trooper now possessed an open channel to Wayne.

My F-150 fit nicely behind three other vehicles in Lottie's drive, an assortment of older sedans. Were we having a tea party or an interview? Oh, forgot. Tea parties came served on rocks around here. In the woods.

Flustered at being late, I almost forgot Lottie told me on the phone to avoid the front entrance. I rushed around until I found a door under the carport. The scent of Confederate jasmine hung thick, the dark vines dominating latticework on the other side. The ceiling rose sixteen or seventeen feet high, and the driveway continued through to the backyard and exited to another street. I was looking at a swath of history where carriages and horses once emptied passengers.

My knock rattled the unlatched screen door. "Hello? Lottie?"

"Come on in." The yell came from way back, and I entered, eager to talk to the farmer's wife. This chat might be a better opening into any wrongdoing than anything Monroe would find.

Of course, the farmer's chat in three hours might prove even better.

The aroma of pound cake and sounds of ladies tittering and the clatter of forks on saucers led me to Lottie and three others huddled around a rustic wooden table for six in the breakfast nook of the kitchen. Their voices echoed off the high ceilings of the hundred-plus-year-old house.

Expecting only Lottie and Ms. Abrams, the others took me aback. I'd so wanted this meeting clandestine. Would've preferred interviewing Ms. Abrams on the phone, like we started to do this morning. Now all these ladies could point at me as their connection to Ag, and regardless how I performed, word might reach Harden before I could justify why I was the *only* person who could've come.

Lottie, in polyester slacks and an oversized short-sleeved blouse, stood and waved me over as if ten people needed shooing in. "Come on, honey. You're not too late that we can't make this happen."

I hoped indeed there was a lot of *this* going to happen. The chair seemed weighed down when I tried to slide out my chair, until a white cat jumped off.

"Oh, sorry. Meant to put that cat out." Lottie scooted to the swinging kitchen door and softly booted the animal through. I took in the room. Such a serious topic amongst eggs in a basket on the counter, lemon-yellow curtains, and Easter lilies in a pitcher on the table. I then studied the women. "Hello, I'm Carolina Slade. Which one of you is Mrs. Cassie Abrams?"

The one who raised her hand held the coarsest stare. Gray-headed, hair up in a bun, the charcoal pants outfit hinted her new role as widow. "I am she. And you have some accounting to do."

"Pardon me?" This tea felt more like an ambush. Made me wonder how much Lottie had exacerbated her story to draw this crew. Though Newberrian long and far, she also represented this town's homespun version of paparazzi. I cut a glance at Lottie who snapped her attention to Cassie, who chose to continue speaking in lieu of letting me give the accounting she'd just demanded.

"That vamp y'all put in your office here. Despicable. Manipulative. You planted her, I say. Using her ways to entice our men to come in, sign on more debt, then y'all take all this credit for serving Newberry. Even confiscate our land." She shed a lone tear, brusquely wiping it aside.

"Oh, Cassie," cooed the short, squatty lady, hair coifed into a pin-curl do, a style my grandmother might've worn.

I had to rein in this conversation and get to the point. "First," I said, sitting proper in my chair, "let me express again how sorry I am for your loss, Ms. Abrams."

"Thank you," she replied.

I eased only the slightest forward, hands clasped on the table. "As for Cricket Carson, never met the woman until yesterday, so excuse me if I seem ignorant. Clue me in. Let's see what I can do to help."

Without a doubt, Cricket represented the woman they loved to hate. Question was whether she'd done anything other than be born pretty and choose to work for Agriculture. I suspected grief spoke louder in Cassie's words than anything else, in spite of her very real venom.

The woman petting the widow quit and sat back, having shown me she'd performed her role and commiserated properly. The empathetic lady sat next to Lottie. Tall, totally white-headed, in a soft aqua blouse I'd guess matched a skirt or pants underneath the table. Her mouth pinched at the sight of me.

Tough audience.

I reached to accept the iced tea and cake Lottie slid before me. "Please tell me about yourselves. Are you all farmers' wives?"

Lottie beckoned to the stumpy one who'd coddled Mrs. Abrams. "This is Phoebe Hite." Then she motioned to the thinner lady. "And this is Faye Boland. All are . . . or were . . . married to a farmer. But the three also belong to the Friends of the Library."

Obviously, a moniker they wore proudly. Teasing off a piece of cake, I swallowed it with my tea, trying not to let the homespun aroma of vanilla in the kitchen take the edge out of what I came to do. "Thanks for having me," I said, omitting the part where Lottie practically ordered me to appear. "I expected only two of you, not four."

Cassie leaned toward me. "Lottie *said* we were members of the Friends of the Library. We specialize in the mystery genre with a wealth of knowledge amongst us. Of course we would all attend. We recognize the need for an inquiry."

Okay. No point in joking about whether they leaned Agatha Christie or Patricia Cornwell. Definitely not the European frankness of Stieg Larsson. They might take me wrong, or worse, take me seriously and launch into analysis of Hoyt's case based on analyses they'd read.

Cassie twisted her head toward one lady, then the other. "These are my closest friends. They are familiar with Hoyt and his ways. They understood him and understand how detectives work."

So we were doing this. "Ma'am," I said. "As mystery aficionados, you understand the need for absolute secrecy."

Big nods all around.

I instinctively glanced at the closed door then back at the ladies. "We don't need this discussion to spread across the community."

"Agreed," Cassie said.

Good, less adversarial. "Your husband died of a heart attack, right?" I asked.

"Oh yes. That's the ultimate conclusion," Cassie said. "But he wouldn't have had the heart attack *without the sex.*" Her finger tapped the table with each of the last three words. "He'd been warned not to use that pill because of his heart. And how he got his hands on it is beyond me. That's a *major* part of this case. Who gave him Viagra and how many times?"

I froze at that sideways type of rationale. Yet I smiled. "Ma'am. I thought this meeting centered on Hoyt's dealings with the Department of Agriculture. And Cricket's misappropriations."

"It does," she said.

I cast Lottie a *help me* look.

"Let's allow Faye her thoughts," Lottie said, in an attempt to steer the talk.

"Your county manager," Faye began dryly, "offers financial assistance to our men."

My nod hung in the air a moment, then I gave it to her. "Yes, and?"

"She is too pretty."

"She's indeed attractive."

"Hoyt died before he had to sell his land," Faye said, "but my husband let go of a fifty-acre piece he had no business letting loose of. All because he mortgaged it in exchange for one of y'all's programs she coaxed him into."

Cassie reached over and smacked the table hard, right in front of my plate. "I may *still* have to sell. I can't farm my place alone, but that Cricket girl will damn sure make me pay back her damn money."

Lottie's impatience surfaced itself way quicker than mine. "She's saying that men go in and get loans and subsidies from the government that they have no business getting. She reels them in with her wiles, and they fall for it. Then she talks them into paying her off early a short time later. Is that about right, ladies?"

No mention of kickbacks or bribes.

I still wasn't getting it, but I wanted more about Faye's fifty acres. "Faye, did Agriculture take your land?"

She spit out the word. "No."

"Who did your husband sell it to?"

Tossing her head, she answered, "Some LMC, LCC, I can't recall."

"LLC?" I asked.

She shrugged.

"And it gets worse," the squattier Phoebe said, a dramatic huff in her delivery, like Aunt Pittypat in *Gone with the Wind*. "Our farm was paid for before my husband mortgaged our hundred and twenty acres. Then he died of a heart attack."

No way I asked about Viagra again.

Phoebe continued both speaking and stroking Cassie's sleeve. "Thank goodness my son swooped in and took over, but not many are that lucky."

I stemmed a patronizing smile. The husbands could've just been wheeling and dealing without their wives' consent. The profession tested anyone, but the oddity remained that farmers didn't readily sell their land.

My muted phone vibrated from beside my plate. Cassie lasered a stare at me. No way would I answer that call, but I worried that Harden hunted me down.

Phoebe's chin bounced once. "They, meaning at least a dozen farmers I'm aware of, would preen and line up for the next program. She entertained them, I say." Another puff for emphasis.

"Entertained how?" I asked. "It might have just been good lending on her part. Just helping."

Phoebe rolled her eyes. Lottie donned a smirk, as though enjoying the potential for smut talk. Cassie finally dabbed her eyes. Of course, she missed her husband, if for no reason other than the income potential.

And nobody answered my question.

"Entertained how?" I repeated. "What is it you think she did short of giving your menfolk the financial assistance they asked? If Cricket doled out money they were not qualified for, then we may have a genuine issue. Where are the facts?"

Did I honestly just say *menfolk*?

A text came in. Then another. I put the phone in my purse.

But seriously, what would Cricket have to gain? Kickbacks from loan funds made the most sense, but in a tech world, kickbacks were ballsy. That would make this Wayne's case in a heartbeat. I still saw the sex aspect as half envy and half myth and leading me to nothing nefarious.

Cassie scowled. "You're the best they have?" She recoiled in disgust. "You missed my point. The Viagra is the key. Go to every doctor in this area and demand the identities, then compare them to your government records. Or just pull up one of those databases you have. FDA does food and drugs. This qualifies under both." She lightly smacked the table, a habit, apparently. "You'll have those bastard pill suppliers cornered, then they'll give their customers. Then we'll nail down all our men and when they screwed who, and if coerced to do it in order to get Agriculture money. Easy answers."

Force-fed sex by Cricket then force-fed dollars. Though accustomed to conspiracy theories, words escaped me at the obtuseness of this one.

Lottie eyed me with amusement. The others, however, waited stoically. Maybe not stoically in Phoebe's case; she stared more with the gullibility of a third-grade child.

I reached for rationale, stumbled for the right words that would ground this conversation in logic. Cassie and Phoebe had lost husbands. To these ladies, Agriculture ruined their lives. None of that should be taken lightly.

"Ma'am, Food and Drug Administration would address Viagra, not Agriculture."

"Then why do they oversee food?" Faye exclaimed.

"They watch over *some* parts of food, but not all." I'd picked the wrong part to explain.

Cassie rolled her head around her shoulders. "I never heard of anything so silly."

"Anyway," I started, "we already have a man over here, analyzing files. Do you want to give names of farmers who you think fall into this, um, coerced category? I'll have him hone in on them with Cricket none the wiser." I bounced a glance off each lady. "Assuming you promise me you'll keep this quiet. You've read enough mysteries to understand that loose lips can—"

"Sink ships!" Phoebe threw at me.

I smiled. "Yes, but loose lips also can unravel an examination and make the guilty party or parties aware. That makes an inquiry more difficult if not impossible when those parties go underground or hide the proof."

The four slowly bobbled their heads.

"Lottie, do you have any paper? I want each lady to write down names. Names of farmers who might've been taken advantage of or anyone who may be in cahoots with Cricket."

She scooted over to her junk drawer and extracted a pad. "I'll jot it down for them."

"No," I said, reaching over and collecting the plates and silverware. Handing them to Lottie, I left the tea glasses. "Let each lady make her own list. And since I'm new here, I won't recognize handwriting. And don't sign your names."

Lottie passed out paper and pens.

"Remember," I said. "Give me a list of farmers who've been affected and anyone working with Cricket." I took a second's pause. "And then, once you're through with that, add a third list."

I let them scribble a moment. "Finally, note anyone who might be Cricket's enemy."

"Ooh," escaped from every one of them.

"Yes," Lottie said.

"Like a real mystery," Phoebe added.

Cassie just wrote.

Faye, however, appeared to ponder.

"Miss Faye?" I queried. "Do you have a question?"

She stared down that long thin nose of hers. "That would mean our names could be on that list."

God help me.

Lottie shook her head. "Leave your names off, if you like. I'm not adding mine."

And with that they seemed to agree and begin writing again.

Cassie folded her paper four ways and slid it to me. The others ladies watched and did the same. Then making a flamboyant acknowledgement of their anonymity, I shuffled them, stacked them, and tucked them in my purse.

"Aren't you going to read them?" Faye asked.

"Not here," I said.

"Why?" Phoebe exclaimed.

"I'm sure you ladies realize, being so well-read in crime fiction, that if I analyzed the lists aloud and discussed them in front of you, I'd be able to read your expressions and deduce who wrote what."

Cassie whispered, "Yes," and glanced at each of her friends for concurrence.

"Smart," Phoebe said low.

"What now?" Faye asked.

I brushed off some crumbs into my hand, rose, and deposited them into the sink. Then I pulled business cards from the outside pocket of my purse. "You deal with me and only me. Don't bother our guy. I will, however, have access to the federal agent we have to relay our information." In an afterthought, I turned to Cassie. "Of course, you continue to help Deputy Royce in his work if requested."

"Of course," she said.

Lottie now expressed surprise. "Why a federal agent?"

"Those are the guys with guns and badges who can actually arrest people."

They dwelled on that, while I began to think these lists might give Monroe more focus in his effort.

"You can't arrest criminals?" Cassie asked.

"No, ma'am." Not that I wouldn't love to.

They seemed to deflate.

"But I can tell them *who* to arrest."

They perked back up.

After another twenty minutes of general chatter from the ladies, I gleaned nothing unusual and only a repeated message that women hated Cricket. Occasionally Lorena Carson's name came up, Cricket's mother, but more in the vein of she should've raised her daughter better.

The time was now after five. I'd missed lunch, and the slice of pound cake hadn't totally filled the void. "Gotta go, ladies." Purse slung over my shoulder, I leaned on my chair. "One last thing, though. If y'all see me around town, we never met."

Again, they agreed as one voice. These three had been close a long time, it seemed. Made the whole situation sadder, but at least they had each other.

Thank goodness my truck sat parked in the back, allowing me to leave first. Weaving my way through what resembled rush-hour traffic in this tiny town, I reached US 76, the back way from Newberry to my lake house east of Chapin.

I felt like I'd fallen out of the pages of some quaint cozy mystery tale, the kind without blood, no real danger, and nosy characters stumbling over clues. While accusations pointed to financial impropriety by an Agriculture employee, somehow these ladies thought that crime should lead to Hoyt's death from Viagra. In reality, pushing loans and Hoyt's death by extramarital sex might have nothing to do with one another. The accusations and suspicions could be Cassie's way to grieve and absolve her husband for acting on his urges, and like they had for decades, her friends felt loyal to her cause.

I couldn't help but reach across to my purse on the seat and fumble to retrieve the papers.

Glancing up and down, from the road to the paper held up over the steering wheel, I already recognized Lottie's from her looping handwriting noted back at the radio station. I threw it down and groped for another piece. Cassie had sat next to me, so the left-handed slant stood out as hers. Didn't really matter who was the author of the other two lists. The farmer names were mostly the same on the four papers, but the dozen names would go to Monroe. Tomorrow his day would take on fresh purpose.

One question, however, proved worthless. Under *Anyone who might be Cricket's enemy,* there were no names. Just simply four versions of *everybody.*

Tomorrow I'd reconnect with Lottie to better interpret this Newberry-esque desire to paint with such a broad brush. Maybe she could clarify more about this urge to tar and feather Cricket that had started with the radio call.

Harden had rewarded Cricket with pomp and circumstance at the radio station, and some kind of employee award check, I'm sure. He wasn't stupid. He didn't want too much scrutiny on his star employee. He'd sent Monroe, who Cricket would be less likely to influence with a wink and a smile. Actually, I suspected if Monroe found anything at all, Harden could easily squelch it.

Appointed politicians like Harden Harris lived for reputation. Monroe and I held no respect for the man, and he sensed it. But if Agriculture suffered financial impropriety, somebody's head would roll. Washington would look at Harden, but he sure as hell wouldn't go down for it. He'd riffle through his Rolodex of usual suspects beginning with Monroe and me. Monroe because Harden had strategically placed him in Newberry in hopes of finding nothing. Me, because I'd been sucked in by Lottie's claim that Cassie would talk to me or no one.

Damned if I did something and damned if I didn't. Here I stood, between a rock and a hard place, no pun intended.

And with nothing accomplished other than putting my job at risk and placating some country women with lists and talk of mystery, I had to break loose and head back toward Columbia, over an hour away, with an hour and fifteen minutes to get there. I prayed my mystery farmer showed up and showed up with enough substantive information to matter. Because I would have to test the speed laws on Interstate 26 if I was going to make it in time.

Chapter 8

I COULDN'T PUSH the speed limit while driving in the town of Newberry, but my impatient foot tested my common sense with taps on the gas. Small towns thrived on ticket revenue. However, once I left town, and buildings stretched too far apart to see their neighbor, my foot gave my Ford the go ahead. I stayed five miles over the limit to the interstate, then ten all the way to the state capital.

Even after my near miss earlier, I tried redialing the farmer while driving, to tell him I was hauling butt to our six o'clock meeting. Which suddenly made me wonder how he got my number. Lottie? Didn't think so. She was supposed to be a reporter, and they usually held sources sacrosanct.

No answer, and only a canned voicemail response without name or identity. "Hey," I said. "This is Carolina Slade from earlier. On my way, so sit tight. Might be five or ten minutes late, but trust me, I'm coming, and my attention will be all yours."

Over the top? Too late now. I hung up, noticed I'd slowed, and pushed my truck back up to eighty.

The clogged artery of vehicles started a mile west of Irmo. *Please, please keep moving.* My off ramp was two miles ahead, the Lowe's parking lot a quarter mile to the left of that. Travel turned sluggish, my eagerness putting me on the bumper of a mini-church bus with no wiggle room around it. Two minutes after six.

Come on!

Traffic stopped. Crap, I could see the exit ramp.

Creep, creep, stop. Crawl, crawl, stop. Finally, I scooted around to the right, thankful I had a truck, and traveled part on grass and part on asphalt, past the stalled cars, until I reached the ramp. Of course a red light at the top of the ramp. Fingers tapping.

I tried not to think about the fact the man hadn't called, but did anyway, then consoled myself he was simply patiently waiting.

Through that light then running through an amber light, I peeled into the Lowe's parking lot. How the hell would I find him? Wait, he was supposed to find me. I circled the lot once more, parked in a far slot out in the open, then I shut off the truck. And sat. Six fifteen.

I would give someone that sort of leeway, but this was a nervous sort who refused me his name. A farmer who probably breathed relief when six o'clock came around, and I wasn't there.

No, give the guy a chance. He might be picking up a certain type of screw to repair a barn hinge, or lumber for a rotted piece of pen.

By seven, I'd called him six times, texted five, and sadly given up. I cranked up the engine and headed home, running through the conversation in my head with Lottie. She had to be the source for the farmer getting my phone number. She had to know who it was.

FOUR ACRES IN SIZE, my place at Catfish Cove held ample room to roam, fish, garden, and escape family squabbles. Ironically, as I drove in, Wayne weighed heavy on my mind. It was either think about him or the farmer I'd missed. Should've left Lottie's earlier.

The sight of Bug draped across my daughter, their feet dangling off the sides of our old treehouse wedged between two hickory trees, blew my thoughts of work out of the water. My flustered mother-self argued with the investigator, and the mother won. I would leave them alone . . . for now.

Parked in the garage, I wanted to hide from the world awhile. Not confront Ivy, not think of Wayne, avoid whatever scrutiny Ally would throw at me. Dark. I closed my eyes. No worries. Nothing but the occasional pop of the car cooling.

Then a flash of Harden ruined it. Calm gone, I picked up my phone, finally daring to read the texts that came in on the way home, my churning imagination about my boss sending my pulse hammering at what he might have sent. Damn, I hated that he affected me this way.

But the first text came from Ally, telling me to stop on the way home for milk. Crap. Let them drink root beer. We always stocked up on that. And one day of water wouldn't hurt them with breakfast. Ally'd probably give the kids coffee anyway.

The second text, however, stole my breath. Harden. Or rather his secretary, asking whether to place me on sick or vacation leave for taking off early, which meant someone asked for me. I texted back one word, *vacation*, trying to be semi-honest.

The jolt of concern gave my stomach a flip.

And the sickly sensation flipped my mind from one issue to the next . . . the *P* issue.

Regular as a rooster crowing sunup, my periods didn't merit a calendar. They came and went. Always the same. Making the calculation easy. A chill shot through my chest at the answer. Seven, maybe eight weeks late. Shit! No friggin' way. No f'in friggin' way.

Glancing back at the door leading into the house, I reached for my purse to find a real calendar on my phone. But I fumbled, sending lipstick, emery boards, and packets of fake sugar across the floorboard. Retrieving my phone, I clicked into my app and scrolled back.

Oh. *That* weekend. That long three-day weekend Ally took the kids to see my parents. Too much bourbon at Wayne's. The pills back at the lake. Shit . . . shit, shit, shit.

With shaking hands, I scooped everything up fast and hugged my purse, willing nerves to settle.

Jesus. Should I stop taking the pills now? Will it do something bad if I *am* pregnant? With the uncertainty of a young girl, I took out my phone and Googled pregnancy and the pill, then stopped. *Pull your act together and research this later.* Ally could read me like a book most days, and she had to have heard the garage door. Take a deep breath and go inside.

The door from the garage opened to the kitchen. Ally worked on making a baked pork roast into pulled pork barbecue, a dish I'd only recently gone back to eating after my ordeal with two crusty hog farmers who tried to do me in, among other nasty things. The hogs wound up gnawing on the remains of one.

Act normal. What the hell *was* normal?

"What kind of sauce?" I asked, dropping my purse on the counter.

My sister's hands worked furiously at dissecting the meat. "Mustard. My favorite. You're late."

"Sorry, last minute call at work." I slipped a piece and dipped it into the sauce. "Bug staying for dinner?"

Please say no.

"You should call me when that happens. Ivy asked, and I said okay."

Of course, she did. And I should've at least texted. The last thing I wanted to do was take my sister for granted even if we didn't always agree about how to raise my kids. I mean, she made good barbecue.

Ally stopped, fingers greasy, and gave me a big sigh and all her attention. "She thinks you hate him."

"She's right." The pig rocked, so I stole another bite.

She shook her head, disappointed. Made me feel like she'd replaced me as the mother who knows best.

"What?" I asked, irritated.

"Give her a chance to muddle through this."

Uh, unh. No way. "He's the one I don't want to give the chance to. The chance to get in her shorts, in her blouse, in her bedroom. The chance to make little Bugs. And you"—I thumped her on the head—"should recall your own stunts. And how Daddy ran one of those idiots down at his home and got into it with the boy's dad in their front yard. How far did that guy get? First base? Third? Home run?"

She finished the pork, tossed the fatty stuff into the trash, and went to the sink. "Put some soap in my hands," she said.

I turned on the water and did as asked. "I don't want her getting hurt," I said.

"She needs to get hurt, Sis. At least a little."

I threw Ally a dish towel. "But not pregnant."

Ally shrugged and went back to dinner prep. Peering out the sliding glass door, unable to stare my sister in the eye, I looked around for my son. "Where's Zack?" Even with his wild side, he made me whole.

"He's outside somewhere."

I moved into the dining room which gave me a clearer view of the treehouse side of the yard. Bug's and Ivy's feet still swung where they were before, but up in an old one-man deer stand in the back corner of the yard, Zack held binoculars, eyes on his sister.

A boy on a mission. My kind of kid.

If I weren't avoiding Wayne I'd call him and brag.

I went to the bedroom to change. With Bug not exactly a guest I'd dress for, I reached for my favorite sweatpants, the gray ones with the beige paint stain on one thigh from redoing my bathroom. Threw on my Clemson tee.

Wayne's case in the field meant no sign of him tonight, which sort of left me empty as I walked past his empty chair. Both Ivy and Ally gave my outfit a second notice, but there was something about eating in the outdoors that kept malice tempered.

Metal chairs scraped on the cement floor. Our frequent chickadees chirped from the holly bushes, a few having left liquid presents along the backs of two chairs. The ones occupied by Bug and Zack. The latter didn't care; the former looked to Ivy to take care of the mess.

Ivy leaped, starting to wait on the boy again until I stared at Bug. My mind melding worked, and he used a napkin to clean the poop, though he acted pained at the effort.

"What grade are you in, Bug?" I asked after he sat back down.

"Tenth," he said.

"You doing all right with it?"

A one-shouldered shrug. "Depends on what you call all right."

Would've been humorous if he hadn't been serious. "Well, let's see . . . are you passing?"

He crammed mashed potatoes in his mouth and spoke into his plate. "Oh yeah. I'm not failing or anything. I'll be a junior next year."

"So, the top of your class, huh?"

His astringent look tugged me oh so wrong. "Not even close," he said. "But it's not like college is in my plans. When I graduate high school, academia is history." He laughed hard and clipped. "Get it? History? Academia?"

I turned to a squirming Ivy, whose complexion just about matched the tiny roses in her shirt. "Oh yeah, Bug. I get a lot more than you think."

"Mom," Ivy pleaded.

"Yes, Ivy?" The intense attention unnerved her.

"Um, Sis." Ally nudged me under the table.

"Hold on," I said. "My daughter has something important to say."

Ivy dropped her fork and threw her napkin. "Why do you manage to ruin everything in my life?"

"It's called a mother gene," I said. "My mother did it to me, as hers did for her."

"Carolina," Ally urged.

Standing, Ivy tugged Bug's sleeve, a clear command to leave.

But Bug shirked loose, his interest on his barbecue. "Not after I waited this long to eat. I'm starved."

Everybody's brow arched, to include Ivy's. She'd played her highest card only to get bested by both her mother and her beau. My heart hurt a bit for her, watching her mentally figure what to do next.

Ally kicked me under the table. I kicked her back. I'd already intended to shut up.

The doorbell rang.

"That's odd." I stood and went inside. It was eight at night down a road without street lights. Anyone who came here was either invited or very lost. That's why I kept a .22 atop the china cabinet about eight feet from the front door. For security and the occasional snake. Of either variety.

The lead glass in the oval cutout of my door distorted the appearance of the man on the front stoop, but I still recognized the white hair.

"Monroe?" Door agape, I stood back to let him in, embarrassed now at my dingy attire . . . and disturbed he was even here. He hadn't been over in at least six months, and he had better manners than to arrive unannounced this late on a Wednesday night.

"Come on in," I said. "What's wrong? You had anything to eat?"

He strode in stiff, pent up, and nervous. "Slade, we've got to talk."

"Obviously."

Ally peered in from the back porch, Zack beside her.

"Can you take care of the kids and Bug?" I asked my sister. "Come on, Monroe. Let's go down to the dock."

He had to have found something on Cricket. Something dire from his behavior.

I detoured to the refrigerator and pulled out a Diet Coke for the teetotaler. After grabbing the scribbled lists acquired at Lottie's, I led him down the boat ramp to the dock, noticing how anxious he acted, his gaze on his feet, his steps purposeful.

The temperate April weather and pollen gave everything a soft green cast, and the final daffodil blooms flaunted their best, but they wasted their finery on us. I sat on one end of a bench in the gazebo and he on the other, then I gave him a moment.

Water lapped beneath the dock, and thirty yards out two wood ducks paddled by. The day had hovered between cool and warm, depending on whether you sat in the sun. This late, a spring chill slid in off the water, making me glad I had on the sweats.

"Tell me what happened," I said. "Did you call Wayne?"

"*I said* I'd call you first."

His snap caught me off guard, so I let him make the next move. Taking the Coke to his lips with one hand, he gave me a manila envelope with the other.

Fingerprints came to mind . . . gloves . . . then I pictured Wayne laughing at me for overthinking this. Turning the envelope, I noted no address or markings, then opened it.

An eight-by-ten photograph of Monroe taken almost to the back of him. He had hands on either side of a young lady maybe thirtyish molded back against his government car. Mouth-to-mouth with no daylight whatsoever in between. Belly to belly. Chest to chest.

I tried to ignore the little sting in me that he'd gotten it on with some slip of a girl, and that he was fifteen years older than she appeared to be. But hey, far be it from me to tell a man who he dated when I'd already told him he couldn't date me.

I noted his blush and gave him a more serious once over. This wasn't a simple social moment though I was stymied what else it could be. "Was this taken today?" I asked. The picture showed he wore what he had on right now.

He nodded. "Right before dinner. I just met her today in the office. That's in the restaurant parking lot."

I slapped his leg slightly with the back of my hand, trying to reassure him. "So what? Someone caught you making out in a parking lot. You haven't killed anyone."

"Turn it over," he said harshly.

In a fine-tipped Sharpie, someone had written, "Leave Newberry."

Staring up at his pasty appearance, I realized now how shaken he was. I studied the writing again, then the image. "Who took the picture?"

He moaned. "Have no idea."

"Who gave you the picture?"

"A waitress, when she delivered my meal."

Odd. "Sure you didn't misconstrue—"

"Can't I just tell you about it first before you come to conclusions, Slade?"

I sat back and nodded. "Sure. Sorry. Tell me."

Monroe and I went way back in an unconditional friendship. At work, heck, at most anything, he caught my back and I caught his. We were both considered quite straight-laced once upon a time. Total rule book followers. Seemed like eons ago since life had been that simple.

When I entered the dark side of investigations, however, especially after my first case when agents temporarily labeled me contriving, my name couldn't shed the tarnish, and my reputation took a beating. Monroe, by association, lost some of his luster.

We usually ignored what people thought these days. Me more than he, however, since I'd had way more practice.

He voiced his fear. "I think she set me up, and I can't figure out why."

"Find anything in your inquiry?"

"Not really."

I slapped at a young mosquito. "You sure she didn't just like you then change her mind?"

He gave me an *are you kidding* look. Yeah, that sounded kooky to me, too, after I said it.

We sat there pondering. Monroe embarrassed and mystified.

"Call Wayne," he finally said.

"Let's think about this a moment," I replied.

"No, I want to hear his thoughts," he said. "Do I go back in the morning, or not?"

I sure wish Harden had sent me instead. "Monroe, once the IG gets involved, they can take over. How many times have we had this conversation? Let's consider the what ifs—"

He set his can down hard. "I said call him. Come on, Slade. Get over yourself."

For a minute all I could do was stare, hurt, waiting for an apology.

But he didn't back down. My friend was damn worried, and he expected me to be, too.

Yeah, time to call Wayne.

Chapter 9

SEATED ON THE dock at my lake home, I couldn't deny the fact Wayne was our best next move. The photograph taken in Newberry upset Monroe, and he was impatient for guidance.

"My phone's up at the house," I said.

He tossed me his, clearly wanting me to make the call to Wayne instead of him.

"Yo, Monroe," Wayne answered. Then in a second too long of silence, said, "Something wrong with Slade?"

"Why would that be his only reason to call you?" I asked.

"Is *he* okay since you're calling on *his* phone?"

"We're both fine. Where are you?" Road noises sounded in the background, so he wasn't home yet.

"On I-20. Ten miles from I-26. Why?"

Monroe had turned his attention to the water, what I always did when events weighed on my mind. But he still listened.

"Can you come to the house?" I asked. "Monroe has a dilemma."

Monroe spun around. "I can meet him in Columbia and save him time."

I shook my head. Wayne could grab dinner with the *three* of us discussing this. And Wayne's involvement would be because of Monroe's need, not mine.

Wayne paused. I assumed thinking. "Newberry flare up already?"

"Maybe. Don't have all the details, but it's Monroe, you know?"

"Yeah, I know."

Was that a standup acknowledgement of Monroe as deserving of our help or a thinly veiled regret of how close I was to him? At the moment I didn't care. Wayne would be here in under a half hour, and that's what mattered.

A pontoon with running lights entered the cove, realized it had no pass-through, then slowly pivoted around. With way more power than needed, the captain gunned it back to deeper water. The wake rolled toward us, sending the dock in a rocking, creaking reaction. Monroe grabbed his seat.

I was used to it. "Idiots. This is a no wake zone."

We sat there until the movement eased, more listening to nature than watching now the sun was down, but the moon rose high, giving everything around us a glow.

"Can't be that bad, Monroe," I finally said.

"Well, it's more embarrassing than anything else."

"You kissed a girl. God, if fraternization was a crime, I'd have a life sentence."

He cleared his throat. He'd long since finished his Coke. "In this climate of harassment? I'm worried."

Footsteps turned our attention to the boat ramp.

"Hey Momma," Zack said, stepping onto the dock to retrieve his rod and reel. "Wish Mr. Wayne had come tonight."

"As a matter of fact, he changed his mind. He'll be here in a minute. Why?"

Zack wound his line around his pole. "I get to tell him that I spit in Bug's drink at dinner. He'll think that's awesome."

Monroe laughed.

"Not cool," I said, while thinking it hilarious. "Don't bank on Mr. Wayne giving you a high five over it, either, Zack. How about running back up that hill and getting Mr. Monroe another Coke? Bring me a root beer, if you don't mind. Then head to bed."

"But I just got down here!"

I gave him my don't-mess-with-Momma look.

He headed back up the drive. "Y'all just don't want me to hear grown-up talk."

"That and we're thirsty," I said louder as he trudged off. "Thank you," I yelled.

"He's like you," Monroe said.

I assumed my best innocence pose, fingertips on my chest. "Why, I've never spit in a drink in my life, sir."

"Not that you haven't thought about it."

"Okay, ice is broken," I said. "I want the entire instant replay of today."

He collapsed a little, shoulders looser. "I was at a desk outside Cricket's office. I'd just delved into Hoyt Abram's file when a friend of Cricket's came in."

I listened. "Okay."

"She was, well, you see what she is . . . in that picture."

Picking back up the photo, I studied the girl, grateful I'd installed good lights down here at the water. "About thirty. Dark hair pulled back with stylish clips. *Very* cute. Wish I could wear a skirt like that." I grinned to lighten the moment. "And she caught your eye."

He squinted at me. "Anyway, she visited with Cricket then came out. It was getting on in the afternoon, around four. She offered to meet me for dinner. I had no other plans. We asked Cricket if she wanted to come, but she declined. I would've too in her shoes, having had me in her business all day."

I leaned an elbow on the dock's railing. Totally innocent thus far, except for the threat on the back of the photo. I prayed this, whatever this was, had a simple explanation, with Monroe worrying too much.

"Cricket told me I ought to go," he said. "The girl said she'd meet me in an hour, then when I finished, I drove the mile over there. No sooner had I gotten out of my car and shut the door, she attacked me!"

I held up the photo. "She's under you, dude."

"Exactly," he said, his hand dotting his exclamation. "She had me pinned, then she grabbed my shirt and flipped us over until our positions were swapped. I landed with my hands on the car trying not to crush her."

"Maybe she's just amorous." But I did not discount she'd had a photographer in the shadows, and Cricket had conveniently left herself out of the equation.

"Well, when she finished, um . . ."

"Swapping spit," I added, fighting to lighten the conversation.

He frowned. "We go inside and order. I'm nervous, she's giggly. She gets up and goes to the restroom. They deliver only my meal, mind you . . . not hers, and underneath mine is this envelope."

I waved the photo. "And she never came back."

He shook his head. "No."

"Hmm."

"What does *hmm* mean?"

No doubt a set up. At least one other person involved, assuming the waitress and the photographer were one and the same. The kisser could've just paid the waitress to cancel her order and deliver the envelope.

"Does this girl have a name?" I asked.

"Ginger."

"Last name?"

"I don't remember it."

"She's brunette, Monroe."

He scratched his nose. "So?"

"Ginger is often reserved to, um, redheads? I'm not sure you got her real name. Remember anything else?"

"She smelled nice."

Monroe was such an easy mark. "Did you see anyone with a camera?" I asked.

"No."

"Describe the waitress."

"Younger than Ginger. Blonde, nice looking but no bombshell. Short, in jeans, a tee shirt with the diner's name on it, and a little apron with pockets. College student age maybe?"

"Not bad on the details, dude," I said. "Did you ask her what the envelope was for?"

"No, figured her for only the hired help. So I stayed and ate my dinner, hoping somebody would come along and explain things, but nobody did."

Kudos to him for that much, but he really should've talked to every-one and anyone there once it became clear the envelope wasn't an overture to a meeting. But Monroe wasn't me. From his hangdog appearance, he likely realized what he should've done in hindsight.

"Where the heck are our drinks? Zack?" I yelled up the hill.

I heard Wayne's boots before I saw him, his hands full of drinks, his dinner balanced atop them. "Here they are," he said.

Approaching him, I sought remnants of our quasi-fuss from last night. Instead, he acted business as usual, as if nothing had taken place. I relieved him of half the burden, and he sat in the corner of the dock next to me, Monroe across from us. Wayne offered one of the barbecue sandwiches to Monroe, who declined.

Then as Wayne ate, Monroe repeated the story. Unfortunately, like me, Wayne couldn't hold back a grin at the parking lot smooch in the photo. Monroe blushed for the umpteenth time.

"First," Wayne said, swallowing a bite. "Don't fall for it again. Second, go back and continue your review. Let's see what happens." He flipped the picture over and pulled out a pen. "Mind if I keep this for a while?"

"Um, guess not," Monroe said, then a thought hit him. "Wait, I'm bait?"

Wayne wrote the date on the back and signed his name, then slid the photo back into the envelope. "Only if you look at it that way." Then he set down his plate on the bench, emptied like the man missed lunch. "But nobody's in jeopardy. Act like nothing happened." He shrugged. "Note how Cricket acts when you show back up, then later, ask her about Ginger."

Wayne stretched out all long and lean in his boots, back against the railing. Like we never argued. Like the trooper hadn't connected with him. I dared to feel relief Wayne's card got tossed and the trooper never called.

"I'm not sure about this pretense," Monroe mumbled.

Wayne dipped his head toward my friend. "Just tell it like it is. Tell her Ginger stood you up and didn't even leave you a glass slipper. Get her full name, where she lives, her phone number. Ought to be interesting seeing how Cricket reacts. Then call me with the info, assuming she gives you anything."

Just what I would've done if I'd been there. "Also, call Wayne or me if it gets hairy."

Monroe stiffened. "Hairy?"

"I mean, if Cricket comes onto you, or someone flattens your tires, or Ginger's boyfriend barges in, or—"

Wayne raised a hand in stop sign pose, his voice firm. "Slade, stop it. You're embellishing."

"Always be prepared." I glowered then a small splash made me peer over the railing into the water. I'd have a great time watching Cricket twist on the line if it were me trying to reel her in.

Wayne sat up. "Let's concentrate on you then." He pointed at me with his beer hand. "You have more to worry about. I wish you were doing the audit, but Monroe's our guy with boots on the ground this time."

Did he just compliment me?

"Thanks," Monroe said.

"Nothing against you," Wayne added, but turned back to me. "Keep things open with Lottie, but avoid anyone who might be a target, like Cricket or this Ginger woman. Maintain your distance but keep that grip on Lottie."

Since when did he encourage me? "Harden doesn't want me involved."

"Since when has any director stopped you? Lottie's already proven she's an armory of information, making her your CI, Slade. Your cooperating individual. You don't pass them around like cards. You keep a tight rein on them, or they can screw things up." He pointed at me again. "You were one of the worst CIs I ever had to work with because you ran so damn rogue."

Nice to hear. "But I solved the case."

His expression turned tight. "You stumbled through it and almost got yourself killed."

My rogueness, as he put it, had saved my children, my life, and both our jobs.

But I hadn't thought of Lottie as a legit CI. My jokes today over pound cake took a more ominous meaning, and next time we chatted, I'd lean harder on her about keeping discreet. "Well, I have information to share, too." I extracted the four pieces of paper from my back pocket. "Here are names certain ladies think might've been conned into Agriculture assistance, then taken advantage of. Including the dead farmer. And a live farmer called me anonymously today asking to meet."

What was that odd look on Wayne? Curiosity with a hint of admiration? I could only hope. This wasn't my first rodeo anymore.

Monroe sat up to see the papers better, squinting in the shadows in spite of the spotlights. "What ladies?"

"Lottie, Hoyt's widow, and two of the widow's friends. Three of the four are farmers' wives."

Monroe, buoyed now that he didn't feel like the lead honcho on all this, snapped pictures of each list on his phone. "Added to my to-do list for tomorrow. Who's the farmer you met?"

"Well," and I wished I'd just kept quiet about him. "He didn't show up when I arrived to meet him."

"Just a moment," Wayne said. "You went along to meet someone you had no idea who he was?" He shook his head, disbelief and annoyance in his eyes. "Do I have to explain the hazards involved in that stunt?"

"It was nothing," I scolded back. "And it was in the Lowe's parking lot on Harbison Boulevard. A hundred people coming and going all around, so—"

"A lot of people doesn't mean anyone would come to your aid, Butterbean." He stared harder. "Will you ever learn?"

Heat rose into my cheeks. From compliment to being reprimanded in front of Monroe in a few short minutes. I'm not sure it was a land speed record, but I had whiplash. For about five minutes we three sat quietly, pretending to settle down, but experience told me neither Wayne nor I did so.

"So what do I do tomorrow?" Monroe finally asked.

"Avoid the restaurant," Wayne said. "Which one was it, by the way?"

"The Jezebel," my colleague said.

Root beer spit out my nose. Wayne roared with laughter. An ice breaker.

Monroe turned three shades of red, and I felt bad, but a restaurant named after a whore seemed so apropos.

Zack appeared out of nowhere, probably unbeknownst to Ally. My boy's first cast took his lure out past the end of the dock as he pretended he had every right to be out this late.

"Zack, I told you to get inside," I said. "It's late, and you can't see what you're doing anyway."

"Aww, Momma," he whined.

"Go. Now," I ordered, and my son reeled in and trudged up the hill.

"He's getting good with that rod and reel," Wayne said. "And he's flustered with ol' Bud."

"Bug," I corrected. "Did Zack tell you what he did?"

Wayne snorted softly. "Oh yeah. He told me."

"Don't condone that behavior, please," I said.

"What? Being sneaky? Getting even? Taking risks?" Wayne reached over and squeezed my knee like we hadn't just minced words. "I don't have to teach him a damn bit of that. He gets it naturally, Butterbean."

He sure was good at making up. I, however, had a more difficult time letting go of a hurt. In my opinion, he often didn't take our arguments seriously, blowing them off sometimes. Part of trying to decide our future was deciding whether two such different people could coexist.

Tomorrow I planned to research the list of farmers, then since Wayne advised I keep up with Lottie, invite her to lunch and scout out Jezebel's. And be quiet about it.

"I got a call today about a traffic ticket you almost got," Wayne said, snapping me back to the present. "Seems a certain trooper met my fi—"

"So I got pulled over," I interrupted. "We can discuss it later."

He gazed down his nose, and Monroe saw it, the corner of his mouth rising in fun at the idea I'd gotten caught getting a ticket. But he didn't know the half of it.

"You don't want to hear what the trooper had to say about you?" Wayne asked, fully aware the word *fiancé* was part of the message.

I stood and dusted my bottom off. "Either of you want another sandwich? A drink?"

There was something terribly awkward about Wayne maybe using the word fiancé in front of Monroe. And I couldn't fathom how ridiculously thorny it would be when Wayne could reference me as his baby's momma-to-be.

A sense of the future closing in around me made me suddenly care about plans and options I no longer had and never really wanted.

Wayne must've seen me shiver, and misunderstood. "You cold?" Then he reached to do just that . . . close his arms around me, wrapping me in the future.

Ever the alpha, Wayne didn't think twice about what Monroe would feel seeing affection between us. Monroe diverted attention back to the cove.

I changed the conversation. "We haven't talked about Harden. What if he finds all this out?"

Wayne only hugged me tighter. "Maybe Monroe can change all that with his investigation."

His investigation. Monroe took a glance back at me, understanding how that comment jabbed, sorry for how difficult it was for me to be chained to a desk. Then I reminded myself—this wasn't one person's investigation. We'd both have to work hard to stay ahead of Harden. And we'd rely on Wayne for guidance.

Then for some stupid reason I teared up.

At Wayne? At Monroe? At Harden? At my daughter choosing a boyfriend I'd rather use as gator bait? At the fear of a pregnancy?

"What is this?" Wayne asked, touching my chin.

I recoiled, lost for words.

Both men held concerned expressions, afraid to make the emotional woman articulate her feelings, so I gave them the answer all men hated to hear. "Nothing's the matter," and clammed up.

No man ever understood what to say to that.

After some palpable silence, Monroe rose. "Let me go, especially if I've got to be in Newberry in the morning."

I stepped over and gave him a hug. "You'll do fine, dude."

He, however, leaned into the hug, whispering, "I'm not trying to come between you two . . . as much as I'd like to."

"I know," I whispered back, then let him loose. How noble to voice his concern for me with Wayne an arm's length away. Made me love my work buddy even more.

Walking up hill toward the house, Wayne peeled off and escorted Monroe to his car while I headed to the porch, then inside. Ivy's muffled singing voice came from the shower. Zack made crashing noises, playing in his room. Ally folded clothes in the laundry.

We were a good enough family, weren't we? With or without Wayne. Damn, I craved a bourbon so bad, but settled for another root beer and returned to the porch, because I understood the lawman well enough to expect him to be back for another go at a conversation. The ring, the trooper, the word fiancé . . . the case. All the above?

I fumed at the roller-coastering that pregnancy forced on women.

Boots sounded on the sidewalk before I caught his slightly salt-and-peppered head of hair appear over the tops of the bushes. "Slade, you back here?"

My pulse quickened as I tried to guess what would come next. "Yeah."

He appeared. "Don't worry, I'm not going to give you a ration of crap about the trooper."

I tapped my bottle on the chair arm.

"You did what I suggested and used my card, though I worry why he stopped you in the first place. You went off the road?"

"And right back on again," I said. "Nothing and nobody hurt."

I could see the restraint in his face. "Well, you're not wearing the ring, so I assume you used fiancé as a convenience."

Hearing him word it that way sent shame over me. I could argue that I'd regretted it the minute I said it, or that it was just as good as his business card, but neither sounded right. "Sorry," was all I could think of to say.

"What's wrong with you?" he asked. "You're moody as hell. Am I that big a nuisance to you lately?"

How was I supposed to answer that? I couldn't. I didn't.

"You act scared to death of something," he added, and waited, searching me for a response he could read.

Fact was, I *was* scared. Of being his wife after failing at marriage before. Of being pregnant. Of Harden getting even in some way I didn't see coming.

"Butterbean, I can't help you if I don't understand what the problem is."

My silence only accented the fact there was a problem. Just which one did I hit him with? The most obvious was the pregnancy, but since I had ice cold feet on that issue, I went with the old standby. "I'm second fiddle again on a case."

He scowled. "That's what you're going with? The case?"

I sipped my root beer, beats thundering in my ears.

"Honey, we've got a good thing going, when you let it happen," he said with deep concern. "But if you don't trust me well enough to be honest, then I can't do a damn thing to help." He stood.

My heart flipped. What should I say? What could I say that didn't sound desperate? And I hadn't confirmed a pregnancy. A missed period could be no more than stress, regardless how my gut told me otherwise.

"Well," and he slapped his hands once on his legs. "Can't talk to myself, can I? Call me when you're up to a conversation." His lope down the stairs seem weighted. "Oh, I have to say one more thing here that should go without saying. And you've been doing your job long enough to appreciate it."

"We can't let personal get in the way of our work."

His brow raised. "Ah, she speaks."

That sort of pissed me off.

"Well," he said as he reached the last step, "if we can't put this personal . . . whatever it is . . . aside, then we can't operate together on cases. Tuck that away for thought, Slade. When you make up your mind how I rank, let me know. I can transfer out in the blink of an eye."

And he left.

Transfer?

Chapter 10

WAKING UP EARLY and lethargic, I dragged myself into the shower where my thoughts gelled best. Only as they came together, they brought back only clarity of a night gone wrong with Wayne. I should've just told him everything on my mind. In the light of day, I found no logic for why I hadn't.

Thursday. Almost the weekend, but Newberry beckoned, and again I had to come up with some creative sidestepping to excuse myself out of the state office. Hearing Monroe's story, I had to see Jezebel's, study how the photo went down, and lay eyes on these people. Wayne told me not to involve myself into anything yet. Background only, he'd said. I was inclined to listen to him.

I couldn't fathom him transferring from Columbia . . . from me.

Water ran through my hair, across my head, and down my neck, and I closed my eyes to bask in it for a second . . . trying to soothe my aching heart. The world seemed to shift. As I opened my eyes, suds ran into them, stinging. I reached for the walls to steady myself, then out of the blue I puked on my feet.

Hand against the tiles, still spitting after revisiting last night's dinner three times, I shakily stooped down for a plastic cup kept in the shower for Saturday bathtub scrubbing. The disinfectant cleanser smell made me gag yet again. Fill and pour. Fill and pour. As I made sure all the giblets and pieces disappeared down the drain, I resisted the urge to cry.

I felt ill, and confirming the reason why wouldn't make me feel better.

Last night, Wayne had left crestfallen when I hadn't opened up, but he wouldn't leave me in peace for long. The man wouldn't let me stall now that he was questioning how I really felt about him, and I couldn't find the words he really needed to hear. This was not how I'd wanted to marry him. *Shotgun wedding at age forty.* Mom would be proud.

Resisting the urge to call for my sister, I got out, toweled off, and threw on a robe. Way too leery of a repeat performance, I eased back into bed. No way I'd sleep. Or so I thought. I woke up to Ally pounding on my door and my pillow wet from my hair.

"You're late," she hollered. "The kids already left. Here's your coffee."

I leaped up and opened the door. "Crap. Thanks."

She eyed me up and down. "Wait, you were up?"

"No," I said, taking a swig and running to the bathroom. "I laid back down and fell asleep. Darn it. Look at my hair." I'd neglected to rinse all the shampoo out, and clumps of stiff hair stuck out all which-away on my head. I jumped back under the water.

Ally yelled over the shower noise. "What's going on with you, Carolina?"

I sudsed up with double the shampoo. "Quit calling me that. What time is it?"

"It's your name, and it's ten till eight. What's up, um, Older Sister?" she said.

Traffic calculations put me in to work around nine, at best. Towel around me, I ran into my closet, its door directly off the bathroom. Thank goodness for a simple wardrobe. Today I grabbed navy slacks with a blouse and jacket instead of a sweater. Just in case a flush surprised me and I needed to cool off fast. Items clutched, I ran out and threw them across the unmade bed.

When I reentered the bathroom in my underwear, Ally propped against the counter. I directed the blow dryer at her for fun . . . pretending to act normal.

"You didn't answer me, Older Sister."

"I overslept, Einstein. And I'll take Carolina over that."

"But the magic question is why," she hollered. "I heard you in the shower earlier. You forget my bedroom is on the other side of your bathroom wall."

We both waited for me to finish with the hairdryer. Clips held my hair back, then double-checking the fast swath of mascara in the mirror, I grabbed my purse and coffee cup. Thank God the coffee was staying down.

"Carolina . . ."

I pivoted in my rush to get my clothes and spouted, "Ally, don't pry."

"Fine," she replied. "You'll have to tell me soon enough."

I threw my damp towel at her for the wash. "Think that all you want."

She caught it. "I hope you're making up with Wayne today. You treated him like crap last night."

That stopped me in my tracks. "You listened? What the hell, Ally."

"You were bad, Big Sister. The guy's awesome, and for some reason you're blind to his remarkable patience in dealing with you. Nobody, including him, can stay that way for long."

"You're out of line."

"Huh, whatever," she sassed back as she sauntered out of my bedroom. "Look in the mirror."

AT THE OFFICE, I dove into research. Each day, no, each hour lately, seemed to stack one worry atop another. Might as well use the energy to mine the database on the dozen names the ladies gave me at Lottie's, taking my mind off baggage. However, I still had to question whether this list-collection I'd winged on the fly was nothing other than sour grapes because their *menfolk* had wandering eyes.

And that farmer who dodged me still wouldn't return my calls.

I wanted to run my research, and the farmer, by Lottie. She might not be Newberry's brainiac of agriculture, but she apparently had inroads to more info than the average resident via her heritage, reporting talents, and most likely her husband's knowledge as an attorney. Not that he told her everything. If I were him I wouldn't. The fact she yakked to me said enough.

The men on this list had history of being loosely attached to Agriculture, meaning they were in the more passive programs like Conservation Reserve and reported their planted acreage just in case a program came along they couldn't refuse. They received an annual rental payment for not farming environmentally sensitive land. Instead, they put acreage into pines or used it for another purpose that would assist the environment. Only fools didn't jump on that deal.

A couple of the men had old emergency loans, but nothing big. Drought, hurricane, whatever, deemed them eligible for low interest money for their losses. They hadn't been involved with Agriculture at all before then. The most stable farmers preferred to rely upon crop insurance.

Regardless of how much Agriculture promoted itself as a great friend and support, few farmers wanted to be indebted to Uncle Sam. The old saying used to label us as "the lender of last resort." While we weren't allowed to say that anymore, it pretty much remained true.

Unlike most farmers, all twelve on my list showed unusual renewed interest in real estate loans. More financial involvement was something a farmer typically outgrew as they aged. Two of these were in their fifties. The rest were north of sixty.

"Ahem."

"Jesus!" I almost fell off my chair and under my desk. Harden posed at the edge of my desk all reared back, paunch out, arms crossed. And at my eye level, that bottom button above his belt was undone, showing his undershirt.

"You wouldn't be so damn surprised if you weren't up to something," he said.

Heart thumping, surprise punching an already unhappy stomach, I exhaled. "It's called concentration. What do you want?"

Luckily the department's IT people required computer screens facing away from whoever might walk in. Still, I *accidentally* hit the keyboard and strategically brought up the screensaver.

"I'm out of the office this afternoon," he said. "Meeting a congress person in Anderson."

Trying not to shrug, I cared little of the man's schedule unless it took him out of my hair.

"Care to come with me?" he asked, taking a swipe at a lock of his crossover fallen from place.

Harden was about as slick as Elmer's Glue. "The last time you invited me somewhere you parked me in the lobby. I'll pass," I said.

His eyes narrowed. "What if I order you?"

"Since I have no idea what you're meeting them about—"

"She invited me to some function to give a twenty-minute talk."

"Ah," I said, avoiding the smirk that he'd proven my suspicion. "So you bring your token 'female colleague' with you, and you think your congresswoman isn't going to read through that? With me all bored and, once again, sitting in a chair in a corner?"

We withstood firm across from each other. I could almost hear his brain train-wrecking over all the politically-correct phrases in his head.

I opened my drawer and reached for my purse. "Fine. You need a woman, you got a woman. But don't be surprised if she attempts to converse with me about stuff like kids, planning dinners . . . or maybe even what I do for the agency. Might be entertaining talking investigations with a state congresswoman." I glanced up. "Have you already signed out a car?"

"Never mind," he said. "You have work to do, plus we might be late."

"Yes, sir," I said, though the words were to his back. He'd already left my office. And he never knew I was late to work. Not that he couldn't still check up on me from Anderson if I left for Newberry. That I feared more.

The corner of my computer screen read eleven twenty. I located Lottie's number and then called. Might be time to put her on speed dial.

My CI answered lively. "Lottie Bledsoe. How may I help you?"

"Sounds like you need me in your contacts list so you see me coming, Lottie. It's Slade."

"Hey, child. We enjoyed having you over yesterday."

I picked out a fresh notebook from a drawer, just for this case. "Hmm. Is that sarcasm or do I not quite speak Newberry-ese?"

The guffaw sounded positive. "You made for great talk after you left. That's a big plus in their lives."

"I wasn't sure what their mood would be, considering Ms. Abrams just lost her husband." And the interrogation I got before I'd barely put my butt in the kitchen chair.

"No, honey, you're good." Her laughter settled down. "Whatcha need?"

"I want to treat you to lunch. At Jezebel's Diner."

"Huh," she said. "Why Jezebel's, if I may be so bold as to ask?"

I retrieved my purse. "I'll make that clear when I meet you at the diner. I'm leaving now, so give me an hour." The time I figured it would take *without* getting pulled over again.

I MADE GOOD TIME, but if not for an extra wide spot near the road that reached into the sidewalk, my truck wouldn't have fit in the tiny parking lot. Fords were a popular truck in these parts, and my generic bumper stickers fit in—Clemson football, the South Carolina flag, Certified SC Grown, and Ducks Unlimited. Everything that would fit in rural South Carolina. Nothing that would tell people where I lived.

Jezebel's sat on a corner in the heart of town, large picture windows facing both Main and a side street. The six-foot panes angled outward toward the top, with mismatched pots of dieffenbachia, snake plants, and aloe vera inside on the long window sills. A sad, wilted peace lily propped against the glass, as if discarded from a recent funeral.

I entered and spotted Lottie already seated against the interior wall, out of sight from street strollers. Her tired blonde dye job showed four inches of gray roots, and today she wore polyester pants and an oversized floral blouse.

Homey smells drifted from the kitchen rather than burger grease. In the back, ladies talked over the low whirl of a noisy ceiling fan.

The 1950s design of the place wasn't the feigned retro of contemporary eateries triggering our nostalgia for profit. This place still boasted original Formica and tube-steel tables and chairs with legs worn into the floor. Faded turquoise starbursts were more like smudges on white linoleum tiles.

I slid out a chair. "Thought I was supposed to be the one with her back against the wall to see the door."

"People don't always like what I do either," she said, handing me a one-page plastic-covered menu from behind the napkin holder. "Here you go. I don't need it."

A young blonde thing fitting Monroe's description of who served him his photograph, set two waters on the table. "Hey, Miss Lottie."

"Hey yourself, Tina."

Not gushy, but familiar enough.

"Y'all ready to order?" Tina had no pad. Just waited for our answers.

"Chicken salad. No crackers," Lottie said.

Tina turned to me.

"What's your favorite?" I asked.

"The BLT. If you like Reubens, I hear they're good," Tina said. "A lot of older people order that."

The girl appeared clueless to her insult, so I let it go. "Give me the BLT then. But before you go, have we met?"

She seemed puzzled. "Don't think so."

"You work here for suppers too or just lunch?" I asked.

She laughed once. "I work whenever Miss Lorena wants me and sometimes when she don't. Saving for school. That high school diploma ain't all it's cracked up to be when you're paying bills."

"She's a hard worker, too," Lottie said with a matronly smile.

Tina flipped back to the job. "Sweet tea for both?"

We nodded, and the girl swirled and disappeared into the kitchen, me trying to recall if I ever had thighs that smooth.

Other than two ladies chattering obliviously, a lone man dined near the front window, and an elderly woman, easily eighty, huddled in the back corner on the window side. "We missed the lunch rush?" I said, sipping water.

"For what it is." Lottie seemed in no hurry to talk. "We'll chat once lunch is delivered."

Tina showed up in no time balancing two plates and two glasses of tea. "There and there," she said. "You ladies enjoy."

Lottie gave Tina time to leave. "What did you think about the lists? Good idea you had yesterday. Really broke the ice."

I lifted a bread slice on one of my triangle sandwiches and deemed the food appealing. "When they showed a love of mysteries, and since they acted a bit tight-lipped, I went with them writing down clues instead."

"Well, you're a hit," Lottie said.

Something different about the bacon married the mayo and tomato down pat. The white bread clinched the sandwich. I wiped my mouth. "How many people have you given my phone number to?"

Lottie studied her chicken salad. "Why? Is there a problem with giving it out? Thought you'd want an open line to solve our problem."

Evasive. "I did. I do. But someone claiming to be a farmer said he'd meet me last night and never showed. You wouldn't happen to know who he was, would you?" After all, she claimed ownership of anyone and everything Newberrian.

She shook her head. "Sorry. You've stumped me there." She shoved another bite in.

I shrugged. "Back to your house. There were twelve names on your lists. You said you talked long after I left, so y'all discussed them."

Lottie waved her hand, mouth full.

"Take your time," I said. "I'm trying to determine who has the darkest secrets that could involve my agency, and how far would they go to keep those secrets quiet." I didn't specify inside or outside Agriculture.

From the window corner about twelve feet from us, the old woman spoke. Thinking she referenced us, I turned to her, but she spoke down into what appeared to be a small ten-inch handheld device.

"That's her soap opera," Lottie said, pushing her chicken salad around. "Hmm, got a bad pecan in that last bite. Gotta ask Lorena who she's getting her nuts from."

"Thought that woman was listening to us," I said.

"That's Aunt Sis, and that's her table. Every day. She's Cricket's great aunt, Lorena's momma's sister with dementia." Lottie raised her voice. "Hey, Aunt Sis!"

Head up, the woman hunted for the source of her name.

Lottie waved big. "Over here, Aunt Sis."

They connected, exchanged smiles, then Aunt Sis's eyes snapped back to her story like a magnet.

"They just leave her sitting there?" I felt sorry for her at a table of one.

With a light shrug, Lottie puckered. "She's all right. Wanders from one of Lorena's six business establishments to the next, up and down Main Street. The employees keep a watch on her, each place with a special corner for her. She just walks around with that mini-TV in her hand." Lottie leaned over and lowered her voice. "But she has ears like a radio antenna."

"She hardly senses we're here."

"Honey . . . she's a lightning rod for gossip, or used to be, so no sense thinking that part of her ain't still active. Of course, nobody understands half of what she says, so nobody takes her serious." Lottie regarded the old woman sadly. "She used to be the mayor's secretary, had a charm that made her the unspoken ambassador to this town. I think she was an actress in her late teens, or tried to be. A beauty, in a Vivien Leigh kind of way."

I tried to picture Aunt Sis sixty years younger.

"Bless her heart," Lottie added.

"Bless her heart," I repeated under my breath. Now, back to business. "So, any specifics on the farmers?"

Lottie washed down a bite with tea, then whispered, "We feel there's collusion between Cricket and her mom."

Not what I asked, but okay. "Her mom's involved in Agriculture's business?"

Lottie tucked her chin back, like a chicken. "Slade! She's a real estate broker and owns all kinds of land and property. Why wouldn't Cricket and her momma work each other's assets?"

"Still not hearing details, Lottie." She chose to stare at her plate for a moment, so I picked at the last half of my sandwich, the first now sitting like unbaked dough in my belly.

I liked a real estate angle. In my debut case in Charleston County, I noted a trend with a small number of landowners losing acreage. Courthouse records, a map, and a ballpoint pen revealed a geographic commonality. Didn't take much more study to note that someone offed retired farmers with paid-for tracts because of a future highway deal to the beaches. An unofficial and very illegal sort of eminent domain action, as it turned out.

"Where can I get a map of the county?" I asked.

Lottie got up and walked to the glassed-in dessert display that separated the dining area from the kitchen. "Y'all got any county maps?" she hollered.

I cringed, but I was learning who Lottie was.

Tina appeared, wiping her hands. "No, ma'am, but Miss Lorena's bound to have some at her office. Want me to call and ask?"

"No, honey. I'll get one. Thanks." She returned.

I noted Aunt Sis watching us, and I smiled back. She didn't reciprocate.

Instead of sitting, Lottie reached down and wiped her mouth with a napkin. "I'm about done. You?"

"Yes."

"Want to walk down to the real estate office with me? It's about four storefronts down."

She started to grab her purse strap off the back of her chair. I motioned one-handed to the side, for her to take her seat. "What?" she whispered, easing down.

Covert she wasn't, that's for sure. "All I've got is a horny dead farmer and an irate radio caller. That's not a lot to pin a case on," I said, hesitant to mention Ginger, Tina, or the photograph. Not sure of Lottie's closeness to the players after seeing her warmth toward Tina.

Lottie smacked and gave me a sigh. "Slade, I listen to these women day in and day out, and umpteen times after church on Sunday. They are seriously concerned."

"Names, Lottie. Dates. What deals?"

Her mouth pursed this way, then that, Lottie studying the street through the front window behind me. Hesitant to talk or frustrated, I could not tell. "We gave you names."

"We need more, but tell you what," I said. "You see what you can find out about the people involved since they trust you. I'll delve more into the loans and sales for a pattern, but I'll walk down to the real estate office by myself. Otherwise the minute someone notices either of us snooping, we're both incriminated. But I have another question. Which farmer did you give my number to?"

"Not sure I'm following you," she said, though I read the opposite in her manner.

"A farmer who wouldn't identify himself asked to meet with me but didn't show," I said.

She waved her hand. "Oh, no telling. I've been handing out your number to anybody who might make use of it. You handle whistleblowers, right? Bet I've given it to two dozen people since we met on Tuesday and I got your cell phone. Before that, I told them your office number."

Fabulous. A dead end. Nothing to do now but head to the real estate office. Alone.

I'd sort of shifted to straddling the fence about Cricket being so heinous. Not that she couldn't be. And her mother was a power player in this little town. By association that could mean Cricket as well. Blatantly strutting around the county with Lottie as my guide could create a stir and leave Lottie vulnerable, too. The guilty tended to overreact, and Lottie had to live here. I didn't.

I decided not to let my CI go before picking her brain one last time. "Are you familiar with anyone named Ginger?"

"Cricket's friend. Lorena's real estate agent."

I needed more answers like *that*. "Yesterday, she hit on our Ag representative, here, in this parking lot. Then he got a threat delivered while he ate dinner. Would she do anything like that?"

"Not sure about the threat." Then Lottie's laugh came out almost dirty. "But could be her style. Ginger makes the rounds. Drives her husband crazy."

Shit! "Husband?"

"Oh yes. He broke his hand not six months ago, and most say it was from putting some poor sap in the hospital. Tell your friend to steer clear of that one. I'll tell you one thing about that girl, though."

"What?"

"She's Lorena's right-hand salesperson. You cringe if she's representing a buyer, because no telling what she'll do to consummate that sale, if you catch my drift."

Oh man, I had to talk to Monroe. "Anything new about Hoyt and the Tea Table?"

Her snigger came low and phlegmy. "The story they're going with is that Hoyt met a girl out there. Fibers on him may have been from a blanket. Tea spilled on it and him. No doubt as to the heart attack. Viagra confirmed." She spoke softer. "Kind of a romantic morning tryst, but I doubt romance had a damn thing to do with it. Laying on the hard ground is not the whim of a middle-aged woman. No, that old codger let his urges run off with him with some nymph, is my guess."

Who said those north of thirty couldn't embrace urges with vigor? A whole weekend of urges and vigor may have landed me in my yet-to-be-validated predicament.

"Crazier ways to die," I said more polite than serious because dying from Viagra while having tea on a rock with a hooker pretty much topped my list of crazy.

Chapter 11

AFTER GIVING LOTTIE time to reach her car, I headed the other direction to Main Street. Newberry could almost be Mayberry from its down-home appearance. A few storefronts begged for tenants, but the majority showed life, as in the lights were on and doors open, but foot traffic both east and west wasn't ten people. The town didn't appear prime for a property scam, but the rural parts of the county might be another story.

Lorena Carson owned six Main Street properties, per Lottie, and I found them impossible to miss. Especially since "Proudly sponsored by Carson" shined in four-inch gold letters across a logo of the Newberry Opera House's tower in the window of each store. Even the six awnings matched in a red and rusty-orange stripe pattern, complementing the brick and red-roof design. So sure of her foothold that she practically claimed the opera house as her own.

That 130-foot tower defined Newberry's crowning landmark, restored in the nineties under the notion its rejuvenation would lift the entire town. However, I knew through work this town was harshly impacted by the interstate built in the sixties being a tad too far to bring traffic to the community.

Agriculture strived to understand its rural communities and what they needed, and Newberry had its struggles when it came to progressive development. A tug of war existed between wanting more for the town and wanting the town to be left alone. A bittersweet sort of dilemma one couldn't help but feel walking down its Main Street.

After passing the Carson antique/art gallery displaying a phenomenal, head-turning debutante portrait of Cricket in a formal gown, I found the hardware store, gift and interior design store, and insurance agency. I deduced the last red and orange awning on the street to be my point of interest.

Carson Real Estate. I swung the door open, and a soft doorbell sounded in another room. Crisp air conditioning caressed my skin, warmed from walking. A female voice sounded from the back. "Working on the hundred, like always. Let me call you back. Think I heard somebody come in."

Electronic screens hung on either side of the small lobby touting what had sold and what opportunities still existed: Lake Murray, rolling farmland, upscale homes, and empty commercial buildings. The obvious drawing cards to the community were Newberry College, the Opera House, then the lake. A mattress factory and an orchid nursery. Not enough demand for real estate professionals to fight over the properties, making one think this Carson ran the show without much competition.

"May I help you?"

I turned toward the lilting voice . . . and saw the girl from Monroe's photo. The brunette crushed a sleeveless shift, the two-tone pattern darting to make her size eight figure come off as a four. I'd kill to wear either size anywhere near that well.

"Hey," I said. "The waitress at Jezebel's said I could get a county map here? I believe her name was Tina."

The agent reached under the counter and came up with a folded road map. "Here you go. Anything in particular you're in the market for?"

"Not really." I stepped over and accepted the map, sniffing surreptitiously to detect why Monroe said she smelled so good. "Just trying to learn the lay of the land to even decide if I'm interested."

"Be glad to show you the area." She studied me, trying to decipher my real story, and I tried to picture her smothering Monroe with those lips, wondering how he felt having that body rubbing his. Couldn't have been all that tortuous for either of them.

I held out my hand. "Carolina Slade," I said.

"Ginger Oliver," she replied with a smile to light a room.

I reached up and lifted a piece of my hair. "Ginger?"

A smirk. A rather precious smirk. "My mother loved Ginger on *Gilligan's Island*. I was born with reddish sort of hair, so there you go. Who could guess I would turn into a Mary Ann?"

I chuckled out of courtesy.

"Yeah," she said. "That joke's getting rather dated. You'd be surprised how many people never heard of the show."

Her cell phone rang, and she held up a finger begging for a moment. I gave a *sure thing* nod and pretended to study the map, not fully extending it because I never could fold those things right.

"Oh, you didn't. Cecil, what the hell were you thinking?" Each word rising in pitch, the last word ending on shrill. Then she lowered her voice and whispered, "Shit. It was just a . . . work thing. Damn it, you are the biggest pain in my ass."

My phone rang. Monroe, probably from the local Agriculture office. Moving as far as I could toward the door, I took the call. "Hey. What's up?"

"So much for being bait," he said through a thick accent, people in the background almost talking over him. "Ginger's husband, yeah, you heard right, husband, just marched in and punched me in the face. Cricket stopped him from tearing into me a second time."

Adrenaline flowed through me. Without thinking, I spun around toward the real estate agent, fighting not to march over there and slap the bitch.

She forced a smile then mouthed, *Sorry, I need to take this.*

I mouthed, *No problem.*

My back to her again, I returned attention to my buddy. "Are you all right?"

"Broken nose," he said. "Can you notify the office? They won't let me drive to the hospital."

"They who?"

"The police, Slade. I was assaulted."

Right. The timing of all this seemed awkward yet convenient.

"The clerk here called 911," he continued. "Glad she did."

"Me, too." I turned and glanced at an animated Ginger, now a ten-foot-taller bitch in my mind. "Did an ambulance show up or just the cops?"

Cricket called Monroe in the distance.

"Just a sec," then Monroe muffled the phone but soon returned. "Cricket's taking me to the hospital. I hit my head on the floor when I went down."

That answered my question about the ambulance. "To hell with her. I'll be right over." A piece of me regretted not calling Monroe an hour earlier, when I first learned of the husband through Lottie. And the husband had to be Cecil on the phone with Ginger.

Which made me want to confront Ginger tenfold.

"Not sure I can wait an hour, Slade," Monroe said.

"I'm not a mile from you," I said. "Sit tight." My adrenaline built. "Did you return the favor to Cecil by any chance?"

Silence. "How did you know his name was Cecil?" he asked.

"See you in a minute." I hung up and eyed Ginger. Who was eying me. Both of us with unsaid words on our tongues. She really didn't want to hear mine.

"I completely forgot I had a showing," she said. "Do you mind if we reschedule?"

I held up my phone. "Seems I've had an appointment appear on my radar as well, so sure. No doubt we'll revisit, because I have some questions I understand only you can answer."

Code for we both needed to head to Cricket's office and the fracas.

Ginger reached out. "Here's my card." Ever the sales agent.

Sliding it in my pocket, I reached out to shake hands. She took it, and I wanted to crunch down hard . . . wishing I could break a few bones. I didn't. Yeah, Ginger and I would have another moment.

"Hope to see you soon," she said. I fast-walked out the front, and she scurried out the rear.

We entered the parking lot from two different directions. While I got out, she remained in her vehicle, probably juggling whether to be seen rescuing her hubby from the cops in the presence of a potential customer. I almost wished she would come in. Instead, she left. *Yeah, you better.*

A lone police car parked in the lot outside the USDA building. We leased the place long-term, therefore, making this federal property. I entered, intending to use that fact.

Inside, an officer lorded over a seated Cecil.

Surely Ginger could do better than him. Her first impression struck anyone as professional. Cecil, however, appeared to be a greasy, part-time mechanic for a grungy cement-block garage where cars they couldn't fix sat rusting in the yard.

Bet her momma and daddy were disappointed. He sure didn't fit the Carson image.

Monroe sat in a clerical chair, head tilted, a bloodied ice-towel across his nose. He still held his cell phone in his hand.

I showed my Agriculture badge, the one with no arrest power. Plastic, but put it in a leather case like Wayne's, and it never ceased to amaze me how many people bowed out of my way. I pulled a chair next to Monroe. "Wow, I bet that'll be pretty in a few hours."

"I ought to punch *Wayne* in the nose," he said, stuffy and congested.

"He wasn't the one putting moves on Ginger in the parking lot," I told him under my breath, attempting humor. I lifted the edge of the towel and grimaced. Someone would have to reset it. My guess was a sucker punch, with Monroe being about as big and nice a sucker as one could find.

And I wanted to hug him to me, apologizing to my core. The minute Lottie said Ginger had a bad-tempered husband I should've called him. At least texted. Again, Monroe paying the price for being thrown under the bus by my feud with Harden. Rubbing his arm, I said, "I'm so sorry, dude. This is my fault."

"In a way, yes," he said.

I wilted. Didn't expect that, but I'd asked for it.

"But I did accept dinner with her, so some of this is on me. She led me on, and I followed like a puppy." He shifted the towel and tried to sniffle. "Like I said, she smelled good."

Leaning over, I whispered, "Just met her, by the way. She *is* rather hot."

That drew a smile.

I patted Monroe on the leg then walked over to the officer guarding Cecil. Time to tend to business and avenge my buddy. Again, introduced myself with my badge, then I gave the uniform my card. "We want this man charged with trespassing."

"It's just Cecil Oliver," the badge said. "Does something stupid like this about every six months. More flash of temper than intent to do bodily harm."

I nodded toward Monroe. "That's not bodily harm?"

The officer raised a brow in acknowledgment.

"And nobody ever presses charges against this guy?" I asked.

The officer shook his head.

"Guess this will be a new experience for him then," I said. "And once his victim, Mr. Prevatte, is medically tended and off the pain killers, he'll be in touch about whether he wants to press charges for assault."

Cecil's growl came with a country twang. "That man came on to my wife. I saw the pictures."

"What pictures?" How many people had seen pictures of that kiss?

"On her camera," he answered. "Only three, but condemning nonetheless."

The intellectual wording sounded foreign from that mouth. "*Nonetheless,*" I echoed with sarcasm. "Regardless of what you think took place, you had no right to injure this man."

I returned attention to Monroe, sick of Ginger's twit of a husband. Cecil exhaled loud for my notice, but he was no longer worth the conversation. Not after hurting my friend.

The officer helped Cecil up. "Guess you're getting locked up."

Grumbling, the cuffed redneck stood. "This ain't right, Tom," he said. "I was the one wronged."

"Not for me to say," the officer said, and they exited the building.

Cricket hurried out of her office, bag slung over her shoulder. "Monroe, I cleared my schedule this afternoon. Let's get you to the hospital." She stutter-stepped to a halt. "Oh, Ms. Slade."

I wasn't the state director, but amongst the Agriculture employees, in the confines of South Carolina, my presence held a smidge of authority. Assuming Harden hadn't diluted it during his lunch with Cricket after the radio show, but Harden wasn't here now.

"Ms. Carson," I said. "I'll take Monroe, but you're welcome to follow. We might need to have a chat."

Even flustered, Cricket pulled off cute, but my gut held a grudge now, and my common sense tugged at me like a cranky three-year-old wanting the forbidden piece of candy. Toddlers could be relentless. This little size six stack of sweetness in front of me was about to run out of cute and didn't know it.

By now, poor Cricket probably regretted that award. Without it, we wouldn't have been the wiser about the irate radio caller and Hoyt's death. I never would've met Lottie and heard the whisperings of a small-town scandal. And with Ginger's antics, maybe the waitress's cooperation, and Cecil's timely temper against a federal employee, Cricket had earned not only my attention, but possibly the inspector general's. I couldn't wait to get home tonight and tell Wayne that it looked like we'd be working a joint case again. Surely there was enough here that even Harden would see the sense of having me involved.

I assisted Monroe to his feet. "The camera," he whispered, his glances toward a small camera on the desk before him.

Without question, I moved to block Cricket's view, disappearing the camera into my bag. "My paperwork," Monroe said in his normal, yet thick, stifled voice. "Slide everything in my briefcase."

I looked around the desk where he was, recognizing nothing in his handwriting.

"Oh, he worked back here," Cricket said, heading to the rear. "I'll do it."

"No, that's okay," I said, thinking the subject of an investigation shouldn't be handling the evidence.

Quickly, I trotted back to Monroe's work space and found the briefcase wide open next to an open file and a notebook. Other files stacked to the side. I threw the one file and notepad in the case, locked it, and ran back out.

Cricket acted lost but aiming to help. "Did you want to take my farmer files, too?" she asked.

"No, we're good," I said.

En route to Newberry General, I called the State Office.

Angela answered, the state director's secretary. She had loved me under the last two bosses but hid her affection under Harden's leadership. He tended to notice who played on Team Slade.

"I'm taking Monroe to the hospital," I said, leaving off where we were or how I got there. "He has a broken nose. Heard from Harden?" Good thing everyone already assumed I'd be the first person Monroe would call in an emergency.

"Oh my, well, tell him we're thinking about him," she said, ever courteous.

"He can't communicate well at the moment, so I'm to tell you he'll be taking sick leave tomorrow. Good thing it's Friday. Depends on what the doc says as to whether he'll be in Monday."

"Of course, of course," she replied.

I hung up, and Monroe groaned.

"What's wrong?" I sped up the truck.

"Should I hire an attorney? To press charges or something?"

"No, you don't need an attorney. The government has lawyers for us when we're injured while in the line of duty. But don't worry about it until after we get you looked at."

Parked, I ran around to help him out.

He refused my assistance. "Harden will do the math about you being here, Slade. And I broke my nose, not my legs. I can walk."

He was right on both counts.

They whisked him into the ER, leaving me to find a chair. Only one other family in the waiting area, so I had my pick of seats. As I sat, the glass doors parted, and after saying "hey" to the nurses, Cricket came in and assumed a place across from me.

Still revved up from my friend taking a beating, I needed some place to toss my energy, so I stared at the girl. She glanced up once, then let her attention dart to the ubiquitous waiting room television.

That's right, girl. What the hell are you up to?

Harden might have done his damnedest to undercut my reputation and to label me a conniving troublemaker, but he hadn't succeeded completely. Especially since anyone who'd been with Ag more than a minute realized Harden's behavior was payback for how I'd jailed his friends.

Even so, I didn't have many staunch allies in the agency for fear the tide would turn, and they'd find themselves on the wrong side of Harden or one of my cases. A lonely job, but somebody had to do it. Besides, I enjoyed sleuthing a lot more than being anybody's pal. No, correct that . . . I enjoyed meting justice.

With Monroe potentially sidelined, Harden would need a body to put his Newberry review back to order. I hoped I would be that body. Nobody else was up to speed *but* me.

I looked at Cricket. *Seize the moment.* Time to oil these cogs of mine and test out my rusty scrutinizing talents. Time to nudge Miss Debutante of Newberry and see what she was made of.

Chapter 12

THE EMERGENCY room echoed with emptiness. Nothing between Cricket and me other than beige linoleum, that infamous antiseptic smell, and the voices from a house rehab show on a flat screen in the corner.

"They say anything about Mr. Prevatte?" Cricket asked, her hands wedged between her knees. Her tiny feet fast-tapped on the floor.

"We barely got here," I replied. "He's still in the examining room."

"Oh, okay."

Nerves. Good.

An impromptu audit like Monroe's often drove a county manager nuts, and by my very presence in Newberry, Cricket would assume me in on it. But I worried more that attention would shift off the case and onto a jealousy-driven assault of a federal employee than I was about being outed.

While Cricket and I sat alone, now would be the best time to put thoughts on record . . . before she had a chance to speak to Ginger, Cecil, or whomever else she needed to mold a tale. I withdrew a notepad from my purse, then my phone. "We need to talk. Mind if I record this?" I set the phone on the arm of the seat beside me.

Cricket hesitated at the request but hadn't the nerve to tell me no. Amazing how often I got my way asking casual permission for something the other party really should have refused. I hadn't done this work for long, but I was learning.

I stated the date, time, and persons present, then swore her to tell the truth, as my training and delegation from the IG dictated. If Cricket cared to lie, I wanted it on record.

"Relay what exactly happened regarding Mr. Monroe Prevatte today," I said. "What did you see?"

"Nothing," she replied, solid and professional. "I came out after the scuffle ended."

Monroe had said she pulled Cecil off him. "Who called the police?"

"My clerk."

"Were you surprised to see Mr. Prevatte come back to your office today?"

The shift in questioning threw her off. "Uh . . . um, no."

Which meant yes.

"Ginger's rather high strung, Ms. Slade," she volunteered. "She likes making Cecil jealous."

"And who is Ginger?" I asked, like I never heard of the woman, glad Cricket felt the urge to spill information before being asked for it.

Her head tilted at what she assumed I already knew. "Um, she works for my mother as a real estate agent. We're also friends since we're close to the same age."

With a nod, I acted newly informed. "And Cecil is . . .?"

"Ginger's husband."

"Gotcha. That's all this amounted to? Jealousy?"

Relief fleeted in her eyes at the hope this questioning could be so simple. "Yes, ma'am. Or rather, I believe so."

"This sort of thing has happened before with Cecil?"

She laughed. "Oh yes. Happens every few months with that moron. Gotta show his woman his Neanderthal side."

"In your office?"

"Oh," and she shook her head. "No, ma'am."

"Does Cecil do business with any of your farmers?"

The lack of immediate response indicated she had to debate her answer. Words weren't the only damning tool in an interview.

"Cricket, come on now." I looked at her as I would a child lying about homework. "You grew up around here. You know the farmers and you know Ginger, and it sounds like you're familiar enough with Cecil. That award Monday said you were good at your job, so, I'd expect you to be quite knowledgeable about these folks."

But instead of being concerned about the accusation, she smiled with condescension. "You're making this too complicated, Ms. Slade. Apparently, Mr. Prevatte saw something he liked. Ginger took him up on the offer. Cecil took issue. That's all."

That's all, huh? "Let's start at the beginning again."

She didn't argue, and we revisited the questions in different order. I noted her mannerisms but learned nothing new. Or I wasn't reading the girl as well as I liked.

"I warned Mr. Prevatte that Ginger could be flighty," she said.

"Did you tell him Ginger was married?" I asked.

"Figured that was between them," she said. "Mr. Prevatte must've felt her appealing enough to take the risk. He put his hands on her." She glanced toward the television. "Or so I heard."

My pulse accelerated. "From who?"

She looked at me incredulously. "Why, Ginger, of course."

"When did you speak with her?"

"Last night, on the phone." She started to open her cell. "Want the time? How many minutes?"

Useless information volunteered too easily. "No thanks." I flipped a page. "Why did Ginger call you?"

"She was upset."

"Exactly what did she say?"

Her thin frown flashed a sense of impatience. "That dinner turned into a hands-on she didn't appreciate so she ditched him."

Lying witch. Unless Ginger did the lying.

I numbered another line. "Why didn't you go to dinner with Ginger and Mr. Prevatte yesterday?"

She crossed her legs. "Not invited."

"According to Mr. Prevatte you were."

"Then maybe I don't remember."

In a counter move I uncrossed my legs and leaned toward her. "Which is it, Cricket? You weren't invited or you don't remember?"

She riveted a hard stare. "I don't recall."

I blinked a couple times, staring back, before returning to my notes. "Tell me about the pictures of Mr. Prevatte and Ginger that Cecil Oliver mentioned."

"No idea."

Maybe Cricket had arranged for the pictures. Maybe not. Made me wonder who the camera in my purse belonged to.

Surprisingly, pity filled her expression. "I'm really sorry about all this."

"We all are." I ended the recording, slid the phone in my bag, and relaxed back, afraid to push harder. I wanted to ask Monroe more questions, study the camera, talk to Lottie. Eventually catch up to Ginger.

"Why are you here, Ms. Slade?" Cricket asked, her voice suddenly edgy. "For real, why are you snooping? Harden forewarned me about Monroe coming, but nothing about you."

Not *Mr. Harris* or *Mr. Prevatte.* Miss Priss no longer oozed sugarplum sweet with the recorder gone. "I'm not at liberty to say," I replied.

"Maybe I'll call and ask."

From witch to bitch. "Mr. Harris is in Anderson today, but his secretary will gladly take a message."

"Maybe I can call his cell."

Monroe exited and we rose to greet him. The bandage consumed half his face, his eyes beginning to darken.

"Geez, Monroe," I said, taking his arm.

"You okay?" Cricket asked.

He waved her off and turned to me. "Can we go? They gave me something for the pain, so I guess you're driving."

Cricket moved in front of his line of vision. "I can get somebody to help deliver your car home, Mr. Prevatte."

Yeah, like I wanted strangers to find where he lived, or more probably where I lived, because Monroe needed tending. That meant in Zack's room, at least for the weekend. "I'll retrieve it, Ms. Carson. Please inform Ginger we'll be back with more questions."

That quieted her. She said goodbye and left before we ever made it to my truck. Once inside and buckled in, I turned to Monroe. "Before you get totally knocked out from those pills, talk to me. What did you find in the files?" I made a whirlwind spin with my index finger. "All this is getting a little too weird, dude."

"The eight files I researched, before being so rudely interrupted by Ginger's *husband*," he began, then he seemed to fade into introspection. He'd emphasized the word *husband* with slur and a hint of swagger. Already drunk on meds.

I reminded him of where he left off. "The eight files?"

"They sold land."

"Which means what, Monroe?"

"Just didn't see the need." He smacked his limp hand on the seat. "Can we talk details another time? I don't think I'm making sense." He tugged on the neck of his shirt. "Turn the air on."

April temperatures outside only hit seventy, but if Monroe wanted the air, he'd get the air. Reaching over, I directed a vent on him.

"Can't breathe," he said, dabbing around his nose bandage. "And it's hot."

"Of course, you can't breathe," I said. "And put that other vent on you."

We traveled another ten miles. He coughed, and it sounded strained. Every third or fourth breath gurgled. He laid his head against the passenger window.

"Poor Monroe," I said low.

"Poor me," he repeated in a whisper.

I didn't like his look, but the hospital released him. Ally already prepped Zack's room at my request. I imagined Wayne's face clouding over at the news of my male buddy spending the night, but logic ruled the cowboy. Sometimes painfully so.

Just a few miles from Chapin, Monroe's head remained rested against the glass. Suddenly, he lurched forward, unmistakable sounds of nausea climbing to get out. "Slade–" He clamped hands over his mouth.

"Hold on," I said, pulling onto the side of the road. I ran around the truck, through thigh-high weeds, and opened Monroe's door. Without the presence of mind to undo his seatbelt, he leaned over and released what smelled like coffee and bad lunch meat across the truck's footboard, splashing chunks and liquid onto the ground . . . and my feet.

Eyes watering, he gazed up pitifully sick at me. Which didn't stop me from pivoting to vomit into a ditch.

When I returned, Monroe's complexion held an unnatural color, and his breathing scared me. "Sorry, but I don't feel right, Slade."

"You don't look right, either," I replied, and jumped behind the wheel, gas pedal pressed hard, my mouth tasting like my kitchen trash.

Too far from Newberry and way too distant from Columbia, I high-tailed it to the closest urgent care which happened to be in Chapin. For the second time of the day, I sat in a small-town hospital lobby, only this time six miles from my house. I texted Wayne. With no vending machines in sight, I begged an ice-cold Coke off a nurse, with the excuse I couldn't handle the sight of bodily fluids. She admitted I looked pale.

This time *my* foot tapped the linoleum floor. Nervous about Monroe and a possible concussion. Nervous about my own shower episode this morning and the repeat on the side of the road. Nervous about Cricket's threat to call Harden, and her boldness in the threat. Nervous about whether Bug had reached third base with my daughter today.

From that laundry list, thinking about work seemed easiest— a problem I could be most proactive about.

The generic black-on-white wall clock read five after six. After finishing the Coke, I laid my head back and shut my eyes. There, in all my sitting and forced contemplation, I came to a conclusion. I'd quit ignoring my instincts a long time ago. Newberry was worth going to war with Harden. He'd accuse me of overreacting. I'd accuse him of dismissing my experienced conclusion for spite. He'd allege I thought too highly of myself. I'd play my trump card and suggest he might be hiding something about Cricket's activities, because he didn't want the publicity of his having rewarded a girl involved in fraud.

A tap on my forehead woke me up. "How's Monroe?" Wayne took the chair beside me.

"Haven't heard," I said, stretching with a yawn. "What time is it?"

"Six thirty. You have a peaky sort of look about you. Hard day?"

I pointed to my shoes, twisting my ankles this way, then that. "Yeah. Nothing like getting puked on."

He gave me a once over, testing a sniff. Expecting a joke, I found myself disappointed when he failed to crack a smile.

"Let me get the scoop on things back there," he said, rising.

Wayne could do that. He'd done it with me, twice, wading past desks, through doors, and into exam rooms with a gentle demand to be brought up to speed. Nurses loved him. Not just because of the whole magnetic badge bunny thing, but because he presented a damn fine package with his stature, the scruffy beard, and the wide, substantive shoulders. The voice of an Alpha male, toned down just enough to show he cared.

He came right back. "They said give Monroe a half hour to forty-five minutes. Not enough time to grab dinner."

"I wouldn't want to leave him anyway," I said. "Did you see him?"

"Yeah, just a second. Don't think he saw me." He sat where Cricket had reared back and crossed a leg over a knee, just waiting.

Still tense with me. "Why are they keeping him?" I asked. You'd think he'd volunteer the information.

"He had an allergic reaction to the shot they gave him in Newberry. Said you got him here just in time. His airways were swelling."

Kudos to me. "Good thing I was in Newberry," I said. "Good thing he didn't have to rely on Cricket. Not sure how that would've gone down."

He went still for a while. "Monroe's out of commission," he finally said, "and he really has no business going back to Newberry."

"A given." I waited. So much effort for so little conversation.

"Well, I received a call this afternoon."

Pressure built in my chest. I reached for my empty Coke can and drank the last few drops, just to do something. Mustn't show weakness, right? "I need another drink."

"Damn it, Slade, just pay attention."

Wow, okay. My threat level rose to orange with my first thought being the transfer he threatened the night before. My biggest concern outside of him getting hurt on the job.

"Your illustrious boss asked if I could look into Newberry," he said.

Oh. The duo together again. The CI and her lawman. What wonderful timing—we could barely talk to each other without snapping. "Okay, so we have to stifle the personal and focus. I told you I got that last night."

He didn't fuss back. Instead, was that . . . pity?

"What?" I asked.

"He wants me without you," he said. "Made it darn clear."

I fell back. "What?"

He snatched a glance at the television on the wall. "You seriously can't act surprised, Slade."

"Not an act, I assure you. But . . ."

"But what?" he asked, staring back at me. "He's the state director."

Exactly. Now I really wondered what was going on. Nobody gave the IG a free rein in one of their offices. What was Harden up to? Or worse, what had Monroe gotten himself involved in?

And most of all . . . "What aren't you telling me, Wayne?"

He rested an arm across the back of a neighboring chair. "I said you aren't involved."

"But I've been working this case. So has Monroe."

"You were off-book, and Monroe's been removed."

A low-grade heat rose through me. "But I have more intel on this than anyone. I'm an asset."

Settling his gaze back on the television, his mouth tightened.

I fingernail-tapped the arm of my chair in a nervous rhythm. "Don't tell me we're back to you holding back . . . and me trying to be good enough to be looped in on the information."

"Babe," he said, a tad exasperated, then paused as if catching himself with the endearment.

My stare riveted on his. "What?"

He shook his head. "I cannot tell you the details without making you angry."

"*Angrier*," I corrected. "It's about Monroe, isn't it?"

I bet Ivy's college fund on the idea that bitch took the offensive, designed a diversion of some kind, then called Harden. Shit. Maybe Monroe did need a lawyer. If the government considered Monroe functioning outside the scope of duty, they'd refuse to represent him.

Wayne started to shake his head and caught himself. He wiped his beard. Ordinarily I loved that beard.

Then the photograph of Monroe and Ginger flashed to mind. "Wait a minute. You kept Monroe's photo."

He scratched the beard this time. A tell. And boy, I sure could read him. "Not only that," I said, "but you signed and dated the picture into evidence." My voice raised. "You expected this to escalate."

"It had strong potential to, so yes," he said. "No point in that picture getting passed around, maybe lost."

With an exhale, I whispered, "Son of a bitch. Cricket turned this all on Monroe as a diversion." Our interview took on new meaning. "What time did Harden call you today?"

"Around three."

Before my interview with Cricket. About the time I spoke to Cecil. While Cricket was conveniently out of sight in her office.

This was a setup, and when Monroe didn't honor the warning to get gone and stay gone, she, they, whomever, took it to another level. And they dumped on the poor guy who would've given Cricket and her office the fairest shake out of all of us. Possibly to take attention off whatever this other thing was.

Wayne's touch of my hand stole my attention back. "Harden threw some serious attitude at me about you being in Newberry already," he said. "Be glad you've got me and not some other agent out of Atlanta on this. Your snooping got you cut out of the equation, Butterbean."

I already figured that but didn't appreciate hearing it. "So, what are you doing next?"

He blew out once. "Don't, Slade. The case is with the IG now, under my oversight. People scrutinize the two of us enough as it is. You're not privy just because you're dating me."

His remark punched me in the gut. I understood the rules of investigation and how those rules could be bent, or selective. Sometimes the rules didn't even work. How many damn nights had we held that discussion over bourbons, to include the night I think I got pregnant.

I pouted, because I could help, damn it. Monroe was as innocent as the day was long, and I felt responsible. Plus, this had been an incredibly complicated day.

"You're too close to Monroe," he said. Like he read my mind.

"Is that the agent or the boyfriend talking?"

"Thought you called me fiancé to that trooper." He smiled, his baritone drawl choosing now of all times to make peace.

"Go check on Monroe again," I said.

He scooted across the divide and sat beside me with a hand on my leg. "This isn't personal."

"Of course it is. Trust has to be earned," I replied, easing his hand off me. "Guess I just don't pass muster."

Chapter 13

I STARED AWAY from Wayne to the news on the hospital television.

"Not that I'm a Harden Harris fan, but he might be smart calling me in," Wayne said.

Harden and *smart* in the same sentence didn't fly with me. "Quit dangling comments at me if I'm alienated from the case."

Wasn't sure which I was most riled at: the IG, an anti-Slade campaign by Harden, or Wayne's conflict-of-interest argument. Was I too close to Monroe, or had I ventured too close to real answers? The personal and professional aspects of my life held no clean boundaries. Whatever I did with Monroe and Wayne fell into both realms of late.

I tired of the banter, wanting Monroe to get his ass out to the waiting room so we could go.

"You're hardheaded, Slade."

I snapped toward him. "You of all people taught me to capitalize on all potential assets."

"You're Harden's sworn enemy," he said. "I'd have a more level head."

I inhaled in defiance. "That's not so."

"Is so."

Silence filled the space between us.

"Can I ask you about the case?" he asked.

Finally, common sense. I'd cooperate, and hopefully Wayne would leak something in return.

I covered what I thought so far about Newberry. The gossip from the ladies at Lottie's. Cricket acting all saccharin then adversarial, threatening to call Harden after the recording. My short answers turned into a rant about how Monroe stood entrapped, and whatever group activity was going down in this county seemed nervous we'd come to town. I promised to send Wayne the interview recording.

And he gave up nothing.

Agents thought highly of themselves, and I understood why to a certain degree having adopted some of that vanity myself. However,

Wayne would never get through to these wives regardless how good he thought he was. They had a bit of a skewed view of a man's worth. No badge would budge that.

"Tomorrow and Saturday I'm slammed," he said. "But I'll probably go see your friend Cricket on Monday. What does she look like?"

Flatly, I replied, "Brunette and four inches shorter than me. She could walk a runway in the Miss South Carolina State Fair contest. Can't miss her."

He grinned. "Not good enough for Miss America?"

I started to say *a dark-haired Pamela*, but peered at the ER double doors instead. I wasn't that cruel.

Pamela was ex-DEA and the ex-Mrs. Wayne Largo, incarcerated and unable to walk thanks to Wayne's own bullet in our joint operation last August. Wayne had never stopped beating himself up over the unfortunate result of his ex turning criminal, probably never would.

"He ought to be ready by now," I said, and rose to question whomever I could find. "I want to see what kind of shape he's in before we question him."

Wayne's boots hit the linoleum with muted clips. "I'll get him, but he's no good to us tonight. Not after what I saw earlier. Man's on drugs. He's not competent to answer."

And he was right. Monroe soon exited in a wheelchair. "Meet you at the house," Wayne said after assisting him into the truck, not waiting for my reply.

Quietly, I drove toward town then took Old Lexington Road, heading straight to my lake house not ten minutes away. Monroe sat with eyes closed. He seemed so fragile, poor guy. My second-best friend thrown into this mess because of me.

Monroe walked himself inside unaided, with me at his back and Ally opening doors. The kids held tight frowns at his swelling and bruises.

After we settled Monroe in the living room recliner, Ally turned down his bed while I fast-fixed a bowl from the pot of potato soup she'd gone to the trouble of making. I grabbed a bowl of my own and scurried back into the living room to set us both up with a tray. "Ally's a good cook," I said. "But if you can't eat it, we'll find something else."

He deemed the food fitting, moving his spoon like someone with arthritis. "I feel like crap," he finally said with a congested wheeze. His raccoon eyes glanced at me after several bites, and pity overwhelmed me. "Guess you want to hear what I found?" he asked.

"No." I patted his sleeve. "Not tonight. Tomorrow after I get home from work."

He cleaned the bowl, but before I could finish rinsing the dish, he almost dozed off. Ally and I tucked him in bed, Ally shutting the door behind us, blocking the cat from slipping in.

Wayne arrived shortly after with a bag from Monroe's apartment.

"Guy's feeling rough," Ally said.

"Makes me want to smack somebody," I said.

Wayne mumbled, "Another reason I have the case."

"Drop it," I grumbled back, making my family disappear down the hall.

Once alone with me, however, Wayne tried to wrap long arms around me. I moved out of reach. He reeled, hands back as if I were a hot coal. "Just trying," he said.

"Did you suggest to Harden that I not—" but I cut myself short. Of course, he wouldn't ask Harden anything about me, pro or con, without possibly losing the assignment to another agent.

He pretended he didn't hear my slip. "If you want to help, access Newberry's files online tomorrow. Try to see what Monroe was after. You can do that, right?"

"Some files and records, but not all."

"Do what you can." His hands showed his impatience. "Or whatever you feel like. Your call."

At an impasse, we stood two strides apart. I'd do as he requested, because it kept me involved. He'd take my help, but not share in kind.

My hand wandered to my belly before I realized it. I jerked it back. Jesus, he raised his brow.

"Stomach churning. Anyway, tomorrow's a work day," I said in diversion, moving to the front door.

A hint of melancholy built up inside, pushing against the frustration wearing me down. I despised women that fell into hot messes, yet here I was on the brink. I was so much better at my job than personal crap, and these days that wasn't saying much.

When his arm bumped mine at his car, he mistook the gesture as apologetic and swooped me into an embrace. "Please let's don't fight," he said into my hair.

I couldn't breathe, couldn't speak, but my eyes teared fast. About the time I was ready to trust this man with my entire being, we hit a bad patch like Newberry. Or Monroe.

"Monroe sort of wrecks our weekend, doesn't he?" he said, nuzzling my ear. "Unless you get Ally to babysit him Saturday night."

Damn this man. My eyes closed, I fought to ignore his breathing, his lips, his hands sliding around, pretending they weren't familiar with how to crawl under my shirt. The way I already appreciated how he could use that beard.

"Wayne."

He worked around to my other ear, his grip tight. "Hmm?"

He moved to meet me head on, and I allowed one quick kiss. "I think Zack's in the deer stand."

A nosy nine-year-old ebbed his libido, and Wayne squeezed me one more time before reaching for the car door handle. Inside, he lowered the window and regarded me with a hard study. "You're still a little mad."

Why couldn't he see this was more complicated than him taking my case? And why couldn't I use my words to define the issues for him?

A shiver crossed my chest from the night air. "Ever think that Harden might be siccing you on Monroe to get rid of me and throw us off the scent of something else?"

His sigh held a long, low groan in it. "I go where the trail goes, and yes, I suspect he thinks he's using me. But—"

"Nobody uses me," we both said as one. Few men were more self-assured than Wayne Largo.

"So," I added, "no chance he's choosing you over me because I'm more of a threat?"

"Again, you're too close to see clearly," he said.

"Too close to what?"

"Harden, Monroe. You're taking all of this personal."

Disappointment filled me to the brim. "But Monroe got stuck going to Newberry only because of my horrible relationship with Harden."

Wayne looked pained for me. "And I understand that. What the hell's wrong, Slade? Is Harden really eating you up this bad?"

Thank God it was dark. I stepped back into more shadows as the first tear spilled over. "I'm fine. See you later."

Wayne pulled off, his taillights vanishing over the hill of my drive.

I hollered at Zack. "Time to come in."

His flashlight waved.

The moon glistened three-quarters full, and a pair of fox eyes reflected from the edge of the woods. With a deep breath, I inhaled my beloved nature, hoping for the calm it always brought before. Did I see

Wayne hanging Monroe out to dry? No. But I had a burning niggle inside that Monroe was about to get hanged.

Heavy-hearted, I willed myself inside. Maybe I'd go to bed early. After stopping off in the kitchen for a glass of water, I entered my bedroom. Clothes shed and teeth brushed, I headed for the toilet one last time.

A small pink and white box sat on the tank.

In a quick spin, I hurled the pregnancy test under the sink amidst the stack of toilet paper.

Damn you, Ally. Today sucked bad enough already without her hand in it, too.

MY NIGHT LINGERED long, riddled with guilt of what I'd done to Monroe, while second-guessing how I'd behaved with Wayne. Sprinkled with the panic of my unconfirmed condition.

Even rising earlier than usual, by the time I got dressed the next morning, Monroe was up and drinking coffee, enjoying the lake vista out my sliding glass doors. I wanted to escape fast, leave without talk of Newberry.

"This really is a nice place, Slade. Thanks for letting me stay, though I'd be fine at my apartment."

I examined him, dabbing fingers around the bandage, pained at how evil the bruises shined. "Damn, that's ugly. How's it feel?"

"As bad as it appears," he said. "You look tired, though."

"Trouble sleeping. Had your meds?"

He held up his cup. "Yeah, with the coffee. Might sit out on that chaise lounge on your porch in a few minutes and let 'em work."

"Good that you're staying here then," I said, drawing my own cup of caffeine, my eyes feeling puffy and dry. "You picked a pleasant time of year to break your nose. If the pollen starts bothering you, though, for God's sake, come inside." I put a lid on my cup.

Only a steady queasiness this morning. Still, I grabbed an English muffin from the cupboard and popped it in the toaster.

No, I wasn't taking the pregnancy test . . . yet. I remained unsettled about Wayne, and I'd just stress out more confirming a baby on the way, so for everyone's sake, mostly mine, I decided to float the river of denial.

Monroe moved closer. "What are your plans today?"

I smeared peanut butter on the muffin. "Whatever Harden decides I'm capable of doing."

Laying the knife on the counter, I leaned on both hands. While

Monroe wasn't going in, maybe he needed to hear I'd been sidelined. Or did he?

He looked as if he waited for me to form sentences with whatever he read in my eyes.

"Um," I said, "Harden assigned the case to Wayne in lieu of me."

"Why is that?" Hard to tell his reaction through the gauze and swelling.

"I don't like it either, Monroe, but get this . . . Wayne was called before we ever reached the hospital. The first hospital," I added.

He narrowed his eyes, then touched the bandage at the pain.

"What exactly did you uncover over there, Monroe?"

"Just good farmers selling land and paying us off," he said, then set down his cup. "But I found nothing worth the IG's attention, Slade. What aren't you telling me?"

My breakfast-on-the-go ready, I grabbed it with a paper towel. "I'll be late. You know how Harden's riding my butt. We can chat later."

But he approached until we almost touched. "Be late then, damn it. Just tell me the straight, God's honest truth."

Monroe never cussed, and his doubt cut through me like a blade. "Because . . ."

His gaze was penetrating, as if waiting to hear me lie.

"Because I think Cricket reported you," I said. "Said you sexually came on to Ginger, threatened Cricket with a bad audit, and initiated the fight with Cecil."

I expected him to yell *what*, or sling blame toward the proper parties. Instead, he bore a hole in me with a stare I'd never seen before. Then he gave me his back, shoulders slumped.

"We never saw this coming," I said, eager to explain, "and I wish we hadn't told you to go back to Newberry."

He said nothing.

"Wayne won't even let me work alongside him on this one," I added.

Monroe scratched at the edge of his bandage before facing me again. "Why should he?"

That caught me off guard. "To help you. Because I already researched—"

"Stop it, Slade. I went to Newberry in lieu of you going," he said.

Oh, how well I knew that.

He waved with his cup hand. "Harden doesn't trust you, and you don't even try to get along with him. I just happened to be in the room when he picked someone in your stead."

"Wait. That's not completely fair." But it was oh so true.

He cocked his head in warning. "No, you wait. While you're mostly right and *usually* proceed with honorable cause, you fly wild. Sometimes putting yourself in cases you're not assigned to. Sucking in those around you in this . . . vortex you create. This . . ." and he pointed at his nose, "was one of those times. A random caller and jealous farm wives get you all jacked up, and the next thing I'm on leave, black and blue, and under investigation."

The wild I could see, but what did he mean by *usually*? The latter, well, that could be debated, but I was afraid to speak. He had a point to make, and he deserved the floor after what he'd been through.

"So, by me being the last-minute, aim-to-please middle man, I'm the one under scrutiny," he said in summation.

I groped for the right thing to say. "Wayne won't throw you under the bus. I hope you realize that."

"Hmm," he said, retrieving his coffee cup. "Then why do I already feel the tires on my back?"

I stood lost and guilty in the middle of my own kitchen.

"Go on to work," he said. "I'm not sure I'll be here when you get home."

Chapter 14

ON THE WAY downtown, I cared little about the extra traffic. Hair fell in my face, and I grabbed a paperclip out of my cupholder to fasten it out of eyes, moist from feeling sorry for myself. As bad as I felt, I still saw nothing wrong with most of what I'd done. Wayne had even asked me to corral my CI at the start.

Then seated in my office, I couldn't get my head in the game. Never had Monroe distrusted me . . . or intentionally hurt me. I assuaged my guilt for a while by blaming his pain for his atypical conduct, but ultimately concluded he meant every word.

I pulled out the list I'd compiled from the four wives. With papers of other issues strewn across my desk as camouflage, I dove into my online access to Newberry customers.

Fighting to stay too busy to think.

This was the first chance I had to really dig into the facts, but obstacles hit me early on. Screen to screen, some information blocked. Other data nonexistent. Damn it! The federal government went crazy over security, so each of us had only specific and limited access to the full trove of information. An inefficient check and balance system that gave Uncle Sam its sluggish reputation.

Flopping back in my chair I scratched fingers across my scalp. I should've taken Monroe's briefcase and read his notes.

Pivoting my chair around, facing out my tenth-story window, I studied the state capitol's dome and pined a moment for how things used to be. Monroe a long-term friend in another office. Me just helping farmers. Pushing paper and getting home by six to feed little ones. Laundry, dinner, and bed by eleven.

But that lifestyle hadn't worked either. Ask my dead, back-stabbing husband.

Then I met Wayne. The light of my life most of the time . . .

The biggest problem was Harden and how I dealt with him, like Monroe said. But with my boss challenging my every move, how was I supposed to behave? Roll over and take the beatings? Get transferred and curtsey to say thanks? I'd only found intimidation to work against the man. Show fear, and he took advantage.

I spun the chair back around, feeling so damn impotent.

Clicking into one screen, then another, I groaned at another wasted search. Somebody ought to create a proper database, but some congressman somewhere would rather fund research about shrimp on underwater treadmills than aid agriculture. I studied what was there best I could . . . then slowly realized a hint of a trend.

These twelve gentlemen held minimal interest in Agriculture until the last three years. Most in the last two. Within months, less than a year after acquiring the loan, ten of them sold and paid off their debt instead of keeping the land and paying over time. Years back, when dairy subsidies folded, a fair number of farmers sold off like that, but I wasn't aware of any tragic shift in rural South Carolina of late.

Not intimate with the county, I unfolded my new real estate map across my desk, hoping Harden wouldn't pull another surprise drop in. Sparked by what I uncovered in Charleston on my debut case, I took a pen to the roads and highways and tried to note trends for addresses. But undeveloped acreage didn't have a mailing address.

I clicked open the Newberry County government website, praying hard they had an easy way to search deeds. No such luck. Ownership could only be traced by current owner, which I didn't know, addresses I didn't have, or parcel numbers not in my Agriculture database.

Clicking into a different county database, I found land sales per month. That stank, too, but I could guestimate and search for sales based upon when the loans were paid off. I opened the current month. Nothing. Then March. The county was four months behind recording sales.

"Slade?" Whitney rapped on my door. "You going to lunch?"

My wall clock read one fifteen. I'd been at this drudgery for hours. "I'm sort of on a roll here," I lied.

"A girl's got to eat," she said.

The *P* thought instinctively rushed to mind, and I admitted, yeah, I could eat.

I took five minutes to run down to the canteen, buy a Coke and granola bar, and rush back up. Even over my panting, I heard the talk in my office area from down the hall. Whitney . . . and Harden.

I tried to stroll in and not sound breathless, going straight past them to my office. Shit. The map was missing.

Appearing in my doorway, Harden held it up, folded neat and tidy, and smacked it across his palm. "What are you up to?"

The catalyst to all that was wrong with my world today stood front and center looking for ways to make it worse. "It's called work," I said, retreating to behind my desk.

I could shut the door and face-to-face call the man the worst boil on the ass of humanity, but he held the high cards over Monroe's future. And he could, still might, make trouble for Wayne.

"Um, with Monroe hurt, thought I'd be taking the case over," I managed to say.

"Haw, haw." A guttural type of laugh. "On the outs with the boyfriend?"

"He's in the field, why?"

The furrows in his cheek displayed his enjoyment. "For your information, the IG is taking this over."

"What?" I said, fighting to sound surprised. "Why call in an agent? That puts Newberry completely in the IG's hands and out of yours. If they find something, that's blowback on you." Full out truth, really.

"Impropriety's why. Cricket Carson reported Monroe behaving inappropriately with her friend and initiating that fight yesterday. He threatened to ruin her reputation and bragged about his authority to write her up. Everyone likes him too well to send a regular employee. I needed an agent."

Yeah, an agent he thought he could control thanks to me.

I rose to stand up to the imbecile, still in disbelief. "And you believed Cricket?" My temper just wouldn't stay down. "If this is to get at me, just come at me, Harden. Quit this other bullshit. Monroe's sharp and honest to a flaw. He doesn't deserve this." Adrenaline surged, radiating up to my jaws.

He kept slapping my map in his hand, watching me heat up. Through the red of my fury, I pictured them talking, Harden and Wayne. Wondered what Wayne said. What Harden said. What they agreed upon. Wayne's plans. Harden's hidden agenda.

I yearned to claw this bastard's eyes out. Even better, tell him that if my chatty farm wives were right, the ones who would only talk to me . . . if coercion, federal funds, and Little Miss Cricket truly entangled themselves in misbehavior, the worst-case scenario meant racketeering charges. Was he up for that?

He went after Monroe to get at me. And he used Wayne to do it. A warning to the rest of the agency that cooperating with Carolina Slade came with a price.

"You got awful quiet," he said, the smile splitting his face like a watermelon in an August sun.

"Trust me," I said, my respiration stupidly fast. "You don't want to hear what else I have to say." Plus, my career couldn't afford it.

He loafed off, yet his gloat remained.

Falling back into my chair, fists clenched into the arms, again I turned toward the window. I'd only followed Lottie's lead at the radio station. I listened to her protest about what seemed a serious issue. Since when was that wrong?

Since when was my touch considered poison?

Monroe was framed. And the guilt was killing me that he blamed it on me.

Still rattled about Harden sneaking in and stealing my map, I pondered what the hell was expected of me. So stupid the way Harden affected me. Each exposure to his nastiness more irritating than the last. The more definite he was about not wanting me involved, the stronger my compulsion to involve myself became. And . . . the more my insides confused what was spite and what was the right call.

I flung back in my chair. To think I'd never heard of Cricket before Tuesday. Damn, if I didn't want to shove that beauty queen against a tea party rock of her own.

Monroe showing up unexpected for an audit had thrust them into this sort of reaction. Idiotic on their part . . . unless he hit too close to pay dirt. A lot of this mess felt impromptu, though. I mean, versus orchestrated.

And if Miss Cricket wasn't involved, I had three heads and a tail. Plus Lottie was my CI. I knew the women were going to clam up. They'd told me they wouldn't talk to anyone else.

My call to Lottie went to voicemail. "Hey," I said. "Call me." Hanging up, I missed the cradle once.

I flipped into email, killing time, deleting, deleting . . . wishing Lottie would call.

Then it hit me. If events had done an about-face onto Monroe, what was Cecil's status? I Googled the Newberry Police Department on my personal cell, the only phone I used for fear of who noted the numbers I dialed on my work-issued phone.

After three times on hold, I reached the proper authority at the jail. "I'm Carolina Slade with the US Department of Agriculture. I'd like to inquire about Cecil Oliver."

"Cecil Oliver was released yesterday, ma'am."

"Who posted his bail?" I asked.

"I said released, not bailed. Charges were dropped within two hours after he arrived."

No way. "Who the hell decided that?"

"Above my pay grade." He hung up.

Cecil'd been released before Monroe and I reached my house yesterday. No wonder Cricket acted smug once I shut off the recording in the hospital waiting room . . . the recording in which she acted innocent, slighted even, that I doubted her integrity. *The coquette bitch.*

Those wives in Lottie's kitchen felt taken advantage of and had put their fears and concerns in my hands. No telling how many folks Lottie told that I swooped in to right their wrongs. Hadn't I promised I wouldn't let them down?

I needed to go to Newberry. Talk to one of the more stubborn women, maybe with Lottie helping to open the door. Tell Wayne all I learned later. He'd be okay with that. Hopefully.

But if Harden found out, whatever disciplinary action he took against me could be career changing. The biggest challenge. A demotion and transfer at a minimum. The first I could manage. The second . . . well, the kids had come to adore the lake.

Unless he flat-out fired me.

With a heavy heart, I noted the commendation on my wall I was so proud of. That was a thought. The governor's standing job offer to me was still open . . . .

New thought, and one that didn't have me charging off to Newberry but was still keeping my promise. Wayne asked me to look online for data on the farmers. I could run with that as tacit approval to be involved. I returned to the screen, to those farmers, my right hand thoughtlessly doodling their names.

Farmers didn't sell land lightly. The sales appeared irresponsible in terms of personal investment, but far from illegal. Who cared about taking money from people who owned enough not to feel it? Someone had put a lot of thought into hiding a scam in plain sight.

In hindsight, I should've known better than to pick up Monroe after the altercation and show myself to Cricket. I'd blown a cover I could've used now.

"Slade."

Concentration shattered, I leaped up. "Oh good Lord."

Harden's laugh bounced off the confines of my small office. "Caught you again."

"What do you need?" I asked, tamping the temper.

He dropped his backside in the armchair across from my desk. No wonder my hands shook after he did this shit.

"Remember that congresswoman in Anderson?" His arrogance came out thicker than usual. My heart beat double-time beneath my blouse wondering what the hell he was up to.

"Well," he drawled, "she asked if one of my representatives could spend a couple days in her office next week. She's got this local committee called Farm to Table that she'd like a woman's presence. Seems she'd also heard of you."

"After you jogged her memory?" I replied. His half-grin confirmed it. This repetitive getting-even mentality of his wore me out some days, but what tired me most of all was acting like it didn't. "I warned you, if I went up there, we'd talk planning meals, recipes . . . investigations."

With a loose wrist he made a snap motion, finger pointed for emphasis. "And I thank you for that," he said. "Seems meals, recipes, and taking farm commodities into the local restaurants, are part of this group. And," he smiled wide, "there haven't been any investigations in Anderson in ten years. Way back before she took office."

My own words used against me. I sucked in through my teeth. "When?"

"Wednesday of next week."

Shit.

"But preferably Tuesday," he threw in. "To get the lay of the land, so to speak. And on Monday, I need you to—"

"Monday's out," I said. "Family concern. Maybe Tuesday, too."

A wary eye squinted, then he gave a growl of discontent and leaned forward to raise his dough-boy self out of the armchair. "You have your orders. Make it happen."

My cell rang, and I checked caller ID.

Damned if he didn't stand there waiting to see if I'd take the call.

It was Lottie, too.

"You mind?" I asked. "Assuming you were done . . . sir."

He waved as though shooing a gnat. "Take it."

The door almost touched him as I shut it behind his ass . . . and turned the lock.

Lottie's voice hollered from the phone in my hand. "Slade!"

Device to my ear, I counted to five before answering. "Guess you and the ladies heard what happened in the Agriculture office?"

"Yes, yes, yes, but that's not why I'm calling."

Setting the farmer list forefront on my desk, I read it again, the names almost memorized. "Just so you understand, that isn't what occurred, Lottie. Ginger's husband showed up and provoked circumstances, and—"

"Stop talking and listen!" she fussed.

That shut me down. "What's wrong?"

"What's wrong is someone ran my husband off the road last night," she said, her words all jumbled into each other, louder than usual, if that were possible.

"Is he all right?"

She sighed big and hard, sad, so unlike her *here-I-am* boldness. "Yes, thank the Lord he's okay. A knock on the temple and a wrenched wrist from the steering wheel, but I need you here. This afternoon. Say, four? I'll feed you dinner."

"Um, that might be hard for me to pull off, Lottie. For what?"

"I *told* you what happened. Aren't you listening?" The decibels pierced my eardrum. "You're the only detective I know. Bishop, my husband, didn't see the other driver. It was dark and he hit his head, like I said. Told him about you, and we thought you could take a look-see and give us your thoughts."

How could I explain this? "If it's not department related, I don't—"

"Don't give me that bullshit. You're a detective."

"Not exactly."

"She won't come," she said to someone in the background, someone I assumed to be Bishop.

"That's not exactly what I said, Lottie."

"Figures," she came back and said. "Leaving the farmers' wives high and dry, too, I take it? Newberry's problems aren't important enough for your big city ways?" She threw out a loud *harrumph*. "I sure had you pegged differently."

Exasperated, I gave her my own heave-ho of lament. "First, stop interrupting me. Second, I didn't say no." Thought it, but didn't say it.

"Four then?"

"Can't we just wait until the morning?"

In an about-face, Lottie gave me a mother hen cluck. "Sure, hon. Eight?"

I'd been played.

"Okay, eight," I said. "And you better have breakfast ready."

"I warned you about him."

"Him who?"

"Cecil Oliver. Who else would I be talking about?"

Had no clue. I hadn't quite rebounded from the last topic.

"Not surprised," she added.

"Well, we'll talk about him, too, when I get there," I said.

"Suits me. What else is in your plan? My lady friends are waiting."

With a long pause, I thought what to say and what not to.

"I'm not getting any younger," she said.

I debated whether to tell her Wayne had the case. The ladies wouldn't like it. Plus, the Anderson assignment still frosted my pumpkin and would probably do the same to hers.

"Any chance we can meet a couple of those farmers from the list tomorrow?" I finally asked. "The ones with the biggest axes to grind against Agriculture."

"But that's the point," Lottie said. "None of them fuss. It's the wives. Haven't you been paying attention?"

Of course, I had. I was the *only* one in my agency listening. Today was Friday. My time was limited to the weekend, maybe Monday if I called in with my so-called emergency.

"You there?" she asked.

"Yeah, give me a sec," I replied.

Wayne wouldn't appear in Newberry until Monday at the earliest. This is what happened when an agency called on the IG about a time-sensitive issue. He'd work overtime staving off the bleeding of any current cases, so that he could rush elsewhere to do the same to a fresh one. With his territory being the Carolinas, Wayne could spend days on the road crisscrossing between briberies, fraud, embezzlement, or other assorted misconduct as it related to the department.

Which meant I had breathing room and nobody asking where I was. A race to hunt on my own before the lawman stepped in and took over.

"How familiar are you with these wives?" I asked.

"Honey, ain't hardly a woman in the county I ain't on first name basis with."

Glad she was on my side. Glad anybody was on my side.

"Okay, see if you follow me here," I said. "Set me up with the three you trust best, but who also talk farming. Not like Cassie or Phoebe. We need women who not only get their hands dirty but also have access to the books. Can talk numbers. And I need them to open up because of their relationship with you."

"All right," she said. "Let me see what I can wrangle."

Yes. Working my CI, as Wayne would put it. "Any time they want,

I'll be there. And another thing."

"What, honey?"

"You're coming with me, right?"

She laughed. "You wouldn't get to first base without me being there to lob the pitch."

Her humor was nice to hear. "You follow baseball?"

"Atlanta Braves for years, baby."

"I hear that," I said. "Do me one more tiny thing, though."

"If I can."

"Ha, more like if you want to."

"That, too," she said.

I shoved my mini layout of the county aside, pulled off the internet. No way I'd be seen in the map room down the hall, either. "Have me another fold out map when I get there. Somebody stole mine."

Finally some proactive work that mattered. *I'll straighten this out, Monroe.*

Chapter 15

COMING HOME AND finding out that Monroe acted on his threat to leave, hurt more than I thought. I sat with Ally on the back porch after dinner, so damn grateful for the weekend, fighting to act like nothing bothered me.

Ally pointed to the chaise with her wine glass. "Monroe didn't hardly move from that spot till around noon, when he packed up and asked me to take him home."

I turned toward the lake. "Don't blame him, I guess. Man's got to be one big pile of aches. Probably felt uncomfortable in somebody else's house." My friend had never walked off from me. Never been more than miffed at me. Fussed lightly and made jest, but never turned away from me.

Monroe didn't understand how to fight, much less get even. He still had this simplistic belief in right and wrong. Guess I stumbled into his wrong category.

Ally continued filling me in on his meds and what she fixed him for lunch. "Was afraid his refrigerator might be empty so I filled him up before he left," she said. "Kept asking him to stay."

"I appreciate it." She sure had a newfound energy toward Monroe.

The evening had sent a rain shower that quickly left, leaving the air moist.

"Hey," she said, poking her bare toes against my legs propped on the porch railing.

"What?" I cradled a ginger ale. Between nerves and the stomach, dinner amounted to little more than half a peanut butter and jelly sandwich. The aroma of Ally's fried chicken had soured my insides the second I walked through the door.

"Guess you don't have to look at me to listen," she said.

I gave her a sideways glance. In cutoffs and a boatneck cropped tee shirt, three years younger, my sister pulled off perky with minimal effort. Little could weigh her down. After all, what use was a good credit score anyway? But she loved my kids like her own, which made me overlook way more of her sins than I should.

"Good," she said. "Tell me, how do you dangle two boyfriends while I have to settle for the Hallmark Channel?"

"I don't have two boyfriends."

She nudged me again. "So, you and Monroe haven't . . . you know?" Her fingers formed a circle, with another finger moving . . . I got the idea.

I could only shake my head, not really wanting to explain Monroe. How he hung around all chivalrous, wouldn't take another woman seriously in hope I'd tire of Wayne. Because then I'd have to explain how he and Wayne could actually stand in the same room together and talk sports and work. How I couldn't let go of him as a friend.

"Done it only with Wayne?"

"What's your point, Ally?" Though I suspected.

She shifted to the edge of her seat, elbows on her knees, the wine glass holding less than a swallow. "What happened to the pregnancy test?"

"What pregnancy test?"

"You know what I mean."

With a puzzled expression, I gave her a blank stare. "I said, what pregnancy test?"

She froze. "I left it on your toilet tank."

"When was this?"

"Yesterday evening. It couldn't have just walked off."

I flashed surprise. "No, but Ivy could've taken it." I sat erect. "She asked permission to go through my lipsticks." With an inhale, hand over my mouth, I whispered, "Ally? Oh my God. You don't think . . ."

My sister took a second to connect, then paled. "No."

"I *told* you she was too young to date." Then mumbled, "Son of a bitch. What will Mother think?"

Ally tucked her legs up, heels on the seat, and rocked hard. "Oh, God, she'll hate us both. Me she's used to. You . . . that's another story. But poor Ivy." She reached over and clenched my arm. "We've got to be there for her. I can help. You have to teach me diaper changing, but it can't be that hard. Jesus, Jesus, Jesus," she whispered into the evening. Now *she* studied the lake, her brain probably churning like a washing machine.

Served her right. And I'd have let her stew for a lot longer except for the first sign of tears.

"Oh, I can't do this anymore," I said. "I threw the damn box under the sink, Ally."

She turned toward me, pure deer-in-the-headlights frozen. "You bitch," she muttered.

"I'm lucky to have you here with us, but stay out of my business until invited, little sister."

Stomping across the porch, she slung back the sliding door and disappeared inside, giving me the most appropriate, melodramatic slam. Leaving me alone.

I set my glass down and rubbed from my eyes to my chin, wondering how the hell I would handle a baby . . . *my* baby.

Mother Nature had graciously endowed me with regular periods and easy pregnancies. The shock of *what if* had come and gone today coming home. Buried in my thoughts, somewhere between mile marker 101 and 97 on the interstate, I had dared speak the words. *I'm pregnant.*

I didn't need a kit in a pink box to tell me what I already knew. Eight weeks along would be my guess.

So why did I want to call Monroe and share the news when I couldn't even admit it to Ally and she knew . . . sort of?

Because Monroe was safe. My gyroscope. He'd shared all of my successes, most of my failures. Ever the voice of encouragement and reason, he'd say all the right words.

Or was this me being selfish?

Wayne deserves to hear first, Slade.

But that was too scary. I stroked the phone, debating. What the hell. I dialed his number anyway. We could always talk shop.

Ally opened the door.

I mouthed, *Work call.*

"*Humph.* I'd rather clean toilets than listen to that stuff." She left.

Yeah, still sore.

Monroe answered, sounding dull.

"You still feeling rough?" I asked. "I wish you'd stayed the weekend."

"Not in the mood to argue about it," he replied.

"About staying, or about Newberry?"

"Staying," he said. "Ally did her best, making promises of food. Even offered a . . . um . . . sponge bath."

I laughed, uneasy at the mix of my sister's free-wheeling behavior and Monroe's constraints. "She'd probably give it, too."

His silence showed he wasn't up for humor.

This probably wasn't the time to tell him my sister would do him in a heartbeat. Especially after our little chat confirming she discovered Monroe was unclaimed territory. "Anyway," I said, "we need to cover yesterday. More so now than ever."

The season wasn't hot enough to turn muggy yet, so the warm breeze soothed me. Monroe talking would soothe me more.

"Don't feel like work talk," he said.

I pressed on. He needed to be brought up to speed. "But you're important, Monroe. We need you. When you reported to Newberry yesterday morning, how did Cricket react?"

"Do you ever listen?"

My breath caught. He didn't want to talk, or was it he didn't want to talk to me? "Wayne thought—"

"I don't give a rip what Wayne thought or said or did, either, do you understand that?"

His outrage knocked me back . . . hard. "Okay," was all I could manage. My heart pounded so hard it hurt. I caught myself wanting to hear his old voice.

Alone in his apartment, how much of this did he think I caused? Guess I hadn't actually called about Newberry. I'd called wanting forgiveness.

Silence spread out long between us. About the time I started to say good night, he cleared his throat. "Cricket's clerk forewarned her. And Cricket saw Cecil hit me."

He might be coming around. "Did she try to divert your attention from your work?"

"No."

"Did she ask what you were doing?"

"No."

I caught myself trying to come up with yes and no questions to not make him mad. "Have you checked your briefcase? Did I pack everything?"

"Enough," he said.

"I'm trying to help."

"You're fighting your cause, Slade, not worrying about who gets hurt in the process."

A trio of male wood ducks took off after a lone female, and I let the squawks die down in their flight as I let that stinging accusation sink in. Had to be the meds talking, right?

"Monroe—"

He hung up.

Stunned, I felt lost in a vacuum for a minute, the only sound the blood in my ears.

I *was* on his side. I did *not* want him hurt. Why couldn't he see that? So I texted. *May I collect your notes?*

Nothing.

Did you ask for Ginger's full name and phone number? I started to say *like Wayne told you to do,* but stopped.

Nothing.

Damn it, I'm trying to be your friend.

Silence.

I typed, *At least delete all references to Ginger from your phone. Otherwise, it shows an interest in her.*

The crickets made introductory evening noises, and the afternoon drizzle had enticed a tree frog to take up residence behind the grill. Sounds I normally embraced and only irritated me now. I threw the phone on the drink table beside my chair.

Zack opened the sliding glass door and ran past toward the water.

"What are you up to?" I hollered.

My extra decibels spun him around and stopped him cold. "Um, fishing," he said, slowly holding up a plastic bowl with a lid on it. "I got bait this time instead of a lure."

Ally came rushing to the same door. "Zack? You little monster! Stop in your tracks. That's a whole pound of my bacon, young man."

His shoulders drooped. His pinched expression veered from Ally to me, hanging there with the threat of both his overseers mad at him.

I nodded toward my sister. "Son, you owe her an apology."

He started back toward us, but Ally waved him on. "What the heck. Go on."

"Awesome! Thanks, Aunt Ally. Oh Mom," he shouted, his energy having climbed back to full throttle just that quick. "I put rocks in Bug's hubcaps today."

"Boy, don't you damage someone's car," I warned.

"I won't," he said, walking backwards down the hill. "But I'm his worst nightmare, and he doesn't even know it!" Then he disappeared behind bushes, coming out at the boat ramp to the water.

And I wondered what else the kid planned to do and how rogue he'd be to do it.

Sort of like Monroe felt about me. The comparison slammed me. Only I'd never quit loving Zack.

I sank into my chair. Didn't make me feel any better that Ivy and Bug had headed out early on a date before I arrived home. A double punch atop of Monroe's departure.

Ally'd okayed it since it was only a movie and dinner with an eleven o'clock curfew. Supposedly they went to the pizza diner where you picked out the toppings in assembly line fashion. I used to love that place, but now it would remind me of Bug. Ally chuckled and sat in the chair beside me. "Zack's a hoot thinking he's a threat."

"If Ivy gets pregnant, I'll give him full rein to do whatever he wants to Bug," I grumbled.

Ally'd returned to her ripe old carefree self. "Chill out, big sister. And wipe off that scowl. Makes you look ancient."

I felt ancient. "What'll we name Bug Junior? How about Maggot?" I had to joke, because my insides screamed at the crap stacking up in my life. Especially the concept of a grandchild . . . and what it would do to my daughter's future.

"She's had the talk," Ally said firmly. "And she's not stupid."

Maybe not, but Bug wasn't exactly trustworthy manhood.

One thing, however, gave me some sense of consolation. Zack watching from his deer stand demonstrated the need to protect his sister, and that warmed my heart. Give him five years, more height and weight, and he might be a force to be reckoned with.

Just like his momma would try to be in Newberry County. Regardless whether Monroe appreciated it or not. Not like I needed everyone's nod to do what's right.

Zack loved his sister and stepped up as her protector. The Newberry women pleaded with me to help them keep their lands, or unravel the culprits who already took advantage. How could it be anywhere near right to turn my back and pass the baton?

But to do anything meant flying low under Harden's radar.

"Quit worrying so much about Ivy," Ally said. "Those wrinkles around your mouth will stick there."

I got up. If I stayed longer, I'd say too much. "Got a headache. Maybe a shower will help."

Ally retreated to the living room, me to the bedroom. After soaking my head, maybe I'd read a book waiting for Ivy to get home. Wayne might call. We'd awkwardly dance around the case in an attempt to ignore the divide between us. Drying off after the shower, my attention fell on the cabinet under the sink. For the longest time I stood there, daring to glance in the mirror and imagine myself thirty weeks from now. Why drag this out any more? Why not take the test?

Naked and on my knees, I hunted, ultimately dragging everything out from under that sink. Toilet paper. Towels. Q-tips. No sign of the pink box.

"Ally?" I hollered, the echo bouncing off the tile.

Thumps sounded on the carpet as she ran through my bedroom to the bath. She peeked in. "Um, what are you doing?"

Nude amidst strewn cotton balls, shampoos, and washcloths, I looked at her with desire to hear one sure answer to my question. "Did you come in here and take the pregnancy test?"

"Why would I do that? I bought it for you."

"Just answer me, Ally."

Humor left her. "No."

Ivy *had* been in my bathroom. She pilfered my toiletries all the time.

I tried not to crumble in front of my sister. Not to come unraveled because my personal and professional lives were dissolving into something I no longer recognized.

I looked up. Ally had gone. And I grabbed a hand towel out of the disheveled stack on the floor, buried my face, and cried.

Chapter 16

THE NEXT MORNING, Ally rose around six thirty to see me off, in spite of the late night. After my meltdown, she'd retrieved me from the bathroom floor with a warm glass of milk, and we'd torn apart Ivy's bathroom, finding nothing, then put it back to right and waited up for Ivy.

Stoic and unwilling to discuss her date with us, Ivy had fallen asleep by midnight. For fifteen minutes, I'd stood in her doorway watching her chest rise and fall like I had years back at the side of her crib, wondering how I would protect her from *this*. Assuming there was a *this*.

Then after another thorough search under my sink, Ally and I'd talked until two in the morning seated on my bathroom floor. A few tears in the mix.

Now, as the coffee dripped and we fought to open weary eyes, we whispered in the kitchen, my sister positioned to keep an eye on the hallway in case Ivy got up.

"So, we don't ask her about the pregnancy test?" Ally asked.

"Put yourself in her shoes," I said. "What if Mom had asked if you were pregnant when you were fourteen?"

Ally dug two cups out of the dishwasher. "She may have, for all I remember. Ivy's nothing like I was."

I fell back against the cabinet. "Thank God for that." But I softened the quip with a smile. "When exactly did you lose your virginity?"

She put a hint of stevia in my cup and slid it over. A teaspoon and an inch of milk in hers. "Way before you, big sister, that's for dang sure."

I poured the coffee. "Well, I can't figure out the right way to address this. She might only be curious."

"Like I said last night, it might be more that she's freaked that she found a pregger test in her mom's bathroom. You are avoiding the obvious." She walked over and leaned on the bar. "Which begs the question, are you pregnant?"

Hell, she knew anyway. "I think so."

Scrunching up her nose, Ally let loose a tight, controlled squeal. "I knew it!" She ran around to me and hugged. "If this don't make you marry that hunk, nothing will. What's Wayne think about it?"

Uh oh. And Ally wasn't good with secrets. "Haven't told him yet."

Her happy face turned to surprise. "What?"

"And don't you breathe a word of it!" I said, waving my cup at her. "What if I lose it? It's just eight weeks. And I'm not sure what to do about it yet."

She backed a step. "Do? Carolina, surely you're keeping it! What better family to bring a child into?" She squinted and did a little compact wiggle in place. "I'd help. I'd stick around as long as you wanted me."

"Who says I want you now?"

"Ha ha," she replied. "Been to the doctor?"

"No." These questions felt too weird.

"Well, hell, Sis. No test and no doctor—you just aren't doing this right, are you?"

I almost asked how she knew what right was, but endometriosis killed her chances of children ten years ago. Being full-time nanny to a newborn probably thrilled her silly. I could do worse.

And no, I couldn't terminate a pregnancy. When I spoke about being unsure what to do, I meant about Wayne. About wedding bells. About whether I needed to marry again after the mess of my last marriage. And what the kids would think about another kid mucking up their lives.

Time to go. "No questioning Ivy, you hear me?" I ran water into the cup and laid it in the sink. "And this conversation with Ivy is mine."

"But what if she asks . . . questions?"

"Send her to me."

"Don't you want me to ask if she's . . . active?"

"My job, Ally. Not yours," I said, with the seriousness of a heart attack. "If she's crossed that bridge, she's made adult choices. We'll be there if luck went against her, but she'll have to grow up damn fast in the process." I slung my purse over my shoulder. "But if you get a chance, dig through the trash cans, will you? See if she's used it?"

Ally nodded, somber. "She's awfully young, Sis."

I sighed. "But old enough. See you tonight." I walked toward the garage door, not wanting to reveal too much of the panic clinging to my heart about my baby having grown up too fast and me not having paid enough attention to see it. Fifty pounds of guilt hanging on me.

"Wait," Ally said, scuffing over in her slippers. "Where are you going so early on a Saturday? A morning person you are not, so what's this about?"

"It's important, and it's work. Best you not be able to answer if questioned, Ally."

She sucked in a breath and came close. "This isn't dangerous, is it?" Always her question after she got shot last year interfering in mine and Wayne's business.

"No, but still, I could get in trouble. Okay?"

She saluted me. But as I hurried to my truck I thought I caught her wiping her eyes. *Yeah, I'm worried, too, little sis.*

JUST MINUTES AFTER eight on Saturday morning, I parked half a block from Lottie's. The lot belonged to an unoccupied blond brick building that professed per a faded sign to have once housed historic antiques. Small towns like this maintained a healthy number of antique stores, when they were little more than places to sell your grandmother's estate remnants that family didn't want.

My truck would probably remain safe there for the day. A week ago, I wouldn't have thought twice about where I left it in Newberry, but because of recent undercurrents, hairs danced on the back of my neck. As if I were being watched.

The short walk took me to Lottie's, and again, I approached the more hidden side door under the carport.

"In the kitchen," she shouted to my knock.

Didn't people answer the doors here? What if I'd been an unseemly sort?

Guess unseemly sorts didn't knock. And weren't expected.

I found Lottie at the sink. "Didn't hear you drive up."

"Parked down the street," I said.

Lottie quit rinsing dishes, shook her hands once, and reached for a dishtowel. "You could've parked in the back. We gotta go there anyway. That's where Bishop's car is."

But my parking choice wasn't as much for me as it was for her. If all I heard was true, Cricket gave Agriculture a bad reputation, and most would consider me in the same light. Plus, Cricket and her ilk weren't happy with me either. "Didn't need to announce my business with you," I said.

She flagged the towel in the air. "We're simple people."

Yeah, except for rampant sex, a dead farmer, and suspected fraud.

Hands on her hips. "Oh, we fuss and have our feuds around here, but nothing apocalyptic happens."

Apocalyptic. A sign of the wordsmith in her. But that eager wordsmith could be rather naïve and too close to the locals to see the bad seeds as simply "misguided." I'd seen it before.

"What happened to the breakfast you promised me?"

"You see what time it is?" she exclaimed. "We ate over an hour ago, but," and she half-slid, half-waddled to the microwave and opened the door. "I saved you a cinnamon bun. Made like my grandmama made them. She won ten ribbons with that recipe." She popped the timer for five seconds, then handed me the bun on a thick napkin. I almost drooled on myself with anticipation before I could get the first bite down.

"Well, come on. You can eat and work at the same time." She threw the towel over the faucet, and we exited out the side and headed around back. Parked in the yard was a monstrous car, beneath a white tarp, as if the cover had been custom designed for the vehicle.

She went to one end and lifted the cloth up, flipping it over the trunk to reveal the entire rear end. Running my empty hand over the car's fins, I marveled. "Lottie, what year is this Bel Air?"

"1957, honey. Bishop would pick this baby over me if he had to choose."

While I wasn't an antique car aficionado, the beauty stunned me. Maroon with white triangle darts to the fins. Hardtop. Wide white walls. The crumpled bumper mashed in, two of the four taillights shattered, the trunk cover showing a two-foot dent.

I took another bite, then ran my empty hand across the damage. "These cars are sturdy. Someone had to have rammed him pretty hard. You sure he's okay?"

"Walked to work today to ease out some of the kinks. His office isn't three blocks over. So," she said, moving around the car, lifting more of the tarp in places. "What do you think?"

"He saw nothing?"

She shook her head. "Had his head in his office stuff. It was dark. Felt a bump he fought to control. A second bump that smacked his head into the window while the steering wheel snagged his wrist. He braked before he hit someone's parked car on the side of the road. Only remembers hearing the car zoom past."

"What did the car sound like? Or did it sound like a truck?"

"Hmm," she said, rubbing her chin. "I'll have to ask him."

I stooped closer. Paint transfer. Red. And high. Not a compact car, and without a doubt one with enough substance to knock this heavy car out of control.

"Lottie? Who owns a red pickup?"

She reared her head back like a chicken. "I'll be damned. Guess we missed the red with it being dark last night. Told Bishop you'd figure this out."

"Any idea whose truck?"

"No, but let me cogitate on it awhile." She patted my arm. "You're so smart!"

"Granted, it's just a theory," I said. "Surely the cops saw this damage and thought the same."

"You'd think," she mumbled.

Replacing the tarp over the rear, I wondered how much gas this car guzzled. "Tell all your cousins and nephews on the force."

"I'll do that," she said. "Let's head on out. I can't wait to tell Bishop tonight."

Back inside, Lottie grabbed her purse off an old sideboard in the dining room. "First, I have to drop off some dry cleaning for my husband, then a pound cake for a friend at her work, then we head to Sonny Huneycut's place. If we have time, a couple more farms after that." She made for the door, and I followed.

Great, we ran errands before sleuthing. "Is it wise we be seen?" I asked, nervous we'd appear in the middle of downtown.

Her side door only half caught as she closed it. Instinctively, I reached up and pulled until I heard it latch. She may consider all this a lark, but my experiences led me to remain alert when on a case. I'd been blindsided too many times in my short investigatory career, as evidenced by a few scars, not to respect the wisdom of safety in all its shapes and sizes.

"Honey," she said, plopping into her red Prius, waiting for me to do the same. "You behave normally, or people wonder what you're up to. My husband doesn't understand a quarter of what I get involved in, so when he asks me to carry his cleaning, I do it. Friends expect a pound cake from me in times of need. This one just lost her sister last week, and I said I'd drop by the store today." She cranked up the vehicle. "You can stay in the car if you like, but both these errands together won't take ten minutes."

While I bet ten minutes wasn't anywhere near accurate, no point in arguing with sound logic. She headed up Main Street. As the conspicuous red and rust Carson awnings came into view, I sank lower in my seat.

The dry cleaners took up the corner of Main and an alley-sort of side street, and neighbored up to the Carson hardware store. Lottie parked right in front.

"I'll wait here," I said.

"Suit yourself," she replied and went about her business.

A handful of people wandered the street, peering in store windows. This wasn't exactly New York where window dressings ran into the thousands, but window shopping was a universal hobby. People ogled through glass, even if dusty and smeared with prints. Couldn't help themselves.

Lottie quickly returned, opened the door, and reached into her back seat. "You want to walk with me a block down to deliver this cake or continue to sit here?"

I wasn't sure which was more obvious, being Lottie's shadow or being the strange lady camped in Lottie's hybrid car. "Sit here," I finally said.

"You need the window down? It's warmer than usual today." Without my answer, she got in the front and lowered all the windows. "Back in a sec," she said exiting, sing-song in her words.

I hunkered and tried to blend into the dark interior, occasionally glancing up to check on Lottie's status. Her puffy body walked the one block, then disappeared inside Carson's gift and interior design store. Pulling out my cell, I hunted for a text return from Monroe, having dropped him a short note this morning. A simple query how he was.

No such luck.

Then in an afterthought, I texted Ivy just to ask how her date went. Like Lottie said, acting normal. Being the over-protective mom.

Don't let Ivy realize that I worried my silly head off.

Don't let Monroe realize he'd ripped up my feelings.

No answers from Monroe or Ivy. I yearned to do something about my daughter to settle the unthinkable question, but what? Monroe, well, I wasn't sure how to make him come around.

"Why, hello, Ms. Slade!"

With a flinch, I almost dropped the phone. "Um, hello, ladies."

Phoebe, Cassie, and Faye stooped over to see me. The Newberry Friends of the Library delegates. For being a one-week-old widow, Cassie's pallor had disappeared, leaving rosy cheeks and, dare I say, happiness? Either her marriage had been stale a long time, or these Newberry people were made of some stern stuff. And they'd forgotten I said to walk by if they ever saw me in public.

"Any progress since we met?" Faye asked, a floral silk scarf draped over what appeared to be a new do, ending in a soft knot under her chin.

"We heard what happened in the Agriculture office," Phoebe added, a white button up sweater over a summer pantsuit. "Is your gentleman okay?"

I wished they'd flit on by, not desiring the attention. "My co-worker is recuperating, but his nose is broken."

They gasped in kind, but their pageantry of concern passed quickly. Cassie leaned forward more, her hands on the window lip. "So, what have you been able to find?"

"Can't really say," I replied. "Open investigation. You three understand how that is."

They nodded big and small, Phoebe wide-eyed.

I resisted an intense desire to question them about the farmer list, but Main Street's curb wasn't the place. However, I did toss them a bone. "Are y'all aware of any new farmer targets? Different than . . . the others?"

Faye bowed closer. "No, but that's not how it works. We never hear until it's over."

"Until what's over?"

"The land is confiscated," she said.

"Thought the land was sold by the owners?"

"They didn't want to sell it."

"But who's they?" I asked. "Nobody talks about who snatched their property out from under them."

All three looked around for ears . . . then stiffened.

Aunt Sis, the elder dementia lady from the diner, stood not three feet from them. Frankly, I'd not heard her slip up either, but there she waited, frozen like a statue of Buddha, staring from beneath drooping, shadowed, heavily-mascaraed eyelids.

The temperature hovered in the mid-seventies, but her blouse was pinned at the neck with a silver peacock brooch, covered by a pink crocheted vest, and then covered again by a wilted, midi-length, open-front sweater adorned with a filigreed aqua scarf. If she'd carried grocery sacks or pushed a cart, she'd have made an ornate bag lady.

"Hey, Aunt Sis," Phoebe said. "I like your hat."

The taupe pillbox hat perched on hair the color of sugar. While someone didn't exactly match her wardrobe, they certainly ensured her coiffure met the "ladies who lunch" standard.

Still, even after being addressed, Aunt Sis didn't move.

"Well," Faye said, inching closer to Cassie, "we'll be going. See you another time, Ms. Slade."

They moved on down the sidewalk, parting around Aunt Sis like water meeting a rock.

"Can I help you? Aunt Sis?" The name felt weird to say.

She stared, stationary.

I exited the Prius, thinking I could escort her into the hardware store, but when I reached arm's length of her, she threw up defensive hands. "Oh, oh, oh," she exclaimed, hands up around her ears.

I backed off a few feet. "Can I help you inside?"

She lowered her arms, fists clenched, a scowl darkening her wrinkled skin. "Sex," she said.

Wow. I took another step back. "Ma'am?"

"Sex!" she screamed. "Sex, sex. A hundred sex!"

My gut lurched into my esophagus. Looking up and down the street, I expected a cop to come running, or some Samaritan to rush up and shove me aside. The library ladies scooted in the opposite direction, a block and a half down. "Stop, Aunt Sis," I said, afraid to touch her. "I'm here to help. Where do you need to go?"

Now she pointed a finger at me. "Jezebel."

My heart thumped. Was she calling me a whore? I went with a better interpretation in hope to divert the conversation. "Um, we met at Jezebel's earlier this week."

She raised hands to her temples, shaking her head. "No, no, no." Then glanced up, pleading. "Je-ze-bel," she pined, stretching out the syllables.

Her pleading broke my heart. "What can I do?" I edged closer, hands to myself. "Help me understand."

Four others walked past us, detached, making me marvel at the lack of interest, as if Aunt Sis were nothing more than a street sign. Finally, Lottie appeared out of the gift shop, saw the dilemma, and hurried our way. By the time she reached us, Aunt Sis stared at the ground, posture more stooped than before, and I couldn't help but rub her bony arm.

"What's wrong?" Lottie asked, like confronting a child who'd pouted many times before.

Feeling like I was charged with a crime, I spilled an explanation. "She started talking to me, but she got upset over something I can't identify. She said," and I peered up then down the street, "*sex* several times, referred to a hundred of them, then shouted Jezebel. When I acknowledged we met at the diner, she lost it. I . . . can't figure out what to say."

"Come on, dear." Lottie's arm draped around the old lady and redirected her into the hardware store. I came along, wanting to see how this played out.

Just inside, Lottie hollered, "Hey, one of y'all want to help Aunt Sis to her spot? She's a tad more confused than usual today."

A middle-aged woman appeared and took over, cooing to the old lady. They disappeared into the back, Aunt Sis glancing once over her shoulder at us. Lottie and I returned to the car.

"She seemed mighty upset that I couldn't connect," I said, buckling up.

Lottie pulled onto Main and headed east. "Must be one of her bad times. Sometimes she's almost her old self, chatting up a storm, the old flirt. Then she's in the Twilight Zone. You can tell when something's bothering her, because she walks. From one store to the other, like the exercise helps her work through a problem. I swear some days she puts in three miles."

"Keeps her healthy, I guess."

"Or she remembers an old habit," Lottie said. "There's a reason they called women *street walkers* years back."

"Okay, that sounds like gossip," I said, not liking the slander.

"Steeped in a bit of the truth, my dear," she replied.

We passed a string of those white mini-mansion houses with azaleas and unfurled American flags. Lottie raised our windows and sped up.

"But she called me Jezebel," I said. "And she repeated the word *sex*. That's just weird."

Lottie passed a car way faster than I would have and, of course, waved. "Honey, who knows. She once passed for a beauty and courted her fair share of gentlemen in these parts. Married and unmarried. And Jezebel could mean the diner, or the old tale in Nell Graydon's book, or an old Bible lesson."

"What book?"

"*Another Jezebel*," she said. "True story, too. Published back in the fifties. About a Yankee woman who traveled South to find her a wealthy landowner. Supposedly the harlot spent a lot of time in Newberry County availing herself to the men. The railroad and prostitutes had a heavy hand in defining this area, though most of us won't admit it."

"Like the Bible's Jezebel," I said.

"Pretty much. Regardless, sane days are gone for our little old lady, bless her heart." She honked and waved at a passing car.

"Bless her heart," I echoed while wondering how many more residents would recall seeing me before the day was through, simply because nobody passed Lottie discreetly.

What was with all the sexual references in this community? I never would've guessed this sleepy town exuded hormones in spades.

A farmer dying having sex in the woods. Ginger chasing Monroe. A diner named after a whore. And an old lady out of her mind shouting about sins of the flesh as if everyone had syphilis.

Chapter 17

LOTTIE VEERED RIGHT onto the 76 Bypass. "Aunt Sis creeps you out, doesn't she?"

I peered around the car's interior, as if hunting for something and kinda dodging her scrutiny. "An old lady shouting sex in my face? No, don't see why that should bother anybody."

But the word *sex* particularly gnawed at me. Guilt niggling at having taught Ivy not to have pre-marital sex . . . and me getting caught doing the same. "You didn't bring me another highway department map, did you?" I asked.

She pointed to the glove box.

After unfolding the two-by-three-foot map, I folded it smaller to the part we traveled. "How far out, and who're we seeing?"

The bypass became Highway 76. What the heck? Straight ahead thirty miles or a little less was my house on the lake. "You knew I lived outside Chapin, right? Please tell me why we didn't just meet each other at this farmer's place and not risk being seen by everyone all over town?"

"One car and discretion," she said, not with sass, but with plenty of business.

"Discretion. Right."

She sniffed at me. "If I recall, you asked that I lead this trek, missie. These people identify with Lottie Bledsoe, so the idea of meeting them is supposed to be mine. I invited *you* along."

Yep, everyone would hear about me before the day was out.

We soon turned north on a two-lane, which I recognized would take us closer to the interstate. A few miles up, she slowed and eased onto an asphalt drive. About five hundred feet in, we parked outside a homestead farmhouse I'd sell my soul to own.

I mean . . . we'd passed sensors anchored in brick back at the open gate. This was the kind of homestead farmhouse that only bigger money could buy.

A historical, two-story Civil War era home, in immaculate condition. Wrap-around porch on three sides with a green metal roof.

Spindle décor skirting the eaves. Dang, had to be eight fireplaces in the house. A barn and bunkhouse-looking affair in the back. A pond to the south. Man, oh man. Not the level of farmer we normally catered to.

I exited the car, my first instinct being what level of political connection lived in that amazing house. Farmers played politics like nobody's business. "Damn, Lottie."

This wasn't some two-bit concern. If this was the level farmer being scammed, why hadn't this crap reached the governor and hit the f'in fan? What was big enough to hush an agricultural powerhouse like this? If I screwed this up, I wouldn't have just Harden on my butt.

A woman in her seventies came out the door in khakis, a white cotton shirt, and leather flats, though the diamonds on her necklace and finger shone past the attempt at understatement. A graceful beauty about her. "Lottie? How're you doing? Thought you'd be a bit earlier, but the banana bread ought to still be warm enough to eat." A very dignified voice with a soft, pleasant, educated Carolina drawl. One you'd love to read you a story.

Introductions were made, and I became acquainted with Glory Huneycut, wife of Sonny. I thought I detected a hint of scrutiny from our hostess but passed it off as my employer affiliation. Regardless, she escorted us in with all the etiquette a woman would show to her closest lady friends. We settled around a polished dark oak kitchen table fit for ten but set with place mats for three. The air hung thick with the scent of butter, sugar, and bananas. We settled on the thick-cushioned high-back chairs.

I tried not to crane my neck taking in the décor. Six bedrooms maybe? God, I'd hate to have to clean all these bathrooms. A crystal fixture over the kitchen table? What the hell hung in the dining room? "Your home is fabulous, Mrs. Huneycut." *Please, give me a tour?*

"We like it here," she replied as she set before us two heated muffins, filled coffee cups, then stepped aside to pull the doors leading to the hallway closed. Then she assumed her seat, back straight, and set her sights on Lottie. "What're you up to, my friend?"

Oh yeah, I wasn't welcome. No wonder Lottie said she had to come along. From the poor waitress in Jezebel's to the lofty owners of the Huneycut estate, I guess Lottie did relate to everyone in this county.

Lottie leaned her ample bosom on the table. "Like I told you on the phone, Ms. Slade here is taking a gander at activity in our county. Odd activity. When I saw her coming at it from the men's side of things, I suggested that the wives might have a better handle, if you catch my drift."

The woman had a wisdom in her eyes, along with a glimpse of consternation. "Why am I supposed to trust Agriculture people after we lost fifty acres?"

She shifted her stiffness to me now, making me hesitate. Eating finger food while talking fraud and racketeering just didn't jibe. I took a bite out of respect, swallowed, then pushed the plate back. "Ms. Huneycut, what happened, why do I need to talk to the wives, and why is the department at fault?"

Short and sweet. Like the muffin growing cold on my plate.

In under an hour, we learned that Sonny was approached by Cricket, advised that Agriculture had some easy money, at insane rates if land was used as collateral, and he said sure. Then a year later, Sonny sold the mortgaged fifty-acre tract to satisfy the debt.

"Makes no sense," Glory said. "He won't talk about it. We've been married for forty-five years, and the man's never kept secrets from me." She took a sip from her cup. "Because of our past, and the trust between us, I gave him this one. It wasn't like we couldn't afford to cut back or that we didn't need to at our ages, but he acted like he'd failed at something. Not like Sonny at all."

She rose, topped off her coffee, and stirred milk into it. We just waited, because she seemed to need the moment. But when she returned, she'd lost some of her starch.

"Anything else?" I asked. "How much money, for instance?"

She studied Lottie over the top of her cup. My partner gave a subtle nod. I acted like I didn't see.

"Well, it was family land, in his name only," she said, "and I'm sure the facts are in the courthouse, but the place was worth four hundred thousand."

"And he sold it for how much?" I asked.

"Three hundred," she replied.

"You're sure about the value?" A lot of folks exaggerated the value of their property, and few people left a hundred grand on the table.

"Assessed value, so what does that tell you?" She almost snapped, but she was too dignified for the question to be much of a goad.

But her point was taken. Assessed value always fell on the conservative side compared to appraised value. The Huneycuts lost *more* than the hundred-thousand-dollar difference.

But farmers could be just as criminal in their actions as a government employee. "What did he use the money for?"

"Paid off all our debt and upgraded two pieces of equipment."

Legit if she weren't lying. A lot of money. And a lot of equity in that land. If I understood anything about agriculture, it was that farmers loved their dirt. "Why didn't he just sell it at full value?"

"He said it had to sell quick, and he had a hot buyer."

Sonny wouldn't be where he was without knowing better. I wasn't swallowing this any more than the muffin. Stunned at the plantation when we pulled up, I'd left my notebook in the car. I couldn't afford to break the conversation to retrieve it, not without risking Glory having second thoughts about talking to me.

"See?" Lottie said to me.

No, I didn't see. All I heard were some inane facts that didn't explain why an established rural entrepreneur threw away money and land. "Who bought the place for so cheap?"

"Some corporation," Glory said. "That's all I've been told, and if it makes Sonny sleep easier at night, that's fine."

I altered my questions, presenting them differently, comparing answers, but the story stuck, and Glory grew impatient at my querying.

And my worry increased. If this sort of deal was a trend, we had a problem. But I couldn't take Lottie's word for it that the Huneycut situation was one of many. I needed proof, and interviews. Because I still saw only bad choices and nothing illegal.

Which would make Monroe madder he'd sacrificed for naught, and Harden delirious I'd been wrong.

Crime normally meant bad loans, delinquent loans, crooked farmers. Instead, we had wealthy producers who paid off early. Not a red flag. At least not to the average person. I, however, sensed an abundance of opportunity for someone to capitalize on land deals, with Cricket in the midst of it all. No way she couldn't be. So what leverage, exactly, was a young slip of a thing using against accomplished farmers?

Not quite yet Wayne's territory, but close. Federal agents preferred those like me to uncover the facts, letting them later nail the culprits. Sort of thankless for me and chest-thumping for them, but regardless, I rocked on, in the name of Monroe.

Lottie and I left the farm barely an hour after we arrived, but Glory Huneycut politely showed us the door with little else to tell. I found the notepad, wrote down the time and a brief recollection of events. Then while we covered a few miles, I studied the map. Lottie had marked the property for me.

I wondered what the neighbors thought. In rural areas, everyone kept a hawk's eye on which tracts sold to whom. You couldn't predict when a contractor or outside developer might slink in and turn a pastoral setting into something filled with city idiots trying to call a subdivision *living in the country.*

We soon turned at a mailbox adorned with wooden legs, nose, and horns, painted like a black cow. Charming. This house sat considerably back off the road, maybe fifteen hundred feet, and the cattle guard we crossed entering the drive told me this guy wasn't just about row crops. The cattle we passed appeared to be strapping, glistening, black Angus. Prime beef on the hoof.

We drove by a collection of three standing about ten feet off the drive, sullenly chewing their cud. "Beautiful, right?" Lottie said.

"Gorgeous." I did a quick count of fifty head on a well-tended fescue field.

"This couple's real active on the Internet," she said. "People are all about beef with no additives these days."

"Yeah," I said, but all I could think about was how much I'd love to live here. Since when was Newberry so bucolic?

Lottie'd texted our next visitor upon leaving the Huneycuts, and when we arrived, a lithe, middle-aged woman waited in scuffed boots, jeans, and a coral Henley. She rose from an old swing, ducking under a drooped limb from the white oak tree behind it. Her cropped salt-and-pepper curls hugged her head, probably to fit best under the wide-brimmed woven hat in her hand.

Here was a woman accustomed to sweat, dung, and dirt.

"June, you look like we interrupted something," Lottie said, walking up for a hug.

"Putting in the vegetable garden out behind the house." The woman welcomed her with open arms. "But good to see you. I needed a break."

Lottie squeezed, pulled back, and swooped her hand out. "Carolina Slade, this is June Sterling. Her husband's Jerry Sterling. This is Double J farm."

I reached out for a shake, and the woman accepted the grip with vigor. "Nice to meet you," she said. I liked her.

We entered the turn of the century home with Victorian overtones both inside and out. Dark woodwork and colors of cream and yellow gave everything a sepia look. Antiques of mahogany and cherry in nooks and corners. Tatted lace curtains. Understated elegance, which told me June might be the same.

No sign of Jerry, and instead of a kitchen table meet and greet, June took us to the back porch with iced tea and a bowl of oatmeal cookies out of a bag. Welcoming us, but likewise stating she was a busy woman and didn't have all day to gab.

She settled in a rocker obviously hers and propped boots up on a stool kept just for that purpose judging from its dents and dust. "Like I told you on the phone, Lottie, the loss of our forty-two acres is not a palatable subject, and I'm not sure how much I can help you." She laid her head back and started the chair moving.

"What I'm hearing," I started, "is that several farms lost acreage in some sort of deal with Ag. We're trying to determine if these deals appear to be any type of misrepresentation." I glanced at Lottie. "I heard there's a bit of ill will about it all."

June rocked harder. "Can't speak about others, but I'm not happy. No, ma'am, I'm not."

"Not happy about what in particular?" I asked.

She turned toward me, dimples showing though her jaw tightened. "Jerry hears from a neighbor about a low interest loan, that he doesn't have to mortgage but one tract of land and not even the house, so he applied. Against my wishes, mind you, because that land was free and clear and contained one of our best pastures." She stopped to chomp a cookie, and I let her chew on it awhile. I assumed she debated how much else to say, and I didn't want to interfere in her willingness to say it. "Eighteen months later," she said, "he's selling the place for twenty percent under market value. Without asking me. We'd used the loan money to build a new barn, purchase brood stock, pay off other loans, and even redo a pond. Had a good rate on the loan, but he insisted on selling the land."

"Didn't that strike you—"

"Odd?" An anger flashed in her hazel eyes. "Of course, it did. I harassed the hell out of Jerry for weeks after, but, well," and she paused. "I needn't go into the environment around here during that time."

I bet she gave her man hell. "How long ago was this?"

"Six months. I'm done nagging, but I see the pain in his eyes every time he rides by that tract. He might as well have sacrificed a piece of his heart." The chair went back to rocking. "A stupid, stupid decision."

What was making these men come off their land, while ignoring their long-time brides pleading them not to?

The cookies tasted fair being store-bought, but I reached for another to be courteous. A breeze drifted in from the west, across us. "He couldn't explain why? You aren't owners of such a grand farm by making such irrational choices."

The doorbell rang. June started to get up, but a male voice yelled from inside. "I'll get it. You just visit with Lottie." No mention of me.

With a scowl, June lowered back down but tilted her head, listening. "Thought he was taking a nap." Not uncommon for a farmer to work from sun-up, then take an afternoon break when the heat was at its peak.

Neither Lottie nor I spoke, nibbling on our cookies. I wisely withheld questioning until we could tell where Jerry wound up once he answered the door.

But June suddenly leaped up and quickly shed her boots. In socked feet streaked with garden dirt, she eased inside.

With a brow, I raised a silent question to Lottie, then stared at the screen door where June had disappeared after one-handedly easing it closed behind her. Instincts nudged me to follow, and when I covertly reentered the house, Lottie trailed my heel.

We found June hiding in the dining room, mashed against her tasteful wallpaper, her fingers relaxing the curtain back to see.

I assumed a similar stance next to the partner window, choosing to squint through the lace instead. Without a window of her own, Lottie squatted under the window I occupied, her knees popping and clearly protesting the move. June glanced at me at the noise, and I just shook my head.

Cricket stood on the front steps. "Now, Jerry, all I'm saying—"

Jerry's grip of her elbow interrupted the thought, however, and he escorted her from the house, grumbling something about "I told you not to . . ." But then I couldn't hear. They walked past the four-foot-wide oak to what seemed to be Cricket's car, parked next to Lottie's.

"What the hell is that bitch doing here?" June said under her breath.

I liked this woman even more.

Back to watching Cricket, I struggled to read her intention. Definitely not angry, but not confident, either. The messenger getting shot, maybe? Or a girl in over her head . . . trying to keep all the frayed ends in order. Not exactly what I expected out of her, but I'd not expected her to show up, either.

Jerry, however, was damn easy to read from his red complexion to the jabbing motions at Cricket.

"Well, she sees we're here," Lottie said, pointing to her Prius.

"No," I whispered, "she thinks *you're* here. Innocent enough to explain, too, so don't overthink this." But my gaze shifted back to June. Her teeth clenched, the sinew in her neck taut against her jugular. She withheld a huge chunk of this story.

Jerry's actions telegraphed anti-Cricket, so I doubted he'd rat us out, but what brought Cricket out here?

Or had one of the Huneycuts maybe called her? Making me intensely eager to learn what could be so damn bad as to make such connected farmers this fearful?

"What else happened, June?" I kept a hushed level. "What compromised Jerry to give up the place?"

"I promised not to say."

"Promised not to say what?" Lottie asked from below me.

June glared down at the woman on her floor. "And nothing, Lottie. A promise is a promise, especially to your husband. We've partnered on this farm since our twenties, and we're not letting a tawdry piece of gossip come between us. So don't even go there, you hear?"

"Okay, okay," Lottie said, then stared up at me. "What do you think?"

I shook my head again. Like I'd discuss what I thought in front of June. However, the comment about tawdry gossip made me recall Hoyt Abrams . . . and wonder. I peered out the window again. "Cricket's leaving."

"And Jerry's coming in," June hissed and backed toward the kitchen.

Giving Lottie a hand, I raised her to her feet then yanked her toward the back porch. Outside, she wheeled herself around to plop into a chair. I resumed my old seat. Panting, Lottie pumped her rocker, her unassuming effort an utter failure.

Which didn't matter, because Jerry didn't show . . . and neither did June.

"Who was at the door?" I heard June say inside.

Lottie and I stopped our chairs to hear.

"Cricket Carson," Jerry said with a growl.

"Wish you'd let me handle her," June said.

"Don't want to give her the satisfaction of insulting you, my sweet," the husband said.

"Not a possibility," the wife replied. Then silence. And more silence. And me envisioning what was going down in that silence.

My heart pitty-patted. Maybe a husband and wife so devoted to each other that in spite of a nasty, uninvited guest, they gave each other pure respect, and maybe a kiss or two. And at their age, the love felt all the richer.

An ideal couple, standing staunch against some power that failed to shake their foundation.

I gripped my shirt, an ache rising into my throat. This was rapidly turning into a do-or-die situation. Fight to expose what *might* be a land grab operation or turn my back on couples like this. Listen to Monroe's criticism and Harden's orders to bow out . . . or continue following my CI the town crier, into some abyss of gossip, praying it held substance.

Nothing like having my job on the line.

Chapter 18

FIVE MINUTES PASSED. Lottie and I couldn't leave the porch and drive off without a goodbye, but June seemed in no hurry to return to us. I rocked and sent texts to Monroe and Ivy, then one to Ally.

One missed call from Wayne with a voicemail and a promise to see me tomorrow. Glad to hear the day was my own, though my thoughts about this close farm couple gave me a longing for my lawman and his south Alabama drawl. A dirty longing making me realize my hormones sneaked up on me these days. In hindsight, I wasn't being very likeable to the guy.

Hell, I was beginning to not like myself.

Ally texted that Ivy went out with her insect boyfriend. The shortness of the night before hung heavy on me, and I rubbed my eyes. God, I worried about my daughter.

When will they be home? I texted back.

It's Saturday, Sis, she replied.

That isn't a time.

Both of us were concerned. Both of us held the same ugliness in our heads about Bug's hands on our girl.

When you coming home? she asked.

Not sure yet.

Ally often tattled to Wayne, not that he asked her to. Just who she was. I already worried about her spilling our talk last night.

I shifted texts to my daughter. *Ivy? Report in, please.*

Act normal, like Lottie said to do.

Do you ever report in to me? came the reply.

Do you want to live to your next birthday? I typed.

Aunt Ally said I could go out with Bug. Said you were working anyway.

ETA to home?

10-ish? she replied.

8-ish, I countered.

Can he stay til 10 if we're home?

If I can see you.

A delay. *You gotta be home to see me.*

I didn't answer that.

The screen door opened and June came out, pink-cheeked, picking up her boots on the way to her rocker.

"Everything all right?" Lottie asked.

No more anger; a more contented peace-of-mind in its place. "Fine and dandy," June answered. "You heard everything I did. I told you, we put this behind us. Now, I hate to cut our visit short, ladies, but I've got six more rows to plant before dinner." She snatched the laces in place and rose.

She'd regrouped and pushed us away after a discussion with Jerry.

I held out my card. "Call if you think of anything."

Without acknowledgment, she tucked it in her back jeans pocket and slid on gardening gloves.

"Let's head to our next farm, Lottie." I appeared to finish my drink, waiting for June to ask which farm. Instead, she marched down the steps to the back yard, minding her own business and probably wishing I would mind mine.

Lottie and I walked around the house to the car, backed out, and headed toward the county highway. No sign of Jerry.

"Gotta love those two," Lottie said. "Like a romance novel."

"Charming," I said, staring at the cattle that hadn't moved much since we'd come in. "Sure wish I knew what made them keep their mouths shut. How'd these women talk to you? You're the press."

"Church, mostly," she said, "but honey, I don't know much more than you do. The ladies just fuss that something ought to be done. Guess I'm the mouthpiece they hope can get that something done, because I don't have a man in that fight, or land to take."

Not that anyone hadn't run her husband off the road.

"I really thought they'd say more to you, though," she added. She hollered *hey* to some man on a tractor who couldn't possibly hear her, her hand out the window waving over the top of the Prius. He waved back.

"But in the radio station," I said, a bit bummed at not having more progress, "you said they wanted to talk. So far, the ones who talk don't know enough to make a difference, and the ones who have the facts won't talk."

I could confront Cricket, but you never interview a target until you have your ducks in a row. I resigned myself to spending the upcoming week in courthouse records, then remembered the congresswoman in the upstate waiting for me on Tuesday. Crap.

A text came in that I ignored, just as Lottie turned left into another drive not a mile from June's. Instead of looking, I reopened the map. "Lottie? Mark all these farms. Don't forget the Abrams."

She stopped in the dirt drive and pointed. "There, there, oh, just give me your pen."

The marks noted sales north of Highway 76 within five miles from each other. In a county as big as Newberry, I found the locations anything but coincidental.

Dumb of me not to make Lottie note these farm addresses from day one. I received another text but couldn't stop staring a hole into that map, reaching for a revelation that wouldn't come.

Lots of factors to consider. The type of farming on each place. Proximity to highway or water. The interstate. Without a doubt, I needed to learn who bought these tracts, then dissect who *they* were.

"Oh, sugar," Lottie whispered.

"What?" I asked, hearing another text, wondering if Monroe had finally decided to respond while hoping Wayne hadn't.

A silver Lexus slowed, coming from the farm we'd turned into. It eased to a stop, door to door with Lottie. "Why Lottie Bledsoe, what brings you out here?" The driver's voice dripped with coquettish sarcasm.

Lottie's hands remained tight on the wheel, the most nervous I'd seen her since we met. "Verna and I go back to high school," she said.

The woman tsked once. "Silly Milly, I know that." She looked over her shoulder toward the farm house. "She's not there, so you're wasting your time."

Lottie couldn't seem to find her words.

Then the woman peered around Lottie, at me. "And who do we have here?"

I waited to be introduced, but Lottie remained speechless. "Hey, I'm Carolina Slade. Met Lottie last week at the radio station. She's a grand tour guide, and I love your county."

The woman's chin raised. "Ah, the Agriculture headhunter."

Wow, I did *not* like this woman. "Correct," I said, plastering the stiffest, come-and-get-me smile I could muster. "But you have me at a disadvantage, ma'am. I feel you're someone I should be acquainted with." Two could play this passive aggressive Southern game.

"So sorry." She leaned over the open window. "I'm Lorena Carson, Cricket's mother. I've heard a lot about you."

"Likewise," I said, wondering why the self-adorned queen bee of everything Newberry had to visit the farmer we needed to see. And her daughter visit another. I pushed the question that Lottie should've been crazy eager to ask. "What brings you out here?"

"Verna and I serve on the same Sunday school committee." Lorena softly touched her collarbone in dramatic pause, and I recognized where Cricket got her ways. "I must admit I've neglected my part on a project we share, but I missed her. What about you ladies?"

Bless her heart, I thought, and not in a good way. I nudged Lottie. Damn it, she needed to contribute to this charade, too.

"Oh, I'm considering a story about our high school," Lottie blurted. "Verna talked all about being a world-traveler when she graduated. Who'd have thought she'd wind up staying in her own backyard?"

Lorena nodded with a suspicious nonchalance. "You always did like your stories."

Poor Lottie remained hesitant.

"Ah, well," and Lorena tilted her head toward the highway. "Got a business to run. Some of us just can't be still, isn't that right, Ms. Slade? Duty calls."

I bobbled my eyebrows. "Hey, I'm just a salaried government flunky. Saturday's nothing more than a day off."

"Well, see y'all." And without waiting for our response, she headed the Lexus toward the road, dust kicking up from her heavy foot.

Lottie eased the Prius forward. "Now she's aware we're out here."

"So what?" I tried to trivialize Mama Carson's appearance for Lottie's sake. However, the woman had sure demanded respect for her presence, and Lottie had bowed down and canonized it. As someone who sassed the state director and had bested the state's governor and his entire family, I tended to slough off social or political status. Hard-working farmers like the Huneycuts and Sterlings impressed me more.

"Well, if Verna's not here, we can turn around," Lottie said.

I really wanted to talk to this third farm wife . . . about the need for Lorena to come out on the peak day for real estate agents. "Let's check for ourselves."

The driveway wound to a circular affair in front of a rambling red brick house that stretched out like a cat across a deep green centipede lawn. The center rose to a second story that probably contained at least a couple bedrooms, but the intensity of the place was its wide, continuous footprint. The porch wrapping around the front and two sides took up more square footage than my entire house. Eight pin oaks held respected, measured spots across the lot. Once again, I was struck by the comparison to the more austere homes of our average client.

"Hmm," Lottie said, as we crawled out. We strolled to the door, me taking in the affluence and breaking the hell out of the *Thou shalt not covet* commandment. Lottie rang the bell.

I dared peer in a window behind a rocker. Lights off.

"She confirmed the appointment," Lottie said.

"Maybe Lorena lied." I tried the glass door. It opened, and a note fluttered to our feet; its masking tape hadn't been up to the task of grasping the wooden door.

Forgot an appointment, Lottie. So sorry. Verna.

"Forgot, my ass," Lottie grumbled.

Agreed. "Oh well, if nobody's here, then they won't mind if we look around."

But Lottie reared back and bellowed. "We know you're in there, Verna!"

"Lorena said she wasn't," I said low.

With a scowl and a yank of my sleeve, Lottie gave her head a quick shake at me. "Your car's still here, Verna! And Troy's truck." She reached in her purse for her cell, scrolled, and sent a call. "The Blue Danube" rang inside.

A mild squeak of the door caught our attention. "You're the major pain in the ass, Lottie. Didn't you see the note?"

"And yet you stand here bitching at us, Verna," Lottie said. "What's going on? I can tell your panties are in a knot."

Verna remained on the other side of the glass. "I didn't meet Lorena."

"What?" Lottie exclaimed, dryness in her wit. "You're not on a Sunday school committee with her?"

With a rush of words, Verna pulled the door back. "You think I'd volunteer to work with her? God help me, but even in church I can't forgive that bitch, so why the heck do you think I'd work alongside her?"

"Precisely," Lottie said. "So why was she here?"

Ordinarily, I would've held out my hand to shake, but I just slid a step closer. "Hello. I'm Carolina Slade."

"Oh yeah," Lottie said. "This is my friend from Agriculture. She's someone I—"

Verna shut the door. I thought I heard it latch.

Lottie reverted to yelling again. "Get your fanny back out here!"

The muffled voice sounded just on the other side of the door. "I'm not talking to anyone from that outfit."

"You'd rather meet with Lorena?"

"Troy met Lorena, not me," came the holler from within. "I hid."

"Seems she rather prefers hiding," I said to my partner.

Lottie leaned sideways close to my ear. "Because of her husband. I'll tell you later." Then she turned back to the door. "Come out, or we'll just go talk to Troy. He's probably heard us already."

I almost felt bad at the bullying.

"I'll stand up to him if you won't," Lottie yelled again. "The sooner you talk, the sooner we get out of here. Slade's a friend trying to dig into what happened around here. Ain't nothing to be ashamed of."

Verna widened the opening.

"Well, come on out, you twit." Lottie opened the screen door and shoved open the wooden. "What the hell's wrong with you?"

Verna came out on the porch. Not as firm a stature as one would think of a farm wife, she stood six inches shorter than I did, but easily weighed as much, and I wasn't thin by a long shot. A sweet appearance with mild makeup on a complexion accustomed to the sun, interrupted by crow's feet and wrinkles that had taken up permanent residence around her mouth. A chin-length bob of gray and white.

But fearful. Of me. And most likely because we arrived on Lorena Carson's coattails . . . and I worked with Cricket.

"Did Lorena Carson threaten your husband?" I asked, because clearly, the wives seemed to be on the outside looking in.

"How am I supposed to trust you?" she asked, leery, defensive.

"Because she's with me," Lottie said. "She's one of the good ones. Rounded up all sorts of criminal elements across this state. She's like the Columbo of rural South Carolina. She's kicked butt from Beaufort to Clemson. She's—"

"Let's don't overdo it," I mumbled, then to Verna said, "What did Lorena want?"

Verna walked over to a double swing on chains and eased onto the plaid cushion. Lottie sat in a rocker. I stood and anxiously waited, because this was the first person who seemed halfway willing to give us anything other than *I can't tell you* or *I don't know*.

She covered the same rundown as the others. Quick loan, then quick payoff when it appeared completely unnecessary.

"What made Troy sell?" I asked again.

"Something he's ashamed to say," she said. "So I shouldn't say for him."

I tired of this echo. "Lorena handled the sale, didn't she?" And probably all the others. Surely Wayne could subpoena those records if I showed him a corrupt pattern.

Verna shrugged.

"Did someone catch Troy being unfaithful to you?"

Slowly, Verna nodded in the positive about Troy's indiscretion.

"And by chance, did anyone blackmail him?" I asked.

"He swore he didn't do anything," she blurted, shaking the swing off its rhythm.

Lottie made dismissal hand movements. "Then how can he be blackmailed? We're talking about Troy here."

Verna folded her plump middle best she could to lean over in Lottie's space. "I was firmly told to not tell *you* anything."

Lottie acted sort of hurt, though I knew better. "But you said to come over."

"That was this morning." Verna put a big period on that last sentence, because she lay back against the swing and looked out across the wide lawn toward a fresh-tilled field.

I eased in front of her line of sight. "What changed your mind about meeting with us?"

A boom of a voice sent me a foot off the floor. "What're you doing here?"

Lottie remained seated, having seen Troy Zeller approach from around the house. I still shook.

A beast of a man, even in his sixties, I dared guess he measured a couple inches taller than Wayne. Bald, wearing overalls, he projected blue-collar, rough neck instead of the affluent owner of the four-thousand square foot manor Verna wouldn't let us inside of.

"Troy," Verna said, halting as if testing his temper. "They didn't know not to come."

"What, you forgot how to dial a damn phone?" he yelled.

Over the top, in my opinion. "Hey, we didn't come here to get her in trouble," I said. "We came to help. Passed Lorena Carson on the way in, too, so what's up?"

His eyes widened, then fell to a squint. "Not your problem. Told that bitch I wasn't taking her shit anymore, and she got the message loud and Windex clear."

Moisture fell down Verna's cheeks.

And Troy noticed, because the flash of worry surprised me. Yet his machismo kept his feet planted in the well-fertilized grass to save face in front of us.

"Go," he said.

"Hold on, Troy," Lottie started. "We were only trying—"

"Are you deaf or just dense, Lottie?"

Tugging my partner's skirt, I beckoned for her to retreat. Squeezing around Troy as he stomped up the steps, she and I made for the car as the couple disappeared inside. "Hold on," I said and stopped under one of the trees. "Listen."

While we couldn't hear Verna, I doubted Troy Zeller knew how to whisper. "She wants to fuck with me again?" he yelled. "I told her to give it her best. She thinks too much of her daughter to mess with me anymore." Quiet for a few seconds, which I assumed meant Verna talking. Then we heard Troy. "And those two women best not come back, you got it? I'm in no mood to share my shit with that gossip monger, and why the hell would I talk to anyone from Agriculture?"

This time Lottie tugged at me. "I've heard enough."

We jumped into the Prius and rode in silence.

Lottie finally spoke. "He's rough, maybe a bit rowdy, Slade, but he loves Verna."

"I'm still on the fence about that," I said, watching fields roll by.

She drove subdued. "That's why she came to me, worried about how this affected him. He's a hard man, but they've been married for over thirty years."

A lot of women stayed married to their abusers, but whether they lived in marital bliss wasn't my concern. What *was* my concern was what railroaded these men into selling their acreage. Time to learn to whom. And with Carson Real Estate so prominent in the county, how would they not be part of these transactions?

This day wore on me now, and with lunch having come and gone, I yearned for home. Remembering my phone, I noted four texts.

The oldest from Harden. *Are you in Newberry?*

How the hell would he even know to ask? On a Saturday, no less. I told Lottie we'd seen too many people. I deleted the message and would feign ignorance on Monday. The problem with using my personal phone for office business: the boss having the number.

Still nothing from Monroe. He'd never stonewalled me like this before.

I flipped to Wayne's. *Finished early. See you tonight.*

Well, hell. That would be awkward.

His text went on. *BTW, Ivy called. You and I need to talk.*

Shit! My stomach flipped once, then twice, then the cookies and muffins from the day almost came back up. Ivy never called Wayne. Talk about what? My pregnancy? Hers? The illusive pink test kit? *Oh, my dear Lord.*

"You all right, hon?" Lottie glanced over.

"I gotta get home," I said.

She added another five miles per hour. "Emergency?"

With a pointed finger, I shouted, "Faster, Lottie, damn. You're related to the cops around here, so use the hell out of the privilege."

"No need to—"

"Lottie, please!"

Lottie gunned the gas. I lifted my phone again, almost afraid to read the final text.

From Ally. *You might want to get home. Something's up with Ivy.*

You think? My little sister, the queen of understatement.

Chapter 19

WE REACHED LOTTIE'S driveway, and I leaped out of the car. "Thanks, I'll be back in touch tomorrow." Maybe a lie, uncertain what my tomorrow would be like after a night I couldn't predict. How much had Wayne and Ally withheld from me about Ivy, knowing good and well I would rush home?

"Is someone hurt?" she gasped.

"No, but . . ."

She relaxed. "Thank God for that. Please let me wrap up the last cinnamon bun to take with you. Somehow I think you could use it."

"Lottie, I've got to go."

However, she'd already left me in the drive. I followed her, if for no reason than to speed her up.

As the microwave ran, I stared out the kitchen window at the covered Bel Air when a hand rubbed my back. "Honey, something sure knocked the ice cream off your cone. What is it?"

Oh, how badly I wanted to unload on her. This sudden expression of mama tendencies reached out to me, and I barely stopped from turning around to collect me some. I hadn't been nice to my family of late, and at the moment I felt adrift. Couldn't talk to Ally about Wayne . . . or Monroe. Hadn't found the nerve to tell Wayne about the pregnancy yet. I was worrying myself sick about Ivy.

"My boss is none too happy about my being here." Truth. My personal business had no room under this roof. Regardless how friendly she was, Lottie's role remained as my cooperating individual, and I had to keep this professional.

Her rubbing turned into a double pat. "Sit. I'll pour you a glass of milk."

I spun. "I don't have time to sit, Lottie."

With little baby nods that said she understood, she wrapped up my bun in a tea towel probably used for biscuits. "Will you come back on Monday?" she asked.

"Not sure. You'll see a federal agent from the Inspector General's

Office though. This crap with Cecil sort of snatched this affair out of my hands."

Lottie shook the wrapped bun at me before handing it over. "As planned by Cricket, honey. Your man with the nose made her nervous."

"Let me run. Got fires at home." I took the towel and stepped to the door. "Thanks so much."

She just waved with a soft, understanding smile.

Outside, I fast-walked down the steps under the carport, about to come out from behind the jasmine snaking up the trellis . . . until a car pulled in the drive. A silver Lexus. I darted behind a plant, then scooted back inside.

I whispered breathless as I shut the door behind me. "Lorena just pulled up."

A knock sounded on the front door.

She calmly brushed her hands over the sink. "She won't bite, Slade. Go ahead and leave, if you need to."

"No," I said, "check it out. I want to hear. Then I've *got* to go." I wanted to beat Wayne home, maybe see Ivy alone before he arrived, though I had no friggin' idea what to say to her. But I wouldn't have another chance to hear about Lorena's nosiness firsthand, either.

Lottie disappeared, and her words traveled back, following the natural air flow designed for these older houses for our intense summer heat. "Wasn't expecting to see you. Want to come on in? Need some tea? Coffee?"

Thinking I recalled the layout of the high-ceiling, hundred-plus-year-old home, I doubled back to the side door. Then sidling along the china-covered buffet in the dining room, I made my way to a spot just left of the hallway arch.

The Newberry queen stood not six feet from me, facing Lottie . . . and Lottie facing me, prattling on. "You've never set foot here for a book club, birthday party, fundraiser, or Bible study, Lorena. You don't sit near me in church, and we've never broken bread together. So, why is it I have the honor of chatting with you twice in one day?"

Lorena tsked, her purse hanging in the crook of one arm. "I imagine fate put us at Verna's, but seeing you made me realize I needed to place an ad with the radio station. It's April, and the market wakes up about now."

"Why not call the radio station?"

Up north, Lottie would've thrown the woman out in a slurry of cursing and ill wishes. Not in Dixie. Even without witnesses, women volleyed niceties laced with acid. This was a face-off, with undertones and unspoken messages both would surely understand.

If I slid out now, I could text my apologies to Lottie on the way home.

"Oh," Lorena said, as if in sudden afterthought. "How's Bishop? And honey," she added, brushing Lottie's arm, "how bad's that gorgeous Bel Air? What a sin to tap that baby." Her body cocked a hip, and I imagined the mask of faux concern.

Lottie's patience wore thinner. "He's fine. The car's fine. I'll tell him you asked. What else can I do for you?"

I mouthed, *I'm going*, but couldn't tell if she noticed.

"Where's your companion?" Lorena asked.

To that I froze.

"Honey, we just saw each other." The agent tapped her temple. "Aunt Sis plays these games with me all day long, so don't think you can best me."

"Slade's a friend," Lottie said, dodging the question.

With a small puff, the real estate agent rolled her head once in disbelief. "You're going with that? Seriously, Lottie, who do you think you're talking to?"

Lottie re-crossed her arms. "I'm quite familiar with who's standing in my living room, pretending to show concern, pretending to order an ad, pretending she hasn't been keeping up with my whereabouts all day long." She leaned in. "Nervous about Ms. Slade being in town?"

Uh oh, don't go there, Lottie. Please don't go there.

"And why would that be a concern?" the queen asked.

"Because people aren't falling for your cover-up."

Shut up, Lottie. I peeked out only to jerk back when Lottie made eye contact.

Which made Lorena start to turn. "Is she still here?"

Holding my breath, I tiptoed backwards around the corner, toward the kitchen exit. Lottie ignored the question.

"Anyway, let me tell you this before I go," Lorena said. "You've known this Carolina Slade for how long? A week?"

My name stopped me in my tracks.

"Maybe."

"Lottie, you do not want to be on the wrong side of things if Agriculture sticks its nose into this county's business."

"Agriculture helped mold this county," Lottie said. "And news is news, or have you forgotten what I do for a living?"

One of them opened the front door. *Don't go, don't go. Let me get out and get gone first.*

"Oh, I haven't forgotten a thing," Lorena said. "Just making sure *you* haven't. The Bledsoes may have been around longer than the Carsons, but me and mine stand a few rungs higher on the ladder, my dear."

"Oh, look at the clock," Lottie said. "It's past time for you to go."

I eased over, then gently pushed the screen open. Ever so softly, I laid it back in place . . . and ran my butt off.

Like a soldier scrambling from cover to cover, I made my way up Main Street toward my truck, hiding behind clumps of blooming white spirea bushes in one yard and azaleas in another. Slumping, I scurried alongside three vehicles parked on the street. Finally reaching the truck, I leaped in, belted in, and cranked up before noticing the flyer on my windshield. I stretched around, barely reaching the paper, and drew it inside.

Let Ginger show you Newberry real estate.

There she stood all sassy in a jade polyester dress hugging her curves, her hand resting on a Carson Realty sign. A blood red smooch of a lipstick mark on the back, with the words, "Let's meet."

Like hell. No telling what she'd pull over on me, or who'd be in the wings with the camera.

The camera! Was it still in my purse?

I rummaged and found it, one of those compact things not much bigger than my cell phone. Waiting for the camera to power on, I kept an eye on the street, in my mirror, half expecting Ginger to appear. Or Lorena to slide her Lexus in beside me.

These small town hussies gave me the creeps.

Thank God for digital. I flipped through pictures. Maybe a hundred of them. Six of Monroe and Ginger in the parking lot. Admittedly, someone chose the most perfectly posed to blow up and gift to Monroe. The others appeared more awkward than provocative, showing Ginger maneuvering Monroe. Monroe acting shocked. Yep. These told a lot better story.

Bet somebody wondered where this camera was. And whose was it? Ginger's? Monroe never said how it found its way to the front office, onto the desk I swiped it from. Cecil mentioned pictures, so I could assume Ginger's, if he brought it to the office, but if Cricket was involved, it could just as easily be hers.

My head was screwed on so lopsided of late thanks to hormones,

Ivy, Monroe . . . Wayne. Not only had I forgotten about the camera, but now I wasn't sure what to do with it. I had no subpoena. Were the pictures even usable now? Tainted evidence of some sort? Maybe for a court case, but not likely for an internal inquiry of Monroe.

I continued through the inventory, glancing up every dozen pics or so. Some of houses, but most of forests, dirt roads, fences, and pastures. Farm land. Acres and acres. Even locals would struggle identifying where these were with few distinguishing features. Made me wish I'd made Lottie take me to the sold tracts themselves as well as meet the farmers' wives.

Other than the pics of Monroe, which couldn't hurt his case, in my opinion, the other real estate pics mattered little.

The silver streak caught my eye. Son of a biscuit, was that the Lexus? I stared. It slowed. I wasn't waiting to see.

Backing up the truck, I took off east on Main, just over the speed limit, right on Adelaide, then home free on Highway 76 toward my place.

That's when I let loose a breath. Who feared a real estate lady? Me. Her crew had sure done a number on Monroe. Better stupid than screwed over.

Thirty plus miles to the house. I had to tell Wayne every detail about Newberry and give him the camera and wondered if my taking it screwed things up.

Most of the reason I accepted the special projects representative job, which sorely needed a shorter name, and something other than *headhunter*, was the challenge. The puzzle game. The whodunit mystery that called to me. But this time, amidst all the saccharin charm and makeup, behind the coy flirtations and unspoken nuances of the suspects, some sixth sense told me to be damn afraid of something. The one lesson I did adopt from Wayne was listening to my gut. Instinct, he said. A trait we all possessed but few acknowledged.

Or was I just hating on Lorena because of her association with Cricket?

I approached Little Mountain. Halfway home, and I shifted gears. The wives we met today acted so differently than Cassie, Phoebe, and Faye. While I hadn't seen financial records, Lottie's three from the kitchen seemed from a lower social caste, their land losses hampering their livelihoods. They also couldn't talk what happened between their husbands and Agriculture. But the more lucrative three farmers and their more educated wives feared talking.

I'd be curious as to a time line. Were the rich farmers dealt with first, or last, or just whenever?

About five miles from my lake house, the conversations I rushed home to have sprang back to mind. Wayne about Ivy. Ally about Ivy. Ivy about Bug.

Do as I say, not as I do. Daddy instilled that in me from the time I could utter my first defiant *No*. How was I to address sex with Ivy when her mother hadn't practiced what she preached? I was sucking at motherhood.

Suddenly arriving home held less appeal.

Chapter 20

BUG'S CAR IN MY drive instantly pissed me off, and Wayne's car made me feel like a latecomer to a surprise party. I strode in the house, regardless, braced for an onslaught from anyone breathing about how I hadn't done my job as a mother.

Ally barely said hey when I walked in. Oddly reticent, she'd ordered pizza, and they'd already eaten. No television in the background. I could even hear the clock in the hallway, for God's sake. Where was Ivy?

Wayne slid open the sliding door, and my heart thumped into my ribs. "Thought I heard your car," he said.

Why wasn't he more worried? I'd died a thousand times since leaving Newberry. Composed a hundred speeches, none of which I could see me saying to Ivy's face. "Where is she?"

"The treehouse," he said. "She and Bug—"

With a turn, I fast-walked to the kitchen door.

Wayne followed. I spun on him. "No, this is my job." No double meaning there, no sir-ee.

He gave me a soft scowl. "Overreacting some, are we?"

I scowled at him.

"I may not be a parent," he said, "but I appreciate how to approach someone who holds more cards than I do. Tread carefully. You want me to tell you what she said first?"

Did I? "Let me see what she tells me first," I said. Not the way I'd handle a person of interest, but pride wanted to see if Ivy would tell me what she'd already told Wayne.

Her recent desire to hide in the treehouse already worried me. A place for secret clubs and hiding favorite toys, for Zack. Ivy'd never liked it before Bug.

In the fifty yards to the treehouse, I debated. Yell her name or slink up the stairs? So many visions in my head I hoped I wouldn't see.

Halfway up the stairs to the six-by-six room with a hickory tree running through the middle of it, the wood creaked beneath me.

"Zack, you little runt," Ivy yelled. "You better not be out there."

I gave it up and showed myself.

"Mom?"

They sat on a quilt. My grandmother's quilt, no less. Bug's back against the corner and Ivy seated between his legs, her back to him. Fully clothed. Couldn't tell if any buttons were misaligned because he had his buggy arms around her, and her arms wrapped over his.

Ivy leaped up and straightened her clothes anyway, which only threw fuel on my fret. "How about knocking next time?" she griped.

"It's a treehouse, not a motel room," I said, then wanted to kick myself for the comparison.

Her eyes widened. "We weren't doing anything."

I started to add *yet*.

"When will you trust me?" Her voice had a crack to it. "You forget how old I am. How old were you when you had your first boy?"

What did she mean by *had*? Gripping the door to the house, I didn't enter. "I'm not the topic here." *Was I handling this right?*

She stepped closer. "Seriously, you sneaked over here to, what, catch us screwing?"

Oh Lord, please erase the sound of that word falling out of my daughter's mouth.

With no means to exit this tawdry drama except to run over me, Bug held his ground, but his eyes almost popped out. "Wait a minute. We haven't been . . . I mean, we didn't . . . ."

"You can thank your bloody stars you haven't," I said. "Cross that line, Buggy Boy, and you won't see what hit you."

"Mom! Stop *testing* me!"

The air crackled with our tension. Ivy's chest heaved.

Why I stood there all demanding and confrontational, I couldn't say, because neither Wayne nor Ally had yet voiced their concerns. Without the context behind their texts, and standing here with these two kids gawking at me like this, I'd overreacted on what was seen, heard, and imagined in my head. Breaking off the face-off, I left Ivy for the house. Hands fisted, I mentally imagined how to correct myself, or regain footing as someone Ivy could come to with her problems. Instead of her mom's boyfriend.

Into the house past Wayne, past Ally, and into my bathroom, I soon squeezed into yoga tights and a long-sleeve tee. Leaning on the counter, staring in the mirror, the throbbing in my neck palpable. What had I become? My hand fell to my midsection.

I couldn't think straight.

What the hell would I even wear as time went on? I hated what pregnant women wore these days. Stretchy spandex over protruding bellies, navels clearly outies or innies.

Not the problem right now.

But the image threw my heartbeat into overtime, and a vise squeezed between my shoulder blades. Frantic dialogue I'd rehashed in my ride home flooded back in. Dialogue for Ivy about motherhood . . . for Wayne about fatherhood. None of it fitting. Ivy would sequester herself in her room, avoiding that discussion. Wayne, however, waited outside in the living room.

I laid my head on the counter. Why was this bothering me so? I'd rather take a bullet than juggle all this personal stuff all at one time.

Too old to have another kid. The current kids too old to want a sibling. Monroe hating me. Wayne, who'd actually been pretty damn nice in spite of my knee-jerk reactions to everything, but who might not be quite ready to be a parent. And Lottie. Regardless of her tough persona, she worried me. With her husband's car rear-ended, someone hated her, and the timing pointed straight to my having gotten involved in Newberry.

Who needed to bring a kid into this kind of life? Which increasingly looked to be a life involving people who wielded knives and guns and could follow you home.

A soft tap sounded on my door. "Carolina?"

I lifted my head. "What?"

Ally let herself in, still tentative. "You okay?"

"Pickle smackin' hunky dory, baby sister. Life's a bowl full of f'in cherries."

That shut her up.

"Monroe call?" I asked.

"Why would he call me?" she replied, bewildered.

"Because—" I stopped myself from mentioning her crush on him. "What is it, Ally?"

"I couldn't find the pink box."

Bless me, she didn't say *pregnancy test.* "Thanks."

She moved to the door. "You better get out there. He's wondering."

I took a fat-belly inhale and let it out slowly. "Yep."

"You getting ready to tell him?" she murmured.

"Have no damn clue."

"Okay," she said, and left, with me close behind.

Leaning against the sliding glass door to the porch, Wayne looked up from checking his phone and stood straight. "Come on out to the porch. We need to talk."

No shit, lawman. Again, heart in my throat.

As I lowered into my regular chair, feet up on a small table, I hunted for the child I hadn't seen. Zack stood between soup cans of bacon and worms as he cast off the dock into the underwater channel that ran into the cove.

"Here," Wayne said, setting my plate on the table between our chairs. "Eat."

Two cheesy, meat and veggie slices with breadsticks on the side. They'd been nuked from the state of the crust. Wayne threw feet up on the rail like usual. I couldn't read him.

I handed him the flyer.

"What's this?" he asked, flipping it over twice.

"Found it on my windshield today."

He eyed me. "You didn't meet her, did you?"

"No. Thought you'd growl about me going to Newberry first."

"You went to Newberry?" Then he snorted once before taking a swig of his beer.

We ate watching Zack until he gathered up his tackle and disappeared out of our sight.

"Still going to Newberry Monday?" I asked.

This was how it went. I find the cases, research their worth, then smile as I hand them over to the real agent to clean up and get credit for a job well done. I had taken the job clear on what to expect, so what more did I want? Congratulations? Maybe. More of a partnership? Without a doubt.

"Yup, be there Monday," he said.

"Do you need my input?"

With a strong side glance, he studied me. "Say what's on your mind."

Took half an hour, but I managed to cover Lottie, her three Friends of the Library, the three farm visits, Cricket, Lorena, then Bishop Bledsoe's Bel Air mishap. And for good measure, I threw in my disjointed analysis. "Someone's baiting farmers and blackmailing them into selling their land to them. I'll give you three guesses where the clues start, and the first two guesses don't count."

"Cricket Carson," he said.

"Unless she's working for somebody else. Haven't found time to comb the courthouse for the buyer or buyers."

His beer bottle swung, held by the neck with two fingers. "Unless it's the middle man doing the con."

"Lorena? Or Ginger?"

"Or someone not so obvious or quite so local." His mind already orchestrated what to say to whom and when. He was so much better at that part than I was. "Monroe's car's still in Newberry," I said.

He kept his attention on the lake.

"Don't think he ought to go back there," I added.

He finished the beer and nodded. "Agreed."

The wall remained, and I wondered how long it would stand fast. "Ten thirty tomorrow we go get Monroe's car?" I asked. Already had the keys.

"Ten thirty," he said. Succinct. Dispassionate.

At least we weren't fighting. I tired of fighting.

Reaching over, I rubbed Wayne's denim-covered leg. Fingernails meeting the inside seam of his jeans, I rode the line up and down his upper leg. "You will take care of Monroe, right?"

That drew a half-grin from him.

Unexpectedly made me hot as well.

His hand covered mine and stopped the action. "Yeah, but Slade," he said, "I have to operate business as usual. If I show any sign of compromise, Harden will report me, and you do *not* want some inexperienced agent on this. Not only can't I afford to jeopardize my credibility, but Monroe can't afford some guy in here who might want to make a name for himself. Or woman. Oh yeah, I can seriously see them sending a female in their attempt to balance the scales."

"Since when do you worry about Harden?"

He lowered his feet, and his voice went deeper. "Since he threatened to transfer you if I didn't handle this right."

I stiffened. "What exactly does that mean?"

"Just what it sounds like."

"He can't do that—threaten an agent. Can't you report him to your headquarters?" Wayne being threatened by my lard-ass boss, and the lawman listening. Way too wild to fathom.

Up went Wayne's feet, back on the porch railing. "We parted amicably. Even talked football."

Which riled me. "Let me see if I got this right. *I'm going to transfer your girlfriend if you don't crucify her friend Monroe. By the way, how 'bout those Tigers?*"

"Just said I'd do my job, then smoothed things between us with small talk." A slight tease of a look at me. "Part of the reason you make this job harder than it has to be is that you function in a straight line,

Butterbean. I didn't agree, yet he thinks I cooperated."

"Oh." I noted the use of my pet name. "So that's a yes on Monroe? You'll take care of him?"

"I'll do what's right."

"All our jobs are on your shoulders," I said.

"What, you don't trust me?"

"I'd sleep easier on the front line."

"So that's a no?"

Not what I meant. "Imagine if I were handling things and you were told to sit out," I explained. "And consider how poor Monroe feels? He's completely maligned, sidelined, and blaming me for it." The last fell out rushed and louder than I planned.

We let the subject fade off and chill in the evening breeze.

"About Ivy," Wayne started. "I'm worried about . . . have you had the sex talk with her?"

Finally.

"Of course. Years ago." Ally handled that, actually, but regardless, my daughter understood where babies came from. Not that knowledge was power when hormones stirred like a blender on puree. I was proof of that.

Clearly uncertain, Wayne hunted for words. God help me, if the subject weren't so dire, I'd enjoy watching him squirm.

"She had this box," he started.

Oh shit. "Box? She showed you?"

He sat up and peered around the corner of the yard, toward the treehouse. "A pregnancy test, and yes, she showed me."

My heart tried to kick out my ribs. I perched on the end of my seat. "Used?"

"No."

My eyes rolled up. Thank the entire heavenly host.

Sort of. If she didn't need it, she'd wonder why it existed in our house . . . in my bathroom.

Wayne had no kids, had little experience with any other than mine. Call me a coward, but I gambled and bought time by playing to Wayne's ignorance. "Tell me what she said," I replied, all matronly.

"Okay," he said, placing his empty on the floor and rubbing his hands across his jeans. "She said she found the box in the house. I'm thinking Ally got it for her?"

Oh wow. Hadn't thought of that angle. The lawman's investigative skills sort of mislead him in this instance, but okay. "What did you say?"

His mouth flattened. "I asked her whose neck did I need to break?"

The laugh blurted out, a release valve for my tension. "Oh, tactful, Cowboy. To which Ivy replied . . . what?"

"I feel odd telling you this."

"I've probably heard worse." I'd probably lied about worse, but still, I prepped for any shock.

He ventured on. "She said she was embarrassed that you didn't trust her to control her . . . urges. That you bought the test, or told Ally to, expecting her to make a mistake."

Didn't see that coming, either. And didn't expect to feel guilty she was right.

"I told her to come to you with this," he continued, gaze seeking affirmation or dissatisfaction. "But she feared you'd lecture her. I told her you were bigger than that. That you'd rather talk it out than be surprised." And he stared, seated stiff in his chair, feet flat on the porch. "Tell me I handled that right, Slade."

My hand went up to cover my mouth. Tears puddled.

"What?" His eyes widened. "Did I mess that up?"

I left my chair and threw my arms around his neck.

He pulled me back. "Did I get it wrong?"

"Damn fine job, Lawman." Maybe he *could* handle the news now. "Wayne," I said, looking him in the eye, attempting a softer stance. "I-—"

"Mom!"

The cry came from the drive, sitting me upright, Wayne's arms sliding down to my waist. "What?" I shouted.

Ivy stomped into view, up the stairs, and posed with her feet shoulder apart and hands on hips. "Your son has done it again."

"And your brother." Zack hadn't been seen in a while. "What's wrong? Where's Bug?" I took a second to analyze her for any amorous wear and tear.

"Bug left, and he's none too happy. You," and she pointed at me like an Uncle Sam Wants You poster, "need to discipline that boy. He tell you what he did?"

Wayne wasn't hiding his smirk well, so I tried to paint a look of seriousness out of respect for Ivy. "What?"

"He put a damn fish under Bug's car seat."

"Don't curse, Ivy," I said.

"Shouldn't have hurt anything," Wayne said.

Ivy clenched her jaw. "He did it like two hours ago. The windows were up, it got hot. It stinks! I was mortified! This has got to stop, Mom."

"I agree," I said.

She gawked at me. "Good. How?"

"I'll speak with him."

Slinging arms out to her side, she seethed, cheeks flushed. "What's the use? You think your baby boy's sweet, but let me date a boy that doesn't meet your standards and I'm a pariah."

Stung, I stood, at the same time marveling at her vocabulary and how we were almost the same height. "No, you're not a pariah, baby." I reached to stroke her hair, and she backed up two steps. The flash across her eyes indicated a red-hot message dying to get out.

"Two words," she shouted. "Pregnancy test."

Mouth agape, my words evaporated.

My phone rang. Monroe. My attention moved between phone and my daughter.

"It's work as usual," she said. "Whatever." With a flip of her hand, she ended our chat and darted into the house.

Still staring where Ivy left, I blindly lifted the phone to my ear. "Monroe?"

His tone made me cringe. "Thanks again, Slade. I'm on administrative leave as of five minutes ago."

"What?"

"Yeah. Tell Wayne if he doesn't fix this, his girlfriend and I are through. I'd transfer except this will be on my record until it's cleared, assuming I'm exonerated. And stay out of it, if you don't mind. For my sake, for my career's sake, if that still means anything to you."

"Monroe—"

"Don't, Slade. Just don't." He hung up.

Ally came to the door. "What did you say to Ivy? I told you she's fragile right now. Went and locked herself in the shower."

I sank to my chair, fingers to my temples.

Wayne leaned over. "What did Monroe need?"

"Nothing from me," I said only for his ears. "Ever," I whispered only for mine.

Chapter 21

WAYNE HAD THREATENED to ask for a transfer, Monroe fumed he would transfer if he could, and now Harden wanted to send me to Timbuktu if Wayne didn't *properly* handle Newberry. In a month somebody, if not everyone, would most likely have new marching orders, thanks to me.

Every damn thing I'd touched since that stupid radio show had gone sour. I could blame Lottie for drawing me in, but I could've told her no. A decision Harden would take full advantage of before all this was over with, against me or Monroe. Somehow Wayne would land on his feet. Just maybe not in Columbia.

A loss I wasn't sure I was ready to accept.

"Slade," Wayne said, gently laying hands on my knees. "What the hell is going on?"

"You said you'd be willing to leave, which I contribute to our screwed-up marriage proposal issue as much as Newberry. Ivy and Bug . . . the pregnancy test." And with that I hesitated, unwilling to take a crying jag, which I suddenly realized I'd fallen into, and turn it into a you're-going-to-be-a-father announcement.

He'd taken his hands off and sat, watching me with quite the experienced eye. "What else?"

I hiccupped, almost in shock that he didn't try to comfort me. Rather, Wayne waited, understanding me well enough to see the tug-of-war taking place. A tug-of-war in my head over which *what else* to say. If I mentioned my pregnancy, he'd write off my errant querying to hormones. The other, however, tore me up more.

"It's Monroe, isn't it?" Wayne said.

Silent tears spilled over my cheeks. "Yes."

A huge exhale from the cowboy. "Should've guessed."

I was lost what to say to that. Or understand how Wayne interpreted it. Mine and Monroe's history dated prior to Wayne, but not the same way. A die-hard buddy on one side and a lover on the other. Monroe being the buddy I couldn't toss just because I had another man in my life. A friend who understood me in some ways and on many levels that Wayne didn't.

Now my choices had damaged Monroe professionally as well as physically. Maybe to the point of no return, and that simply sliced through me like a saber.

But if Wayne couldn't accept my friend as part of my package, well . . . hell, I didn't know.

"Let me take the proposal off your list, then," he said.

With a hitch, my breath caught.

Palms up, he stood, then he lowered a hand out to me to rise as well. "Come here."

Tentatively, I accepted, studying him for a sign of what was to come. Scared shitless this was a goodbye.

"Let's start over," he said, not hugging, just talking. "No obligations. No deadlines. No proposal. I'll even take the ring back."

"Wayne," I started, unsure what to say next.

"No," he said. "This isn't punishment. Consider it my way of taking some of the load off you . . . for now. After Monroe's troubles are solved, we can talk. Maybe decide how this thing between us ought to go."

Jesus. What was I supposed to say to that?

"What do you say?" he asked.

"I, uh . . . don't . . . hmm." Yeah, I sounded like a dolt. Felt like a complete ass.

Karma was a bitch.

"Pick you up in the morning," he said. "Ten thirty, right?"

"Yeah," I said. "Ten thirty."

And he left.

I sank back onto my seat, returning my attention to the water . . . to Monroe . . . to my big, unforeseeable future.

A half hour later, Ally poked her head out the door. "Where's Wayne?"

With a shrug I pulled a leg under me.

"Oh," she replied, knowing better than to ask another question on that topic. "Well, Ivy went to bed early, which means she's texting with friends. Off in another galaxy. Since it's Saturday, I was about to offer my babysitting services so you could have a night with Wayne, but guess I'm too late."

You're not the only one.

FIVE MINUTES EARLY, Wayne arrived in my drive the next morning. With butterflies in my stomach keeping the baby company, I was ready early, too. Would we talk relationship, or had Wayne's withdrawal meant no discussion at all? And could we discuss Monroe without resentment on either side? We drove through a Sonic for breakfast burritos and Tater Tots, and then hit the road toward Newberry.

"About my rescinding the proposal." He bit into his burrito, driving with one hand. He took an exceptionally long time chewing a bite. "What if I left the ring at your house? For safekeeping?"

Sounded like neither one of us slept well last night. "I'd be happy to watch over it for you," I said, playing along, though I wasn't sure we were ready to revisit this subject so soon. One missed night of nookie didn't seem long enough to intelligently contemplate a path forward.

"Hide it somewhere, if you don't mind," he said. Then, "Thanks."

We rode in silence for miles.

"You okay?" he asked. "I mean, after last night."

"Nothing a night's sleep couldn't fix."

Well, that answer sucked. He could read it as sarcasm, or take it as an insult. Truth be told, I spent my night pondering how to raise a baby alone and how I'd ruined everything with Wayne.

Personal talk wasn't my strong suit today. Better we just deal with Monroe, the guy who'd taken the beating, literally and figuratively, for taking our advice. Wayne would have time to think, I'd have time to collect myself, and Monroe might have his life back in order. My buddy had become an unexpected wedge between the lawman and me. Not good. And part of getting to the place Wayne and I could openly and honestly deal with that wedge meant getting to the bottom of this case.

More silence. All the way to the Newberry exit. Something radiated off Wayne, which I hoped wasn't resentment and was just wariness, and he probably sensed a same wariness off me as well. We approached the town limits. "Where we going?" he asked.

"Main Street. Go through that light and keep straight."

The closer we cruised toward the heart of Newberry, the more the little hairs on my arms prickled over some zealous Southern ladies who I suspected compromised families for land. One made loans. Two were real estate agents. There wasn't exactly a great logical dilemma as to who had a hand in the transactions.

"Pull in here," I said, pointing to Lottie's white-columned home.

He did as told. "Monroe parked here?"

"No. I want you to meet Lottie Bledsoe. Your assignment is to address the claim that Monroe acted with impropriety. I don't want us to lose sight of why Monroe was even over here, and this lady was the catalyst that sparked our interest."

His lack of response told me he recognized some of my deductive reasoning.

Nobody answered the side door, and when I tried it, a lock held. Good. Maybe Lorena coming by made Lottie think twice about security. It was a quarter to twelve, and she was probably still at church.

"Come around back," I said, leading Wayne to the Bel Air.

Once removing the tarp, he whistled. "Now that's a nice car."

"Lottie's husband was run off the road, and Lorena Carson made fun of it to Lottie."

His look at me communicated he needed more.

"Bishop didn't see who it was, but we think it was a red truck. So keep your eyes open while you're over here. Someone might be sending a message to Lottie. Heck, Lorena all but did standing in this house yesterday."

Since I had him in Newberry, I wanted to feed him everything in my head from my feelings to a description of each and every person who'd been mentioned to me or crossed my path. I wanted him eager to pounce and dig down deep . . . picking up where I left off.

"You need to find out who bought this land," I said. "I don't care what Harden wants, while you're in the thick of this town, find out what Cricket is up to."

His head tilted down. "I think I can handle it."

I shrugged. "No doubt, but people are afraid to talk around here."

"I've run up against that before, too, Slade."

"Wayne," and I sighed. "I'm not competing with you. I'm giving you a head start. There are a lot of women involved here, on the good and bad side, and I might have a better handle on where their heads are, okay?"

Standing there in Lottie's back yard, silence fell between us again. God, I wish we could start this day over. The week. The month.

"So where's Monroe's car?" he finally asked.

We left and soon pulled into the small parking lot for the one-story blond brick building that housed Agriculture as well as insurance and surveyor's offices. Monroe's car, a gray government Taurus, remained where I last saw it, on the front row against the curb, close to the entrance.

Another car parked beside it. A cobalt blue Honda.

We parked beside Monroe's vehicle, and I fetched the Taurus' keys from my purse and handed them to Wayne.

Government offices took on a different personality on weekends since federal employees were staunch Monday through Friday grunts. Most of us could be deemed loyal enough to come in for the odd exception, but for the most part, these buildings sat like churches on Mondays, empty and dark.

Wayne walked over to the waiting car, getting in to crank it, while I strode to the main entrance of the small group of offices.

"Where you going?" he asked.

"To check the door. See who might be here." But I slowed upon approach. The main door hung ajar.

I toed it open, afraid to touch anything, and went inside. The office stood immediately on my right. Through the square glass window, clearly, the lights were on. No doubt that was Cricket's car outside. What could she be up to?

Using my shirt, I turned the doorknob. Not locked. If I were trying to cover up paperwork before an agent arrived in my office, damned if I'd leave the place wide open, but Cricket wouldn't expect us on a Sunday. Most anyone else would be in church evidenced by parking lots crammed with cars on the way in. Smart time to shred documents.

But I couldn't hear anything.

Moving through the lobby, the room seemed stifling for April, an odor like someone's refrigerator went on the fritz, making me sniffle. Maybe the power went out over the weekend for a while and came back on. Stealthy on my feet, I eased past furniture, avoiding a bump into anything, damn excited about the possibility of catching Miss Homecoming Queen destroying evidence.

Turning the corner to the two private offices, one of which Monroe used while he was here, I noted the quiet . . . and Cricket's door half open. Still, listening, I heard nothing.

"Cricket?"

Guess nobody was here. The car maybe parked outside when she caught a ride with someone else or had a dead battery. Regardless, tomorrow I'd gladly write Cricket up for leaving the office wide open and ripe for plundering.

I entered her office . . . and gagged.

My pulse hammered in my ears. The rank aroma caught me only a split second before the vision that would remain with me forever.

Wrists bound with white cotton cord anchored to the opposite legs of her desk, arms spread, Cricket lay bent over her desk. Or someone I assumed was Cricket. The body resembled hers, the crime in her office, but the victim wore a black garbage bag over her head. Her shirt remained on her back, but was sliced open down the front and fabric splayed to both sides. The body was nude from the waist down with jeans kicked against the wall. My insides knotted at the apparent scene of a rape . . . and murder.

Afraid to breathe in the fetid aroma, my hand cupped over nose and mouth, eyes watering for no reason other than horror. Who did this . . . oh my God, who ran loose after *having* done this?

No point checking for life. Not with that purple, waxy complexion. Not that I could make myself touch a body so obviously in rigor mortis.

I backed out, clumsily, trying desperately not to touch a thing. "Wayne!" Misjudging the doorway, my heel caught on the frame, sending me onto my backside. Panic surged, and I crab-walked backwards until I could stand up holding onto a chair.

I spun and bolted through the lobby outside. "Wayne!"

He rushed to meet me, gripping my upper arms. "Jesus, Slade, you're white as a sheet." He glanced over at the door. "What happened?"

Swallowing bile, I gripped his shirt. "Cricket's dead. And it didn't just happen from the look of her." Another spasm roiled bile back up into my throat.

"Over here," he said, and led me to the grass where I upchucked every bite of that egg and cheese burrito. But before I could finish puking the Tater Tots, Wayne left and rushed inside.

Spitting out the final touches of breakfast, I wiped my mouth on my sleeve and ran back to the building. Wayne yelled unseen from the private offices before I could get past the lobby counter. "Don't come in, Slade. Get back outside and keep everyone but uniforms out of here. I just called the locals, and I'm calling my people. We don't need you or anyone else trampling the crime scene, so get out there and protect it. Until someone else takes over, take down names and badge numbers."

Badges. This was one of those times when his badge trumped mine, and for once I didn't care. I would do as I was told, shaking hands and all.

However, I didn't have to do much for long. Not twenty seconds later, a siren cut the air. The light strobed between buildings until it reached our street. The vehicle's shocks bobbed once coming in the lot, and again as it came to a halt at the curb. Instinctively I took a step back.

Another siren screamed. Then a third.

The black-uniformed officer exited his car not bothering with the cap. "Who are you?"

"Carolina Slade, United States Department of Agriculture." I hated how weak I sounded. "I'm with Senior Special Agent Wayne Largo who's inside." In an afterthought, I flashed my abbreviated version of a badge that let me do internal investigations. "We came to pick up one of our government cars here, and I found the door open. Then I discovered . . ." My gaze roved to the building, the image revisiting my mind's eye, "our employee dead."

His eyes narrowed, querying.

"Cricket Carson. I believe she was raped as well."

"Son of a bitch," he said, trotting toward the building. "Guard this door," he shouted back as he disappeared inside. Crap, I read his name but not his badge number.

Up came flashing car number two, then three. It was about to get bat-shit crazy around here, and I took my phone to its notebook app to record all the names and badges.

But the Newberry PD took control, then deputies from the Sheriff's Office swarmed in to include Lottie's nephew and Royce whom we met at Hoyt Abrams' death scene at Tarleton's Tea Table Rock. I was relieved of the lone duty I'd been assigned.

So I located a spot under a willow-oak about twenty yards from my car and took a seat in the shade. Present if someone needed a rep from Agriculture, invisible if not. A place to collect myself. Good Lord, what had gone down in that office last night?

Yeah, I was curious, who wouldn't be? But I also couldn't stop the minor tremors in my arms, or the vision reappearing in my head.

The coroner appeared about the same time Lottie did, with whom I assumed was Bishop at her side. They scurried over. From the tie on him and the floral, belted dress and black patent short heels on her, they'd come from church.

"Slade, oh Slade," she fretted, craning her neck as if attempting to see through brick. "I heard someone say someone shot Cricket."

The grapevine already twisting and distorting, probably from Lottie's too-quick-to-talk nephew. "I didn't see a bullet wound. Let's wait for the coroner."

She turned. "You found her?"

"Yeah," and blew out. Admitting I saw the scene seemed to warrant it. I couldn't get the stench out of my nose . . . or the sourness out of my gut. "You got a mint?"

Lottie waved frantically at Bishop to hand her the purse he'd been toting for her. She rummaged through and pulled out a striped peppermint. Peeling off the aged cellophane, I popped it in my mouth, trying not to chew it up too fast.

"Tell me about it," Lottie said, extracting her phone.

I shook my head. "Nope, sorry. Pending investigation."

She drew back. "Are you serious?" She plopped a chunky hand on her chest. "It's me."

"Wish I could, but you of all people understand why."

With a stare of disbelief, she attempted to wear me down with innocent then straight on questions. Tenacious. My attention diverted to the fast-growing collection of vehicles as a silver Lexus honked its horn. The car sped in, stopped without finding a parking spot, and Lorena Carson swooped out, her door swinging hard enough to pop the hinges, leaving Aunt Sis in the passenger seat.

"Cricket? Cricket?"

A uniform stopped her, leaned over, and spoke in her ear.

However, Lorena shoved him aside and fought to break through the sea of cops. "I have the right to see. Don't I have the right to tell y'all whether it's her? Because it's not her, I'm telling you. She went to Columbia yesterday and isn't expected back until today. She has a friend getting married. They went shopping." She tried to pull loose from a deputy now restraining her. With a wrench of her arm and torque of her shoulders, she freed herself. "Do you hear me? She's shopping for a damn bridesmaid dress!"

Each of her words cracked more. Wincing, the deputy obviously hated his task at the moment.

But the cobalt Honda spoke clearly enough.

Blocked from entering, Lorena's chest heaved. Church bells rang from another church letting out. The nosy kept piling into the parking lot.

However, when Lorena peered up once, coming out of her wad of tissues to wipe her eye, she saw me. Then struck out in my direction.

With maybe thirty onlookers and more arriving, Newberrians watched in anticipation. The closer she strode, the tenser I got. No denying this Newberry County icon intended to rain havoc and God-knows-what accusations on Lottie Bledsoe's strange friend hiding under the tree.

Everything I'd ever wished on Bug paled in comparison to what this woman probably wished on me.

Chapter 22

AS LORENA CARSON approached me still classy from church, damned if Lottie, Bishop, and a small group of others backed away. When the tree hit my back, I realized I had, too.

"Why are *you* here?" Her words could etch glass.

"To pick up our employee's car left the other day."

She stepped closer. Close enough for me to feel cornered, itching to thrust her back. Dozens of eyes on us and not a soul offering to intercede. But if I reacted, I'd be the heavy, obviously her the victim, and no telling what part of all that would wind up in the Newberry paper . . . or Harden's voicemail. My angst had me thinking too fast, imagining all sorts of plots.

"What do you know about this?" she demanded so up in my face her coffee breath made my stomach roil.

No way on Earth would I tell her I saw Cricket trussed up and violated, a bag over her head . . . naked. "Like I said, I just came to pick up a car."

"Humph." She pivoted and parked herself under the edge of the oak tree's shade, phone to her ear, hand mildly shaking.

"Hey, baby." She nodded emphatically at those closest to her and pointed to the phone screen showing the call picked up. Pity all around. I wondered which uniform held the other end.

Everyone stared, each leaning to hear. The silence interrupted only by a breeze softly rustling the spring leaves overhead.

"Hello? Cricket? Speak to me, darling. This is your mother. Quit playing games."

Whispers ensued around the crowd while Lorena waited. Then frowning, she barked at the person on the other end. "Who are you? Let me talk to Cricket." Her color drained. "Senior special agent who?"

Wayne had drawn the short straw.

"Why, I saw her yesterday afternoon," Lorena said. "She'd reached her friend's house, and they were headed out shopping, then eating downtown, staying out late."

Cricket probably spoke to her mom not long after I saw her at the Sterling farm. Oh God. The last time we saw Cricket alive was from our hiding spot behind lace curtains in June Sterling's dining room, eavesdropping on Mr. Sterling's scolding to the girl. How absurd it felt now.

The warm body yesterday versus the cold body in the office. Regret, guilt, not sure what, racked me.

"No, I haven't called the friend. But I will. She'll clear all this up." Lottie listened. "Oh, stop this," she ordered across the phone, but strength ebbed from her voice. And she hadn't asked why the agent held Cricket's phone. "No, I'm standing in the damn parking lot outside her workplace." She choked a swallow, the *damn* not carrying the weight it should.

What mother watching couldn't ache for that woman?

The chief of police exited the building, scanned the area, then headed in our direction. She saw him, read his eyes, and with a soft *flump*, settled to the ground. With reservation a couple women instinctively reached out and started forward, only to be stopped by others around them. People selfishly honed in on the Newberry matron, afraid to get that close to the throne.

With effort, I pulled my gaze off Lorena's sad public display of loss and canvassed the crowd. Like an arsonist and his fire, the killer might be watching the drama play out. Amongst this throng, all dressed in their Sunday finest as if honoring Cricket in a pre-funeral showing, might be the sick individual who did this. Drawing out my phone, I took shots of the pockets of gathered folks and noted the red pickup truck.

Parked amidst the myriad of other cars and trucks, the red Chevy, a nineties model, sat innocent enough. I couldn't check out its bumper yet, not standing in the eye of the storm.

The chief had helped Lorena up and escorted her inside and out of sight, probably to the restroom. Her absence only raised the level of chatter.

Lottie rematerialized. "I just can't be hating on the woman today." Bishop rubbed her back. Not a man of many words, apparently.

A spring breeze blew through the area, with a few ladies holding down skirts, anchoring hats. I realized I hadn't seen women wearing hats since Sunday school summers at my grandmother's farm in Mississippi, but here they seemed to grip the old South ways as hard as they held onto each other in time of need. While also standing their ground to see what's going on so as to have firsthand knowledge at the next bridge game.

Aunt Sis roamed the grounds, stopping periodically to listen to one clutch of onlookers, then wandering to another. She often bumped people, and the person would give her a pat on the shoulder or a one-armed hug then send her on her way. Ginger included. With Cecil behind her, his scowl indicated he didn't hug old people.

Ginger's crisp stature had grabbed my attention with the clean lines of a navy-blue dress and two-toned spectator heels that pumped up her calves. Her figure caught gazes of half the males in the parking lot as she ricocheted like a pinball, asking questions. Cecil cleaned up decent on Sunday in sport coat and creased slacks, but not enough to bridge the obvious gap between their social leagues. Either he was really great at something that turned her on, or she wasn't all she was cracked up to be. Or maybe they were high school sweethearts who jumped the broomstick a bit too soon. Thus, Cecil's jealousy issues.

I wondered if Ginger knew more about why Cricket was alone in the office?

Only worry could have made the agent that animated and frustrated, fast-walking person to person, each nod and shake making her eyes puffier. Cecil seemed cooler than a spouse should be . . . but then I thought of my ex. Nothing like being hooked to a man jealous of his wife's job.

The barbaric savagery of Cricket's demise gave me no solace, and I felt remorse at having bashed her before. Any male Newberrian could be guilty, here, and watching.

Regardless, nobody deserved what went down in that office.

Someone pointed toward the tree, toward me. I needed to find someplace else to stand.

Jitters came and went all over me, repeating their paths under my skin. I'd rather be proactive and moving than standing here recalling Cricket's pallor.

"Ginger," I called, but Cecil turned first. I'd love to pin this on him.

Ginger swung around, tiny tears glistening on her lashes.

"Sorry about Cricket," I said, approaching.

She punched my shoulder. "Don't pretend you care. Don't even think about it."

Did she seriously hit me? Reaching for my shoulder, I glowered. Fighting the flare of temper, I braced my stance. "I still can feel badly for you, for Lorena, and for anyone who knew her. And I do."

Arm reared back, she poised her fist. "I swear, I ought to . . ."

Cecil grabbed her elbow. Tempers apparently ran rampant in their family. With the threat contained, I dared ask my questions.

"Were you aware of her plans with a friend? Were you that friend by any chance?"

She barked back. "We can have different friends, or hasn't that crossed your pea brain?"

I hushed and cooled my jets. Shock made people act oddly, and I'd give her the latitude to be inappropriate and hold judgment at bay. Yeah, a mixed bag of feelings going on in that realtor's head.

"Is that her in there or not?" she asked. "Everyone keeps saying your name."

"We're all waiting for answers," I said.

Cecil turned to watch the uniforms.

"Got your message on my truck, Ginger," I said. "What did you want?"

"Kiss my ass," she said with a growl.

Not as distracted as he appeared, Cecil nudged his wife. "What message did you give *this* bitch?"

"A surprisingly personal one," I said without thinking, "unless she leaves lipstick kisses on all her messages." Then I eyed her. "You did recognize my truck, right?"

Perhaps I delivered a little too much sarcasm, but these two had ripped Monroe's life apart, and my nerves weren't exactly on their best behavior.

Ginger spun and left, Cecil nagging at her. She mumbled, "Shut up. We're here for Cricket."

A touching couple. And my hands still trembled.

Aunt Sis bumbled by, talking to herself. "Jezebels for a hundred. One hundred Jezebels. Not Cricket, not Cricket, not Cricket."

Oh, the poor thing even in her fog realized something was amiss. I couldn't help it. At the risk of being called whore again, I laid my hand on her upper arm and rubbed. "Aunt Sis, are you okay?"

For a moment, her rheumy eyes didn't seem so lost. They bored into mine, straight on staring. My pity for her drove into my soul. "I'm so sorry," I said.

Her head shook slowly side to side. "They wouldn't listen to me," she said. "They cost us our Cricket."

Whoa, complete sentences. Snagging my phone to record this woman attempting to make sense, I tried to keep the conversation going. "Who cost you, Aunt Sis?" My fingers darted across the screen, hitting the wrong app, starting over. "Can you tell me who you're talking about?"

"One hundred. The Jezebels. They knew better." Tears spilled down her cheeks.

Back to broken phrases. Patting the woman again, I canvassed the parking lot. Where was Lottie?

I caught her working the uniforms for a story. "Lottie?"

She twisted toward me. I pointed at Aunt Sis. Nodding, she motioned to her husband to go retrieve the lady.

No. I shook my head and hard pointed at her. *You,* I mouthed.

She likewise mouthed, *one minute* and held up a finger.

My career, both before and after I became a special projects representative, had introduced me to the peculiarities of these tiny, rural towns. Each had its own politics, social strata, the gyrations of which often traced back to which ancestor did what, or went to jail for. The fact it had been a hundred and fifty years prior meant little to dispel feuds. That's how I saw this place with its engrained social gymnastics. I struggled to note every glance and attempt to understand the language.

Aunt Sis hovered near me, holding one hand in the other. Her thumb pressed her opposite palm, divulging the turbulence in that petite, bag-lady body.

I eased my hand up and down her arm while attempting to create a suspect list. All I could think of was farmers. Maybe their wives, but with the rape I couldn't see a woman involved.

"What?" Lottie said, catching me by surprise.

I pulled my arms back over my middle, then undid them, wondering if the action was instinctive in light of all the trauma here . . . a protection move. What if thoughts and visions found their way into the developing mind of the baby I carried?

"Um, Aunt Sis here is beside herself," I said. "She might need someone more familiar since Lorena is, sort of, indisposed?"

"Cricket," was all the old aunt could say, dragging the syllables out.

"Come on, sugar." Lottie directed the woman by the shoulders back toward the crowd, most likely to those more familiar to her. But as Aunt Sis left, she peered repeatedly over her shoulder, nodding at me.

Why did I feel as if I'd been handed the baton in a relay race?

With no task, I sat back down under the tree. Why had Cricket lied to her mother? I'd seen her alive yesterday between one and two, and considering the fact that full rigor mortis took place about twelve hours after death, I assumed she'd designed an alibi to cover her trip to the office. Which stymied me since I had figured mother and daughter were in cahoots. If Wayne wasn't looking at Cricket hard before, he would be now. If only we'd looked harder, and sooner, because Cricket might still be alive.

I'd tried. Damn, I'd tried. Or so I told myself.

Sort this through. Unlike the way cable television presented mysteries, murder was not the norm for white collar crime. Leaving me to wonder if we had more than one crime afoot, with Cricket simply being in the wrong place at the wrong time. What were the odds of that?

I shivered again in spite of the warmth, the sun golden on what should've been a pristine spring Sunday when everyone kicked back with family in the first short sleeves of the season.

The crowd stubbornly hung thick, and I continued to study the male faces. My thin knowledge of the men prohibited any sort of educated guess, and nobody looked the sort to tie up that tiny wisp of a girl, then maliciously bang her while she presumably suffocated. That took a demented lunatic, and the thought of him enjoying this melee in front of the building, maybe even envisioning it as a performance in his honor, terrified me to my bones.

Wayne exited and, hand over his eyes to block the sun, hunted for me. Relieved, I jumped up and hustled toward him, but he motioned to go back. Upon reaching me, he draped an arm and took us to the other side of the tree to avoid onlookers already eying his badge hung on the outside of his belt.

"I took pictures of the crowd," I said, eager to help.

"Great. You didn't touch anything inside?" he asked.

I shook my head. "Not the first thing. Even opened the door with my shirt tail."

"Good."

"Wayne?" I asked. "Am I right that she was bagged and then raped?"

"Looks like it but can't say for certain yet. She damn sure took a beating."

My hand went to my mouth. Unable not to, I mentally slid into her shoes. The jolt, the rape, the suffocation. I'd seen enough death in my last couple of years to last me to my own, but this one topped them all. From Wayne's far-off look, he seemed to feel it, too.

Wayne massaged my shoulder, like he needed to let my thoughts sink in before continuing. "I told the Newberry PD that we had jurisdiction but would like to pursue a joint investigation. The US attorney wants the case. The chief has a personal friend with state law enforcement, so SLED will be here soon."

Still couldn't believe the turn this day had taken. The massage felt good on tense muscles.

"You'll have to update me again on your farmers, Slade. And introduce me to your friend Lottie."

"Just tell me when, Lawman."

He reached around and crushed me to his chest. "Later, when I get free from here, which might not be for a couple hours. Stakes are pretty high now, so please be careful. None of your haphazard stunts." He pushed me out and held me in front of him. "Promise me. We have no idea what's going on."

"I promise."

He seemed so appreciative of me. Maybe thankful. "I've got to get to Cricket's mother and interview her while she's vulnerable. To establish a timeline."

"I have a pretty good timeline of my own about all of this," I said, then took a chance. "Why not let me come in?"

I expected the are-you-kidding-me look. Didn't expect his answer. "Don't speak unless spoken to, and stay out of sight," he said. "They have her in the ladies' room. I'll leave the door open, and you stay in the hall. If you hear anything, no matter how extraordinary, keep quiet. We'll compare notes later. You hear?"

I recalled only one other time like this. In Beaufort when he interviewed the kid running a tomato packing shed. That was the first time I watched him suck information out of a reluctant witness. And the real estate bent of this case reminded me of our bribery case in Charleston County, but his inclusion of me this time gave me my first sense of real partnership.

He was letting me be a player.

"Can you wear that pretend badge of yours?" he asked.

My heart skipped a beat. "Yeah, I think so." I dug in my pocket for it.

"Good. Less questions raised that way."

The chief might notice, maybe even SLED, but if Wayne said wear the badge, I'd wear the badge.

Damn . . . I'd never worn it before.

Took me a second to attach it, then we headed up the sidewalk.

"Wait," I said. "What should I pay attention to? What do I listen for?" I swallowed, agog he'd let me into this LEO world as almost one of their own.

"Missteps and lies," he said. "The chief has a long personal connection. I've only heard of her by reputation through you and Monroe. You, however, have some insight from previous conversations the rest of us don't have."

I nodded, afraid to feel important but eager to have a part.

We entered the building, the officer on guard holding open the door. My nerves a jitter, I followed Wayne until he pointed where to stand. He entered the restroom and propped the door ajar.

I flattened against the wall, feeling momentarily dirty taking advantage of a mother's tragedy. But if Cricket died because of her work, and Lorena had been involved in that work in any way, now was the perfect time to make the mother talk—when her heart was broken, when her guard was down, when whatever crime she'd baked up in Newberry meant nothing after the loss of her child.

Chapter 23

AS I PRESSED against the paneled wall in the hall outside, the Newberry chief introduced Wayne to Lorena inside the ladies' room. All the other offices in the shared complex were closed with it being Sunday. Wayne expressed his condolences, then wasted no time with further niceties. Firm and benign, he started with, "Was your daughter in the habit of coming into the office after hours to work?"

Lorena's voice spoke thick from crying. "She only lives a couple miles from here."

"Please answer the question, ma'am."

Damn, Wayne. While I understood his stoic nature, my heart couldn't help but commiserate.

"Give me my daughter's phone," she demanded. "And let me out of here so I can go to her house." When nobody immediately acted, she cleared her throat. Then again. "Sometimes she worked late, especially when her headquarters gave her ridiculous deadlines." Some contempt there, though shaky in delivery.

Wayne continued. "Did your daughter have boyfriends, an ex?"

"No. She worked too hard."

Well, Harden *had* given her an award for all that hard work. Footsteps sounded on the floor tile down the hall, but they went into Cricket's office.

"Had she spoken about anyone with a grudge against her?" he asked.

I noted his use of *anyone* instead of *any man*, then heard Lorena's quick defiant *harrumph*. "You aren't from here, or you'd hear how ridiculous that sounds. Everybody loves her. Everybody. She's the sweetheart of Newberry. Her heart and soul is with these farmers . . . her way of honoring her deceased father." Sounded like the radio show. She sniffled, but her words still held tears. "We used to be a dairy family and lived north of Pomaria."

Wayne pushed on. "Everyone love you as well? No toes stepped on in your real estate business?"

"Um, no."

Hesitation. So unlike the stonewall Lorena Carson I'd heard of.

"You're in real estate, I understand? That's a field that full of mines," he said harder. "Are you positive none of your deals have hurt someone?"

She gave no response.

And a thought smacked me. What if someone held Lorena hostage? Not figuratively, but professionally. What if someone higher than Lorena pulled strings? Wayne had dropped that hint on my back porch just a day ago . . . about Cricket being a pawn. Well, maybe Lorena was one, too.

"Who might harm Cricket to get at you?" he asked.

Better. *Come on, Wayne.* I tried to envision his expression. I craved to see hers.

"Nobody would come at me," she said, in a sad, half-assed effort to push back, still protecting that image. Had to be a habit of hers and a burden to bear incessantly polishing that brand.

"Who got ruffled from a price too high or appraisal too low?" he prodded. "We're only trying to find the animal who did this."

The word exploded from her. "Nobody! You stupid son-of-a-bitch, my daughter is in Columbia. There's a mistake here."

"Lorena," said the chief. "Cricket is not at home. She's dead, horribly dead in her office. Now's the time for you to come clean and answer the agent."

"I am answering him," she yelled. "You *know* me, Chuck. I cherish this county. Everything I *do* is for this county. Cricket, too. Who would mind that?"

"Then what about that sale last year when the buyer reported you to the real estate commission?" the chief asked. "Or the time they threw eggs at your office? Or the rotted pumpkins on the doorstep of each of your establishments?"

"The first was deemed unfounded. The other two . . . juvenile." She almost spat the last word. I turned over, flattening my stomach against the wall instead of my back for a change, doing anything to hear better.

"Unsatisfied customers, Lorena. Just like the man asked you about. Didn't you receive threatening emails? A dead bird in the mail?"

I tapped a soft fist repeatedly against my thigh. Ask the damn question, Wayne . . . Chief. Ditch the disgruntled customer concept and think deeper.

I flipped around again, daring a step closer to the door. Geez, I wish

I could see her. See how her eyes darted, if they instinctively moved to the door, seeking escape.

They went on another five minutes, but Lorena held her course as the most reputable trusted person in town with no skeletons in her closet, and only minor "nothing to see here" incidents. Her daughter was painted as the most worshiped young thing Newberry'd ever seen. A message spread way too thick to be believed, too thin a fabric of hubris not see through. The Carson image could not be challenged while Lorena breathed.

Would take somebody mighty powerful to control this woman. The conversation was waning, and like Wayne had said, the time was prime to make Lorena talk. For her, no considerations could be more important than her *missing* daughter.

I texted Wayne. *Can you come out a second?*

After a few long seconds, the lawman's boots echoed on the tile as he exited. "I scotched down the hall and whispered. "Why aren't you making her talk? She's dodging your questions."

"Don't you ever do that to me again," he mad-whispered back.

"You asked me to listen. This is my opinion from listening."

"Slade," Wayne warned. "It's a process. Don't toy with the momentum nor guess my motive." He started to leave.

"She's powerful. Brilliant. She sits on Newberry's throne. Who is so almighty that someone would make her jeopardize all of that and then kill her daughter for not cooperating?"

He stood there speechless, staring at me. "You think I don't know all this?"

He returned to the bathroom.

Lorena spoke to him in an eerie, low, firm voice. "I don't talk without speaking to Cricket."

"Lorena," the chief said, using her name tactfully as we all had, "Cricket is not coming home."

I couldn't help but peek in. She threw one fist on her hip and stiffly pointed to the men. "Frankly, I don't have to talk to any of you. I'm going home. Cricket usually comes over for Sunday dinner anyway. Imagine your expressions when my daughter is found whipping up potatoes to go with the pork loin I bought yesterday."

Wayne held up the phone as a reminder.

She reached to snare the device.

"Cricket just left it at work. You're all mistaken," she said, reading the unspoken tragedy in their eyes, drawing on what dignity she could muster. "Fine. Show me the body. I'll kill this gossip deader than dead right here and now."

Wayne looked to the chief. I would, too, letting the uniform familiar with the woman bridge the gap between reality and desperate belief.

"It's still a crime scene," he said.

"Then . . . it's not Cricket."

The chief reached for her. "Oh, honey, don't do this to yourself."

She backed up, bumping into a stall. "Don't touch me."

"Remember how I taught Cricket Sunday school?" he asked, sounding more like a favorite grandfather. "And how she climbed my fence to steal my summer plums? How I gave her and her date a police escort to the prom?"

Whimpers.

"It's her, Lorena."

A sob quickly swallowed. "Let me go back there, Chuck."

"Sorry, honey, the coroner has responsibilities."

Lorena Carson was no dummy. I wiped an errant tear and gave her five seconds to figure it out.

"Oh, no, *no*," she said. "Cut my baby up?" Each word escalated. "Are you out of your minds?" Screeching now.

When the wailing began, Wayne exited, took my arm, and slid us out of the building.

People scattered out of our way at the shade tree, and I put the tree trunk between us and the majority of folks trying to read our lips. Surely some of them had heard Lorena there at the end. "Any of these people might be mad at this woman," I said.

"Besides the farmers?" he asked. "And what the hell was that back there?"

"I'm sorry. You said this was a prime chance, and I had these thoughts I thought you needed to hear. I only—"

"Abused a very liberal opportunity I afforded you to learn from. Damn it, Slade!" He stared up into the overhanging branches, as if he couldn't look at me.

So I fought to regain ground. "Everyone assumes because she's full of herself that she's in charge. I say Cricket's death could mean more layers to this mess."

His answer sounded tired, yet judicial. "She'll be interviewed again, Slade, but how am I supposed to trust you in critical moments like that?"

"But," and I looked sideways at him, "like you said, best to interrogate her while she's vulnerable."

"She wasn't responding, and your interruption probably cinched that she won't today."

He was right. And I'd stretched the chasm between us in my overzealous need to, what, be in charge? I colored outside the lines at times, but I seemed to be blind to where the lines were the last few days. Not that my questions didn't have merit. "There's somebody else involved here. My gut's been telling me it's some big buyer with a lot of clout, but could be somebody else representing the buyer. But there's more to this case we haven't scratched the surface of yet." I picked a piece of bark off the old oak. "Maybe they're after Lorena. Like a mob thing."

He shifted his stance. "You're saying this was a hit for the Carsons not playing nice?"

Thank the Lord he was listening to me again. "Maybe. But we start with the farmers, get them talking. I'm still thinking this is a land grab with more farmers than I'm aware of, maybe more than Lottie can name. This place could be a *Murder on the Orient Express*, for all we know." Had I motor-mouthed too much?

Wayne leaned on the tree. Yep, I'd lost ground again.

"Can you say it's not?" I said, palms out. "Start with Troy Zeller. Hot-headed. Mad as hell about losing a tract of land. Yesterday we overheard him threatening to hurt Cricket to get to Lorena if she didn't let him alone."

His eyes narrowed. "We'll talk more, Slade, but I have to get back to work."

"Hey." I pinched his sleeve, just enough. "Sorry."

He gave me a worn sigh. "You just don't listen sometimes. You about screwed things up in there. I specifically asked you to just stay quiet and out of sight, yet you . . ." He pushed off the tree. "I've got to go."

I didn't let go. "Why not go after Zeller right now? He's a clear threat."

Pointing back toward the building, his voice dropped, hinting with condescension. "That body in there is talking to us more at the moment. Give me an hour. Then we'll talk about your so-called theories."

So-called theories? "Need me to do anything out here?"

"Nope."

"What am I supposed to do?"

"Wait," he said.

"So, no point in wearing the badge anymore, huh?"

"Not that I can see."

Wonderful. And my boss would go ballistic about me even being here. Between news and politics, somebody could call him, meaning he'd be calling me. Where would Wayne stand on that? "What about Harden?"

He turned toward the building. "He doesn't tell me how to investigate. This is murder. You have integral insight into this case, directional information I may need, and until I say otherwise, you're involved. Just stay out of the way until I call for you."

Rather bittersweet.

I turned aside, thinking our conversation ended and reached into my purse for my cell. A big hand reached around me and clamped my purse back shut. "Do not call Monroe."

Surely Monroe needed an update? He was a player. He'd paid a price for being here in my stead.

Wayne stooped over. "He's a suspect now. See? You're not thinking."

I may not be getting procedures correct, but I knew my friend. "Monroe wouldn't dream of doing anything like this."

"You and I understand that, but a third party might not. We'll get to him, but we handle this professionally, or I boot you out of the picture altogether. Got it?"

Admitting he was right gave me a traitorous feel toward Monroe. "Fine."

"Gotta go. Where will you be?"

"With Lottie. She's my CI. Might as well use her."

"Don't—"

"I realize she's a reporter. I realize she can't be trusted. I realize this is an open investigation."

He started to remind me of something else, then strode off. With purpose.

Without a hug.

I wasn't totally discarded, at least for the time being. I'd felt rather innovative having struck out on my own yesterday to visit farms, sharing muffins with the Friends of the Library around Lottie's kitchen table. My independent nature gathered intel and paid off to a certain degree . . . assuming it hadn't prompted Cricket's death. If not for me, we wouldn't even be in Newberry.

Which might be a good thing . . . or a bad thing.

Standing alone, a shiver ran up my spine but wouldn't dissipate this time. Seeing Cricket so violated kept coming back around, frightening me. Regardless what she'd done, innocent or not, she didn't deserve . . . that. The image of her over that desk, dead for hours . . . I shook again, fighting tears I refused to shed. A horrible, edgy fear I hadn't allowed before, crept over me now that the adrenaline had ebbed.

I turned my back to the remaining crowd, one hand digging fingernails into the bark. Regroup. What was I thinking before that vision slithered in and took me over?

With a huge inhale, I held it, then released. Glancing back at the crowd, I hollered, "Lottie," and waved for her to join me.

That's when I noticed the red pickup was gone along with half the crowd and my chance to tell who owned it.

Chapter 24

BISHOP BLEDSOE MUST'VE received orders to remain behind, but he watched his wife scurry across the parking lot toward me as fast as her black patent pumps and panty hose would allow. "How's it going in there?" Lottie asked with an eager breathlessness.

"As well as could be expected," I said. "Listen, you can name everyone here, right?" I scanned the area for effect though I knew nary a soul except Bishop. Even Ginger had left. And if Lottie helped me, I'd leave, too. "Is the county's clerk of court here?"

"You mean right now?"

No, Lottie, two hours ago. I looked at my watch for effect. "Yes, right now."

Lottie shook her blonde-gray curls. "I don't think so. She might've been a while ago."

A woman. Good. I hoped she wasn't too anal about rules. "Where does she live?"

Lottie gave me an are-you-kidding stare. "Why?"

"I'm tired of being in the dark about who bought these plots of land." Newberry's online database left a lot to be desired. I could learn more, faster, with hands on paper in this county. "Take me to her, if you don't mind."

"Ooh, does this have something to do with Cricket?"

"Maybe," I replied, seeking that middle, ambiguous, unrevealing stance with her that I promised Wayne to maintain.

But Lottie wasn't passing up the chance to shadow me. "Your car or mine?"

"Yours," I said. "I'll never get my vehicle out of here." Plus, Lottie's probably carried more clout. Everyone knew that red Prius. And the way some of these people felt about Agriculture, why not lead with whatever advantage I could get.

Not a mile and a few blocks off, tucked quiet and oblivious to the chaos behind us, we parked outside a two-story brick home. The clerk of court answered the door, leaving the screen latched. In jeans, with kids yelling in the background, the fiftyish woman quickly explained they were grilling hot dogs for the grands and not easily convinced to leave all that and open up her office for us.

"But Cricket was found dead in her office," Lottie said.

The politician threw her Easter bunny dishtowel over her shoulder. "I drove by earlier, and I hear you, Lottie, but what can't wait to tomorrow? We're expecting sixteen people in the next hour, and I'm still making the potato salad."

Lottie leaned in. "Ooh, love your recipe, by the way. Tasted it at the church potluck last month."

I'd left the badge on my waistband and rested hands on my belt, trying to appear as firm and purposeful as possible. "You can call the police chief if you need confirmation, but I can't begin to explain how urgent this is without divulging too much. Newberry has a killer on the loose, and the records in your office may help us with one of the threads we're trying to unravel."

Still wiping hands on her towel, she remained behind the screen door, unconvinced. "Think of the precedent this would set. I'd have people calling on me weekends, holidays, and nights if it got around."

"Think of how you helping solve a murder will look next election cycle," Lottie said low. "And I'll owe you a pound cake."

Twenty minutes later, we were inside. The clerk waited, even offered to help, for about a half hour, then returned home, but not before ordering the security guard to camp inside the door and lock up when we left. I let Lottie assist since she originated the complaint. She would've researched who bought these parcels if I hadn't, anyway. Reporters excelled at digging.

We hit pay dirt.

Divergent Investments, Incorporated. The same illegible signature on all the land documents. The typed version, however, read Samuel T. Baldweaven. The corporation established itself in Delaware, along with the majority of the country's corporations, to include shells, which this one could easily be. While still working in Charleston, I learned through a bankruptcy case that Delaware's government thrived on the fact they were the state of choice when it came time to choose a legal headquarters for an entity. No way I could convince those gatekeepers to go in on a Sunday and tell me who the board was for Divergent Investments. Bet their information was better found online than Newberry, though. A to-do item for tonight.

"Where are these other farmers we didn't visit?" I moved to peer over Lottie's shoulder.

"Got your map?" she asked.

Crumpled from being in my purse, I spread it out on the huge table made for paralegals and title searchers who slaved hours in this room for attorneys. Lottie read the legal description of one, then leaned over with a pencil and starred its location. Then again two more times.

"Obvious pattern," I said. Three farms wasn't a coincidence, but now we had a dozen. Just like we'd noticed yesterday while in the field, all tracts stood on either side of Interstate 26, with US Highway 176 the northern perimeter and US Highway 76 the southern. A swath leading from Newberry toward Columbia. The newly added dots were just more dots in the swath.

The sort of thing Monroe would've uncovered if allowed to follow through. The answers I would've discovered the first day, if allowed to go in full bore instead of snooping around and pretending I wasn't.

"What's being planned in this area?" I asked.

She shook her head. "Nothing, and I have a cousin on county council. He'd hear long before the average person around here."

I folded up the map. "Maybe he doesn't feel comfortable telling you."

With a grin and nod of her head, she closed the book before her. "Honey, with what I have on that man? He'd give me his wife's social security, VISA, and driver's license numbers if I asked. He comes over to the house once a month for dinner to keep me from including him in any of my articles, unless he wants to be mentioned, in which case he brings the wine." She noted my stare, and added, "But I can ask him."

"Please do," I said, checking a new text on my phone.

Where are you? About done here.

We weren't done, though. *Give me a half hour*, I texted.

To do what? What are you up to?

I didn't have time to explain per text, and right now Wayne was not in an explanation mood. I typed back. *On my way there now.* I had enough info for a start and knew where to come back on Monday. Hopefully together. Hopefully back on the same path, as a team.

I hadn't been so harum-scarum since my first case, making me wonder if hormones made that big a difference in my ability to discern priorities. Whatever the reason, I needed to regain Wayne's trust.

Five minutes later, Lottie dropped me off at the crime scene. People were gone from the parking lot, with only cop cars remaining: state, county, and local. Monroe's Taurus and Cricket's cobalt Honda, too.

Standing on the edge of the curb, Wayne spoke with the chief along with another couple of uniforms. When I walked toward them, he shook hands, left, and met me. Almost like he didn't want me to speak to them. "Get in my car. Best we not leave it," he said. "You're becoming a celebrity around here."

I slid in the car and buckled up. "And you aren't?" A six-foot agent with a scruffy beard and wide shoulders, who filled out jeans like nobody's business. And the cowboy boots. Like he wouldn't stand out. To women, anyway.

"Where we eating?" he asked, pausing at the lot's exit for my answer.

"Aren't we driving Monroe's car back?"

He shook his head. "That burrito disappeared a long time ago. I need to talk to you, and it might as well be while we grab food." All business.

I wasn't in the mood to eat but agreed we needed to talk. "Then probably anywhere but Jezebel's," I said. "There's Figaro's but not sure we're dressed for there. I saw a sandwich place on Main and a couple places on the edge of town."

Wayne leaned on the steering wheel. "Where's Jezebel's?"

Obviously he needed reminding. "Lorena Carson owns it, Wayne. We can't go there."

"Sure we can."

I pointed and read off the number of blocks then, squinting, asked, "What's your angle?"

"No angle. Just want to see where Monroe's problem began."

We'd morphed from a land scam to the assault of a federal employee to a murder. Wayne was shrewd enough to understand that this originated with the gossip of farm wives, but we needed to sync up. What he knew from the murder scene. What I gathered from the courthouse. What we still needed to research via Delaware.

We arrived, parked, and entered the restaurant so aptly named for a woman who capitalized on men, sabotaged a landowner for not worshipping as she dictated, then had him put to death. A woman who primped and dolled up, stereotyping prostitutes as painted ladies. Guess high school Sunday school did stick with me.

A creepy parallel to the goings-on in Newberry County.

A black wreath already hung on the glass door—probably on all the Carson businesses. We grabbed a table against the wall, like I had with Lottie before. Aunt Sis sat at her seat, her mini-television going. Tina visited the old lady's table and asked her to turn the volume down, then reached over and did it for her when the woman paid her no mind.

"You sure this is right?" I whispered.

"You think they'll poison us?" he asked, picking up and flipping around the one-sheet menu.

"Not sure I can truthfully answer that." I glanced around the small restaurant to see who might be studying us. Nobody I recognized but Aunt Sis.

Tina came over, her hesitation ever so slight at the sight of me, but any concern about me vanished once she laid eyes on Wayne. "Hey, welcome to Jezebel's," she said. "You're new."

No doubt she'd crawl in his lap at the mildest invitation. Made me want to say, "He's the father of my unborn child," but I got over the urge. This case was postponing that announcement even more since I could see this man sending me home out of harm's way if he knew. We ordered, and Wayne received a double-dose of I-get-off-work-at-five look from the girl as she returned to the kitchen. I shook my head.

He grinned back. Shameless. Making me wish we were still sort of engaged.

"What'd you do all afternoon?" he asked, though his gaze wandered often off me and across the room, toward the back, through the windows to the street. The average Joe would've been insulted, but I understood his ears were still on me. "I told you to back off," he added.

I ignored the remark. "Found more farmers and maybe a trend," I said, explaining about Divergent Investments. "And all the tracts fall in a strip of land following the interstate, bordered between Highways 176 and 76 between here and Columbia."

I covered the farmers again, their wives, wondering if Lorena's real estate company handled all the sales. The confounded secrecy of these landowners when it came to the rhyme or reason the land was sold . . . the debts paid off way early . . . the sales prices too low.

"You're missing something here," he said, buttering some bread.

Which made me realize we hadn't gotten warm bread and whipped butter last week. Was this a Sunday thing, or a hot customer thing? If a photo came along with the food, I was storming back into the kitchen and shoving little Miss Tina against a wall.

"How can we learn if Lorena handled the sales?" I asked. Neither Lorena nor Ginger would tell me at this stage of the game. I was public enemy number one. Then the light came on. "The attorneys closing the loans. They took the paperwork to the courthouse for recording, as well as performed the title work. The agency could be on their closing statements with distribution of the real estate commission."

He pointed at me with his second piece of bread. "Bingo."

"Damn, can't make that clerk of court woman let us back in today. I'll put Lottie on that in the morning."

"Good use of a CI." He slid the wrapped bread toward me. "We need to talk about Troy Zeller."

Aunt Sis gave a small whoop from her table. Diners' heads swiveled, but she remained affixed to her screen.

"Zeller said he'd control Lorena by threatening Cricket and is clearly one of the farmers involved. Lottie and I skedaddled when he got his dander up."

Wayne's forehead knotted. "You actually heard him threaten Lorena?"

"No, heard him brag about it after she left."

"Then we deal with what we know. The utterance of a threat trumps hints and suspicions." He leaned back as Tina arrived with his Sunday special meatloaf, mashed potatoes, and gravy.

Tina kept side glancing at him even as she slid my plate of pork roast and wild rice toward me, my palm stopping the slide towards my lap.

"Holler if I can get you anything else," she cooed, then left.

"That's Tina, the girl who delivered Monroe's picture," I whispered over my food.

He looked at her then dug into his meatloaf as if starved. When I didn't start, he pointed to my plate. "It'll get cold."

When I didn't immediately pick up my fork, he stopped. "What is with you and food here lately? You pig out one day and can't eat another?"

Oh crap. Did he suspect? "Nothing," I said. "Why are you wolfing it down?"

He swallowed, still eying me, then put his phone to his ear. "I'm headed out to Troy Zeller's place. Told the chief I'd get information from you then follow him out to the farm."

Wait, what? "Am I going?"

He shook his head. "Not after the last stunt. I asked you to stay outside and you couldn't do it, so why should I bring you to pick up a potential killer?"

Damn. "Wayne."

"Don't *Wayne* me," he said, chowing down.

Being pumped for information and kicked to the curb raised my blood pressure. "So I just sit here until you finish up?"

"Nope," he said. "You have Monroe's keys. Go get his car and head on home. I'll drop you off to get it if you eat fast enough."

"Never mind," I said, less worried he thought me pregnant. Slowly I slathered butter on a roll. "I'll find my own way back."

Tina started to come over, but once she caught my stare, she suddenly paid attention to another table.

Chapter 25

WAYNE JUMPED UP from his seat at Jezebel's and met the chief outside. With the restaurant bounded on two sides by glass, all the diners turned heads at the uniform and the guy with the badge on his belt.

I continued eating my meal, miffed at Wayne blowing me off. Almost delighted he might have thought me preggers, and now completely assured he didn't have a clue. That information would be mine to deliver at the time of my choosing. *You aren't in charge of that piece of intel, Lawman.*

The more I thought about it, the more I was sure that Lorena felt pressure from somebody to do whatever it was she was doing. Cricket had been involved, maybe coerced as well.

Cricket might've even talked easier than her mother, but it took the murder to make people sit up and take notice. Damn shame.

Wayne came back in. Guess they weren't going after Troy Zeller right now. Too bad Wayne scarfed down his dinner for no good reason.

I hoped he got heartburn.

"Come on. You're coming with us," he said.

Still demanding. "Sorry, I didn't hear you, Cowboy."

"Yes, you did, and please, would you like to come with us?" he asked, amending his delivery. "We want to pick up both Mr. and Mrs. Zeller, in separate cars, and they don't have a female officer on hand."

Took herculean restraint not to leap up and grab my purse, but I delayed a moment to wipe my mouth on a napkin before following him outside. The chief waited with another officer, and with a nod, they got in their vehicle. Joy of joys, I was riding with Wayne.

"Exactly why am I needed?" I asked after five miles of silence. I wanted him to say it.

"You've met these people. Troy is a hothead from what both you and the chief say, so I'll escort him back with the officer. You'll ride with the chief with Mrs. Zeller back to the station where we'll interview them."

"So how do I treat this? Do I talk to her? Do I—"

"We're simply offering rides to two cooperating individuals, so say as little as possible."

"I'm just the settling influence on her?"

"You got it."

We rode again in silence, neither of us at ease, both of us more lost in the situation at hand.

At a crossroad, a red pickup behind a semi caught my eye, but I could not see the driver, and he didn't follow. I pulled out my phone to check out the pictures of people, cars, and the license tag I took of the red truck back at the crime scene. I scrolled through twenty pictures, half of them blurred in my enthusiasm to be clandestine, including the one of the red truck. Damn.

By the time we arrived at the Zeller farm, I'd seen three such vehicles. During another case I'd become paranoid about black SUVs. Now I saw red trucks.

I'd been right about the black SUV.

When we arrived at the farm, the pressure hung thick on the porch when the chief asked for Troy. We were welcomed inside nice enough, but the flush in Verna's cheeks and the furrowed brow on Troy indicated some serious, long-playing conflict. I doubted they went to church this morning.

"Need you to come with us, Troy," the chief said. "We have a few questions, and I think you know why."

Verna shuttered, gripping the back of a kitchen chair as if it held her up. "He's been here for the last three days."

"Shut up, Verna," Troy said, and she cringed.

Lottie'd said he cherished Verna, but this behavior didn't jibe with her statement.

But they went without incident, Troy hesitating when he and his wife were split up, one in each car. Almost as if he might change his mind.

Verna sniffled soft tears in the back seat of the cruiser the whole way in. I held back questions, but several times I turned and looked at her, trying to communicate I was on her side. I wasn't so sure I was on Troy's.

But I'd become one of the bad guys to Verna. When all this was over, maybe I could make her understand. With Lottie's help.

At the station, they escorted Verna into one room and Troy into another, Wayne disappearing with the latter. At Verna's door, the chief waved at me. "You coming?"

He didn't have to ask twice.

The chief jumped right in. "Verna, guess you heard Cricket Carson was murdered."

She nodded, staring into her lap.

"Most people would immediately ask what that had to do with them," he continued, "but I don't have to ask that, do I?"

She didn't respond.

"Why was Lorena at your home yesterday?" he asked.

"I didn't talk to her."

"But Troy did," he added.

"Because I didn't want to talk to her," she said. "He was protecting me from her."

The chief cocked a brow. "Protecting you? From what? Some sort of physical threat?"

"He said I didn't need to know."

But I bet she did.

While I wanted to free up Verna from some of this stress, Lottie and I had left her arguing with Troy, with the topic being about getting Lorena off his back.

FOR A HALF HOUR, the chief covered when Lorena drove out to the farm, and why she would make that visit. Each time with no change in her story. I confirmed when Lorena left, trying to add credence to Verna's statement, but from there on out, I was as in the dark yet intrigued as the chief as to what went down.

For a change, I kept quiet.

"We fussed after she left, or rather, after Lottie and Ms. Slade left," she said. "Troy wasn't happy that any of y'all came out," she added.

"Did Troy threaten Lorena?" the chief asked.

"He told me he did."

"What happened from then until the next morning?" he asked.

A pen and pad lay on the corner of the table, presumably for Verna to write a statement. She wasn't writing, and I itched to, so I slid it over and took notes.

I wrote what she said, then with stars at the bottom of the page, noted what still hadn't been asked. Like why were Verna and Troy at odds about Lorena in the first place?

Freshly scolded from interrupting the last interview, I held my tongue, but once again, there were questions not being asked. Yearning to doodle, I held back, in case the chief wanted my notes.

Basically, Troy went to the barn mad and worked on equipment. Verna remained inside and served supper around five. She drank two glasses of wine after a nasty argument with Troy over the land deal, which she again refused to claim much knowledge of. Finally, some mention of it, but the chief didn't ask for details of the deal. *Come on!*

Verna remained inside the house, probably having more wine, was my guess, while Troy went back to the barn. She retired to bed early and woke to him making coffee.

"Ms. Slade? You have any questions?"

Almost jumping at the surprise invitation, I nodded. "What is Lorena holding over Troy's head?" I asked. "She has dirt on him, Verna. Just like the other farmers I talked to. He took out a loan with Cricket that he didn't need, then sold land he didn't want to sell, selling it at a ridiculous price. Something he has a right to be furious about, but instead he stews about it."

Tears dripped down her cheeks. "He won't tell me," she said.

"Were both Lorena and Cricket involved in Troy's loan deal?"

"I said I wasn't involved."

"But you suspect," I replied.

She openly wept. "He swears he hasn't slept with anyone."

"What's that got to do with Lorena?" Then I stopped. "Was he accused of sleeping with Cricket?"

"Oh, oh, I can't see that," Verna said. "Not at all."

But sex was a factor. My wheels turned, rethinking the Sterlings, the Huneycuts. Some pieces trying to fit together. What Ginger had tried to do to Monroe.

We bled Verna dry with little to go on except for the fact she went to bed early and could not account for her husband's whereabouts until early the next day. Leaving her with a cup of coffee and a box of tissues, the chief and I exited.

We tapped on the door where Wayne interviewed Troy, and the lawman stepped out. We took the conversation down the hall to an empty office. "What you got?" he asked.

I covered Verna's version of the time frame.

Scratching his neck, Wayne weighed the message. "Basically what Troy had to say. No evidence of subterfuge, but fact is neither one can account for the other that night."

"But she went to bed tipsy," I said. "He could've gone out and back and her not be the wiser, but I don't see them trying to cover anything. The stories seem consistent."

The chief offered me coffee from a pot in the corner, and I refused. "I've known Troy since we were teens," he said. "He owns a temper, no doubt, but while I've never seen him put a hand on a man or woman, he's still the most likely suspect."

That he knew of. "So why did Troy threaten Lorena?" I asked.

Wayne looked miffed. "Refuses to say he did, therefore, he has nothing to say about anything real estate connected."

"Of course not," I said. "Paints some serious motive on himself if he does." I sat in a wooden chair most likely older than I was. "So what now?"

The chief sipped his coffee, staring at Wayne. "Can't file charges, Mr. Special Agent. I say we gotta let him go."

A few moments later, after Wayne threw a last couple of questions at Troy, to no avail, the husband came out in the hallway. I retrieved Verna. Warily, both approached each other, the wife way more concerned than the man. No rush to hug. No hurry to assure each other they were loyal to the end. Frankly, I'd hate to be under their roof tonight. Especially if I were Verna.

All of us moved toward the lobby. "We're not filing charges," Wayne said, "but don't either of you leave the county." Then to Troy, he asked, "What's your cell number?"

Troy grumped it out. Wayne dialed. The phone rang in Troy's coat pocket.

"Well, get it," Wayne said, and Troy slowly retrieved it, a man not accustomed to being told what to do.

Pointing at his own phone, Wayne's eyes narrowed. "If you see that number or the police department's number, you answer. You don't want me having to hunt you down. That clear?"

Troy stared hard. "Clear."

He reached over to touch his wife's upper arm, and for a second I registered tenderness. Not sure.

"Whoa, my man, what the hell's going on?" came a voice from behind me.

With a scowl Troy watched Cecil Oliver stride over and reach out for a shake, his other hand gripping the farmer's shoulder. "You all right?" the mechanic asked. "The rumor mill has gone berserk about you."

Wayne looked to me for direction.

Ginger didn't follow her husband, going straight to the counter, demanding someone inform her of whatever it was she wanted. "This is

Cecil Oliver, the man who punched Monroe," I told the lawman.

A darkness rolled into Wayne's expression. "Senior Special Agent Wayne Largo," he said, hand out for an introduction. When Cecil hesitated to react in kind, Wayne reached over and forced the man to shake his grip . . . then reeled him in. "What are you doing here?"

Cecil forced his grip loose. "My wife, if it were any of your concern. Cricket was her best friend."

"Ah," Wayne replied. "Which does make you, and your wife, my concern. That and the assault of a federal employee." He turned to the chief. "Could I borrow your interview room again?"

Cecil's eyes widened like saucers. "Hey, this is harassment. I came so Ginger could ask what's been done about Cricket. Lorena would want her to."

"Lorena can check for herself," I said.

"And you can spare ten minutes," Wayne added, and with the barest of strength on the mechanic's arm, escorted him into the room where we'd interviewed Verna.

I started to follow, but my phone rang. Harden.

Then as the chief accompanied Troy and Verna out the door, I retreated to the other interview room, taking a call that could dictate whether I needed to bother reporting to work in the morning.

"What the ever-loving hell's going on in Newberry, Slade? I have to hear it on the news? And now my phone's ringing off the hook, damn reporters. Why haven't you called me? And your boyfriend won't answer his goddamn phone."

Truth was I should've called him. And Wayne actually should've taken the call. But neither of us wanted to juggle Harden's interference with everything else on our plates. He added nothing worthwhile and just wasn't that important.

"Everything happened so fast, Harden," I said, easing the door shut. "Wayne and I were retrieving Monroe's government car from the Newberry office, and . . . well, I found Cricket dead."

"And you never thought I needed to be informed?"

I sighed hard into the phone for his benefit. "You ever found a body?"

He grumbled, "Well, no."

"Then you wouldn't understand. Wayne's had his hands full, and I've been running errands for him. He's interviewing a suspect right now, so no, he hasn't had a single moment to answer your call. Cricket Carson's dead. It's a fluid situation."

I was breathless by the end. If Harden was as heartless as I pegged him to be, I'd be disciplined again by dawn.

"That's all you can tell me?" he asked, his voice surprisingly calm.

"Um, yes."

"How's the mother?" he asked tentatively, as if he cared.

"Angry, in denial, I think."

"Yes, yes, I can understand that."

Was that sympathy? Damn. Where did this side of the ogre come from? Guilt started crawling inside me, making me second-guess my hate for Harden Harris, but I checked it. Too much water under that bridge for one sympathetic thought to erase.

"Well, tell Largo if he needs anything, call me, day or night," he said. "And you give him whatever assistance he calls for. Clear your calendar. Your assignment's Newberry. Just keep me in the loop."

Says the man who hadn't let me touch investigations for eight months?

"I'll tell him," I said. Shock maybe? Or trying to avoid his obstructionist, bad guy persona for image's sake? To the press maybe, but why to me?

I hung up stunned and headed to the interrogation room in hopes of catching Wayne grilling the ass who shoved the wedge between Monroe and me. However, before I could touch the handle, Wayne exited with Cecil. That didn't last long.

Cecil brushed against me, taking me off balance and back into the wall. "Ginger?" he shouted, "Let's *go!*"

"I'm warning you, Oliver," Wayne said firmly. "You all right?" he asked me.

But I was watching Ginger, and she wasn't leaving without an explanation. Leaning over, Cecil apparently told her enough to raise her wrath. "They did what?" she screeched.

She started to head in our direction, but Cecil snatched her by the arm, almost taking her down. "I said let's go." Yeah, that grip would leave a bruise.

"Lorena's hearing about this," she yelled, then yanking herself free of her husband's grip, she pushed him aside and marched out. After a snarl at us, he left, too.

Wayne shook his head.

That couple made me nervous. "What did you ask him?"

"Same as I would anyone. Where he was from noon yesterday to noon today. He had good alibis with witnesses, assuming he wasn't lying. We'll check him out."

"And her," I said. "We've got to get around to interviewing Ginger. Surely she's full of information."

It was nearing dark, and I wasn't so sure I wanted to walk the streets of Newberry alone anymore. "What now?" I asked Wayne.

"We get Monroe's car," he said. "Then interview him when we deliver it."

He said *we*. And since this was Monroe, I'd hold Wayne to that. And I wouldn't be standing in some hallway when it went down, either.

We headed to Columbia in separate cars. I enjoyed thinking about Monroe in peace.

And about a killer who might not be done with his mission . . . because we had no clue what the mission was. Along with so many other people in this town with so many creepy personal agendas.

Chapter 26

AFTER TEN AT NIGHT, weary from a long day of death, interviews, and confrontation, I climbed the barely lit stairs behind Wayne to the second-floor apartments of Monroe's complex. We discussed no plan on how to speak to Monroe, and Wayne probably expected I'd concede to him. Frankly, I hadn't decided what to say, either, wishing we'd waited until the next day. Wayne knocked on door number 47.

"How are we handling this?" I asked Wayne, just as Monroe opened his apartment door, the bruises on his nose colorful. The swelling was down enough for me to see the indignation even at night in the dim porch light.

"I don't feel like your company," he said.

"Well, you've got it regardless," Wayne said, stern and un-company-like. "You letting us in?"

"Like I have a choice?" Monroe left us standing on the threshold.

In sweatpants and bare feet, a tee shirt from the 2009 Spoleto Festival in Charleston, he hadn't washed his hair since maybe when he left my house on Friday.

"You haven't even listened to why we're here," I said, coming inside.

"Whatever it is, I'm not in the mood for it." He plopped on his sofa without offering us a seat.

We sat anyway, me on the other end of the sofa and Wayne in the armchair. The place smelled like fast food, chicken maybe, though I caught pizza in the mix as well. "You heard about what happened in Newberry?" Wayne asked.

Monroe stared as if he might be deceived. Guess trust still wasn't his thing. "Why, someone else get punched?"

"First tell me where you've been since yesterday noon," Wayne asked.

"Nice way to encourage cooperation," I mumbled.

Monroe turned attention to me, puzzled, his scowl signaling a deepening distrust. "Not until you tell me what you're talking about.

Don't you dare play me, Slade. You either, Wayne. I deserve way better from the two of you, and if you can't respect me any more than that, any more than you already have, well . . ."

"Monroe, someone raped and murdered Cricket in her office last night," I said, before Wayne could throw another stern, unfeeling jab.

But Wayne didn't miss a beat. "Did you do it?"

"Wha . . . you . . . hell, no, I didn't do it!" Monroe's stare flitted from Wayne to me and back again, shock in his energy. "Y'all think I could do something like that? Why would I—" Then eyes wide, a revelation scared him. "Oh damn. Damn! It might look that way, but," and he turned to Wayne. "Honest to God, I didn't do it."

Which meant a lot coming from Monroe, a man who never cursed or took the Lord's name in vain.

"Do *you* think I did it?" he asked me, voice bouncing off his ceiling.

I shook my head and softly replied, "Of course not."

"What about you?" he said to Wayne, his voice much higher than usual. "Why are you even here except to accuse me?"

Wayne held his own, without emotion. "No, I don't think you did it, but I had to see your reaction. Now, we eliminate you as a suspect to avoid any scrutiny. Anyone see you in the last twenty-four hours?"

Monroe's shoulders released a bit. "I slept in. Been binge-watching *Breaking Bad*. Half the night and most of today." His head drooped. "Oh no, that's not good either, is it?"

"Watching cable the whole time?" Wayne asked.

"The whole time. This is just great."

Wayne laid elbows on his knees. "Quit whining, Monroe, and think. You had to eat. Did you cook or order out? Or better yet, go out and get it?"

Flustered more than I'd ever seen him, Monroe stared down at his toes in the carpet. "Wait. I ordered pizza last night, so there's that delivery guy. Crap, what if we can't find him?"

"Keep going," Wayne said.

"And ordered chicken wings earlier today, was just about to order from them again." He looked up, worried. "Does any of that help?"

I inched closer on the sofa. "Sure it does, Monroe. You have receipts?"

He jumped up. "Yep, on the bar here. And . . . and I used my debit card."

"Fine." Wayne walked to him and patted him on the shoulder. "I know you didn't have anything to do with it. You were a victim in all this, but we don't want others to have a concern with you, and fact is, we need you back at work."

Monroe gave us the biggest heave-ho of relief. "But Harden placed me on admin leave. I can't go back to work."

"I think we can fix that," I said, and pushed past Wayne, wrapping arms around my friend. "Harden's given us carte blanche to deal with Newberry. He was even nice about it." I leaned back and looked up at Monroe. "So please don't be mad anymore."

He hugged me back, and some of my stress slid off. We were buds again.

"Give me those receipts," Wayne said. "Get me a list of calls made with whom and when. I want everything you did, said, hell, thought, throughout this weekend."

Suddenly I wasn't quite so angry with Wayne.

"Monroe," I said, "may I see the notes in your briefcase?"

He headed to his bedroom. Upon returning, he laid the case on the kitchen table.

Pilfering through the papers, he lifted a particular piece. "This isn't mine, though. Seems to be a list of names."

"Give it here." I took it and read the handwritten note aloud.

Gathered for the 100. 20 names. Buyer: Divergent Investments. I'm sorry. CC

Then came the list of twenty, scribbled almost illegibly, as if in a hurry. Monroe's presence had unnerved Cricket, and I suspect if he'd stayed longer, she might've confessed her role in whatever was going on.

I immediately recognized farmers I'd met, and a couple whose widows I'd spoken with. But the list totaled twenty, more than Lottie and I had defined in the clerk of court's office.

"What's one hundred mean?" Wayne asked.

"No way there are a hundred farmers around here involved with the kind of land deal I've been hearing about," I said. "This thing would've exploded a long time ago. I think we're dealing with just the twenty."

"Monroe?" Wayne asked. "Any clue?"

"None," he said.

The memory started small, niggling, growing. I'd heard of the hundred. Not once but several times, and from two different people. Ginger mentioned it when I first met her at the real estate office, when she thought I wasn't hearing her on the phone. *Not in the hundred*, she'd said.

Then Aunt Sis. *The hundred. Jezebel's. A hundred Jezebels.* I presumed she spoke of harlots or preached the Bible. But living with the Carsons, even with Alzheimer's Swiss-cheesing her brain, she had to absorb some of those conversations, overheard business dealings and plans afoot. Who would pay her any mind when she couldn't communicate intelligently?

Had she been trying to speak to me all this time?

"Why didn't Cricket just tell me?" Monroe said. "We were together almost two days."

"Why not tell me when I interviewed her in the hospital?" I added.

Wayne took the note. "It's hard to turn against your own mother."

"Unless, like I keep saying, someone higher than Lorena had them tied up," I said. "And Ginger might not have been the dear friend she professed to be. More like a watch dog for the mother. Maybe the reason Monroe got threatened, then punched, because someone worried Cricket might talk."

Maybe Cricket tried to be good, and I'd been too quick to judge at the radio station and in the hospital. I hurt for her even more atop the guilt. However, I seethed that Lorena Carson would willfully get involved in corruption that sucked in her daughter.

Monroe went around the bar to the refrigerator and pulled out three soft drinks. "What does this mean?"

"Means we're headed back to Newberry in the morning," I said, taking the drink, "unless our illustrious federal agent doesn't want us involved. After all, he hasn't exactly enjoyed my contributions today." I elbowed Monroe, with a quick glance at the lawman. "My badge isn't real, you know."

Wayne stared, soft drink resting on the bar. "All three of us need to be in Newberry in the morning."

"I'm sorry, what was that again?" I asked.

Relaxing back against the counter, Monroe remained on the outside looking in, as always. "Sounds like I missed a fun day with you two love birds."

"You have no idea," Wayne said.

"What love birds?" I added. "Wayne cut us loose and made us free spirits."

Why I spit that out, I couldn't say.

The lawman lasered a hard stare at me, jaw tensing under the skin.

Monroe spoke up, in his third-wheel, I-did-not-just-hear-that way he did so well. "My, it's getting on past eleven. What time are we leaving for Newberry in the morning?"

"I'll pick you up at seven, Monroe," Wayne said, gaze still aimed at me.

"And I'll meet you two in Newberry, at eight. Now, which one of you is taking me home?" I said, knowing good and well that Wayne wouldn't dare let Monroe do it. Not after I'd announced I was fair game.

He shouldn't have said it if he didn't mean it.

And I should've taken the proposal more seriously. We were both idiots, and truthfully, I didn't want Monroe to take me home. I'd hoped after the day's chaos, and our disjointed act of working together, that Wayne would want to have a moment alone. See if I was okay after such a shock or something. Commend me for seizing the time to grab Lottie and search the courthouse. Just want to be with me and talk shop, collect all I knew . . . ask my opinion. Say he wished we weren't arguing and could start over again.

But all the way home, he said nothing.

"You all right?" I asked.

"Yeah, why wouldn't I be?"

Aren't you going to ask if I'm all right?

Almost midnight, my patience wore thin, my bones tired. "Just something to ask after such a fright. Long day and all."

"I guess," he said, staring at the interstate harder than he needed to. The closest vehicle drove a quarter mile ahead.

"Sorry about the Lorena interview," I added.

His sigh almost fogged up the glass. "My fault. Shouldn't have asked you in the first place."

I waited for the period on that thought: *Because you aren't trained, Slade.* And though he didn't say it, I'd bet two pay checks he thought it.

Truth was I wasn't trained like him, and my bullying to play like the big boys often set us back.

Yeah, silence might be best for the rest of the way home.

WHEN THE VISIONS of Cricket's blue skin didn't wake me up, the memory of the death smells did. Six times I bolted awake, and six times it took me a half hour to fight back to sleep. I counted backwards from a hundred, only to recall the hints in Cricket's note that had been mixed-up in the briefcase papers. Then I shifted to thoughts of Ivy . . . wondered if Ivy saw me anything like Lorena as a mother.

By morning, my eyelids weighed a pound each, yet I swung feet out of bed and to the floor just to be rid of the tossing and turning that made me feel worse.

I'd taken a shower last night to be rid of the day's nastiness, but if I didn't take another this morning, I'd never wake up. However, as energy creeped back into me, I wondered what Lorena was doing at this moment, empty that her daughter was never coming over for another Sunday dinner. No elaborate marriage with all of Newberry present. No grandchildren. Her husband and only child gone. How did someone go on after all of that?

Today might even be the best day to confront Lorena, as manipulative and cruel as that sounded. Her soul destroyed, her family decimated, she practically had nothing to lose in spilling reality to Wayne. Or me. Assuming she hadn't hired an attorney.

Though I couldn't see Wayne authorizing me in the same room as Lorena.

On the way home, last night's awkwardness in his car left me kiss-less and alone on my doorstep, watching his Explorer drive off. No walking me to the door. Whether he behaved like this because of the case or because he'd had enough of us, I couldn't say, and for the first time I wondered if I'd pushed the cowboy a tad too far. Like, beyond-return too far.

Maybe that question would be answered today. I threw on black slacks, with a white blouse and a maroon cardigan easily shed as the spring day warmed up. Flats. Always flats. Heels ever reminding me of a mother I never saw eye-to-eye with.

Then I headed back to the scene of the crime.

I thought I'd be early, but Wayne's government Impala already parked outside Cricket's office. With no desire to enter that building again, with yesterday's visual oh so vivid in my head, I texted Wayne. My mission clear, I left Wayne and Monroe auditing files and making calls, and headed to the courthouse to massage this list of twenty farmers, grateful for once for the grunt work.

If Cecil dared to came back to see Monroe again, he'd leave in Wayne's cuffs, so they'd be okay. And I made sure I stuck close to groups, phone at the ready, with the guard in the courthouse made aware who I was and what I was there for.

After several hours of record searching, I called Lottie and arranged a lunch date. While I preferred another restaurant, I went with Jezebel's yet again, for no reason other than to see which characters came and went, and who it bothered I was back in town. Wayne had predicted correctly I'd become a celebrity from the second glances I received in the courthouse, and my insides stayed a bit keyed up at the constant reminders.

Almost noon straight up, I packed up my research and drove to meet Lottie. Though only three blocks over from the courthouse, I wasn't comfortable with making myself such an easy target for slurs, confrontations, or worse, by walking out in the open.

Still, I beat Lottie there and waited for our table to come open back in the corner, stomach growling at the wafts of burgers, onion rings, pot roast, and gravy. The wait wasn't long with diners coming and going on their lunch hour, so about the time Lottie hustled in the front door, Tina escorted me to our table of preference. As usual, Aunt Sis sat at hers, in the opposite corner, her pastel garb a bit brighter today. I wondered who dressed her every morning, or if they gave any sort of effort.

We ordered two chicken salads, hopefully with better pecans this time for Lottie's sake, then I laid out the map along with Cricket's list of names.

"Show me these," I said low.

"Oh my, did not know about the Reeses." She inhaled with surprise and looked at me with amazement. "Or the Hankersons. Where did you get these names?"

"Shh," I said. "From Cricket, before she died. Mark them, please. And have you heard anyone mention *the hundred*?"

"Oh my goodness," she kept saying, shaking her head while dotting the map. All still within the same swath as the others. But when I described Cricket's comment, she shook her head harder. "No way that's a hundred farmers."

"Just what I thought." We moved the map around, noting distances, highways, seeking clues.

Then it hit me. "Lottie, a hundred doesn't reference people." My empty belly took a flip. "It's the difference between Highways 176 and 76. A hundred." I traced the map's marked region, nodding to my county expert across the table. "Is one hundred a nickname for that area of the county we've been studying?"

Lottie shook her head. "Could be just something Lorena came up with." Her eyes got all googly and wide. "Maybe it's Lorena's codename for all these sales. A secret name for some master plan."

I grimaced. "You watch mysteries, don't you?"

"The hundred." Aunt Sis must've been listening. "The Jezebels, the hundred," she said toward us, but more like staring past us at the wall.

I rose and went to her table, started to sit but decided to keep my distance and stooped instead. "Aunt Sis. What's the hundred?"

"Cricket," she said, mewling, agitation rolling off her along with her double dose of White Shoulders perfume.

"Yes, ma'am." Poor woman was likely overlooked in all the mourning, and I yearned to scoop her up in a hug. "I'm so sorry about Cricket."

A tear fell from her red, droopy lids, and for a moment she made straight-on eye contact. "Bad, bad women."

"Which women?" I asked. "Lorena? Ginger? Who else?"

Her gaze held fast. "They tricked men."

"So sorry, Aunt Sis." Though the full meaning of the trickery escaped me. I took her hand. "What did they do?"

The front door opened, the entering couple arguing, not caring who heard. Aunt Sis retreated into herself and fell back into the show on her mini-television, though her lips kept moving, repeating *Jezebel.*

"I'm picking up lunch for Lorena and me and taking it back. Quit dogging my heels, Cecil."

The man was practically Velcroed to her side. "Like you don't give me reason. How many *have* you screwed?"

"Shut up," she hissed.

Lottie quickly folded up the map, and I returned to the table, wishing Aunt Sis would hush. We could still hear her.

"Oooh, look at who we have here." Cecil slinked toward us. "The cow detective. With Lottie Bledsoe, our own scuttlebutt whore."

Lottie didn't back down. "We're just having lunch, Cecil."

Ginger, however, went for her phone. "Lorena, you'll never guess who we caught collaborating in your own diner, of all places." She paused. "Nope, Lottie and that Slade woman. And they've stirred up Aunt Sis. Yep. I'm sure they'd love to see you." Her grin spread cagey and sly.

I stood, instantly concerned we could wind up in the center of a brouhaha. "Lottie, I believe it's time to go."

Cecil bent from his waist, jabbing his finger. "Sit your asses down. If my wife wants you to stay, you'll stay."

But I remained on my feet. "I'm leaving, Mr. Oliver. Don't push me. Do you really want to assault another federal employee? Or face federal kidnapping charges? With all these glass windows and so many witnesses?"

One occupied table rose, the two individuals scooting out the door, shrinking my witness list. Upon their disappearance, Cecil shoved me in the chest as if proving witnesses didn't matter any longer. I grabbed the table edge to avoid missing the chair.

Lottie pointed her finger at the mechanic. "Cecil Oliver, you best rethink what you're doing."

"Shut up, old woman. There are consequences for people like you and your husband who stick their noses into other folks' business."

With that, Lottie shushed, her fire extinguished by the threat.

With a shove of her own, Ginger moved her husband aside. "Haven't you gotten yourself into enough trouble? Shut up. Just go on back to work. Lorena will handle it."

With a venom in his expression, he leered in Ginger's face. "All the trouble is because you're spreading your legs for Lorena and whatever man she signs a contract with."

Ginger paled. "That's not what's going on, Cecil. Jesus, you're so damn stupid."

"Stupid, huh? We'll see who's stupid when queen bee Carson gets down here, and I make her fess up to the shit she's making you do."

"Damn it, I'm not doing anything," Ginger yelled.

The bell on the door tinkled, and Lorena walked in. Haggard. While an extra layer of makeup attempted to hide the grief, it failed to camouflage the fury.

Ginger pointed at us, as if she needed to.

Lottie balled up in her seat, elbows in, fists tucked against her chest. No back up at all.

Lorena's stormy, rancorous stare honed in on me and me alone.

Phone behind me in my hand, hitting buttons from memory, I hit the call button, praying Wayne'd been the last person I called . . . wondering what kind of weapon Lorena might be hiding, and how long last night she stewed over using it.

Standing between Aunt Sis's table and Lottie's, I prayed my phone maintained an open channel to Wayne so he could hear all of this.

Tina trotted out of the kitchen, a tray of two entrees on her shoulder, then halted at the sight of Carson management in the middle of Jezebel's floor. Another couple took advantage of the diverted attention and darted out the front, then a lone gentleman. No more customers left.

Bewildered, the waitress laid the tray down on the counter and backed up, though too curious to completely disappear.

Dressed professionally, daring to appear in town and demonstrate she was not prostrate with grief, Lorena remained only momentarily distracted by her waitress. Quickly she returned her attention to me. "What the hell are you doing in my diner, Ms. Slade?"

Ginger crossed her arms, watching the show, a half-sneer clear and smug. Cecil stood in the center of the diner listening, an eagerness in his expression. This was a game to them. Drama from a front row seat.

I remained standing, feeling safer on the balls of my feet, grateful nobody brandished a weapon. I wasn't far from darting out the door myself, with or without Lottie. "Just trying to help, Ms. Carson," I said, while trying to time my escape.

This morning I'd hoped she might be more attuned to divulging secrets with all her family gone, but that wasn't happening now, not with this audience. Her temperament dictated quite the opposite, actually. The woman was made of strong, sinewy stuff.

Taut and slow, she moved forward, like a violin bow, sending chills into me. Unpredictable.

Muscles tense, I started mapping out the best way to run out the door for real . . . and who I'd knock aside in the process.

"You have interfered one time too many!" she yelled. All of us jumped, most taking a step back from her. Including me.

"I've just been doing my job," I managed to say. *Wow, that sounded lame.*

With a snap of her head, she disagreed. "You were not supposed to be here, were you? Yet you came anyway. One sneaky move after another, underhanded, without the authority to investigate my Cricket." That scowl could've fried a brick. "I know your boss. If it's the last thing I do, I'll take your job." Then she spread her arms. "You are the catalyst to all leading up to this day. To my daughter's pending funeral."

I shook my head. "Ma'am, I had nothing to do with your daughter's death. We're still trying to uncover who did it. Agriculture appreciated Cricket. We gave her an award just a week ago on the radio show and are so appreciative of her talents, her contributions." I took a breath, hearing it quiver. "You should be proud."

You should be ashamed, was more like it.

"No," she screamed, and I withdrew into myself as if dodging a rock. "You do *not* get to talk about my daughter."

Then the front glass door opened. Dumbfounded anyone would enter this mayhem, everyone took a pause to identify this poor soul stumbling into a bad scene.

Huge, filling up the opening from shoulder to shoulder, the sixty-something farmer made his way into the diner. His coat seemed warm for the weather, but otherwise he appeared like he'd stepped off a tractor and come in for a meal. "I'm looking for you, Lorena," he said, and turned the *Open* sign on the door to *Closed.*

Chapter 27

I TURNED AND RAN toward the kitchen, but Tina zigged in my path. We bounced off each other, her against the counter, and me against the brick wall.

"Nobody leaves, agriculture lady," Troy said, not loud, but concrete solid enough to make me not think twice about a second attempt to escape.

"You can't keep us against our will, Troy," I said, frozen and afraid to go back into the dining area where my chances for freedom became nil.

He shook his head. "Got no interest in you, but I need time to deal with Ms. Carson without any of you running off grabbing the police." After a quick study of the room, measuring, Troy pulled a short-barreled, pump-action shotgun out from under his coat. No stock. I'd never seen anything like it.

Squeals and gasps panned the scene, and I almost crawled under the nearest table. Ginger moved toward Cecil, who didn't give a damn about his wife, instead his scowl bearing down on the farmer. Aunt Sis watched without any apparent concern.

Lorena didn't flinch, but her momentum had stalled in all this, like she wasn't sure how Troy Zeller fit into the setting. She remained stiff, resolute.

"Now, Ms. Slade, get back in the dining room and stay quiet," Troy ordered.

With all eyes on me, I slid back over to my chair next to Lottie. She reached over and patted my leg under the table, her quivering unmistakable. "I'm sorry," she said.

I gave her a meager shake of my head that none of this was her fault.

"You're an idiot," Lorena said to the man.

Troy released a small growl. "Not arguing with you about that, Lorena. A huge idiot, which I owe a lot to you."

Relieved to have the attention no longer on me, with shaky hands under the table, I studied my phone. Damn, I hadn't hit the right button before. Quickly, I called Wayne, lowered the sound, and slid the device into my cardigan's pocket—the mic directed up—and prayed he wouldn't yell loud enough to be heard. Likewise, that he wouldn't hang up.

"Just leave, Troy," Lorena said.

"Don't think so." His bass, monotone reply chilled us all.

"What about Verna?" came the voice from beside me. Took a second for me to fathom that my huddled friend had dared to enter the exchange. "Thought you loved her."

Wheeling, Troy bellowed, "You don't get to talk about my wife!"

Lottie cringed and spoke no more.

My anxiety in overdrive, I smelled trouble. Not little trouble, or small-town fussy trouble, but roiling danger. Surely nobody thought they were holding anyone against their will, but by definition we sure were smack dab in the middle of a hostage situation.

"Come out here where I can see you, too, waitress," Troy said, enough irritation in his voice to explain his patience wore thin. Tina scooted over near Aunt Sis, sat, and hugged the poor old soul.

The entire room now knew to stay where they were. Yep, nobody failed to see we were hostages now.

"Don't make a federal case out of all this," Lorena said.

Too late. This squabble, small-town scandal, whatever-the-hell conflict these people held had long ago crossed into that territory. Not that it crossed their minds . . . not that they would care. Bad blood, imagined and real, had spilled one time too many for anyone to consider right or wrong, or whose jurisdiction it fell into.

Troy stood about ten feet from Lorena, with Ginger and Cecil about four feet on the other side of her. Lottie and I at one table. Tina and Aunt Sis at another.

"Hey, girl," Troy said, his strong voice not needing to yell. "You, waitress."

"Her name's Tina," Lorena spouted.

He waved the gun loosely around the room, not at anyone, but just because he had it in his hand. "Close these blinds," he ordered.

Poor Tina looked about to faint, but she began at the window nearest her, behind Aunt Sis, and made the rounds. Toward Main Street, covering that glass. Then parallel to Main, lowering blinds on that whole wall of glass, except for the front door which had no cover at all. Unexpectedly, she proved adept at the task, operating quickly, each of us watching, waiting, praying someone outside saw and wondered. As she reached the brick wall and turned toward Troy, I caught sight of a red truck . . . wondering whose it was, and if whoever was inside with us.

And I was dying to check my phone.

I sat with the brick wall behind me, the kitchen to my right. Tina walked from that corner, diagonally toward Troy to reach Aunt Sis's table back nearer the kitchen, opposite from Lottie and me. But as she neared him, he silently motioned for her to stand against the glass instead. Then he motioned for Ginger and Lorena to do the same.

"I will not," Lorena protested, ramrod stiff and uncompromising.

"Shut up and do it," he said.

Ginger took her arm, and both moved beside Tina.

Cecil, however, eased toward my table, only for Troy to shake his head and motion again toward Tina. Cecil relocated in their direction but didn't back up against the window like the women. I recognized a man sizing up the opposition . . . hunting for opportunity.

Lottie and I pretended we were invisible. I barely breathed.

With his legs braced shoulder-width apart, Troy lowered the gun, as if he'd set up the room like he wanted. He stood directly in my line of sight of the door, but not completely blocking my view outside. Cars went by, a couple of people walked past, nobody looking in.

Troy's enormity reminded me of some rustic, justice-seeking vigilante in overalls. Fearful but in an anti-hero sort of way. A barrel-chested, broad-shouldered Clint Eastwood without hair. Scary, with a sense of justification. Or maybe that was because he hadn't lined me up against the wall with the folks he counted responsible for his troubles.

"My wife's home packing, Lorena," he said. "People already calling my farm and canceling orders for my beef. News already out I'm a murderer." He turned toward Lottie. "Thanks for stirring things up, newspaper woman. And you." He bellowed the last word, giving me a jolt. "Federal agents interrogated me, accused me of murder."

Again with the shotgun gesture, at my partner and me. When we didn't stand, he sighed with impatience. "Up!" Waving the gun. "Against the wall with the others."

Lottie's complexion was pale as the tablecloth. I worried she wouldn't be able to move on her own, so I assisted her, then arm in arm, we circumnavigated a couple of tables and joined the group.

He watched, and I could almost feel the hum of nerves in the man. Unless those were my own.

"Someone's trying to set my ass up for killing Cricket," he said.

Stepping out, Lorena fisted her hands, Ginger reaching for a sleeve to bring her back in line. "You threaten me, threaten *her*, then she's dead." Her arms vibrating, she pulled loose from Ginger. "Who the hell else could it be but you, Troy? Our contract didn't justify killing my daughter."

With a swing of the gun, he motioned toward Ginger, who ducked then squatted to half her height. "You have your slut come on to me, give me a blow job, take a pic, and force me to sell my property. Of course, I'm going to take issue, and damn right I'll hold a fuckin' grudge."

Lorena angrily wiped tears off her cheeks. Then with a voice filled with rage cried, "But not Cricket. None of that warranted her dying."

The tough shell had cracked. I wasn't even sure the woman was in her right mind, and who could blame her. Her kingdom was crashing down.

Troy's face darkened as if her emotions only infuriated him more.

"She was only doing what I told her to do," Lorena continued, fighting hard not to crumble to pieces. "And I was only doing what I was told to do."

Bull's-eye. My suspicion validated. "By whom?" I asked, before I could advise myself now was not the time. Panic zinged through me at being so dense.

And as expected, the entire room of folks turned to me, like I'd lost my mind. Maybe I had. I kept going when Troy didn't aim the gun at me. "Who's pulling your strings, Lorena? I don't think Mr. Zeller killed Cricket. So who did?"

Frankly, I wasn't a hundred percent sure Troy hadn't killed Cricket, but the method in which she died didn't match the person Lottie had described to me before. I never saw the loving husband in him that Lottie professed existed, but more so, the cold, calculated nature of the crime clashed with his bull-in-a-china-shop approach.

In other words, that guy in Cricket's office wouldn't be standing here not sure what the hell he wanted to do.

I wasn't convinced Lorena thought Troy did it, either, and was more certain she just wanted to lash out. That she mourned her daughter and rued her choices was obvious. She wanted an excuse to turn attention from the fact that her scheme had tragically backfired.

Troy reached into his pocket, and I defensively turned to the side in case it was a pistol. But instead of a weapon, he extracted a ring.

"You bastard!" Lorena lunged at Troy, whose exaggerated shrug only shoved her back into a table. She didn't go down, but she leaned over the table, her bravado gone. "That only proves you did it," she said, weeping. "Cricket always wore that ring on a chain around her neck. It was her father's 4-H ring." And with that she sobbed.

And I recalled seeing that ring around Cricket's neck at the radio station. She'd held it admirably in her hand, explaining to the radio audience how it had been her father's.

If Troy hadn't had his left side to the front door and his attention on Lorena, he would've seen the two police cruisers go by. Hoping down to my core that they were setting up, I tried not to stare, tried not to give our captor any indication that the cavalry may have arrived.

Then I saw Wayne peer in through the front door glass about halfway down, below line of sight to avoid immediate detection, and my heart almost hurt at the relief.

Troy was still studying the ring. "Found it in my coat pocket this morning. Wasn't mine, and I didn't put it there." His gaze rose to meet Lorena's. "How'd you plant it?"

This moment was critical. Before cops busted in, or however they intended to play this out, we could draw some conclusions here. We didn't need some small-town SWAT team taking the man down before we learned what happened. "You wore that coat yesterday?" I asked, thinking I remembered it.

"Yes," he said.

"Where did you go Sunday other than to the police station with us?" I asked.

He lasered on me. Good. "Nowhere," he said.

"You stupid idiot." Lorena used the table and pushed back up tall. "You think a cop planted it? One of *our* cops? God, I gave you more credit than you're worth."

Troy stopped and pondered, and I could sense him replaying yesterday evening. I had been there, and more than cops had crossed the farmer's path.

Troy looked over . . . at Cecil.

Which puzzled Lorena. She followed Troy's stare twice, missing the point.

But I got it.

"Y'all were there," I said, motioning at Ginger, then Cecil.

"So were you," Ginger spouted.

But I paid more attention to Cecil.

He stiffened, with a twitchy shrug. "Why you looking at me, bitch?"

I shook Lottie's grip off my arm and took a step forward. "You made a concerted effort to speak to Troy," I said. "Shook his hand, patted his back, practically hugged the guy. Troy didn't seem too natural about accepting that hug."

Troy slowly swung the shotgun around toward Cecil, but crazily, the mechanic remained honed on me, his accuser.

"You're just trying to take attention off yourself," Cecil said. "You came to town trying to fire Cricket."

"So now you think I killed her?"

He shrugged in a who-knows manner.

For a split second I debated on how far to go, how ugly to speak in front of a hurting mother. Making a decision, I went for it. "You slapped her around first."

Cheeks tear-streaked, Lorena listened. So did Troy, as if eager for the story.

"You stripped her, tied her bent over the desk," I continued.

Ginger gasped, hand over her mouth. Lottie held onto Aunt Sis, gathering her into a protective hug.

"You raped her . . . then suffocated her with a garbage bag."

I heard whimpers and wasn't sure from whom because there were so many. Hating being the one to release details, I wanted to hold attention, buy time for the cops outside, and judge from the reactions if what my gut told me was right.

Cecil wasn't moving. And he hadn't protested.

Before I could warn Troy not to, he relaxed his weapon. Cecil grabbed it loose, and with a shoulder shove, toppled the big man back over a table.

I couldn't tell who was more willing to kill whom. Cecil a rapist and murderer. Ginger a whore. And Lorena guilty as the mastermind of a plan that went bad. And Troy, losing both land and his marriage, having nothing left to live for.

Lorena made the next move. In spite of the gun, she rushed toward her daughter's killer, but Ginger held her back when Cecil leveled the shotgun on Lorena.

"You degenerate piece of trash," she screeched. "You degrade and defile my daughter and then murder her?"

Ginger, tears streaking her cheeks, her grip tighter on her boss, yelled, "Cecil, put that damn gun down."

Tight-jawed and red-faced, Cecil's temper flared. "You believe this?

You have no evidence, no reason to believe these accusations, but because that bitch you work for says it, you assume it's true. You worthless sluts are the architects of this entire mess. Everything bad in this town occurred by your hands in one way or another."

Bent over at the waist, he spit out his wrath. "You pimped out my wife." He kept the gun on Lorena but turned next to his bride. "And you, you cheap whore."

Jezebel couldn't help but come to mind, and suddenly I sensed that Aunt Sis had done her damnedest to tell me about way more than Bible stories.

"I wasn't the only one," Ginger said, and pointed at Tina. "She helped."

Tina crouched to the floor, shivering, head in her hands.

Around the edges of the blinds, I noticed people darting outside.

"I don't give a damn if Tina's the bicycle that every man in the county rides, she's not my wife. You are!" Cecil declared.

Says the rapist. He hadn't confessed, but I knew. My gut knew.

But if this volatile room didn't settle down, someone in here was getting hurt . . . or killed.

"Cecil," I said softly, to keep him from arguing with the two women intent on antagonizing him. "You're at a turning point here. There's no direct evidence you did anything except punch my employee in the nose." *Except maybe forensic evidence in Cricket's office. I could only hope.* "You pull that trigger, and you're a dead man. You will not walk out of here alive. Is that really what you want? Or do you want to live to tell your story?"

His stillness told me he pondered my logic. But in a sudden interest, Cecil scanned the room, measuring where each of us was. Troy had remained on the floor, watching the spectacle, the closest to the door.

"The ag lady makes sense," Troy said. "Nobody can prove who put that ring in my pocket. As much as I may not like her, she's right. You shoot, and you're dead meat."

Smart. Cecil would listen more to a man, and Troy had correctly read my effort.

"Lorena," I said, keeping attention off Cecil, in hope he'd lose his itch to pull that trigger. "I chuckle at how shrewd you are. You had the entire room, to include me, pointing at Cecil just to take the spotlight off of you. Like he said, you are the architect of this disaster. You and your co-hort, higher-up, whoever."

"Yeah," Cecil said, waving his weapon. "Maybe you weren't towing the line well enough to suit 'em. They killed Cricket to straighten you out."

Through the ruined mascara and unkempt hair, Lorena flashed a ridiculous smile at me. "You don't know?" Her laugh was painful to hear, sad and untethered. And made me wonder what I overlooked.

I used what we'd learned about the daughter, what had changed my perception. "Cricket tried to tell us in a note, Lorena. She couldn't stand her role in this conspiracy."

Lorena glared, too stubbornly curious as to what I spoke of to shut me up.

"Yes," I said. "I'm aware of twenty farmers and your one hundred code name for the area of land you fought to acquire. We have more intel, but I believe that's information more reserved for the courtroom. If I were you, I'd be trying to talk a deal with Agent Wayne Largo."

Everyone stood petrified, even Aunt Sis, except for her one softly spoken word, "Jezebel."

Laughter bubbled up from Cecil. "Oh damn! I see the light at the end of my tunnel, but you'll probably go to jail over this stinkin' real estate bullshit."

I watched Lorena absorb the truth in Cecil's sarcasm with a hard silence, and what I worried about was a building fury. With a gentle move toward her, I hoped to attract her attention. "Lorena . . ."

But Lorena leaped at the man. I lunged toward her.

And the shotgun blast deafened us all.

Lorena's weight flew back into me, sending me back against window blinds. Cecil studied the weapon with an *oh, crap, what just happened* as I kept Lorena from collapsing to the floor.

The front door glass crashed in, a brick sliding across the fifties linoleum. Instinctively, Cecil swung the barrel toward the cacophony, cycling the weapon to eject the empty hull and chamber a new round. But the battering ram against the back kitchen door snatched his attention around to his right, all of us flinching as the shotgun's muzzle passed over us.

Wayne popped up from behind the counter, his Sig Sauer P220 tight in his hands, aimed straight for Cecil. One shot. In the head. The mechanic's body slumping lifeless to the floor.

Ginger screamed and rushed to her dead husband.

"Everyone stay on the ground, hands raised," Wayne yelled. "Do not move." Then "Target down," to the officers outside.

But I could not oblige him and get my hands up. Lorena, my arms around her, dragged me down, my legs weakened from the shock.

Uniformed officers rushed in.

"Slade?" Lottie crawled on knees to me, hands raised as told, any other time a silly, ridiculous image. "Are you okay?"

I struggled to hear her while listening to my ears ring. "Lorena . . ."

The real estate agent's blood seeped into my clothing, onto my arms, now my legs.

"Slade?" Wayne was suddenly in my line of vision, up close. He felt for a pulse on Lorena, then gently lifted her to the side off me. "Slade, are you hurt?"

Blood everywhere. Warm. All over me. Palms out, hands shaking . . . how was I supposed to tell?

Prodding, feeling, frantically examining me, Wayne took charge, and I let him, my thoughts sluggish, unable to catch up to reality.

"Shit," he whispered. "Get the damn EMT over here. And I mean now!"

I looked at him, puzzled, but when he snared a handful of napkins from the nearby table and pressed hard against my abdomen, the pain made it clear. Lorena hadn't been the only one shot.

Chapter 28

I NEVER PASSED OUT. I also never thought that secondary buck-shot could take a person down. A shiver coursed through me. Then again.

Wayne hovered, yelling over his shoulder every now and then as authorities swept into Jezebel's. Finally, only Cecil, Lorena, and me left on the diner floor, a creepiness that unnerved me. How close had I come to being them?

Then Ivy crossed my mind, and Zack. Then Ally . . . Monroe. My phone. "Wayne," I started.

"I'll handle it."

With a clipped laugh, I gave in. Wayne had no idea what I meant, but he'd do whatever to figure it out and accomplish the task.

I still couldn't fathom dying from a couple of shotgun pellets, but EMTs worked fast, smiling between the frowns and fast hands stopping the bleeding and harnessing me onto a gurney. Wayne couldn't stop scowling, which I understood came from his inability to fix things. The lawman didn't enjoy standing on the sidelines. Medics loaded me into an ambulance they had already staged at the scene before the cops entered the building. Then Wayne hopped in.

"No need to," I started.

"Hush. Just let these guys do their thing," he said and nodded to the medic to shut the door and move out.

"How long and where are we going?" Wayne asked.

"Not far," said the medic. "Newberry Hospital. Don't want to risk the longer distance to Columbia."

Wayne wedged himself in a corner out of the way. In his mid-thirties, the blond, pudgy EMT kept checking vitals, hung a bag of something, and snaked a line into my arm. Then he peppered me with questions.

"Full name?"

"Date of birth?"

"Allergies?"

My torso exposed, the young man cleaned and monitored holes I was afraid to ask about. Then he put some sort of bandage on me in a not-so-delicate manner.

"Sorry, I know," he said. "It hurts. How do you feel?"

"Like I've been shot," I replied.

He laughed. "Like you would know."

I tried to chuckle back and winced. "Shot, stabbed, rammed with a car, and nearly drowned after the boat blew up."

The medic paused and looked back at Wayne. "She a cop?"

Which only made Wayne glance at me and shake his head.

"Girl," the guy said, looking at me in a new light. "Might be time to find another line of work."

Wayne mumbled something.

The medic turned overly attentive to my belly. "This one spot is stubborn."

The lawman peered over to see. I tried not to fret and instead, stared at a smudge on the ceiling of the ambulance, wondering what it was. Then after another twinge of pain, I tried to fight the furrows I felt burying in my forehead.

"Any bleeding disorders?" the guy asked.

I shook my head.

"Are you pregnant or any chance you could be pregnant?"

Leaping at the question, my heart jumped then pounded repeatedly against my ribs. This was not the place . . . nor the time . . . damn, Wayne, why did you have to ride along?

"Ms. Slade? You still with me?"

"Um, yeah. Sorry. What?"

"Any chance you could be pregnant? Have to ask."

I swallowed and uttered, "Not sure."

"Pardon?"

"Not sure," I repeated and shut my eyes, not wanting to look at Wayne.

"Then we'll treat that as a strong possibility."

Good thing they were, when I really hadn't.

Pain started to take over. I turned my attention inward, the medic's question throwing me into an internal panic. They poked, prodded, and bandaged. While so far I hadn't welcomed a baby in my life, the thought of losing it scared the hell out of me now. Along with how Wayne would confront me the second I was stabilized, and we were alone. I didn't expect it to be touchy-feely, and his fear for me would only make him worse.

I WOKE UP WITH Monroe leaning over me. "Told you she was waking up," he said.

Blinking, my focus came and went. Suddenly there was Wayne. "Hey, you back with us?"

"Think so," I said, slowly taking stock of my body parts, moving, waiting to see where I hurt most. "Ouch." Oh yeah. There. Then my eyes flew open.

Was I still pregnant?

Had I been pregnant?

Did I want to hear that answer yet? *No.* I needed time to process. And, for now, I was content with nervous ignorance. One step at a time.

Thank God Monroe was here to keep Wayne from talking about it.

"How are you both back here?" I asked.

Both men smiled, Monroe wider than the other.

"Let me guess," I said, croaking like a frog. "Monroe's the husband, and Wayne flashed the badge."

A half-grin from Wayne told me I guessed right. Did I know my men or what?

"I've been thinking," I said. Actually, I'd dreamed about the case, the shooting. Felt like I'd been dreaming for a week, infusing a sense of urgency in me we'd lost time.

"You've been asleep," Wayne said.

"No, seriously," I croaked again. "Get me some water. I need to tell you what I think." Monroe jumped up for the water, and I scanned the room, assuming you could call it that. A bed surrounded by curtains. "Where are Ally and the kids?"

"They'll be here in an hour or so. Said I'd call when you woke up," Wayne said.

Taking a sip from the cup and straw Monroe held over, I realized how parched I was and took two more then lay back. Monroe reached down and raised the bed.

"Listen, Wayne. There was a higher power pulling Lorena's strings," I said.

"Not your concern," he ordered.

"The hell it's not." My voice was still raspy, but he had to hear this. "Lorena made me realize who had control of her. She talked in the diner."

Both men listened. Finally.

"It's Harden," I said.

Monroe rolled his eyes, his humor evaporated. "Seriously? Are you that blindly against that man to pin Newberry on him? Slade, I think . . . I'm not sure what I think, but it makes me concerned even more about you." He left the bedside. "Do you never listen to yourself?"

"Damn straight I do, and you're biased," I said, voice sounding more like a growl than I intended. "Wayne? Twice she nudged me, mocked me, talked about how I ought to recognize whom else was involved, how she could have my job, how she was aware that I was in Newberry against Harden's orders."

"She said Harden?" he asked.

"No, but who the hell else could she mean?" I pled.

Monroe shoved aside the curtain and left with it billowing behind him.

A nurse came in, checked vitals and the bandage, told me to keep drinking liquids, and left after saying they'd move me to a room in a few minutes. Guess I would be a Newberry guest for a couple days more.

I began doling out instructions the second she disappeared. "Check phone records. Harden's, Lorena's, and Cricket's," I said. "Interrogate Ginger. She's lost her job, her husband, and her best friend. Ought to be ready to spill a zillion secrets wanting to get even with somebody."

Wayne's mouth twisted to the side. "Hmm, never would of thought of all that."

"Don't *hmm* me." I coughed and took another sip of water, throat raw. "The US attorney thought him too minor to prosecute on our first case in Charleston, too tenuous a connection to that shell corporation and that pack of people we put away. Well, he was stupid enough to use the same play out of his playbook, Wayne."

Staring, he chewed the inside of his mouth. I recognized that habit. He was listening.

"At least try to prove me wrong," I said, "but I bet my right arm I'm right."

He took a deep breath. "You so easily could've lost that arm you speak of, not to mention your life."

"But you'll do what I ask?" How could he say no to his girlfriend lying in a hospital bed?

"I will."

"You'll thank me later," I added, telling myself I ought to feel validated. But instead a jittery nervousness built inside my shot-up self, and a silence settled between us as we turned a page.

The elephant entered the room. A baby elephant.

"What did the doctor say?" I asked.

"You had a blighted ovum," he said.

Had. That scared me for reasons I couldn't name. "Meaning . . . what?" *What had I done wrong, or what hadn't I done? What the hell was a blighted ovum?*

Wayne's tone turned gentle. "You were pregnant, but it quit developing."

As though slapped with a wet rag, I sank into my pillow. "Wh-what?" Red-hot fear filled me. "Did the pellets kill it?" Oh dear Jesus. Had I thrown this child into harm's way? Then the loss escalated into worse. "Did it . . . make me so I can't have kids?"

God help me, a month ago I gave no thought to more children, much less the ability to have them. Now . . .

"No, Slade. It's just something that happens. Doc said you have all the symptoms without the embryo."

Empty. God, I felt so damn empty. How could that be when there'd been nothing there?

I'd been so damn sure.

When I looked up to his eyes for reassurance, I didn't understand what I saw.

He shook his head and stood, coming slowly to the side of the bed. It scared the bejeesus out of me because I didn't understand what he meant, or how he felt learning about a potential baby by accident . . . via an accident that could've killed his child if it had existed.

A powerful slow drip of time in those steps.

"Why didn't you tell me the pregnancy kit was yours?" he asked.

I rubbed my temples. My decision of discretion made sense days ago but sounded immature coming from Wayne's lips.

"I was confused, Wayne." Why wasn't he holding me? At least holding my hand? "I didn't want you to feel roped into marrying me."

He scoffed with a bitterness I hated to see, turning his head to the side, hands on his waist . . . unable to look at me.

"Wayne?" Tears welled and threatened to spill. Why hadn't I told him? Right now I felt so damn stupid.

"First, I proposed way before all this," he said. "Is this why you've been so weird of late? Pushing me away?"

"Maybe," I said.

"Leading me to withdraw my proposal?"

I fingered the white sheets. "Guess so."

He nodded, coming to a conclusion I wasn't privy to. I shifted in the bed, stiff, wincing.

"For the record," he said, turning back around, "I like your theory. Explains a lot about Harden, and Ginger ought to be easy to convince to talk. You were right through most of this case."

Okay, we were talking work now? With accolades? I was still too groggy to keep up if he kept doing this back and forth.

"Thanks," I said.

"But I should've been the first person you came to about the other subject." His mouth flatlined. "That hurts so bad, Slade."

I'd give anything for him to call me *Butterbean*.

I couldn't look at him and studied the edge of the curtain, the people walking by. "I'm sorry."

But then he took my hand, and my poor, confused heart leaped.

"Why you can't commit to another marriage . . . maybe I get that," he said. "Don't want to, but it's not my choice. It's just my luck I fell for a woman damaged by some asshole who preceded me. Thought I could make it all better and make you more comfortable with the concept of matrimony."

Oh, I wasn't liking this. "Wayne."

"You put our child in harm's way for selfish reasons."

I could say there was no child, but in theory I had. But who could've predicted Troy's overreaction or Cecil's blind jealousy? And that they'd come together in my presence?

"I had a job to do," I said.

He let loose of my hand. "And you're missing the whole point." Reaching over to the chair, he lifted his windbreaker, the one used to cover his shoulder holster. "Ally will be here any second, and the kids need to see you're okay. I'm headed back to check with the chief and get back to work. If any of this proves like you think, I'll convince Monroe how wise you are." He gave me a weak grin, and I almost cried.

"I was wrong, Wayne."

"Yeah," he said, holding the curtain's edge. "Maybe I was, too."

He left. But I wasn't sure exactly what he might be wrong about, because from where I lay, he'd done the best he could to be the best man I could've ever found.

THE DAY I CAME home from the hospital, Wayne had unearthed enough evidence for them to put Harden on disciplinary leave pending the investigation's completion. But only Monroe showed at the house an hour after I settled on the sofa, an apology and chocolates at the ready.

"You were right at every turn," he said, accepting a coffee and a wide smile from Ally, who took extra time to hand him a napkin before sitting by me. He accepted and doubled down on the remorse. "I feel like a stooge spouting off at you about Harden. You were right. It's crazy how you're usually right, but . . . how do I say this . . .?"

"My unconventional ways disturb you," I said.

"Flying by the seat of your pants is more like it," Ally added. "Shooting in the dark. Shotgunning your approach."

"Really?" I said. "How long did it take for you to come up with those?"

Laughter all around. Refreshing after the last two days of morbid misgivings in which I doubted every decision, sentence, and thought I'd had since the damn radio show ten days ago. Because Wayne had kept his distance.

Not that he hadn't texted. A couple of voicemails. One particularly long email.

Ginger gave in like a Florida sinkhole. A lockbox in a storage closet at Lorena's home revealed a clandestine plan to develop a residential swath toward the interstate. What once was considered too rural to deem habitable to those with Columbia employment, had become a tolerable commute. Not only had Columbia grown out, but so had Irmo and Chapin, the communities in between. Luxury vehicles coddled commuters with satellite amenities and Wi-Fi. Driving forty miles to afford a house in the country became a dream come true to urbanites.

Just like I'd suspected . . . like the Zellers, Sterlings, Huneycuts, and Abrams had dreaded.

At her mother's urging, Cricket connected with farmers, stretching guidelines, enticing them to take out loans while leveraging prime acreage in the *one hundred*. Then within a year of the loan closing, Lorena or Ginger asked the farmers to sell, the prices lowered once they were compromised, to a buyer they weren't allowed to meet. Then utilizing the feminine wiles of Ginger, Tina, and another young lady who worked in another of the Carson establishments, Lorena compromised the men, capturing the misdeed, or appearance of such, in a photo or two like with Monroe. Of course, she quickly learned that the more affluent farmers had the most to lose and proved the easiest to discredit and, therefore, silence.

Between the power of the Carson influence and societal mores, the farmers had remained silent. That many farmers amazed me, many of them secretive for their wives' sakes, as it turned out. In the autumn of their years, they didn't want to fight the scandal.

The unfortunate Mr. Hoyt Abrams found deceased at Tarleton's Tea Table was meeting Tina, but his heart prevented him from consummating the deal, so to speak. And when Monroe's audit delved too close to the truth, with Cricket too nervous to be trusted, Ginger did the same with him. Then when Monroe didn't heed the warning, Cecil appeared with his fists after Ginger conveniently left her camera for her husband to see.

Harden Harris enticed Lorena to coax Cricket into the first deal after having Cricket introduce him to her mother. A favor to help a farmer. The girl, eager for her mother's adoration and boss's approval, made it happen. One turned into two, and Cricket was hooked . . . caught between a rock and a hard place, her mother and her boss. Opening her mouth would ruin her career and her family and sully her in the agricultural community her father loved so.

Poor, poor child.

Personally, I figured Harden attempted to lay out a homecoming for his buddies I'd put in jail via this new deal. So much for that, *buddies.*

And I worried what would happen to poor Aunt Sis.

"Read this." Monroe showed me his phone.

Took care of the SOB who popped you in the nose. You owe me.

From Wayne.

I tried to smile. "Told you he'd take care of you."

The empathy in his eyes told me he'd used the text to bridge the subject. "What happened with Wayne?"

Grimacing, I shrugged. "Lack of communication."

Ally patted me on the leg. "He's not gone and definitely not forgotten. Anyone need more coffee?"

We gave her the affirmative and watched her leave the room.

"You all right?" Monroe asked, starting to reach for me then holding back.

"Yeah, I'll live."

"Says the girl who almost didn't."

"It wasn't that bad."

He tilted his head. "Wayne said otherwise, in quite the concerned manner."

I sighed. "What else did he tell you?"

"About the case? Nothing new, I imagine."

He dodged the question. He was there when they brought me out of surgery. The pretend husband allowed back to be with his pretend wife. Of course, the doctor explained the pregnancy details to him.

Painful for him to hear, I'm sure, and talking to him now about it would only be for my benefit, not his. This time I'd think about him first.

"Momma!"

Ivy rushed in, crying big sloppy sobs. Forgetting my surgery, she leaped onto the sofa and crawled into my lap.

"Slade!" Monroe rose.

Groaning to myself, I clenched my eyes and let the pain pass. "It's okay, Monroe. What is it, baby girl?" I stroked her hair.

Then I pushed my daughter back to peer at her, anguished at her tears . . . then furious at the insect that may have caused them. "Ivy, what is it?"

"Bug."

"Bug what?"

Monroe looked lost.

I gave a mild wave for him to steer clear. This was mother-daughter invitation only.

Sniffling, Ivy rubbed her nose on her shirt sleeve. "We broke up."

"Aww, honey," and I pulled her back to me. "It happens. He was just your first." And the thought of so many subsequent heartbreaks only brought me full circle to where I sat today . . . without Wayne.

I hugged her closer, for my own relief as much as her grief. "He find someone else?" The logical conclusion when a sixteen-year-old dumps a girl of fourteen.

"No," she whimpered. "I cut him off."

Cut him off? The phrasing sent a jolt of terror through me, along with all kinds of sexual notions and their consequences.

"Yes," she said, the emotional jag easing off. "He said he was going to get even with Zack." Her eyes tried to fill again. "And he said you were a pain in the ass. Totally unacceptable."

Two cups in her hands, Ally snorted and retreated back into the kitchen. Monroe coughed and excused himself behind her.

But I remained with Ivy, rocking her in her sadness, thanking God for sending Bug on his way. Soothing my daughter for a few days suited me fine, because nothing would soothe me for a while. Not even locking up Harden.

This time I really messed up.

Chapter 29

TWO WEEKS LATER I sipped tea with Lottie over lunch. I was still on leave and had slipped over to Newberry all clandestine-like before reminding myself I had no more reason to sneak. Harden remained on admin leave, with Monroe hand-picked to serve as acting state director in his place.

Monroe was now my boss.

Weird. Not that I wanted the job, but I hadn't expected to see him in it. Time would tell how it affected our relationship . . . and how loose a rein he'd give my special projects representative title.

"The red truck was Cecil's, wasn't it?" I asked Lottie.

She nudged me with a plump elbow. "I keep saying . . . best detective ever!"

"Yeah," I said, pushing around the grapes accenting my scoop of Jezebel's infamous chicken salad. "A sleuthing genius. Took me forever to see my director was behind the crime. Too late for Cricket." And too long to see I was throwing Wayne away.

She gave me a sympathetic pout. "Cecil was a wild card. Not on your scoreboard."

"Yeah." I laid my fork down, with my hunger just not there. Wiping my mouth with my napkin threw me back to Wayne, and the memory of him bearing down on my gut, those white cloths blossoming red from mine and Lorena's blood.

Her foot tapped my chair. "Hey, girl, where'd you go?"

"Sorry, Lottie. Not sure eating here was all that smart. Thought it might help me get my head on straight."

She shoveled the last bite of chicken in her mouth, chewed, then as if reluctant it was her last, she swallowed slowly. "Well, my two-bit psychiatric advice is this. Time heals all. And I still think coming here will help."

"Send me your bill."

That drew a wide smile out of her.

"So," I said, pushing the plate back, but a new waitress instantly popped out of the kitchen and scooped up our dishes before I could finish my sentence.

"Thanks, Maggie," Lottie said.

"Let me guess, you grew up with her mother," I said, elbows on the table.

Lottie scowled. "Honey, I babysat her mother. I grew up with her nana."

Yeah, I needed this homespun woman and her simple, countrified style. No pretenses and all real-life stuff. "Tell me what happened to Aunt Sis. I catch myself worrying about her, and I don't see her here. I can't imagine what goes through her riddled mind these days."

She reached over and touched my arm. "Oh, Slade, you should've called, and I'd have saved you the worry. Aunt Sis is fine."

"Is she in a home?" I asked, ready to ask for the name of the place, to check it out . . . make sure the lady who tried to crack this case open was taken grand care of.

Lottie warmly rubbed where her hand lay. "She's still at Lorena's place, with a full-time nurse who brings her downtown for a few hours a day to keep her routine. As the last heir to the Carson estate, she's more than covered for the rest of her natural years."

Good. "But who's in charge?"

With twinkling eyes, she grinned. "My Bishop petitioned the court for emergency guardianship and won. And I plan to bake her a pound cake once a week. Bishop promised to carry it to her on Mondays. Now, what about that old boss of yours? What are y'all doing with the guy who caused all this?"

Truth there. Lots of truth my agency would be making amends for in this county for years to come thanks to Harden Harris.

"He's out of commission, but his days are numbered. Every officer of this so-called land corporation is being scrutinized, and since most of them probably had no clue what Harden orchestrated down here, they'll probably testify against him."

She bobble-headed at me, satisfied. "And our farmers?"

That part saddened me. Even if Harden went to jail, the problem still existed. Would the corporation be made to make restitution to these farmers, or would these men have to file civil suits that could take years? And if compensated, would they get their land back or just simply be paid the difference in price? "Can't say, Lottie, but when I hear, I'll call."

Which raised a question that still nagged at me. "Did you or didn't you know that farmer who failed to meet with me in the parking lot?"

Her mouth tight, she sighed, giving it up. "Yes. He's kin."

"And?"

"No *and*," she said. "Your boyfriend has his name on his list now so let's just let the poor man be." She hesitated. "Is there any chance he'll get his property back?"

"Like I said, no idea. I hope so."

More nodding. Then we realized we'd run out of things to say. We'd become friends, but somehow we needed space from that friendship, both of us acclimating to a new normal. Both of us wishing we'd acted sooner, done more . . . acted somehow differently enough to keep people from dying.

Cricket would weigh heavy on our minds for a while. Lorena, too.

We hugged and left, her heading up Main Street to embrace her people. The pound cake lady. Me leaving in my truck, headed back to the lake. The investigator.

Or as Wayne would label me, the wannabe . . . not that I didn't get it right most of the time. By the end, anyway . . . often with stitches.

I QUIT BREATHING when I pulled into my drive. Wayne's car waited down near the water. My driveway wove from the road to the house where most folks parked, but it continued down to the ramp beside the dock for those putting in their boat. Nobody drove down there for any other reason. Which told me Wayne wanted to talk.

Legs quivering, I exited the truck and held onto the tailgate for a moment. I hadn't seen him since the hospital. A few back and forths about the case via smartphones, but no meetings, no dinners, no calls for consultation.

A scan of the yard told me the kids were inside, probably Ally's doing. My sister, whose bucket list included marrying me off to Wayne. Bless her.

Finally I made my way down the asphalt, the two hundred feet feeling like a mile. Wayne waited under the gazebo, resting against the opening leading down to the water. Mallards fed off the lake's edge, bottoms up then down, fluttering to shake off the water in between.

No way he didn't hear me drive in.

"Didn't expect to see you here," I said as soon as I thought he could hear me.

"Didn't expect to find you gone," he replied.

Please don't let it start like this. I reached his side and stared out at the lake, too.

I may have won the case, if you could name a winner in such an arena, but I'd come away the loser overall. My personal choices with Wayne had been hit or miss since we'd met, and not coming clean with him the moment I suspected a pregnancy had been wrong. All my second- and third-guessing screwing everything up. My stalling about the ring for eight months hadn't been too wise, either. Oh, how I wished I could roll back the weeks. I'd apologized in the hospital, yet still he'd walked.

He sighed for my benefit, a prologue that scared me to my bones.

"Do I need to apply for a transfer?" he asked. Not adversarial. Just plain spoken.

"I really wish you wouldn't," I managed to say, and then said something that was harder to say than I loved him. "I need you."

Still no glance other than up the cove.

"Do I need to change jobs?" I asked. "With Monroe as director, I'm sure he could find an alternative. Special projects representatives wear lots of hats. They aren't just investigators."

He crossed his arms, still scanning the distance. I lowered myself to the built-in bench lining the gazebo, the day having worn at me a bit.

"I've put in for a partner," he said. "Can't say when or who they'd send."

"We wouldn't have to work every case side by side," I added. "A third party might help."

What were we doing? What was I doing other than paralleling what he said?

But I was afraid to originate a unique thought, afraid to apologize again. Insanely terror-stricken that I'd push him over this last thin hint of a line left between us.

His love was straightforward. Mine not so much, the blame for which was solely my own.

But these goddamn jobs we had. They'd brought us to each other, woven us together, and I was sure he felt as I did, that if either of us compromised our careers for the other, it would be the end of the relationship. The one who sacrificed would eventually resent the other, which continually carried us back to where we stood. Only each time more scarred.

But even more so, what scared me from saying I do? What fear had seized control of my senses such that I'd made ridiculous choices with this man who loved me so? Like Wayne said in the hospital, I was injured from my past. So why couldn't I simply accept Wayne as the solution to overcoming that past?

Afraid of what look I'd get when he finally caved and noticed me, I stared down at my feet, through the cracks in the boards to the water. To the baby bream below. Telling myself not to cry. This decision was all on him, and my chest felt about to explode from the wait.

"Christ, you'll be the death of me," he whispered, then briskly reached down and lifted me to my feet, stealing the breath out of me.

"Listen to me," he said.

I waited.

"I love you," he said.

I nodded, still afraid to mess things up. Still waiting for the but.

"But I'm holding the ring for a while . . . at least as soon as you give it back."

"A proposal do-over," I asked hopefully.

He grinned, and it warmed me . . . an excellent sign. "A do-over," he replied. Then he smothered me, my cheek mashed into his shoulder. His breath into my hair.

"I love you, too, Lawman."

He squeezed me tighter.

"And that sort of hurts," I said.

"Oh damn, sorry, Butterbean."

The nickname almost drew tears out of me. If nothing else told me we'd begun healing, that did.

We hugged for a while, my thoughts coming back, reliving Newberry and all that had brought us to this point, almost splitting us up . . . again. Cricket, the blast, Lorena's blood covering me and the floor.

"You shot him in the head," I said into Wayne's shoulder.

He eased me back. "And your point?"

"I thought LEO's were taught to shoot center mass."

His long stare scared me into thinking I'd messed up again.

"Slade," he said low and slow. "That man had a twelve-gauge. He was still, he was close, and he had to go down. I couldn't afford for him to shoot again." He squeezed me hard again. "I couldn't afford to lose you."

"Zack," Ally yelled from the top of the hill. "I said not yet. And definitely not with the cubed steak I thawed out for dinner!"

My son scampered past Wayne and me to the end of the dock.

"I told 'em y'all would make up," he said and cast out a line. "And I promised not to come out until I saw y'all get mushy."

"We haven't gotten mushy," I scolded. "And your aunt's going to skin your hide for stealing dinner for bait."

"Screw the part about dinner," Wayne said, dragging me to the distant corner of the gazebo. He sat and lowered me gently onto his lap. "Let's prove the kid right and consummate the mushy part."

"Just keep it PG, Cowboy," I said, then kissed him long and hard. Who needed a ring . . . for now?

The End

Acknowledgements

Thanks to every person in Newberry who bought a book, and the number is pretty darn big.

Much appreciation to Audrey Henry, Jan Wicker, Sandra Oliver, and the legion of members who belong to the Newberry Friends of the Library. They took me under their wing, even inviting me as keynote for their annual banquet when *Lowcountry Bribe* came out. There I was, a novice, nervous as a cat, talking to all these ladies who thought I was worth something. Now here we are, with my eighth book, and they are still strong, if not stronger, behind both Carolina Slade and me. I love them to pieces. Along with the chicken salad at the annual banquets, which I've never missed since that first one five years ago. I can never repay you enough.

Sue Summer . . . you are a hoot! From my first WKDK radio interview with you, I've been entranced with Newberry. It reminded me of my grandmother's town, and I caught myself coming back for research, shopping, and dinners just to absorb some of that homespun setting. Such deep history! Your stories could entertain me for hours, and you planted the seed for the setting of *Newberry Sin*. And your pound cakes are to die for.

Thanks to Randy Berry, the owner of Books on Main in Newberry, who's loved my books from day one, hosting multiple book signings and spreading the gospel of Slade.

And bless you Lawman. You're not Wayne, like everybody thinks you are. No, sir, you're so much more.

About the Author

C. HOPE CLARK holds a fascination with the mystery genre and is author of the Carolina Slade Mystery Series as well as the Edisto Island Series, both set in her home state of South Carolina. In her previous federal life, she performed administrative investigations and married the agent she met on a bribery investigation. She enjoys nothing more than editing her books on the back porch with him, overlooking the lake with bourbons in hand. She can be found either on the banks of Lake Murray or Edisto Beach with one or two dachshunds in her lap. Hope is also editor of the award-winning FundsforWriters.com.

C. Hope Clark

Website: chopeclark.com

Twitter: twitter.com/hopeclark

Facebook: facebook.com/chopeclark

Goodreads: goodreads.com/hopeclark

Editor, FundsforWriters: fundsforwriters.com

Made in the USA
Columbia, SC
18 April 2018